The Things She Stole

A Brandon Penny Heist

D.D. Black

A Note from the Author

I spent a lot of time in Portland, Oregon, researching this book. And while most locations are true to life, some details of the setting have been changed.

Any resemblances between characters in this book and actual people is purely coincidental. In other words, I made them all up.

Thanks for reading,

D.D. Black

Chapter One

December 15, 2018

"When was the last time you heard from your mother, Mr. Penny?" Detective Joanne Caraway smiled sweetly, drumming her fingertips on the table. Her manicured nails reflected a patch of fluorescent light that gleamed off the lacquer.

I picked up a box of tissues and passed it back and forth between my hands, biting my lip like I was nervous. When I was ten, my mom's friend Soup taught me the three rules of talking to cops. I'd kept those rules tucked in the back of my mind ever since, so I wasn't nervous. "Don't recall, exactly. Why do you ask?"

The detective's round face was pleasant to look at but would be easy to forget, like the generic mom in the photo that comes with a dollar-store picture frame. It was a *relatable* face, an *approachable* face, one that might belong to a member of my own family. Caraway's wry smile told me there was a whole world behind that face. "*Approximately*, then?"

I tilted my head, squinting one eye like I was trying to remember. "Maybe a few days ago."

She jotted my answer on her notepad. I'd gotten her attention. "A few *days?*"

I shrugged as though none of this mattered.

"So you knew she was back in town?" she asked.

"Sure. We had a quick coffee. Nothing big."

"Do you have a phone number or address where she's staying?"

I set the box of tissues back on the table. "Sorry. She doesn't just hand out that kind of info."

"Did she say why she was back in town after all these years, Mr. Penny?"

I frowned. "It's Brandon. Or Brand. Some people call me Brand."

Caraway smiled again, this time with genuine warmth and a touch of pity, like a girl staring into a cage at the animal rescue shelter. I was the abused dog the pure-hearted girl wanted to save. The detective possessed a nice collection of smiles and had already deployed a few of them for different purposes. This one said, *I know about your past, and I'm sorry.* Her command of smiles would have conned three people out of four, I had to give her that.

I looked away. Slats in the neglected, dusty blinds allowed thin lines of gray sky to show through. Passing cars whooshed and splashed down Madison Street. Rain spattered the window. A wisp of lemony air freshener mingled with the stale aroma of a room that needed airing out. A chair's repeated scraping had scratched through the beige paint on the wall, revealing lines of bare plaster. How many poor saps had squirmed in these cheap office chairs over the years? Enough to leave a mark. The room made me feel insignificant and anonymous, like I might shrink down and fall into a crack in the floor and never come out. That was the point of rooms like this, and the combined pressure of every meeting had worn ruts into the place.

She cleared her throat. "Okay, Brandon. Why's your mother back in town?"

"Could be a lot of reasons."

"Like?"

I sighed, pretending to contemplate. "She always enjoyed the

Festival of Lights at The Grotto. And the big Christmas tree in Pioneer Square. Oh, and there was this sandwich place she loved up on Burnside. Best pastrami on rye you ever had. Slaw, hot mustard." I dropped my head and frowned. "But they closed a few years back. Now there's a Pilates studio on the ground floor and luxury condos on top."

Caraway smiled, less sweetly this time. Her bright blue eyes flashed in a blink-and-ya-miss-it betrayal of something less patient. "I get it, Brandon." She sniffed and the smile was back. "I do. You're a true-blue guy. Your mom abandoned you, but you still love her. Lot of people out there who'd turn their back on their mom for less than what she put you through, but not you." She walked the perimeter of the compact interrogation room, then sat and folded her hands in her lap. "You don't want to get mixed up in whatever she's up to, so why don't you tell me exactly what that is."

When a cop begins a sentence with the phrase, *You don't want to get mixed up in...* what she means is, *Give me what I'm asking for or I'll make sure you get mixed up in this, whether you had anything to do with it or not.* It's meant to be taken as a threat, and that's exactly how I took it.

"I think the sandwich place was called Dexter's. That help?" When she didn't respond, I added, "Like I said, though, they closed a few years back. One of the last holdouts of old Portland. How long you lived here?"

Caraway tapped a thumb on the table. "I've got three sons of my own, Brand. I *understand* that bond. I'm a mother first and a detective second. My oldest is twenty. He loves me like I'm sure you love your mom." Her voice dripped with sentimentality.

I stifled my smile. If she got any more sickly-sweet, she'd hit me with a Care Bear Stare and tell me the true meaning of Christmas.

"She raised you, took care of you. I *get* that. But she committed *murder*." She tried to meet my eyes, but I looked away. "She saw that guy coming through the door and made her decision. You know that. You want to be loyal, but deep down you know that *nothing* makes what she did okay. You're a good enough person to see that."

I looked back at her, hard. She met my gaze steadily and her eyes implored me: *Come clean. Be honest. Help me help you.*

At that moment, I started thinking of her as *Carebear*.

She put a hand on my shoulder. "You're a good enough person to see that what your mother did was not okay, aren't you, Brandon?"

"I am."

"We have reason to believe she's planning a crime." She narrowed her eyes. "Did you know that?"

I perked up. "Knew she was in town. That's it, though. What's the reason?"

She looked at me askew. "What?"

"You said you have *reason to believe* she's planning a crime. What's the reason?"

"Word on the street." *Boy*, she did not like having to answer a question. Her whole vocal tone shifted. *Interesting.*

She returned to her seat and I nodded as though "word on the street" was an acceptable answer. "And the crime?"

"I was hoping *you'd* tell *me*, Brandon." Her voice had lost the last of its sweetness.

"That why you brought me in?"

"We didn't *bring you in*." She pulled out one of her smiles—a disarming grin—and aimed it at me. "I only asked if you'd talk to me."

That was true. When she'd stopped me outside my apartment, she asked me to come downtown for an *interview*. The word *interrogation* never passed her lips. Her choice of words was designed to let me know I wasn't a suspect, to make it clear I wasn't in any trouble. But I knew an interrogation when I saw one.

"Just a friendly conversation," she continued, "I've read your file and it ends about twenty years ago. Now you've got an apartment, a steady job. You're a law-abiding citizen. Probably even have a pretty girlfriend who accepts your past."

"No. I don't." Annoyance had crept into my voice, despite my efforts to stay cool. Bringing up my straight life was a threat, another piece of this interrogation that wasn't an interrogation. It was a way to get leverage, and I wanted to deny her that. It was also true that I didn't have a girlfriend. Not anymore. Jennifer had been the one good thing in my life since I went straight, and I'd managed to screw it up. She'd left me a year ago, and it was probably the right decision.

"Well, like I said, you don't want to get involved in whatever your mother is up to."

I nodded slowly. Clearly Caraway hadn't been tracking me closely or she'd have known I was single, but she was right that I was no longer a thief, though it had been sixteen years, not the twenty her file suggested. I kept a mental tally of the crimes I'd committed, and for the last three years, that number was zero. Even in the thirteen before that, my worst transgression was buying weed, a crime so small it was no longer illegal. The smallest crimes and the biggest crimes are the ones that get legalized. The stuff in the middle is what lands your ass in jail.

I guess that's why I got in her car. Because I was an honest, law-abiding citizen who didn't commit crimes and who cooperated with cops. I went along with her because I didn't want any trouble. Going straight was supposed to keep me safe and out of police stations. Until this morning, it had.

"Odd that she'd return to Portland"—Caraway cocked her head—"after all these years." She let it hang in the air like smoke, more a question than a statement. "Sure you don't know why?" She wagged a finger at me and winked. "And don't tell me about pastrami sandwiches. I loved Dexter's too."

The dusty, lemony air stuck in my throat and I felt short of breath. I never should have brought up Dexter's. Two deep belly breaths calmed me down. "Why's she back in town?" I shrugged. "Dunno if she's a killer, but we both know she's a thief. Lots of things to steal in Portland."

She flashed a white-toothed smile. "Yes. Yes, there are. Look, we know she's done jobs in Washington State, Idaho, far west as Colorado. Picks a new town, comes in for a few days, then disappears again. Never stays more than a few days."

Okay, I thought, *she's assuming I work better on a deadline*. What I said was, "Look, is there something you're asking me to do? Because

I don't understand what you're getting at." I knew what was coming next, but I wanted to make her say it.

"Tell me, Brand, will you help us locate your mother?"

Deep down I always figured I'd end up in a police station again. That's why I kept Soup's three rules at the ready. First, never forget that it's *illegal* for you to lie to cops and *legal* for them to lie to you. It's Interrogation 101: "We have your DNA." "We have your fingerprints." "Your buddy is in the room next door spilling his guts." All perfectly legal lies, according to the Supreme Court. This simple fact creates what Soup liked to call an *asymmetrical situation*. Don't get me wrong—he didn't tell me not to lie to cops. The point was that cops would lie to me if they thought it could help get a confession. Cops love confessions, true or otherwise.

The second rule of talking to cops is both physiological and psychological: Always keep your cool. Cops rarely use lie detectors because they're inadmissible in court, he told me, but they try to read body language at all times, so you need to keep your cool *at all times*. They want you to get angry; they need you to get scared. They want your primitive fight-or-flight drive to kick in so they can manipulate you. If you're scared, you'll say whatever they want if it'll take the fear away. If you're mad, you might forget yourself and hand them a sweet assaulting-an-officer charge. So whatever they say, keep your cool.

The third rule of talking to cops is based on a simple assumption: As much as they'll tell you they're on your side, that everything will be okay as long as you tell the truth, they're lying. So never—under any circumstances—tell the truth.

I stared into Detective Joanne Caraway's kind blue eyes and did what I'd been doing the whole interview, what I'd been doing since she picked me up outside my apartment in Felony Flats. I did what I'd learned to do as a kid.

I lied.

"Absolutely, Detective Caraway. I'll help you find my mom."

∼

On our way out through the lobby, I saw a Gandhi quote stenciled on the wall in a fancy cursive font: *Be The Change You Wish To See in The World.* Taped beneath it was a poster for CrimeStoppers of Oregon, offering a cash reward for anonymous tips leading to arrests. I never met Gandhi, but I knew enough about his experiences with police to doubt he'd have been happy about the placement of his most famous quote.

I stopped at the glass door, turned, and smiled at Caraway, who'd trailed me out of the interrogation room. I nodded at the quote on the wall. "You follow that?"

"I guess, yeah." She gave me an odd look, like she knew something I didn't. Or maybe she knew I was wrong about something. For the first time since we'd met, I couldn't read her.

I'd promised to get in touch with my mom to see what I could find out about her plans. I'd assured Carebear I understood this was a time-sensitive project, since we both knew my mom wouldn't be in town more than a few days. I'd agreed to be in touch by tomorrow night and had dutifully stuffed her business card in my pocket. In essence, I'd promised to snitch. Her look made me wonder whether I was as good a liar as I thought I was.

I stared at her for a long moment, took a final look around the station, and walked into the cold, steady rain.

The Oregonian: December 14, 1998

Fatal shooting at Laurelhurst poker game

Unclear whether robbery or gambling dispute behind killing

by Brian Schmidt

A man was killed Friday night at what police are calling a "private poker game" at a residence in the upscale Laurelhurst neighborhood.

According to investigators, two shots were fired just before nine o'clock on the 600 block of NE Couch Street. The deceased man's name hasn't been released, but investigators believe he worked as a security guard.

Sources say police have yet to determine whether the shooting was the result of a robbery or a dispute among the gamblers. One suspect "believed to have knowledge about the incident" has been taken into custody.

Chapter Two

Portland belongs to the crows. There are some pigeons downtown, a flock of seagulls here and there, but mostly the city is blanketed by a vast murder of scavengers. Crows aren't like pigeons: they're intelligent, they communicate with one another in their own language, and they recognize and remember individual humans. Anywhere you go in Portland, on some branch or wire, the crows have an eye on you.

The same is not true of the police, much as they'd like it to be.

I spotted the tail before I'd made it two blocks from the station. I was on foot, so rather than sending an unmarked car, Carebear had given me a guy in a brown Eisenhower jacket and a baseball cap. The plainclothes officer hung about half a block back and appeared in no real hurry. That was his first mistake. Like me, he didn't have an umbrella, and that was his second mistake. It's a point of pride among Portlanders that we don't carry umbrellas. At the same time, few of us go for long, leisurely strolls in a December downpour, so it made him stand out.

By the time I realized I was thinking of ditching him, I had a solid plan and two backups. That gave me pause. Law-abiding citizens don't ditch police tails. Then again, law-abiding citizens don't spend half an hour lying to a detective, either. But I'd come right into the station when Carebear asked, and criminals don't cooperate with the police in the first place, right? That made me wonder what the hell right Carebear had to put a tail on me, when I hadn't done so much as a misdemeanor in years. She didn't have the moral right, obviously, and she probably didn't have the legal right to pull this KGB shit either, but cops do what they want. What I didn't understand was how she had the professional right, the budgetary right. The guy tailing me was good, which meant he was a trained undercover cop who made a lot more per hour than I did. How was a possible lead on a twenty-year-old murder worth taking up the rest of this guy's day? There were a dozen unsolved murders from this year alone that should have been higher priorities. And yet there he was, stopped twenty feet behind me, carefully retying both of his hiking boots while I thought this through.

I'd learned a lot about Caraway in that interview, more than she'd learned about me. She wasn't to be trusted. That was obvious. The tail confirmed that her whole sweet-and-friendly act was a lie, but his presence also hinted that something else was going on. What that was, I didn't know. If my mother really was in Portland, I wanted to find her. As far as I knew, she hadn't been back in twenty years. But I wanted to find her on my own terms, not as Caraway's tool.

I continued down the block, tracking him in the reflection of a storefront window, then stepped into the shelter of a bus stop where an old woman with a plastic rain bonnet sat patiently, her shoulders hunched over like she was folding in on herself. A car splashed by, spraying a fan of oily water at our feet. I said, "Nice day if it don't rain, huh?"

She looked up with a kind smile, happy someone wanted to make small talk. "Nice day for ducks. I don't mind the rain."

My tail in the Eisenhower jacket had taken refuge under an awning, pretending to look at his phone, hanging back to see if I was really catching a bus.

I smiled at the old lady. "Me neither."

Though I kept him in my periphery, I avoided looking at the tail just as carefully as he avoided looking at me. I waved my transit card past the sensor pillar, which pinged happily and informed me I could ride the buses and trains for the next couple hours.

I waited, looking and not looking. My tail did the same, remaining visibly absorbed in his phone screen until the bus came a couple minutes later. The ad on the side of the bus read: *Straight Talk with Brian White on KPKX Radio. 7-10 AM, Every Weekday.* Brian's handsome brown eyes and smiling face stared through me, and that rattled me more than the cop. Brian White, still out there, still spouting his lock-up-the-homeless routine to fill time between ads on morning drivetime. Brian *goddamn* White, still just living his life.

I forced myself back into the moment, ushering the old woman onto the bus ahead of me.

She patted my hand as she sat in the front row. "You have a ducky day, young man."

I smiled and headed to a seat in the back. My tail was smooth; he boarded without any visible hurry, never looked up from his phone, and stopped a few feet away. He stood with his back to me, but he knew exactly where I was and I couldn't move without him knowing.

I got off the bus just before Burnside, and naturally the cop happened to get off at the same stop. I walked east toward the homeless camp that always appeared under the bridge on rainy days. A tourist family with umbrellas stopped me to ask the way to Voodoo Doughnut, and I pointed them in the right direction. The whole time, never too close but never quite out of sight, the man in the Eisenhower jacket shadowed me. Soon I reached Ankeny Arcade, a small plaza where the Max line crossed beneath the Burnside Bridge.

Like a lot of great American cities, Portland was built on crime. In Portland's past, dudes stole the land, stripped it bare, ground up their workers' bodies in the process, and kept most of the money. You can tell which dudes because they all have streets named after them. Ankeny Arcade, for example, was named for Alexander Postlethwaite Ankeny, considered a hero for his groundbreaking work in the fields of Indian-killing and strip-mining. Like I said, some crimes are so big they're legal.

I had a clear view of the river now, its surface gray-brown and stippled with raindrops. Fifty yards ahead, the homeless encampment sprawled like a flea market under the bridge. The city hated having homeless people there, especially before the holidays when the tourist-friendly Saturday Market was going on a block away. But it was near the downtown homeless shelters, and folks who couldn't get into a shelter always headed for the nearest space out of the rain. A few dozen people milled around, some clustered toward the center of the bridge, trying to stay warm. Some waited for a train to take them someplace else, others just waited. A small murder of crows had gathered near the stairs that led up to Burnside Street—some grabbed bits of damp popcorn from a puddle, others perched on the rail, watching, waiting. I'd always been fond of crows. Not only are they the smartest birds out there—second only to humans in animal intelligence—they're crooks. I liked the way they hung around looking for something to steal, passing word between them in their language of clicks and caws if they found a good mark.

I recognized a yellow tent next to one of the huge structural pillars that held up the bridge. Lucky break. Plan A was a go.

Back when I was a kid, my mom worked with a guy called Mikey Smooth. He liked to say he got the nickname because of how he was with the ladies, but really it was because he could pick a lock faster and smoother than you could pick your teeth. To Mikey, the pins and bolts and springs weren't some frustrating thing to be busted open with a swift kick, they were there to be gently coaxed and caressed, and the pick set was an extension of his hands. But Mikey picked up a heroin habit when he did a jolt inside for burglary, and ever since he'd been unable to get clean. Now he lived under the bridge and everyone called him Mikey Shakes. Mikey Smooth *had* been a burglar, and a damn good one, but he never did the burglary that landed him in the joint. He wasn't dumb enough to break into a house with people in it. Some other crook *was* that dumb, though, and the lady who was home said it was a Black guy. That was enough for the cops to pick him up, and for the lady to ID him at trial.

I sidled up next to the yellow tent and looked toward the river as I pulled out my phone, poked a couple random spots on the screen, and held it like I was making a call. "Hey Mikey," I said to the tent, "you in there?"

"Don't know nobody called Mikey," came Mikey's voice from inside.

"It's cool, man. It's me, Brandon."

"Brandon?" His voice sounded like hell, ragged and weak. Either it had been longer than I thought since I'd seen him last, or he was declining more rapidly. I heard a book thump closed, then some shuffling and squirming as he turned around inside the small tent. Finally, he unzipped a flap and poked his head out. He'd lost weight, and his hair was grayer than I remembered. So was his skin.

I made a show of talking into my phone and not looking at him, making a "be cool" gesture with the hand my tail couldn't see.

He got the signal and didn't look at me either. "What's the matter? You on a job? Thought you was living straight." While he talked, he collected some of his stuff from the tent and carefully zipped it closed.

"I *am* living straight, but I got a cop tailing me anyway. Can you believe that? Plainclothes, baseball cap. My nine o'clock."

Mikey looked without looking, then pulled some change from his pocket and started counting it. "Brown jacket?"

"That's the guy. He's good, and I don't wanna give him a heads-up that I've made him before I ditch. Can you make me invisible for five or six seconds?"

He nodded. "I *could* do that. What's in it for me?"

I didn't get paid for three days, and my phone bill was late already. "Forty bucks?"

"Forty bucks *today*? I can't eat an IOU."

"Back here as soon as I do some business and hit an ATM. End of the day, latest."

"Deal."

I looked down the track like I was waiting for the Max. Sure enough, there was a Red Line train about two blocks away, rolling slowly closer.

I turned back to Mikey Shakes, twisting like I was trying to pop my hip joints. "Can you time it so just when the train—"

"Yo, man," he interrupted, still not looking at me. "I'm not an idiot." As though proving his point, he sauntered past my tail, quietly entering a space that Eisenhower Jacket wasn't monitoring. Wherever it looked like this cop's attention was directed, in reality it was all on me.

Attention's a funny thing. The human brain can only truly focus on one thing at a time, and while it can shift focus very fast, that shifting and refocusing is still a process. That process can be manipulated. Since the cop was focused on me, he didn't even notice Mikey Shakes messing with a trash can behind him. The public garbage cans downtown have little roofs so they don't fill up with rain, and solid exterior shells so they can't be knocked down. But inside those is just a regular aluminum garbage can. If you open up the side, you can take that can right out.

The train slid to a stop under the bridge. Its doors hissed open and dozens of people streamed off—tourists, suburbanites, commuters, old folks, young folks. Just as the human activity was at its peak and the crowd began to block the sightline between my tail and me, Mikey whipped that trash can up over his head and slammed it to the ground with a CRASH so loud it sounded almost like a gunshot.

The entire crowd flinched—all the folks getting off the train, all the folks getting on the train, all the homeless people. Most importantly, my tail looked at Mikey. You can't *not* react to an unexpected loud noise nearby. It's just evolutionary hardwiring. Your brain perceives a threat and you look in the direction of the noise to identify it. When that loud noise happens six feet away, even a well-trained cop looks.

Mikey kicked the can across the train tracks with a series of crashing BANGS, and every crow took off at the same instant. He tilted his head back, shaking a fist at the crows as they disappeared into the sky. "STOP EATING MY TOENAILS AND GRILLED CHEESE!"

Words can slow the human brain, especially if we're alert for danger. We naturally look for meaning, but sentences like the one Mikey shouted to the heavens force us to loop back a couple times. Even though we understand all the words, we can't derive any meaning. This produces a second or two of cognitive error messages. A second or two can be a long time.

By the time my tail turned to find me again, I was gone. His attention had been elsewhere for several seconds, and that was all I'd needed. He looked at the stairs up to the bridge, looked in all the possible directions I could have fled, looked at the doors hissing shut on the train. He wasn't close enough to get to them before they closed and the train started rolling north. He whipped out his cell phone and made a call, presumably telling someone I was on the Red Line and they needed to have another unit catch up to me. He then headed east, the next-most-likely direction I would have gone.

I kept my eye on him until he was out of sight, then squirmed out from beneath the parked car I'd rolled under. I felt more nervous than I should have. It's not illegal to ditch a police tail, so I hadn't committed any crimes yet.

But the thought was already there: *yet*.

For two decades the Portland Police Bureau had loomed like a giant bear in the cave next to me. I tried not to bother it, but I knew that if it woke up hungry and decided to eat me, there was nothing I could do about it. That justified any steps I could take to avoid being eaten. Ditching the tail had been only a first step, but the speed at which I'd fallen back into old habits unnerved me.

My brain was firing in a dozen directions at once. There was no way in hell I was going to help Carebear. But I didn't know how I'd *avoid* helping her. Her subtle threat echoed in the back of my mind: *You don't want to get mixed up in...*

Then there was the fact that my mom was in town. She'd been my life for twelve years, then disappeared from it for twenty. Now she was within miles of me, possibly blocks. Carebear be damned, I had my own reasons for wanting to find her.

I climbed the stairs to the bridge where I would cross the river into Northeast. I had no idea where my mother was, but I knew a guy who might. Soup had been my mom's occasional partner and now owned a pawn shop near my apartment. If she was back in town for a job, he might know why. And if he didn't, he'd know someone who did.

The cold rain had soaked through my shirt by the time I was halfway across the bridge. I stopped under a steel railing to shield my phone from the downpour and tapped out a text. *Hey man, Keyser here. Long time no see. Got some questions about Dolly. Can I come by?*

The Oregonian: December 15, 1998

Robbery seen as motive in Laurelhurst murder

Two intruders broke into home

by Brian Schmidt

According to police, an attempted robbery led to the deadly shooting at a private poker game in the Laurelhurst neighborhood Friday night.

Witnesses who have given statements to investigators claim the game had been going for roughly an hour when two masked intruders broke through the door. In the ensuing chaos, a security guard was shot and killed.

The stakes of the game remain undisclosed, but law enforcement officials believe it was for "big money" since they found several thousand dollars in cash lying on the ground when they arrived on the scene.

A neighbor told The Oregonian the house was used for parties and fundraisers, but they'd never suspected an illegal poker game. "It's a nice neighborhood. Never thought we'd see anything like this around here."

Chapter Three

I didn't usually tense up in anticipation over a possible text because I didn't live a life that could dramatically change with a single message. I left the dramatic stuff behind in my teenage years, like a normal, healthy person. But waiting to hear back from Soup was getting to me. I considered heading straight to his pawn shop, but showing up at his place of business out of the blue to ask about a former partner currently wanted for murder was uncouth, not to mention dangerous. For all I knew, Soup had been hauled in by Caraway, too, or maybe his place was under surveillance. I had to leave the ball in his court.

The sky had settled into its late-afternoon gray, threatening another downpour at any minute. I told myself I'd walk until it started raining hard enough to soak through, then hop on a bus home. I was about to stash my phone when it buzzed with a new text. Not from Soup, but from Jennifer. *Fair warning. I'll be in to pick up my meds tomorrow. Remind me to tell you about this old getaway movie I saw last night. You'd have loved it.*

Jennifer still lived in her little studio apartment above Movie Madness, and still picked up her thyroid meds at Morey's once a month, so I saw her every now and then. Our breakup hadn't been dramatic. No infidelity or wall-punching rages. She'd ended it because I was too screwed up to plan a life with, though her letter had phrased it more delicately. Every time she came into the pharmacy, every time she happened to be working the register when I stopped by to rent a movie, I got a familiar feeling, like I'd just watched *Brokeback Mountain* or Gary Sinise's *Of Mice and Men*. The feeling you have after watching a film that breaks you in just the right way—a little tear in the heart that you can live with, but you know will never go away.

I replied with a thumbs-up emoji, stifling my instinct to tell her about my morning and eager not to seem too eager.

When my phone buzzed again, I assumed it was Jennifer, but this time it was Soup. *Okay. Busy today. Christmas shopping season. Come around closing time.*

That gave me six hours to kill.

After replying to Soup and crossing the river, I passed through Buckman and Sunnyside, then wandered past the pilates studio that took over when Dexter's got priced out of the neighborhood. I wasn't looking for my mom. Even if I'd known what she looked like these days, I wouldn't have been able to find her. Good thieves move in the shadows, and though I didn't know much about my mom anymore, I knew she was a good thief. When I had nothing else to do, sometimes I'd revisit places that held memories to see if they'd changed, or maybe to see if I'd changed. Over the last few years, I'd gotten into the habit of wandering the city, checking out the scenes of crimes I'd read about.

Liquor store robbed at gunpoint by the 84 East onramp. Why not head over there to see what I can see? Escape routes, security cameras, and so on.

Apartment in a condo building downtown taken for a hundred grand in jewelry. That's odd; everyone knows it's easier to rob a home than an apartment with a doorman and security. What was different about this building? Might be fun to take a look.

I was a criminal not doing crimes. Like the retired quarterback who's no longer in the game, all I could do was sit on the sidelines, telling myself I would have done it better. Of course, I'd always hidden these little trips from Jennifer for the same reason I'd never critiqued the tradecraft when we watched crime flicks together. We've all heard a hundred times that honesty is the key to healthy relationships, and it might even be true. I wouldn't know. What I know is that everyone is hiding something, and my love of crime is what I hid. Out of guilt and shame, sure, but mostly because I knew Jennifer could never understand that part of my life.

As I turned into the Laurelhurst neighborhood, I had to admit that I wasn't *not* looking for my mom, either. I strolled down Northeast Glisan Street, wound through the small, curved side streets as I'd done a hundred times before, always steering clear of the block where everything had gone wrong. I wondered whether she was in town to rob one of the stately homes. An antique collection in that wide-porched Craftsman? Maybe a hoard of cash in that neoclassical mansion? Nah, Soup had told me once that she'd graduated up. Jobs with longer timelines and larger payouts. One thing I knew for sure was that she was far beyond the short cons we ran when I was a little kid.

Take this necklace, she'd said. *Take this necklace and hold it, and when I give you the signal, you start acting all sad and sorry.*

That wasn't how it started for her, but it's how it started for me. In some of my earliest memories, I'm sitting on sofas in fancy homes, waiting. Sometimes I read books with thick library stickers on the spines, sometimes I colored in books printed on thin gray paper, and sometimes I just sat, waiting for Mom to finish cleaning the house so we could do something fun. That first time I helped her steal, the lady's couch was white leather. The softest I'd ever felt. We lived a life of particleboard-and-canvas couches that smelled like Goodwill, not soft leather ones that smelled like lavender. I remembered running my hand over it again and again, fascinated by how smooth it was.

Take this necklace and hold it, and when I give you the signal, you start acting all sad and sorry. I'm going to be acting mad and yelling at you, and it's okay if that makes you scared just for now, just here in this room. But remember that after this room, once we have the money, there's no truth in any of that. I act mad the same way I used to act scared when I told people you were sick. Remember that? It was a game, like this. I love you the most and forever, that's the truth. But I'm going to act mad, because that's how we're going to get money today.

I did it, and it worked. I held the necklace and, when the rich lady appeared, my mom yelled at me. *Brand, what are you doing? You KNOW better than to take things that don't belong to you.* Then, turning to the lady, *I'm SO sorry, ma'am. He knows money has been tight and he's... I'm so sorry.* Then back to me, *Brand, this woman is kind enough to let you wait while I clean and... I know you get scared when I talk about the bills, but taking things that don't belong to you isn't the answer!* Then she handed the necklace back to the lady, continuing with her apology, head down in shame.

We got money that day. I don't know how much, but I guess the lady took pity on us. I was almost six years old and we saw *The Addams Family* in the nice downtown theater that night. Mom ordered the big popcorn and Red Vines and I fell in love with Christina Ricci.

When I was too old for our jewelry con to be plausible, my mom came up with another one. At one of her housekeeping jobs, I'd stand lookout while Mom swapped a spare car key for a dummy, or took an impression of it. She'd say, *Stand there with this toy, and if you see or hear anyone coming, drop the toy loudly, right on the tile floor.*

We did that one a few times and, afterward, there'd be plenty of food for a few weeks or our car would start working again. I learned later that she never snuck out at night to pinch the cars herself. All she did was sell the key and the location to a dude who paid her forty percent of whatever he got for it.

By the time I was nine, I'd figured out that Mom was making money in secret ways, and I begged her to let me help. I remember that her "other jobs" seemed mysterious and forbidden. It wasn't that I minded being left with her friend Monica for a few hours, I just wanted to be part of Mom's life, especially the cool, magical part of it.

She finally relented, and that's how I started working auctions. After explaining that an antique auction was where rich people competed to see who'd pay the most for old stuff, Mom dressed me in some of my nicest clothes, and herself in a long coat and low-cut top. The auction display was in a big room with a patterned carpet and fluorescent lights. Must've been a function room at a hotel. Three walls were lined with tables covered with funny-looking objects with little pieces of paper in front of them. The objects weren't interesting, so I studied the people instead.

They were all dressed like the boring people on TV. I understood, in my child-way, that Mom had brought us among our enemies, both because they were boring and because, in her house-cleaning job, she worked for people like that.

After a circuit of the room, she led me into a wide hallway that led to the bathrooms. She squatted down face-to-face with me, and spoke low, *Count to twenty real slow, one-Mississippi, two-Mississippi, and then come out, walk into the door of the auction room, and start making a fuss like we talked about, got it?* When I nodded, she said, louder, *Okay, I guess you're old enough to go in by yourself, I'll wait here!* and ushered me in the men's room door.

I stood in that harsh-lit hotel bathroom, not having to go, counting Mississippis, and getting more and more scared. The boring people in that room didn't seem like they'd care about a strange kid. They might not look at me. If they didn't look, Mom might get caught. Then I had an inspiration, thinking of something that had happened at school a few days earlier, something nobody had looked away from.

Proud of myself, I stuck my index finger up my nose, crooked the tip a little, and *twisted.*

Five seconds later, I was in the doorway of the big room, screeching at the top of my lungs, *Mommy, help! I'm bleeding!*

I was right: everyone looked. A little kid with blood all down the lower half of his face will do that. I half-saw Mom make an almost-invisible swipe with one arm, and then she charged through the crowd and scooped me up. *Oh, sweetie, is your nose bleeding again? Shhhh, it's okay, we'll take care of it.*

She turned almost apologetically to the rest of the room and used the same soothing-a-child tone, *I'm sorry, he gets these sometimes. It's okay.*

Everyone was so relieved to hear that, so glad they could stop worrying about the bloodied child, that we became invisible. Mom took me into the women's restroom and packed my nostril with toilet paper. In the car on the way home, she scolded me for introducing a new element to the plan, for not thinking of whether seeing me bleed would frighten her. But she also let me handle the 18th-century ivory snuffbox she'd pocketed, warning me to be careful because I was holding four months' rent in my hands. I caressed the smooth, delicately engraved curves of the little box. I never saw it again, but I never forgot what it felt like.

After that, Mom cut me out of the deal for a while. She was probably worried that I'd grown old enough to understand what we were doing. By the time I was ten, she'd graduated to selling plans to professional burglars like Mikey Smooth. Layouts, alarm codes, key impressions, travel schedules, that sort of stuff. She was probably the only jugmarker in America with a part-time housekeeping gig.

Problem was, she often suspected her partners were screwing her on the cut, so her next move was to start doing burglaries herself. That was where my love affair with film started. Mom would park me in a movie theater after buying two tickets, then slip out the side door. Most jobs took an hour or less, so she usually made it back before the credits rolled. Movie tickets aren't the best alibi, but they're not the worst. After she started doing burglaries herself, it was only a series of small escalations to get to the "robbing a poker game at gunpoint" stage of the crime life.

As the sky began to darken, I landed back at my apartment in Felony Flats, a neighborhood that's too scary to be gentrified, at least so far. A few years back, the city tried to rebrand the area, because who wants to pay $1,600 a month for a one-bedroom in a neighborhood named for its high crime rate? In the East Portland online community, we had a good time making fun of the city's efforts and coming up with our own name. After taking into account that crime *was* down over the last ten years, we settled on the name "Misdemeanor Meadows."

Despite the name, the neighborhood wasn't too bad. There were fewer shootings than there used to be and my complex was full of mostly friendly neighbors. If you watch *Portlandia* or hear about Portland on the news, you might have a certain picture in your mind. Good beer, local food, tattooed hipsters, indie bookstores, and Antifa clashing with either white supremacists or cops in Waterfront Park, depending on the day. The Portland I inhabited was one of eight-hour shifts, city buses, and a gray rain that owned seven months of the year. TV Portland worried about gluten and microaggressions. My Portland worried about making rent. My Portland worried about getting screwed on overtime, or picking up another shift so the electric company didn't cut the power.

My living room had a TV, a DVD player, a comfy old chair, and three bookshelves filled with way too many books, spilling over onto every horizontal surface. Some were history books—mostly local stuff about Portland and the northwest. Some were fiction—Gillian Flynn, Walter Mosely, John Le Carré. The biggest section was crime—memoirs and studies of bank robbers, con artists, grifters, mobsters, and, of course, everything by Phil Stanford, the legendary crime chronicler of the Rose City. At any given time, half a dozen were library books, and a couple of those were probably overdue.

Every room in my place had a popcorn ceiling, a slapbrush-textured surface with gold flecks that resembled nothing in nature. It hovered over my head at seven-feet-and-change, and its hideous design promised to block sounds from the floor above. I'd heard the pet names "daddy" and "babygirl" from the neighbors upstairs too many times to believe my landlord's assurances about privacy.

I still had two hours to kill, so I cracked an IPA, fell onto my recliner, and flipped on the TV. I knew what movie I'd left in the DVD player. I hit Play, then paused it before the opening credits rolled. I needed this film tonight, but wasn't sure I *wanted* it.

The first time I watched *Paper Moon*, I cried all night. I was thirteen and in a group home at the time. After lights out, I'd sneak down to the rec room and watch the old VHS tapes people had donated over the years. I liked action movies, dramas, comedies, damn near anything as long as it wasn't too old, so a black-and-white film set in the Great Depression wasn't about to catch my interest. That's what I told myself at the time. Now that I'm older and have read a couple books on trauma, I know I had *many* reasons to shy away from a film about a little girl and her dad working as small-time grifters. Then, one fateful night it came down to watching *Aladdin* for the fifth time or biting the bullet and watching *Paper Moon*.

From the second scene—Addie and Mose arguing about whether he'd stolen her money and whether she'd drink her Nehi and eat her Coney Island—it had me. Eighty minutes later, I was cross-legged on the floor, two feet from the TV so I could hear every word without waking anyone up, bathed in the soft gray glow of the screen. As I watched Addie run down the dirt road to reconnect with her dad—maybe to go straight, maybe to live a happy life committing petty crimes—my right sleeve was soaked where I'd wiped my tears. All I could think was, *That's the way things should have gone.* But they didn't.

A dividing line splits my life in two: December 13, 1998. I've heard people talk about how 9/11 was like that for them, how the world is split into *before* and *after* that day. But 9/11 came years after my own divide, and it didn't compete. The distance between being twelve and having a mother and being thirteen without one is a million miles. The country changed in a thousand ways after 9/11, but for me it went on like normal—living in group or foster homes, watching *Paper Moon* over and over, and wondering when my mom would turn around and run toward me down that dirt road.

She never did.

I've watched the film a hundred times since, never with anyone else in the room. I pressed play, and under the twangy piano melody of "It's Only a Paper Moon," the sounds and smells of Felony Flats flowed in around me. Cars whooshed through puddles on Southeast Clinton Street, Mrs. Yang yelled at her husband a floor above, and Jamila banged pots and pans in the sink as she rushed to make an early dinner before her kids got home. Judging by the smells creeping through the crack under my door, it was taco night.

I pulled a long gulp from the beer. On the floor beside my chair sat my box of memories—an old shoebox of newspaper clippings, receipts, a letter or two, and some records I nabbed on my way out of my last foster home. Sometimes at the end of a long, shitty day, I'd thumb through the memories and grasp for the time before. As I watched Mose swindle a guy out of two hundred dollars, my memories drifted to the poker game, when everything went wrong.

The cold air on my cheeks was electric that night, my blood fizzed through my veins, and I felt as though anything was possible. I rode a pawnshop bike that was too small for me, my knees nearly bumping my chest as I pedaled. The puffy jacket and fake freckles painted on my cheeks made me look closer to nine than twelve. Laurelhurst was a neighborhood I normally wouldn't visit, but I coasted down a quiet sidewalk lined with knuckle-trunked trees a hundred years old, and I knew every house on the block. I knew which had kids, which had servants, which had dogs, and whether those dogs were mean or friendly. I was full of a joyous anticipation almost too intense to contain. For the first time, I was the key to the job.

The scene of the crime was a big brick mansion that took up half the block, sprawled out like a fat, sleepy cat. Wrought-iron bars covered the first-floor windows and its arched front door was made of old black wood. I eased off the pedals, slowing to size up the large man guarding the front door. Six feet plus, big around the middle and big through the shoulders too, with huge hands and a neatly trimmed goatee. His eyes tracked to me, the innocent-looking kid on the bike, so I smiled and gave him a little wave. A test.

He grinned and waved back. Jackpot.

I circled the block as quickly as I could, pumping the pedals hard to get back into position, fast enough that I started sweating beneath my jacket, even in the December breeze. All my senses buzzed. I was more awake than I'd ever been. The yellow glow of a streetlight cast cartoony tree-branch shadows along the sidewalk. The street was super quiet, as though the world was holding its breath to see what I'd do next. Even the crows that would normally be cawing and flapping had disappeared, leaving everything still except for the whir of my bike tires over the pavement.

When I made it around the block, I slowed again. On the shadowy side of the hedge next to our target, Mom and Ricky waited. Mom's hair was twisted into a bun and tucked beneath a knitted winter cap. Between that and the heavy coat, you could hardly tell she was a woman, which was part of the point. Ricky wore the same cap and coat, and each had a wool scarf pulled up above their chin.

I gave a thumbs-up as I pedaled by, my heart nearly exploding with pride. They pulled the scarves over their noses and put their hands in their coat pockets. I pedaled faster, breathing harder and building the speed I'd need for the flop. I gave the big guy another wave-and-smile to make sure he was looking at me, then zipped past and hit a driveway to weave the bike onto the sidewalk without losing speed.

Forty yards on, a tree root split the cement. When I reached it, I jerked the handlebars hard so my front wheel hit the root sideways. The bike slammed to a stop beneath me and I rose from the seat. I'd practiced a hundred times in my mind, but my excitement turned to fear as I flew over the front of the bike. My feet tangled in the handlebars. I crashed down on my left shoulder as the bike flipped and landed on top of me.

Letting out a howl of pain, I drew my left knee toward my chest, the howl collapsing into sobbing syllables. *Aaaah-oh-ow-ah-oh-god, that hurrrrrrts!*

Sure enough, heavy footsteps pounded rapidly in my direction, first muffled over grass, then louder as they struck pavement. The security guard was backlit by the mansion's glowing windows as he ran toward me. I looked up at him in tears as two shadows raced around the dark hedge. Mom and Ricky were illuminated for an instant under the porch light before vanishing inside that big arched door.

You okay, kid? asked the big man. *That looked like a rough fall.*

I was just... I was riding... I sobbed, *and I fell, and my leg hurts so bad!*

Okay, it's all right, I know first aid. Lemme look at it.

I pictured that big galoot in a Red Cross class, carefully learning to fix people smaller and more fragile than him. I shook it off and stuck to my prepared lines. *No!* I snapped. *Don't touch it! It hurts!*

It's all right, little man. Just trying to help. Can you tell me where it hurts? His voice was gentle and soft. We'd pegged this guy just right.

I started my next line. *It's my knee, it's—*

CRACK.

Unmistakably a gunshot, unmistakably from the mansion. The guard's head and mine snapped up in unison. For an instant, we shared the same thought: *Something's gone bad-wrong.*

I took another swig of beer, then swirled the remaining half-inch in the bottle. It was my last one. The fridge was damn near empty, so I had to make it count.

I didn't like remembering that night. It made my chest tighten and my temples throb. When something just *ends*, your brain goes back to the time before, and you try to figure out what happened, try to make sense of things, to put the pieces together. But sometimes things *don't* make sense, sometimes the pieces *don't* fit. Sometimes you're just torturing yourself with an endless memory loop that leads back to the moment your whole world broke.

By the time Addie and Mose reunited on the dirt road, it was time to meet Soup. I tossed the shoebox of memories on the floor, flicked off the TV, and headed out into the night.

For the first time in a long time, I had a whisper of hope. It wasn't a hope that everything would get better. Not even that *anything* would get better. If my mom really *was* in town, Soup was my best shot of finding her. I didn't know if seeing her again would break the endless loop of memories or create new ones to take their place, but it promised something different.

The Oregonian, December 17, 1998

Possible shooter identified in Laurelhurst murder

by Brian Schmidt

Police have identified a Portland woman with a known criminal past as a suspect in the shooting that killed one man in the Laurelhurst neighborhood on Friday night. According to sources within the department, Wanda Penny and an accomplice entered the front door of the home at 8:55 PM and demanded the money being gambled in the poker game.

An argument ensued and a security guard burst through the door only a minute or two later. According to an officer who was present at the scene, Ms. Penny shot the guard before escaping. The security guard was pronounced dead at the scene.

The house where the shooting took place is owned by timber heir Martin Seykes, who could not be reached for comment.

The accomplice has yet to be identified.

Chapter Four

Soup's real name was Franklin Kitchens, but the crowd my mom
hung out with when I was a kid didn't like real names. From
what I'd gathered, people swapped the *Franklin* for *Soup*, as in *Soup
Kitchens*. The joke was that he was so cheap he'd eat at soup kitchens
even when he was flush with cash. Whether it was true or not, the
name stuck, and eventually the *Kitchens* fell away. By the time I met
him when I was five or six, everyone called him Soup.

I found him at Ace's Quick Cash, his pawnshop in Felony Flats,
just west of 82nd and only a ten-minute walk from my place. Soup
had bought the store and the apartment above from a lady called
Bonny, who took it over from a guy called Duck. Nobody knew who
Ace was, but the name worked so everyone ran with it.

When I walked in, Soup nodded at me over the shoulder of a
woman haggling for a better price for a watch, claiming it wasn't a real
Rolex. The second hand didn't move right, the engravings on the
winder weren't legit, and there should've been a cyclops lens magni-
fying the date. Soup wasn't having it. The damn thing was real as a
heart attack, and he wanted two grand. It was three minutes past
closing time, but he wasn't about to kick out a potential customer.

Soup was like me, and like my mom as I remembered her, always

32

looking for an angle, always trying to find the edges of legality. There is a kind of mind that hears there's a rule against theft and thinks, *Okay, good to know. That makes sense, stealing is bad.* And then there's a kind of mind that hears there's a rule against theft and thinks, *What definition of theft are you using? What are the edges of this particular rule? How do they catch people who violate it? What are the costs of getting caught versus the chance of getting caught versus the profits of NOT getting caught?* And God help me, I realized when I was still a kid that I didn't have the first kind of mind.

White-collar criminals use the same logic: *How much can I get away with before the law says I'm a thief?* The only difference is that those guys have the political and legal clout to change the rules, and thereby the definition of theft. They know how to make theft legal. We all understand that walking into a neighbor's house and leaving with her stereo is theft, right? But what if the CFO of a small investment firm uses a shell company to purchase a million shares of a fraudulent Chinese solar startup, then pumps the stock to unwitting retirees using an avalanche of buzzwords and straight-up lies? And what if the stock price triples, then the CFO dumps it just before the company—which he knew was a rug-pull all along—goes belly-up? That's illegal, right?

Well, prove it. After taking the marks in the nursing home for half of their retirement accounts, he buys a condo in St. Barths. Meanwhile, if I steal his BMW, I'm looking at three to five years.

Every person walks around full of internal contradictions—little hypocrisies that get them through the day, compromises they've made, or truths they've buried so they can make rent and stay alive. I'm no different. Even though I don't view the rules as a moral code, I mostly follow them anyway. Finding the edges of the law simply comes naturally to me, but that's not the same thing as committing crimes. Like I said, I haven't committed a crime in years. Haven't been involved in anything serious since a sweaty summer night when I was sixteen.

Soup was like me in another way, too. He'd gone straight. Started obeying those made-up rules, or at least most of them. Before he bought Ace's, he dealt weed and occasionally other stuff when it crossed his path. Nothing major, but when Oregon legalized marijuana in 2015, it cut the legs out from under his business. At that point, running a pawn shop made better economic sense. Back when he dealt, I bought from him every once in a while, but I quit smoking when it became legal. I knew a half-dozen guys locked up for it, and it didn't feel right to smoke when my friends were locked away for a "crime" that society had recently decided didn't exist.

The woman walked out after agreeing on a price of eight hundred bucks for the disputed Rolex and promising to return the next morning with the money.

Soup flipped the sign on the glass door to "Closed," then greeted me with a gap-toothed smile and clapped his hands together. "Keyser!"

I acknowledged the nickname with a nod. It was one of the few things I had when I was ten that I still had, at least within the walls of Ace's Quick Cash. I didn't understand when Soup first called me Keyser over twenty years ago, but I rented *The Usual Suspects* on VHS a couple years later and it all made sense.

"Heya, Soup." I stepped up to the glass counter. Twenty handguns with price tags on the trigger guards lay spread out under the glass. To their left lay a selection of engagement rings from engagements that, presumably, hadn't worked out.

"That lady"—he shook his head in disbelief—"you believe that lady? Doesn't she know I have a mortgage to pay on this joint?"

I pressed my hands into the case and peered at the watches to the right of the handguns. "*Is* the Rolex real?"

"What's *that* got to do with anything?"

I laughed, but I wasn't in the mood for small talk. The glass was cold on my fingers and the place smelled of must and rain. I'd been to Ace's to see Soup a hundred times, but this time felt different. "You seen Dolly?"

He sat on an old wooden stool, pulling a plastic toothpick from the pocket of his faux-fur vest. "Right to the point, huh?" He shoved the toothpick into his mouth and squinted, his dark-blue eyes locked on mine, his wrinkled face drawn up in skepticism. He had so many lines around his eyes and on his forehead that he looked like my neighbor's friendly old Shar-Pei.

Soup knew as well as I did that we'd spent the better part of twenty years avoiding the subject of my mother. It wasn't that we never mentioned her, just that we kept it superficial. I'd meet up with him to buy a nickel and he'd say, *Heard Dolly was in Idaho. Gemstones.* Or I'd stop by Ace's and he'd mention, *Guy I know said he did a rare book collection down in Sacramento with your mom. Dolly was the jugmarker on that one.* I'd always say, *Oh,* or *That's cool,* but no more than that. No follow-up questions. I never told him not to talk about her, but I never engaged and eventually he got the picture. We hadn't spoken a word about her in a few years.

I said, "Heard she might be in town." He didn't need to know about my morning.

Soup removed the toothpick from his mouth and pointed it at me. "You *heard?* If she's in town, my bet is she don't want no one hearin' about it."

He had a point. If Carebear was right and my mom was in town for a job, it was a bad sign that anyone had heard anything. If someone's heard something, it means someone screwed up or someone snitched.

Soup pursed his lips. Made me think he'd heard something, but I could tell he hadn't been picked up by Caraway.

"Have you seen her?" I asked again.

He jammed the toothpick back in his mouth and waved a dismissive hand at me. "If she *is* in town, she ain't been in here."

I walked a lap around the small shop, studying the rare coins in a display case and the guitars hanging from the wall behind it, before moving back to the handgun display next to the cash register. "That's it?"

Soup took a silver ring from the case and polished it with a jewelry cloth. "Your mom was a helluva thief. One of the best. And a beauty, too. Everyone thought so. Only woman in the circles I worked, back in the day." He cocked his head to the left like he was looking at a memory. He stared so hard I even turned my head, following his gaze to the wall. "Dolly was a class act. Careful, smart. Always knew what was what before she made a move, always had a backup plan in case something went sideways."

I winced, remembering a cold December night when things went sideways and there'd been no backup plan.

"No drugs, either," he continued. "Half the guys who ended up busted were whacked out on something." Soup was still looking off into the distance, looking at nothing, maybe looking into the past. I knew he missed being a criminal.

Standing in his pawnshop, I couldn't blame him. The corners were dusty, the ceiling water-stained from leaky pipes, and a half-eaten plate of spaghetti sat next to a magazine on a card table in the corner. As a general rule, straight life is boring as hell, probably even more so for Soup than for me because he'd been a criminal most of his life and straight for only a few years. Soup was the dollar-store version of Ray Liotta at the end of *Goodfellas*.

To avoid talking about that, I asked, "You think she never got caught because she didn't do drugs?"

"Part of the reason, but smarts was most of it. Comes to crime, she's a conservative."

That fit with my memory of her, and made it even stranger that she'd come back to the town where she was wanted for murder. "Hear of any jobs going down? The kind of thing she might be interested in?"

"In Portland?" He shrugged. "I can ask around, but no." Soup stepped out from behind the counter and stood next to me. "Still don't know why you're askin', but I've heard things. Rumors. Stuff I ain't told you. Figured you have reasons to not want to know. You want to know now?"

I nodded.

The door clanged and I turned, half-expecting to see the cop I'd ditched that morning. Instead, it was a skeleton of a man, his bony arms visible through a sopping-wet long-sleeved t-shirt. He was bald but had a short beard dyed a striking shade of bright green.

Soup seemed to recognize him. "Told you I don't deal no more, Greenbeard. Hell outta here. I'm closed."

"You got an umbrella?"

Soup frowned, then stomped behind the counter and handed him one. "Four bucks."

The man threw four crumpled ones on the counter and left without another word.

I said, "Who buys an umbrella in Portland?"

"You'd be surprised how many people stop in asking for them." He locked the front door, then used a tissue to pick up the money and slide it under the register. "Can't be too careful. These tweakers are constantly shedding Hep A onto their money, then out to the rest of the world."

"Oh, damn." I paused a half-beat, then asked, "So, 'bout Dolly?"

Soup rested a hand on the glass case that held the guns. "Don't know for sure, but I heard she was doin' higher-end work. Tech. Securities. Maybe even a bank, but I doubt that. She never liked guns, and I don't care how good you plan, a bank job needs guns."

"Bert Spaggiari, 1976," I said reflexively. He and his crew had painted *Without weapons, without hate, without violence* on the walls of the bank vault they emptied. Everyone knew that.

Soup rolled his eyes at me. "Fine, fine. But if you're not pulling the *greatest bank job in history*, it's a gun job, ya little smartass. That's why *I* never did one."

I shoved my hands in the pockets of my wet jeans, trying to figure out what to ask next. Heavy folds of skin half-shielded his eyes, which shone with a bright intelligence. A half-dozen questions occurred to me, questions about the past and about the present.

He watched me thinking, saw me struggling, and put a hand on my forearm. "Brand, tell me straight, how'd you hear she might be in town?"

I tried to play it cool. "Why'd you call her Dolly, anyway?"

He half-grinned. "One reason's because, for a long time, she kept a day job. Heck, you remember all those hours she put in as a house-keeper. Even when she was making enough from, y'know, *jobs*, she still worked a job. We used to tease her about *working nine to five*, and 'Dolly' just sorta stuck."

I remembered driving out to Sellwood and the West Hills in our beat-to-hell Nissan that smelled like wet cigarettes. The rich ladies she cleaned for treated her like a half-trained animal, and their husbands would... "Hang on. You said that was *one reason* you called her Dolly?"

"Well, that figure of hers *was* another."

The way he said it made me uncomfortable, but also sparked a memory. "Oh *damn*." I winced. "I just now got something she said when I was a kid. When she used to do lifts at auctions and stuff, she would wear a long coat and a low-cut top."

"I miss Nineties fashion," Soup mused.

"And when I asked how come, she said it was in case something went wrong, then the mark wouldn't be able to give a description of her face. Didn't get the joke when I was seven." I shook my head.

Soup guffawed. "Like I said, she was smart."

"She never... well, dated any of you guys, did she?"

"Naw," Soup said. "I mean, I think it crossed everyone's mind at least once, but naw. Lotta girls you can date, but not a lot you can do jobs with, y'know? Mostly, it was just that guys in our line of work don't like being second place in a woman's attention. Ego thing, I guess. And she made it clear there was one guy who'd always come first for her, no matter what."

I fidgeted with some lint in my pocket, balling it up tighter and tighter as he spoke. I'd come for information about the present and we were stuck in a past I had no desire to revisit.

"But yeah, once you took dating off the table, Dolly was just... likable. Too many crooks treat every conversation like it's about who's got the biggest johnson. None of that with your mom. Easy to get along with, y'know? We all liked her. And she liked us. Didn't trust us, though. Kept everyone at arm's length. Never had a steady crew." He paused, like he was going to elaborate, then smiled. "We liked you, too. You were the cutest little S.O.B., always sneaking in after your mom told you to go to bed, always asking questions. Little budding criminal mastermind, Keyser Soze. You remember the time I sat you down and told you how to talk to cops?"

"Oh yeah," I said carefully. "I remember that talk."

"Listen, Brand, I don't want to get into your business, but... I know you've been straight a long while now. And I know your mom isn't." He paused like a man gathering up words in a dangerous combination. "I dunno if you're planning on... I have no idea *what* you're planning..."

Fair enough, neither did I. "Just spit it out, Soup."

"If you're thinking of getting in again, maybe that's a decision you should think over... carefully." His voice was cautious.

"What makes you say that?"

"Even good thieves get caught. Ricky Gat, Mikey. Your mom's had some damn close calls. Plus—" he cast an exaggerated, side-to-side look around the store—"you see a pretty wife and smiling kids waiting to hand me a World's Greatest Dad coffee mug? With or without guns, this life ain't the kind you share."

"I'm single now." I'd mentioned Jennifer a few times, but never brought her to meet Soup. Even if we'd stayed together, I never would have. I'd worked like hell to keep my past away from Jennifer. And even though Soup had gone straight, he still sparked a part of me I hadn't wanted her to see. Soup knew me, though, and could probably tell I'd been in love.

He gave me the side-eye, but let it go and began sorting through some red-and-white pawn tickets beside the register.

I cast about for a change of subject, and my brain pinged on a detail, a *"yeah, but"* I'd managed to ignore earlier. "You were wrong before—the biggest bank job in history wasn't in '76, it was in 2003. Spaggiari's crew got ten million. The 2003 job got over a billion in hard cash, none of it ever recovered."

He scowled, willing to argue the point. "I didn't say *biggest*, I said *greatest*. Bert pulled off a beautiful crime. That's not the same as having Iraqi soldiers load pallets of cash onto trucks."

"Fair point," I conceded. "They were obeying Saddam's order. The biggest bank job ever was completely legal."

"All the biggest crimes are. But they're never beautiful."

My head spun with memories and paranoia and I felt myself moving toward the door. I stopped in the middle of the shop. "Will you ask around? I need to find her." I heard the words as though spoken by someone else, as though I'd had to leave my body to ask the question. "Tonight, if possible."

Soup cocked his head to the left and passed the toothpick from hand to hand. Finally, he nodded. Just once, and almost imperceptibly, but it was all I needed.

I unbolted the door and opened it. The bell clanged and a rush of cold, damp air blew in, chilling the sweat on my forehead and knocking me back into my body.

"Hurry," I called back as I walked out into the darkness, scanning for cops. I still had to hit an ATM, then get back to the Burnside Bridge. I owed Mikey Shakes forty bucks, and I'd promised he'd have it today. You never break a promise to someone else in the life. That was another thing I learned growing up.

And now I had Soup's promise.

The Oregonian: December 19, 1998

Laurelhurst murder investigation stalled

Suspect released

by Brian Schmidt

Investigators admitted Thursday that their investigation into the murder in Laurelhurst has slowed due to lack of evidence.

Investigators have been interested in questioning Wanda Penny, who they describe as a "career criminal." Police say no arrest warrant has been issued and they have been unable to locate Penny for questioning. She is believed to have fled the state.

Yesterday, police released an unidentified suspect apprehended only blocks from the site of the murder and attempted robbery on the night of December 13. Though he was described as "somewhat cooperative," no case could be brought against him, according to investigators.

Details are still emerging, but The Oregonian has learned that his name was officially withheld under Measure 11, meaning he was under fifteen years old.

Chapter Five

The intensity of the previous day receded when I began my shift at Morey's Pharmacy. As much as I'd felt things viscerally as a kid, I rarely felt much of anything as an adult. And my job was the perfect place not to feel anything. Eight-hour shift after eight-hour shift, my life had become an exercise in banality, an endless parade of pills, sodas, adult diapers, snacks, cigarettes, nicotine patches and, this month, ornaments and Christmas lights.

Problem was, the banality left room for the memories to linger as a quiet dissonance scratching at me from the inside. All I'd heard from Soup was a midnight text: *Still working on it*. I'd considered checking out my mom's favorite haunts or walking by the houses of her old friends, but she was smart, unlikely to do anything so obvious. In the end, I couldn't think of anything useful enough to be worth an unexcused absence from work. Two of those in six months gets you fired.

The first difficult customer of the day was confused and distraught about his cholesterol medication. He'd grown more and more agitated as he waited in line. Working the register, you can always tell who has a complaint or question because they fidget and fume, wringing their empty hands. It's a near-universal fact that people who aren't buying anything believe this entitles them to head to the front of the line, but few actually go for it.

This man was in his fifties, tall and barrel-chested, his face red, blotchy, and slightly damp. "I'm having an issue with my Zocor," he growled, leaning heavily on the counter. "I used to be on a different medication for cholesterol, Cresti or something like that, but my—" he visibly stopped himself from swearing—"my insurance company stopped covering it."

"Sorry to hear that."

"Yeah, and this one has a lower copay. That's a big help, but there are some issues."

"Uh-huh."

"Still can't understand how two similar drugs can be priced so differently. Can you?"

For the first few months at Morey's, I'd attempted to explain to customers that I only worked the register. Legally, I couldn't answer questions related to their prescriptions. Soon I realized something: most people didn't want answers. Or, at any rate, they didn't want the answers our pharmacists gave, usually something like, *That's a decision made by the insurance company, we don't set policy.* Or, translated from customer-service-speak, *Yeah, you're getting screwed, and no, there's no way I can help you.*

Most people were like the blotchy-faced man in front of me. They wanted someone who'd listen to them vent. I offered a polite smile because that was my job and it was clear this dude was hurting. "No, sir. I can't understand it."

"The issue though—and I'm sorry, I know there's a line behind me —the issue is stomach pain and skin irritation." He pointed at a dry patch on his face. "So what do you think?"

"Sorry to hear that, sir. Lemme get the pharmacy tech for you."

"Dear God! Dealing with side effects, insurance, and copays will stroke me out long before cholesterol does. Can't *you* help me?"

"I'm just a cashier, sir." I flashed him a sympathetic grimace.

He turned a slow three-sixty, examining everything around him and noticing, for the first time, that he was at the counter *next* to the pharmacy window. "Sorry, you were the only person I saw and"—he scratched the red spot on his face—"it's just that this skin thing..."

I got him the pharmacy tech and rang up antacids and chips and makeup and soda for the folks behind him, listening involuntarily as he retold the story from the beginning.

I sat in the breakroom, thinking about Carebear and the dude—now *dudes*—who were tailing me. I'd picked up the new tail before even leaving for work. My apartment building had one entrance but two exits. The main entrance was on Southeast Clinton Street, but the door at the end of the hall exited into an alley between Clinton and Hult. That was where we took out the trash and recycling. From my living-room window, I had a view of the street out front, and I hadn't picked up anyone there. That didn't mean much, though. I'd assumed there was a guy in a car close enough to monitor the main door in the reflection of a side mirror. First thing when I woke, I'd grabbed the recycling bucket and, bleary-eyed but fully alert, carried it to the alley. Sure enough, at the north end was a man leaning against the wall. He'd turned as soon as the door creaked open. I'd dumped the recycling—making an awful noise as the bottles and cans rattled and jangled in the empty dumpster—then gave the guy a thumbs-up. He knew that I knew he was tailing me, so why not? And I was about to head to work anyway, so I didn't need to ditch him.

What I couldn't figure out was why I was worth tailing in the first place. It wasn't like the PPB had dozens of extra officers waiting around to follow guys like me through every achingly boring step of our daily lives. Police departments have a hierarchy that dictates how they allocate resources. Like most large organizations, the first and most important priority is protecting their own power and budgets. Second is making themselves look good. Preventing crime comes third or lower, so if I warranted a tail, Carebear must have been convinced I knew where my mom was. Hell, Carebear might have believed I was involved in whatever my mom was cooking up. But even that didn't justify the manpower unless my mom was onto something huge. Maybe a massive score was what had brought her back to Portland after twenty years, but nothing I'd heard about my mom carried stakes high enough to warrant two tails.

Or maybe Carebear was chasing the poker game itself. After all, there's no statute of limitations on murder, and Caraway seemed like the type who'd love to see a photo of herself splashed across the front page of *The Oregonian*. I could already see the headline: *Dogged Detective Nabs Wanted Woman in Laurelhurst Poker Game Murder*.

I'd avoided the details of that night for twenty years, but I wasn't going to be able to avoid them forever. Other than the players and my mom, only one person knew what went on inside that room: my mom's partner on the job, Ricky Gat, who was now locked up in OSP. In an hour of sentimentality a couple years back, I'd gotten on his approved visitors list. I'd told myself I'd go out to see him, but the prison was an hour outside town, and I didn't have my own car, and it felt like a hassle, and... between one excuse and another, I'd never visited. As my break ended, I sent Ricky a visitation request through the J-Pay correctional email system.

I was about to head back to the counter when my phone vibrated in my pocket. I'd made my peace a few years back with the fact that, like most Americans, I carried a GPS tracking device around with me at all times. It was Soup. *Dolly wants to chat. Tomorrow at 10 AM?*

I blinked, expecting the message to disappear or morph into something less... immediate. When the message failed to change, I tapped a reply asking where, but deleted it before sending. I doubted anyone was snooping my phone yet, but the possibility made me nervous. I took a deep breath and sent him a message: *I'll drop by later.*

The only problem was that "later" would have to be after my shift ended—six and a half more hours—and I'd already eaten the sandwich I'd planned to save for lunch. Tomorrow I might see my mom for the first time in twenty years, but today I had to keep my job.

To keep tweakers and dealers from sticking us up for oxy or amphetamines, we'd placed a big sign on the counter that explained how the good stuff was in a time-locked safe. It worked well. People believe damn near anything printed in all-caps on a laminated sign. But the "safe" was right up to the bare minimum legal standard of what you could call a "time-locked safe." In fact, it was the same model I'd once picked up for fifty bucks on Craigslist so I'd have something to do with my hands while I watched movies. After I'd busted it a few times, I took to picking up old padlocks and combo locks at the flea market and fiddling with those. I could never afford the safes I really wanted to practice on, and I stopped doing this when Jennifer started spending time at my place.

A couple times a day, I thought about how easy it would be to empty the opioid safe. Deliveries came twice a week, so we never had a huge supply, putting the street value of the contents at only low five figures. And moving that many pills at once would mean taking a hit on price and increasing the risk of pinging a snitch or an undercover cop.

A guy approached the counter, one I'd seen before. He was about my age, but his thin, wispy mustache made him look like a teenager attempting to age up. He always wore an old suit jacket over freshly-ironed designer jeans, and showed up once a month to pick up his grandma's pain meds because she was "too old to do it in person." He was dealing, of course. The prescribing physician on granny's oxycodone had changed four months earlier, and the number of pills increased. For my own amusement, I'd used one of the pharmacy techs' IDs to log in to the system and check out the doc. Turned out he prescribed quite a bit of oxy, Vicodin, plus a fair amount of alprazolam, which suggested he had name recognition in the suburban-wine-mom demographic. Those moms love their Xanax. So, Wispy Mustache's granny wasn't getting her pills, they were paying for his fancy jeans. Maybe she didn't need them anymore. Could even be that she was dead. None of my business either way.

Despite the new, stricter guidelines for prescribing opioids, little had changed. The crooked doctors of the world kept prescribing and the fancy-jeans dudes of the world kept dealing. I sent him away with another ninety pills, idly wondering how he'd move them. Probably through friends and "friends," but if he had a nickel's worth of sense he'd just sell online, where risk plummets and it becomes a nice little home business instead of something that gets you shot. If they'd had the TOR network when I was a kid, a lot of stuff might've been different. But there are a lot of ways stuff might've been different. I tried not to dwell on it.

Jennifer's text had said she might stop by today, and I was embarrassed how much I was looking forward to it. Still, I didn't let myself get too attached to the idea. When it came to errands, Jennifer's best intentions sometimes let her down. She had a pliable sense of time and occasionally let her medication run out because she was too busy or lazy to pick up the refill. When we were dating, I'd picked them up for her. I wasn't a great boyfriend, but I always made sure she had her meds.

She still hadn't shown up by the time I sat at the little table for my afternoon break, and my phone was burning a hole in my hand. I knew Soup wouldn't have given my mom my phone number, and she wouldn't have called me even if he had, but knowing he'd made contact with her changed everything. The feeling that I was being clawed at from the inside intensified. I scrolled through the stats from last night's Blazers game and watched a dude on YouTube bust open a safe using liquid nitrogen. The longer I sat, the worse I felt. Everyone knows that memories live inside us, and I used to think they lived in the brain. But that's wrong. Memories—the painful ones at least—live in the whole body. They latch onto bones, lubricate joints, and burrow into muscle fibers. They swim through blood, and they have teeth. As I sat on that cold plastic chair, alone in the breakroom, they crawled out of their hiding places and into my thoughts.

The little speaker in the corner played a commercial for Michael Carusa's car dealerships. He had five or six of them in the greater

Portland area, and the commercials always started and ended the same way. He'd been using the same cheesy jingle for years: *C-A-R-U-S-A, Drive the car you deserve today!* We weren't allowed to change the radio station because it had been carefully selected to be inoffensive to the greatest number of valued shoppers. So I sat there while the jingle burned a hole through my brain. It was better than the alternative.

C-A-R-U-S-A, Drive the car you deserve today!

Under normal circumstances, Carusa's jingle drove me nuts, but combined with seeing the Brian White billboard on the side of the bus yesterday, I was beginning to wonder whether the world was conspiring against me.

The door swung open and my boss flopped into the seat across from me at the little folding card table. "Been thinking of setting up a new display area." As usual, his voice was full of enthusiasm, as if he was describing the latest episode of his favorite TV show, or his daughter's first steps. Last time I felt that sort of enthusiasm, I was riding my pawnshop bike down a shadowy block in Laurelhurst. "My thinking is, the NFL playoffs are about to start. And what goes with football?"

I shrugged. "Chicken wings?"

He frowned. "Well, sure, but you know as well as me we don't have the permits to sell meat." He waited for me to guess again.

Kevin wasn't a bad guy. He'd been promoted to assistant manager last year and didn't treat me like garbage. He reminded me of this tuna-noodle casserole one of my foster dads used to make. It was cheap and reasonably nutritious, but it was bland and sticky and chewy and always the same. It was a failure of imagination, a pasty rejection of the idea that food could be pleasurable or flavorful. Kevin was the tuna-noodle casserole of people.

Finally, his enthusiastic grin and raised eyebrows got to me. He really wanted me to play this game. God forgive him, I had to admit that his presence was making me feel a little better. "Snacks?" I offered weakly.

He smacked the table with both hands. "Exactly! Chips, soda, popcorn, roasted almonds and beef jerky for the keto people. With the Plaid Pantry right across the street, I figure we can cut into some of their snack market with a football-themed display right out front. Maybe a banner on the side of the building so people can see it as they pull into the lot? Whadya think?"

I almost said something snarky about how if he wants to move chips and popcorn he should get us licensed as a marijuana dispensary, but instead, I smiled. "Sure. Why not?" Then, with as much enthusiasm as I could muster, "I think you should go for it." If a football-themed snack display was all he had to get him juiced, who was I to take that away from him? Plus, I wasn't really one to talk. It wasn't like my life was packed full of excitement.

He gave me a knowing smile and marched out of the break room like a man on a mission. In just under two hours, I'd be done for the day. By then, he'd probably have little paper footballs pinned to the entrance and stacks of Pepsi and racks of chips towering over every person who walked through our sliding doors.

At the end of my shift, I "punched out" by tapping some icons in an app on my phone. We used to use keycards, but the pharmacy phased those out last year after a salesman convinced Kevin that the app was more secure. As though people clocking out late or early was a major security hole that threatened the entire business. And as though a cloud-based, third-party app with fishy security credentials was safer than keycards. It's amazing what a good salesman can convince someone of, especially when it comes to digital security.

Jennifer hadn't come, but I figured she'd be in tomorrow. A year after a breakup, a person isn't supposed to devote this much brain-time to their ex's comings and goings, but I couldn't help it.

I forced her out of my mind as best I could. I couldn't worry about her or her meds right now. I had to go meet Soup, which meant I needed my crime brain. On the curb, I scanned for tails. The purplish-gray sky and the smell of wet pavement meant I'd missed a

49

heavy rain while inside. Eisenhower Jacket Guy was nowhere to be seen, but he might have been in a car nearby. The only sure way to catch a tail was to start moving.

I walked a lap around the block, then headed back into the pharmacy and grabbed my phone from the break room, where I'd left it on purpose. I poked my head back out the front entrance. Everything was still clear. I lapped the block again, checking reflections in shop windows and using the selfie setting on my phone to look behind me once or twice. Nobody watched me but a pair of crows on a phone wire. Maybe the tails had given up. My job was boring as hell, but *watching* me do my job... I laughed at the thought. *Torture.*

I stopped to use the bathroom in a coffee shop, then slipped through the back door into an alley. From there I jogged to the bus stop and waited for the 72 to take me back to Ace's Quick Cash, back to Soup, and one step closer to the meeting I'd longed for.

The meeting I'd dreaded.

Foster Care Placement Questions

DATE:
February 1, 1999

ABOUT CHILD
Name: Brandon Penny
Age: 12
Gender: Male
Siblings: None
School/Daycare: Beaumont

WORKER INFO
Protection Worker: G. Hernandez

MEDICAL CONDITIONS
Allergies: None
Medications: None
Psychological Conditions: Oppositional Defiant Disorder
Drug/alcohol exposure: Minor, no immediate concern

REASON IN CARE
Reason: Arrested, mother is fugitive, no other known relatives.
Date of Apprehension: 12/13/98
First time in care: Yes

FAMILY/KIN
Mom: Wanda Penny (no contact!)
Dad: Unknown
Other kin involved: N/A
Sibling Age and Location: N/A

BEHAVIORS

Aggression/Anger: Mild
Emotionally Sensitive: No
Sleeping: Normal
Toilet Trained: Yes
Interaction with others: Largely OK
Impulse control: High
Property Destruction: Theft
Self-Harm: No
Other: Dishonesty, frequent lying

PLAN OF CARE

Brandon is an intelligent, healthy boy who was deprived of a normal home by his mother's criminal tendencies. If taught normal skills and exposed to the value of honesty and obeying the law, there is no reason he shouldn't become a perfectly normal adult. My recommendation is that Brandon continue with regular schooling, where he should excel if he can learn to work within the boundaries of normal society.

Chapter Six

Steel Bridge looks like a giant H made of rust-pocked gray metal. It's a vertical truss, the type where the span rises straight into the sky when a ship comes through—parallel to the ground instead of tilting up on a joint like most movable bridges. They don't make many vertical trusses anymore, but it's a Portland landmark. As I bounced toward it on the Blue Line, only one of the two towers was visible. The second stood hidden behind the first, making it look more like a crane from an old black-and-white photograph. I rarely took the Blue Line, but it was the cheapest route to the Oregon Zoo.

I'd met with Soup the previous day after taking the long route to Ace's and doubling back a few times. Soup ran a legit business and the last thing I wanted was to show up tailed by cops. He'd danced around the subject of my mom for a while—or maybe *I* had—but after a few minutes of BS, he'd told me to meet her at the mountain goat exhibit near the entrance when the zoo opened the next day. When Soup told me I was going to see my mother for the first time in twenty years, all I could do was stare at a dust ball on the floor, aware of the blank place inside me where the surge of emotion should have appeared, but didn't.

Getting to sleep had been a war. Every little noise grabbed my attention. Across the hall, Jamila kept clinking dishes and turning the water on and off in her sink. Her routine was to wait until the kids went to bed, then turn on a podcast and clean until midnight. She liked her kitchen to sparkle like it had never been used. A floor above me, the new couple was either moving furniture or having vigorous sex. Maybe both. Blocks away, a car alarm went off, but a branch scraping my bedroom window distracted me from it. A car door slammed. My refrigerator hummed as its cooling cycle began. When I finally got to sleep, bad dreams were my reward. Nothing I could remember on waking, just a general sense that terrible things had chased me through the night. Before catching the train, I'd brewed some coffee and toasted a bagel, hoping the routine would chase away the eerie feeling, but the uneasiness remained.

I leaned against the window and pressed my face into the cold glass as Steel Bridge formed its giant H. Below, the Willamette River sparkled in the light of the December sun, specks of yellow gold dappling the dull, brown water. Half an hour from seeing my mom for the first time in twenty years—on a sunny winter day at that—you'd think I'd be reminiscing, focusing on the good memories, or planning what to say. Instead, my brain replayed something that happened when I was thirteen, in my first foster home. Had it been one of the dreams pursuing me as I slept? I wasn't sure. For whatever reason, on a day when I needed to keep it together, a memory that made me feel sick and small and evil was at the top of my brain's playlist, and the damn thing was on loop.

The foster home was run by a couple named Dana and Ben. I was their sixth kid and lived there for most of the year I was thirteen. On the wall of the kitchen they had a bunch of cross-stitch samplers—Bible quotes in blocky letters, black on white.

He that covereth his sins shall not prosper: but whoso confesseth and forsaketh them shall have mercy.
— *Proverbs* 28:13

Train up a child in the way he should go: and when he is old, he will not depart from it.
— *Proverbs* 22:6

Those two were displayed at all times. The rest were there every day *except* when someone from the state came to check on us.

Iron sharpeneth iron; so a man sharpeneth the countenance of his friend.

— Proverbs 27:17

He that spareth his rod hateth his son: but he that loveth him chasteneth him betimes.

— Proverbs 13:24

Foolishness is bound in the heart of a child; but the rod of correction shall drive it far from him.

— Proverbs 22:15

Those last three disappeared from the walls after dinner five times a year, leaving only unfaded rectangles of artificial wood paneling. Among us kids, it was our cue to be on our best behavior because someone from the state was coming the next morning. Dana and Ben took the "rod of correction" the way they took everything else in their reading of the Bible: literally. It was usually a wooden dowel about two feet long, replaced at the hardware store every time they broke one on us. By the time the incident with Tony happened, I'd made its acquaintance more than once. The first time was a mild session for swearing. Second time was rougher—I stole chocolate cake from the fridge after lights-out. They thought their damned rod taught obedience, but all it taught me was fear. So when they found the weed I'd taped to the drainpipe under the sink in the girls' room, yeah, I was scared. They'd found the baggie during an unannounced search of our rooms, riffling through the beds and drawers of the three girls and three boys who were stuck there at the time. They didn't find anything in my stuff—I was too smart for that—but the nickel of stems and bits had fallen off the pipe where I'd taped it. Just before lights-out, they'd brought us all into the family room and told us what they'd found. What bothers me is they didn't even ask whose it was. They'd already decided it was Tony's, based on his past record blended with whatever strain of zealous craziness was already running through their brains. They made us watch as they pulled Tony's pants down, made us watch as Ben laid into him with that stick for what seemed

55

like forever. I tried to look away, but Dana saw me. We weren't allowed to look away. She grabbed my head and turned it back. Most days, she was a decent person, emotionally cold but not hurtful, and a good cook. But when that righteous madness was on her, she'd... well, just for example, she'd force a bunch of children to watch another child's ass beaten bloody.

If they'd asked, I might've confessed. If they'd said specifically, "We are going to brutalize Tony unless someone else admits it was their marijuana," I might have spoken up. I doubt it, though. I was scared. They'd beaten that into me. But I had the chance to say something anyway. I knew what was going to happen the minute they pulled out that baggie, but I let it happen. I could justify it a hundred ways. I didn't even like Tony, me getting beaten would have been just as unfair and cruel, and so on. There are always justifications when you need them, but some stains never wash clean from your conscience. I'll never forget Tony's screams, just like I'll never forget that I pulled that security guard off the door.

"*Now arriving, Washington Park Station,*" the robotic voice said politely from a speaker behind me. "*Exit now for the Oregon Zoo. Doors to my left. Puertas a mi izquierda.*"

On the platform, I stopped in front of a long plastic tube recessed into the stone wall. It was a 100-foot-long core sample taken when the station was created. Marked by strata, it showed the passage of geological time. If its labels were correct, I was two hundred and sixty feet below the surface, standing at a level of the earth that had been formed sixteen million years ago.

The elevator had only two stops. As part of the station's geological theme, the signs referred to the two levels not by conventional floor numbers but by "Sixteen Million Years Ago" and "The Present" for the train station level and surface level, respectively. During the ascent, a digital indicator showed my current position expressed not as a floor number, but as elevation above sea level.

450 feet. 511 feet. 538 feet.

As I rose to the surface, I hoped to feel the weight of the thousands of tons of rock lifting from me like a buoy floating over rising water.

591 feet. 619 feet.

I wanted to step from the elevator into the sunlight changed, light as a feather. My ears popped as the elevator rose, but that brought no relief. The painful pressure was coming from somewhere else.

The Rocky Mountain Goat exhibit was the first thing I saw when I entered the zoo. It was a collection of huge boulders with nearly-sheer sides, surrounded by little patches of nutritious grass. It let the big, shaggy goats show off their ability to clamber around on impossible-seeming ledges and angles, and let kids get close enough to see them well without being able to touch them.

I'd been to the zoo more than once as a kid, and I remembered the boulders as towering monoliths, almost like mountains. Now it was smaller than my memory wanted it to be.

I saw Mom leaning on a sign next to the fence around the boulders. She looked older. Older than my last mental image of her, sure, but also older than I'd expected. On the train, I'd imagined what she'd look like now in an attempt to update the memories in my mind. Actually seeing her forced me to confront that part of me that had been looking for the thirty-year-old mother I'd last seen bolting across that porch in a mask. The adult me knew she'd be older; the twelve-year-old me still expected his mom to be thirty.

Even accounting for her age, she looked good. There weren't many fifty-year-old women in my day-to-day life to use as a comparison, but her face looked bright. Her dark brown hair was tied in a ponytail that brought back so many memories. Now it was streaked with gray at her temples. I watched from fifty yards away, taking her in as her eyes darted from the entryway to the restrooms to the food court to the walkways. She'd missed my entrance and had scanned past me twice. For an instant she looked right at me, then kept scanning. She hadn't recognized me. The pain of it hit hard. Like me, she was looking for someone from twenty years ago.

Her gaze landed on me once more as I approached, and the look in her eyes changed. Searching, then puzzlement. Confusion, followed by recognition. Finally, surprise, but no smile.

I stopped a few yards away.

She looked me up and down. "I was looking for someone younger. I guess you're not twelve anymore."

"I was looking for someone younger, too."

We stared for too long before she smiled and spread her arms for a hug. On my best days I'm uneasy with affection. I pull back into my head and refuse to feel, only to reflect later on what I *might* have been feeling. Despite that, I stepped forward and she pulled me in hard. Before I could pull away, her hand moved around my waist, then slid up my back, tapping and exploring as it moved up to my shoulders.

The three most common places to hide an audio transmitter are on the chest—which she'd ruled out by pressing in close for the hug— the belt, and the back. It wasn't a full search, but she was checking me for a wire.

Twenty years of nothing—not a letter, not a call, not a single moment of contact. The first time my mother had touched me in two damn decades, and she was patting me down to make sure I wasn't a snitch. I'd been of two minds about meeting her. I wanted to see her again, to be her son again, for things to go back to how they'd been. Then there was the fear. I didn't trust her, I knew she wouldn't trust me, and meeting with her could mess up my life even more. The pat down tipped the scale toward fear.

She studied me as we broke apart, head cocked to the side the way she used to do when thinking about a job. She was probably wondering how I'd learned she was in town. Like any good thief, she'd want to know whether I put her job at risk, whether I put *her* at risk. She'd also wonder whether I was already working with the cops. She'd be stupid not to. Good thieves are also good liars, though, and she wouldn't come right out and say any of that.

She said, "Oh my God, how *are* you? I was afraid you wouldn't want to see me, which is why I didn't reach out to you, or anyone." Her tone was earnest and eager, like she was genuinely happy to see me. "There's so much to talk about. I hope you're not..." She trailed off, like she'd run out of sincerity.

She did want to know how I was. But after twenty years, the question, *How are you?* was so laughably inadequate, it left me speechless. A half-dozen answers occurred to me, some honest, some lies. Most dripped with sarcasm.

I leaned on the railing and waited for a goat to lift its head from a patch of grass before I answered. "Good, good. You know. Things are good." For some reason I went with the one answer that wasn't true, wasn't exactly false, and wasn't funny.

Small talk over, she got right to it. "How'd you know I was in town?"

I considered pinning it on Soup, considered saying something to the effect of, *Soup heard it from a guy and mentioned you.* But I couldn't tell a lie involving Soup and I didn't consider telling her about Carebear. "Word gets around, y'know? Be careful."

"Be careful? Brand, c'mon."

She turned toward me, but I kept my eyes on the grazing goat. The phrase *Be careful* had spooked her, but I let it hang there. After a long silence, I turned back. "So why *are* you in town?" I didn't expect the truth, but I hoped to get a read on her.

"Microchips."

I raised an eyebrow. "Yeah?" I was surprised she would want to share what she was up to. Maybe she felt she owed me something for all that had happened in the past.

"Don't look at me like that. I'm..." She sighed. "It's so weird seeing you. So... *something.* Yeah, microchips. A step up from what we used to do, what *I* used to do."

"Valuable?"

"Very. Not like the ones in your phone or laptop. Radiation-resistant, aerospace-quality chips go for sixty grand a pop. Eight display models gets close to half a million—" she shrugged in professional resignation—"or half that, fenced."

I shrugged back. "Huh."

I didn't know whether she was lying about the microchips, but the job yanked my attention away from the questions I'd come wanting to ask, and raised a dozen more. Like I said, certain kinds of minds see the contours of a crime whether they like it or not. *What exact brand of microchips? Are they in a downtown office building, a factory, or one of the new techy loft offices they keep building on the north side of the river? What's security like? Solo job or do you have partners? Do you already have a fence lined up?*

She touched my arm. "I know you're still in touch with Soup." Her tone was light, like she was trying to shift the conversation to small talk. "What about Dougie?"

Dougie was one of her partners from back in the day, and the question was her way of finding out whether I was a criminal. I liked Dougie because he always let me get whatever I wanted at the candy store after a successful job. None of that sugar-gives-you-cavities BS from Dougie. I hadn't seen him in twenty years either.

"I'm not really in touch with anyone other than Soup. Anyone from back then, I mean."

"Good, that's good. What about Ricky?"

"You probably know he's in OSP."

"Heard that. You been to see him?"

"Nah. Haven't seen him since... you know." I couldn't mention that night out loud. And something in me didn't *want* to mention that I'd emailed him the day before. "Mikey Smooth, actually. I *am* in touch with him. He got out. Lives in a tent under the downtown bridge. We call him Mikey Shakes now. Heroin."

She didn't say anything. I couldn't tell if it was because she already knew about Mikey, or if the news simply didn't faze her.

We followed a winding path deeper into the zoo, past the bald eagle exhibit and the black bear habitat. We slowed at a marine area, where penguins floated happily on the water and groomed themselves on low rocks.

I'd gathered my courage as we strolled, and I was about to ask the question I'd been sitting on for twenty years: *What happened that night?* An unexpected sound came from behind us. We swiveled at the same moment. A pine cone skittered over the concrete, scratching the walkway a few yards ahead of a young couple pushing a stroller. My mom stepped out of the way, giving them a wide berth. The couple stopped between us, talking in low voices and pointing at the penguins. Each had one hand on the stroller, the other on a coffee. They peeked into the stroller every few seconds like its contents were the most valuable thing in the world. That's when my throat tightened up and I realized I couldn't ask about that night. Asking would destroy whatever fragile truce we'd managed to construct over the last ten minutes. Or maybe I was just afraid of the answer.

When you're a kid, your mom is just your mom. Who she is and what she does seems normal. As an adult you find out that no, you had a specific mom, full of quirks and particularities that, perhaps, you share. I've read that people who know their grandparents often come to understand how their mom landed her particular quirks, but that doesn't apply to me. Over the last decade, Soup had drawn a vague, black-and-white outline of Wanda Penny that sprang from his adult understanding, one I didn't share. Now, some of the colors were filling in. She wasn't icy, not exactly, but I had the feeling I couldn't reach her, couldn't make any real contact with her. Like she was there and not there at the same time.

I shoved my hands in my coat pockets. The man with the stroller kicked the pine cone again and continued down the path, arm-in-arm with the woman. I let out a breath when they disappeared around a sloping curve that led toward the monkeys.

I heard myself ask, "Where have you been staying?"

"All over. South Dakota at first, then Texas for a bit. New Mexico."

"Working the whole time, or..."

"Here and there, yeah."

Her answers were getting shorter, her tone more clipped. She knew I wasn't wearing a wire, but she still didn't want to share too much.

She pivoted hard to avoid talking about her life or her crimes.

"Married? Girlfriends? Boyfriends? Significant others?" She smiled a conspiratorial smile. "Kids?"

"No kids. No wife. Had a couple girlfriends. Lived with one for a year. Dani. She was a dancer. Ballet."

"What happened?" she asked.

"She gave me her ATM PIN code."

"What? Tell me about that."

I'd gotten out in front of myself, said more than I'd wanted to. Half of what I'd said was true, but I'd been aiming for a hundred percent lies. I'd never dated anyone named Dani, never lived with Jennifer, and she was definitely no dancer. The PIN code part was real, though. One time at a flea market, Jennifer handed me her debit card, told me her PIN, and asked me to run to the ATM to grab sixty bucks. To someone like me, that was the act of an insane person. With her PIN I could get access to her bank account, her identity, everything. I'd tried to convince myself that Jennifer was the normal one so I should just get over it, but some pieces of us are set too deep to wish away. I'd become distant after that day. I found reasons to get in fights, reasons to doubt the relationship. The truth was, I'd become an asshole the moment I realized she trusted me. And now my mom wanted to know that story as though it wasn't part of the life she'd given me.

I was quiet for a long time, pretending to be interested in a penguin waddling from rock to rock. Part of me wanted to shout, *Hmmm, I don't know, maybe I have some issues with women and trust!* What I said was, "Just didn't work out, y'know?"

She leaned on the railing beside me and cocked her head, opening her mouth to speak. Then she looked at the ground. "Sorry about that," she said quietly.

I was five years old when my mom took me to the zoo for the first time. Ricky was with us that day. I remember it clearly because he told me about the legendary case from the seventies when two drunk guys snuck into the zoo to taunt a pair of lions. One fell into the cage and got eaten. His buddy returned the next day and shot both lions with a thirty-ought-six. It was a big deal around Portland at the time.

In retrospect, Ricky and my mom were probably planning a caper while he told me that story and I ran around pointing at stuff and licking my ice cream. It was cold that day, and I felt like I had the whole place to myself. The zoo is Portland's most popular tourist attraction, but crowds are thin most December mornings. That's probably why my mom chose it back then, and now.

"How long are you in town?" I asked.

"First thing Saturday. Leaving right after the job."

"Yeah, *figures*." I didn't mean for it to come out like a knife, or maybe I did.

She frowned. "Want to get together again? We could meet at Dexter's tomorrow and get a sandwich."

"It's gone. Luxury condos now. Basically, just assume anything you used to like in this town is luxury condos now." It came out more bitterly than I'd intended, and I'd been aiming for pretty damn bitter.

She paused as though wincing inside, then tried again, her voice lower. "I really am glad to see you, Brand. Glad to see you grew up into a man and that you're not, well... That you didn't become..."

She was glad I hadn't become a crook, but she didn't know me. She didn't know what the last twenty years had done to me, and I didn't want to tell her. What I wanted more than anything was the answer to one question with two parts: *what happened that night, and why didn't you come for me afterwards?* But desire's a funny thing. I felt like an invisible part of me was reaching out from my body, trying to draw in the thing I wanted from her, but I stayed quiet. As badly as I needed an answer to put me truly and finally at ease, I said nothing. Every unsaid word lodged in my throat, cutting off the air.

A light rain had begun, the kind where it can rain all day and you only get damp. A couple of crows cawed at one another and flapped toward the trees. Too much time had passed. Too much had happened. I knew at least half of what she'd told me was lies, and she likely knew the same about what I'd told her. I gave her a cold look. "Anything else?"

She looked at me for a long time, her eyes sad. "Well, I'll let you make the next move."

I'd wounded her. Good.

We exchanged contact information, but I made her promise not to call me. I doubted Carebear was up on my phone, but it wasn't impossible. Mom had a Nokia 5000-D2 untraceable GSM phone. I'd have to download an encrypted app before I could message her directly.

She hugged me before we parted. She didn't pat me down this time, but my skin burned as I walked through the zoo. I felt the places her hands had pressed my clothes. My upper back, lower back, a spot on my right hip. Every place she'd touched me pulsed with painful heat, as though beaten with a wooden rod.

Chapter Seven

I spent the next morning in a daze, playing snippets of the conversation with my mother over and over in my head. As I rang up multivitamins and Diet Pepsi and cigarettes and opioids, I grasped for meaning in every word choice, every inflection, every look. I wanted to believe I could read her, that I could replay the conversation and figure out where she was telling the truth and where she wasn't. I wanted to believe I could interpret every gesture to read her true feelings, but I couldn't. I didn't know her anymore, and any attempt at interpretation was filtered through memory and trauma and my own messed-up brain. I tried to replay the scene in my head like a movie, but it didn't work. There was no music telling me what to feel, no dominant theme set up in the first act that resolved nicely by the third. Instead, little pieces of our interaction came at me like signposts in a slow-rolling fog, disappearing almost as quickly as they materialized. A snippet of conversation would arise, tinged with significance and meaning, then fade before I got a clear look.

What about Ricky?

First thing Saturday. Leaving right after the job.

I'll let you make the next move.

Underneath it all was pain, and not just the pain I'd lived with the last twenty years. The question I hadn't asked was killing me. *What happened that night, and why didn't you come for me afterwards?*

She probably had various practical answers: *I was on the run. I was suspected of murder. I couldn't get to you.* But those were convenient facts taped over the truth—like when someone breaks up with you, justifying it a hundred different ways when the reality is they don't love you, or they love someone else more.

She simply hadn't come back for me. I didn't even know if she'd gone to our rendezvous spot at Dexter's. I cared about that more than I cared about whether she'd killed a guy, and I still hadn't asked. Maybe I didn't want to know the answer.

I stumbled through the morning, and by one o'clock I felt slightly normal. Though my insides still roiled, I'd decided on a plan. I wasn't going to contact my mom again. I'd call Detective Caraway after work and tell her that, as hard as I'd tried to find my mom, she'd given me a fake number when I met her for coffee, so I'd been unable to reach her since. I wanted to help, but I simply wasn't in contact with the right people any more. After all, I didn't move in those criminal circles. I'd close the conversation by wishing her the best of luck in nabbing my mom and locking her up before she stole again.

But I didn't want Carebear to find her. I figured the most likely outcome was that my mom would steal the microchips—if she'd been telling the truth about the target—and disappear. Maybe in time I'd come to look at the meeting at the zoo as a bittersweet goodbye. The scene in the movie where the characters yearn for resolution, but it just doesn't happen. They part ways, their hearts destined to remain slightly broken. I'd move on with my life without her. I always had before.

That was what I was thinking when I noticed Detective Caraway standing in the pharmacy. I saw her over the hunched head of Ms. Jackson, a ninety-year-old woman who still picked up her prescription in person on the first of each month. She was a sweet old lady who— no joke—tried to tip me with a quarter each time she came in, even though I'd told her a half-dozen times we weren't allowed to accept tips.

I don't know how long Carebear had been watching me when I noticed her. I'd like to think my ability to read cops was better than my ability to read my mom, though, and I could tell she hadn't just walked in. She stood by a rack of hair dye, holding a box with a picture of a good-looking blond dude on it. She caught me noticing her and drew near, waiting for Ms. Jackson to shuffle away with the little white bag that would keep her alive for another month.

I pressed my hands into the counter in front of the cash register as she approached. "Going blonde?" I asked. Carebear didn't seem to follow so I pointed toward the display rack. "You were holding hair dye while pretending not to watch me."

"Very observant, Brand."

"Thanks, I guess?" I opened my eyes wide and cocked my head to the left as though asking, *What are you doing here?*

Carebear leaned on the counter and inspected a salted caramel protein bar—a pseudo-healthy snack that Kevin displayed as an impulse buy after boring me half to death with the plan a couple months earlier. She appeared to study the label like a crime scene. "Nope, too many carbs." She set the bar back in the box and flashed a smile that would have raised a diabetic's blood sugar more than any protein bar. "I came in to see you today, Brandon, because I wondered if you had any information about your mother. It's been two days and, frankly I've been"—she frowned—"*a little disappointed* I haven't heard from you." Coiled outrage oozed from between her teeth on *a little disappointed.*

And, just like that, my decision about my next move evaporated, along with any positive feeling about it. Caraway had shown up at my job, and now my thoughts were chaos and fury. Not only did it piss me off on principle, but my boss was here, and my coworkers. It was threatening on a lot of levels. All the anger and frustration rolling around in my guts found a target.

I shook my head. "Nothing yet." I made my tone optimistic, as if I'd failed to come up with anything, but wasn't done trying. I was a good soldier. "She gave me a fake number the first time we met, turns out."

"Hmm. Isn't that too bad?" She picked up the protein bar again, as though reconsidering.

Early afternoons are slow at the pharmacy. The morning had been brutal, but now the place was mostly empty. Every second Carebear stood there, turning that damn protein bar over in her hands, taunted me. She knew it, too. I'd never wanted a customer to walk in so badly.

I was sure no one had tailed me to the zoo, but maybe they had surveillance on Ace's. Might be Soup's name was in a file somewhere as a known associate of murder suspect Wanda Penny. For them to know I was still in touch with Soup, they'd have had to be tracking me long before my mom reappeared. On a practical level, the PPB just didn't have that level of resources.

The silence got to me, so I threw her a bone. "I asked around, but no one's heard anything. You sure she's still in town? Maybe it was just for a day or something."

"We keep hearing things and, well, I'm worried about you, Brandon." She swept her eyes across the pharmacy like she was surveying the beautiful gardens at my country estate. "You've got a good life. A nice job here. I'd hate to see you get wrapped up with a murderer."

There it was again. The threat designed to sound like a helpful suggestion. I shot a look behind me as the word *murderer* hung in the air. No one here knew about my mother. They didn't know anything about my past. They'd never asked and I'd never volunteered any information. Kevin was nowhere to be seen—he was probably in the back office drawing up a diagram of the New Year's Eve Champagne display he'd run by me at morning break. The pharmacy techs were busy counting pills. An older redhead named Betty was restocking shelves of vitamins nearby, but I didn't think she'd heard.

Carebear had said it just loud enough to communicate a threat. She was here to tell me she could screw up my life if she wanted. How casually she'd said "wrapped up with a murderer," as though she could easily make my mother's crimes my own.

The bell on the front door clanged and Jennifer sauntered in. I'd wanted a customer to come in, but not Jennifer, not now. As usual, she was running at two different speeds, her easy pace conflicting with the hurried look on her face. When we were dating, we'd meet for lunch and she'd say things like, "I have to hurry back" or "I've only got five more minutes," but she could never make her body obey her commands. She'd linger, walk at half speed, pick up a magazine to browse, or have just one more thought about the films of Kathryn Bigelow. Her body moved on its own time. Usually I enjoyed our brief interactions when she came in, but at that moment I couldn't imagine anyone in the world I wanted to see less.

Jennifer's eyes scanned straight to me, and I tried to wrap things up with Carebear as fast as possible. "I don't have anything," I said. "But I'll be sure to let you know just as soon as I hear something." Immediately, I regretted the sarcasm that had crept into my voice.

She shrugged as if it was the response she'd expected. "You sure?" Her tone was flat. Was she baiting me? If she knew about the meeting at the zoo, it meant one of three things: either Soup had snitched on me, his place was bugged, or she had a warrant to get into my phone, as well as the personnel to track it. But there was no chance of the first, and little more of the second and third. And if she *did* know about the zoo, I would have been an accomplice to the crime my mom was planning, and Carebear would have played hardball. I decided this visit was simply a threat. She was pissed I hadn't made progress, pissed I hadn't gotten in touch with her, and wanted me to know she could mess up my life if she felt like it, if I didn't give her what she wanted.

I said, "Been busy, you know?"

"Sure, I know how it is."

"And I'm not in touch with the people my mom used to work with." Jennifer was getting closer, and my voice had dropped to a whisper.

Carebear walked a little circle, pausing to inspect the little booth with the complementary blood-pressure gauge. "These things work?"

I shrugged.

"You know, Brand, one in three police officers has high blood pressure."

"I'd feel just *awful* if your health were anything less than perfect."

She squinted. My sarcasm told her she was getting to me, which was exactly what she wanted. Keeping my cool had been easier in an interrogation room.

Betty emerged from around the corner, pushing a cart of vanilla Slimfast. She stopped next to Caraway. "Can I help you, ma'am?"

"Oh, thanks for asking!" Carebear shook her hand aggressively, which caused Betty to glance over, asking me with her eyes, *Is this weird lady with you?*

Jennifer made it to the counter but stepped to the side. She could see something was going on, and didn't want to make herself part of it. Smart. I met her eyes briefly—she searched mine for answers—then I stared at the floor.

"I'm *fine*," Carebear was saying to Betty. "I just came in to talk with Brandon for a minute."

Betty looked from Carebear to me, then back to Carebear. She put her hands on her hips. "Are you his mom?"

Jennifer's head jerked toward Carebear, who let out a long, forced laugh. I gritted my teeth. Betty's question wasn't ridiculous. Carebear and I didn't look much alike, but we were both white, both had brown hair, and Carebear was in her mid-fifties, around the right age to be my mom. To an untrained observer, her syrupy sweetness might come off as warmth or affection. Combine that with the fact that she'd hung around chatting without buying anything for a few minutes, and the assumption made sense.

Carebear swiped at the air playfully. "No, but I *do* have boys of my own. I'm Detective Caraway of the Portland Police Bureau."

Betty and Jennifer both stepped back instinctively, the way you do when you learn you're talking to a cop, the same way your foot gets lighter when you spot a patrol car on the freeway, even if you're not speeding. My co-worker glanced at me, then smoothed her red apron. "What's going on?"

I carefully avoided Jennifer's eyes and said the first lie that popped into my mind. "Apartment next to mine was broken into a few nights ago. No big deal, but Detective Caraway is following up."

Betty seemed satisfied and turned to her cart. I wondered whether Jennifer knew I was lying, but I wouldn't look at her to find out. If I did, I'd be able to see the answer on her face, and I didn't want to.

Caraway wouldn't let it go. "It's okay, Brandon, you can tell the truth."

Kevin—the man built by God to be an assistant manager— emerged from the back. Always quick to notice anything out of the ordinary, he came up and took off his glasses, looking from me to Caraway.

Time slowed. Betty and Carebear stared at me. Jennifer had stepped back a pace, lingering by the fish oil supplements and pretending not to be eavesdropping.

I noticed my hands, balled into tight fists at my side. *Always keep your cool when talking to a cop*, but I wasn't keeping my cool. My breathing was labored, my belt too tight around my waist. I was sweaty and cold and my throat felt like a desert. "Kevin, this is Detective Caraway from the—"

"Portland Police Bureau," she interrupted, stepping to the counter and shaking Kevin's hand like a car salesman who desperately wanted to give him a great deal on a minivan.

"What's this about?" Kevin asked.

Carebear leaned away, eyed me, smiling. "You want to tell him?"

She'd already called out my lie about the break-in, but I wasn't sure how far she wanted to take this. "You better. I wouldn't know how much I'm allowed to say. To keep within legal limits, I mean."

Kevin looked on earnestly, as though there must be some perfectly reasonable explanation for all of this. His world always had reasonable explanations. One thing I'd learned while dating Jennifer was that not everyone was a liar. One time she'd asked idly what I'd had for lunch and I told her I'd had a burger when the truth was I'd had a burrito. It wasn't about advancing some pro-burger agenda, it was just... natural. I told little lies all the time, always had. By keeping part of myself unknown—even a small part—I was keeping myself safe. It had been a long, slow process to learn that Jennifer wasn't like that. Neither was Kevin.

Carebear, on the other hand, was a liar in word and deed, from top to toe. She picked up the protein bar, passed it from hand to hand, and raised an eyebrow. "These any good?"

Kevin grinned. "Oh yes, I eat one every day and I finished the Portland half-marathon in under two hours. That's why we put them right up front here." Confronted with the chance to make a sale, he seemed to have forgotten that a detective was standing in his store. I avoided looking at Jennifer as he launched into a monologue about simple versus complex carbs like he'd finally found his time to shine.

"Fascinating," Carebear said when Kevin finished. "You've convinced me. I'm no marathoner, but we can all use a little more health in our life." She set three bars on the counter. "Now, let me tell you why I'm here. And I appreciate, Brandon, that you don't want to say too much. Very responsible of you."

Kevin looked at me. "Is Brandon in any kind of trouble?"

I felt Jennifer's eyes on me. I didn't need to glance at her to confirm it. That would have been a mistake anyway, to show Carebear who I glance at when I'm rattled, to put Jennifer on the PPB's radar. Last thing I wanted was to invite this shit into her life.

"Oh, no. Not at all." Caraway smiled as though even the thought of it was the most ridiculous thing in the world. "You see..." she leaned in to read his name tag "...Kevin, I'm investigating a possible theft. You remember the Laurelhurst murder from 1998?"

Kevin looked intrigued. "I don't think so."

"It was all over the news. Late one night, a couple young crooks robbed a friendly little poker game in the Laurelhurst neighborhood." Caraway leaned across the counter, lowering her voice. "But somehow the robbery went bad and one of the thieves shot a security guard. Murdered him in cold blood."

Kevin shook his head. "That's terrible."

Betty moved closer now, fully engaged in the story. "I think I remember that. It was in the papers. They never caught the guy who did it?"

Carebear shook her head. "It *was* terrible. The killer disappeared, but we think *she's* back in town, planning another crime. Now, I may not be the most brilliant detective, but one thing everyone knows about me is that I do my due diligence. Looking through the old files on that night, Brandon's name came up."

A chill moved up my spine. I looked from Carebear to Kevin, whose affable smile had become a frown of concern. Then I risked a glance at Jennifer, whose expression was blank. She usually wore her thoughts on her face, but could become entirely unreadable when she wanted to. It was a kind of forced-neutrality look I usually took to mean she was upset. In truth, I didn't know what it meant. It was like a superpower, one she'd just turned on. She knew a little about my past. I hadn't lied about all of it. But I'd given her the Disney version, where I'd overcome adversity to become a half-decent person. She knew my mom had ditched me, but she didn't know the details.

"Oh, he wasn't *involved*," Carebear continued. She wasn't here to ruin my life, not yet. But she wanted me to know she could do so at any time. "I can't go into all the details, but we thought Brandon might have information about the woman who committed the murder. That's all."

"Is she dangerous?" Kevin asked, looking around his store protectively.

Carebear tapped a protein bar on the side of the cash register. "We have to assume so. All we know right now is that she's in town for a theft of some kind. But she's killed before when someone got in the way." She looked at me. "Any reason to think she wouldn't kill again?"

Her question hung in the air, and suddenly I became aware of the music playing in the store and the sound of the bell ringing as the front door opened.

I looked up, relieved to see a swarm of customers, maybe eight or ten.

"It's the Benson Hill people," Kevin said.

Once a week, a shuttle van brought a dozen seniors from the Benson Hill Retirement Village to pick up meds and do a little shopping. They usually kept us busy for nearly an hour. Betty turned back to her cart and continued filling shelves with the canned shakes.

"I better get back to it," I said to Carebear. "I'll call if I remember anything else."

"Thank you, Brand." She turned to Kevin. "Lovely store you have here. Maybe I'll see you at the marathon next year." She winked.

"It's never too late for fitness," Kevin said.

Detective Caraway made her exit visibly, waving bye-bye to me with the hand holding the stupid nutrition bars. As the door clanged shut, Jennifer came up to talk to me.

She had thick dark hair, dark eyes, and vampire-pale skin, a combination to which I am dangerously susceptible. Pair that with a fierce intelligence and a deep love for movies, and I never stood a chance. That woman messed me up in all the best possible ways. I'd fed her the edited-for-content version of my past because I didn't dare risk losing her over something as small and tacky as the truth. Now she'd overheard a goddamn cop describing a version of my childhood that did not match the one I'd sold her for years. We'd managed to keep a friendly, even slightly flirtatious vibe between us since the breakup, and now I knew that was over. Honest citizens like her didn't flirt with crooks like me.

When she saw no one else was at the counter, she gave me a sympathetic smile. "Wow, the old cop-intimidates-someone-for-information scene. I must've seen a million of those. So, like, I can say with confidence... that one *sucked*."

I laughed involuntarily. I'd been setting myself up for her to rip me a new one, but, typically, she didn't give me what I expected.

"I mean, the scene's not lit well, for a start." She gestured at the godawful fluorescents I lived under for forty hours a week. "But also, what's with the cop character here? There's supposed to be some internal conflict, a little back-and-forth, not just some mean lady in a pantsuit picking on a pharmacy clerk."

She was looking to me to pick up the thread, but I was floored by the kindness she was showing, so the best I could manage was "Yeah, she was no Gene Hackman. Remember *The French Connection?*"

Jennifer smirked, happy I was playing along. "I think she was aiming for *L.A. Confidential* and wound up somewhere around *Paul Blart: Mall Cop.*"

That got a short bark of laughter from me, but I was too keyed up to relax into bantering. "I can't lie," I lied, trying to be honest, "I would have preferred you didn't hear... any of that."

She shrugged diplomatically. "Assuming she was talking about your mom, it didn't match what you've said about your childhood, if that's what you mean. But then, you never said almost anything about your childhood."

I looked down at my hands. "Well, there were reasons for that." Now that she knew I'd been lying to her, she'd tell me she never wanted to talk to me again, and my life would lose those little bright moments of friendliness with my ex.

Instead, she surprised me again, leaning in and lowering her voice. "I mean, I'm not gonna pretend she didn't mention some pretty dark shit. But, like... I wouldn't blame you if you didn't want to talk about dark shit from when you were a kid. I get that. But... I guess..." It was unusual for me, seeing Jennifer squirm on something she was embarrassed to say. "...if you decide you want to talk to someone about it... Y'know, I'm someone."

I nodded, suppressing the urge to comfort her somehow, or spill my guts as she suggested. There were people lining up behind her, and I still had a job. "How about I come by tonight when your shift ends? We can get a beer or whatever."

"If you want to talk," she clarified.

"Yeah, I mean, I should get some stuff off my chest." That was true and felt too much like a lie. "I don't have anyone to talk to about most of it." I added, which was a lie, but felt true.

She turned to leave as the bald guy behind her cleared his throat meaningfully. "I'm off at six." She was long gone by the time I realized she hadn't picked up her meds.

The rest of the shift was a numb slog, even lonelier than usual. Carebear had come to rattle my cage, and it had worked. Now my coworkers looked at me with suspicion and curiosity under a thicker-than-usual layer of fake politeness. I didn't want to imagine what they were saying about me behind my back, so of course I did anyway. By the time I clocked out at five, paranoia and self-loathing had combined to make me certain that in the breakroom, I'd been positively identified as the Zodiac Killer.

Outside, I took a few deep breaths. The sun was already down, and the cool evening air helped clear my head. I could get past the fear and defensiveness Caraway had been trying to provoke, and ask myself why she was provoking it in the first place. Her motives felt personal, her level of concern out of line with the situation, even if she *was* trying to solve a twenty-year-old murder.

I had more questions than answers, but I had to table them for now. Thanks to Carebear rattling my cage, I'd promised to meet Jennifer and try to tell her the truth.

East Side Middle School Weekly, May 11, 1999

Eighth-Graders Stage *Merry Wives of Windsor* to Rave Reviews

By Benny Gillman

The drama class debuted their adaptation of The Merry Wives of Windsor *by William Shakespeare on Friday afternoon at an all-school gathering after lunch, earning praise from students and teachers.*

Seventh-grader Maria Collo enjoyed the show. "It was great," she said after the performance.

Eighth-grader Emily Johnson agreed. "I liked how funny it was when they tricked him into hiding in the gym locker full of smelly clothes."

The play was directed by drama teacher Bethany Ermintrout, who told ESMS Weekly that she and the students updated the story to take place in a modern-day middle school. She said, "I'm so proud of how hard everyone worked."

In the updated version of the play, a spirited young man named Falstaff proclaims his love for two different eighth-grade students, but fails to keep them separated. When they find out about each other, they take revenge, appearing to encourage his affections while tricking him into a series of amusing and embarrassing experiences.

The star of the show was eighth-grader Benjamin Lopez, who played Falstaff. "It was fun," Lopez said after the performance. "I can't wait for our community show on Friday night."

Another member of the cast was eighth-grader Brandon Penny, who played Bardolph, a member of Falstaff's entourage. Penny said, "It was cool. I got to play a thief and a liar."

The Merry Wives of Windsor will be performed at the auditorium on Friday night at six and Saturday afternoon at two. Tickets are $5.

Chapter Eight

There was an hour between the end of my shift and the end of Jennifer's, and the more of that hour I could eat up in travel time, the less of it I could spend thinking, driving myself crazy about the prospect of telling Jennifer the truth. I chose to walk from Morey's to Movie Madness.

Unfortunately, a nice walk on a crisp winter evening is a great time to do some serious thinking, and I found myself reviewing all the lies and half-truths I'd told Jennifer about my upbringing over the years. When she'd asked about my family, I'd always said things like, "My mom did what she had to do," or "She lived a little sideways of the law," or "She disappeared when I was twelve. Had to lam it." I'd deliver the last one like a character in a cheesy eighties cop movie, trying to make light of the situation, as though it didn't really bother me. Once in a while I'd drop a meaningless cliché like, "It hurt, but it was probably for the best." I knew Jennifer didn't buy it, but she never questioned me too hard. Sometimes in relationships you have to allow your partner the little lies that keep them sane. Jennifer had allowed me a lot of those, and she was not going to enjoy learning what they'd been hiding.

Movie Madness is where we met, and one of the reasons we

were still on decent terms. I hear that most cities don't have real video stores anymore, and people have to settle for whatever the streaming services allow them. That must suck, but I wouldn't know what it's like, because I lived a ten-minute bus ride from a store with more titles on hand than every streaming service put together. It's also a film museum with original costumes and artifacts going back to the silent picture days, and it was the item of contention in our breakup. Just like she wasn't going to stop picking up prescriptions at Morey's, I wasn't going to stop renting movies. When she dumped me, I tried turning it into a whole thing. *I was renting movies there for at least a year before you got the job,* I argued pathetically, *so you really ought to quit out of respect for me, so I don't have to run into you every time I want to rent a film.* Divorcing couples fight over custody of the kids, or the dogs, or that expensive vase they bought on their honeymoon in Japan. I tried to start a fight over custody of America's best video store. She'd just laughed at my ridiculous demand. Soon, I was laughing, too. Jennifer was as broke as I was and she needed the job. Plus, she loved movies even more than I did.

She was with a customer when I walked in, so I did a lap and checked out their new memorabilia. They'd added an outfit Liv Tyler wore in *Ad Astra*, plus a leather jacket from the first *Terminator* movie. When Jennifer got free, I ambled up to the counter and handed her the little paper bag with her prescription. Even though I wasn't allowed to, I'd lifted it from the pharmacy section without trouble. "Thought you'd want this. How's the thesis going?"

"Thanks." She raised an eyebrow as if to say, *Fine, if that's how you want to play it.*

My opening was a too-obvious attempt to ease into the topic at hand, but I was genuinely curious about her thesis. She'd been working on the thing since before she dumped me, and I knew the deadline was coming up.

"I changed the title to *Riot Grrls and Tank Girls: 1990s Anarcho-Feminism In Cinema.*" She leaned in. "And did I tell you... no I didn't yet, I haven't told anyone but my mom... I have a good lead on a teaching gig. Film History. Seattle University. They're not the best, but definitely not the worst. Assuming I finish and graduate."

"You will," I said.

"I mean, adjunct professors make bullshit money, but it's a start. And bullshit money is slightly more than I make here, and it feels like... something. It's like the first time I've felt I might actually be able to make a living thinking about movies, writing about movies, talking about movies. If I work it right, even the popcorn will be tax deductible." When she was genuinely excited, Jennifer talked fast, like the words were tripping over themselves in a race out of her mouth. Her unjaded enthusiasm was one of the things I liked about her. "The department chair there—he's the guy who told me about the job—he said he might even be able to help me turn the thesis into a book. Said I have a 'commercial voice,' whatever that means."

Another customer approached the counter and I stared at the back of a DVD case without actually reading it. I was happy for Jennifer. I really was. Sure she got to watch a lot of cool movies for school, but she had to watch a lot of dull ones, too, and I'd seen her work her ass off on enough papers to know that, when she got her degree, it would be well-earned. Still, hearing about her plans stung. It felt like she was moving forward, on to bigger and better things, and I was either standing still or slipping back into my past.

"So," she said when we were alone again. "You want to tell me what that thing at your job was about? The cop?"

"She's a detective."

Jennifer shrugged, then glanced side to side, making sure no one was within earshot. "She was talking about your mom, right?" I appreciated the way she lowered her voice, even though there was no one close by. She knew it was a sensitive subject.

I passed the DVD from hand to hand, avoiding her eyes. "She was."

Jennifer took the DVD and set it behind the counter. "Did your mom really—" she leaned in, lowered her voice to a whisper that tickled my ear —"kill a guy? I mean, I picked up on the fact that she was a thief but..."

A lanky, acne-scarred twenty-something came out from the back, struggling under the weight of a tall box of old VHS tapes. I'd met him before. Aaron, or maybe Andrew.

I felt Jennifer's eyes burn a hole through me, then move to her co-worker. "Allan, anything else you need me to help with before I clock out?"

He set down the box, then said, "Nah, we're in good shape. See you tomorrow."

Jennifer pulled on her coat as we stepped outside. "Hey, walk with me a minute? Trying to get my ten thousand in today."

"Sure," I said, and I let her lead the way.

Jennifer was always talking about getting in better shape, taking ten thousand steps a day. She wore one of those little GPS wrist things to help her keep track, but she never made it to ten thousand, at least not while we were together. Like me, she was far too comfortable on the couch watching movies. We did a lap around the block in silence, Jennifer glancing my way every once in a while. She had this way of looking at me—head cocked to two o'clock, chin slightly upturned—asking the loudest questions without saying a word. The therapists I was forced to see as a kid asked hundreds of questions using thousands of words, dutifully scribbling my nonsense in their notebooks. I didn't hold it against them; they were just doing their jobs. But I never got the sense that they cared as much as Jennifer did with her silent, sideways glance.

I leaned on a tree, trying to push through every lying instinct I had. "You want to hear it for real?"

Jennifer nodded slowly, her face dancing in and out of the light from a streetlamp. "Maybe over a beer? The Horse Brass is right up there."

As usual, today wasn't going to be ten thousand steps, because between counting up steps and having a cold beer at the end of a workday, she was making the sensible choice. That was her little lie in our relationship. She allowed me to stay vague about my mom's criminal past; I allowed her to stay optimistic about hitting ten thousand steps. Maybe the asymmetry there was one of the reasons things didn't work out.

"I could definitely use a beer," I said, and a couple minutes later we were nestled in a booth in a faux-English pub with a rotating microbrew selection that was locally legendary.

She managed to sit on her curiosity until our beers arrived: an IPA for her, a crisp kolsch for me. We each took a sip, and she finally prompted, "So..."

I sighed. "Some of this is, well, it might be a lot." I said it like a warning sign reading *This is your final chance to exit the ride.*

"Whatever your mom did, it's not you. You're not responsible for her crimes, and you're not like her."

I felt myself bridle at the way she'd said *You're not like her.* All she knew about my mom was the bullshit I'd fed her and whatever she'd gleaned from Carebear. In Jennifer's mind, my mother was already a terrible person, a thief and now a murderer, so she had to believe that her ex-boyfriend could never be as bad.

I almost clammed up and bailed on the conversation, but I felt a sick compulsion to tell the truth. It was an uncomfortable feeling for a habitual liar, like I was about to strip naked in the middle of the bar. I shoved my hands into my armpits, hugging myself, looking for any comfort I could find. My eyes on the table, I watched the edge of a cardboard coaster gradually absorb a drop of water. Without listening to myself more than necessary, I walked Jennifer through the short cons my mom and I pulled when I was little, then offered the broad strokes of my mom's bigger jobs. I skimmed over the dirty details, but I didn't lie. I kept my voice steady, monotonous, like an oncologist describing the size and shape of a tumor to a medical panel. Dispassionate. Professional.

Then I got to the night of the poker game—scoping the house, taking the flop off my pawnshop bike, the big security guard running over, and the gunshot.

That damn gunshot.

I hadn't looked directly at Jennifer once. Just as Caraway had a collection of phony smiles, Jennifer had a collection of facial expressions that could light me up like a campfire or hollow me out like a drill bit. She didn't deploy them maliciously, but that made them more powerful. Jennifer was an earnest person, her face an open book most of the time, a poker shark's dream, so I shifted my gaze to my second beer, which had just arrived. To get through this, I had to not know what she was thinking.

I'd gone quiet after mentioning the gunshot, so she reached out and touched my hand gently as I set the beer down. "Then what happened?"

"The guard ran for the door, and I could see from the shadows on the windows that people were moving around inside the mansion. I ducked behind a tree and peeked around it. When the guard reached the open front door..." I paused and felt my fingernails dig into my palms. "Bang. Another gunshot from inside the house. He stopped. Almost turned toward the street. Then his legs collapsed under him. Then he was just lying there on the porch. Dead."

I felt Jennifer wanting to speak, but I had to get through it, so I kept talking, faster and faster, like she had earlier. Except my words weren't propelled by excitement about the future, they were a desperate ejection of my past.

"My mom's partner came out of the door and ran into the shadows. Then my Mom came out. She looked at me and pointed west. Then she ran east like I'd never seen her run before. I couldn't take the bike, its front wheel was shot to hell, so I just ran. Before I'd made it a block, a cop car pulled in front of me, slewing sideways to cut me off. I hooked a left down an alley. The cops were, whatever, fat old guys wearing seatbelts, and hell, I was twelve years old. I was made of lightning and Silly Putty." I chuckled derisively at the image of my younger self, but I wasn't laughing inside. I remembered the speed and power I'd felt that night. "By the time the cops were out of their car, I was in the shadows. Then a second cop car appeared at the end of the alley, hitting me with the high beams. So I went over a fence and cut through a backyard. I remember it had this big treehouse." I'd never told this story to anyone in detail, and it was stirring up a lot of well-settled mud. I remembered feeling mad at that treehouse, that some rich kid got it built for him and probably never even used it. I'd never thought about that flash of envy consciously, but there it was in my memory.

"Anyway, the cops were yelling at each other behind me, all loud and authoritative, and I was almost to the next street. The block ahead was bathed in red-and-blue lights, so I knew I wasn't out of it yet, and I jumped over this ornamental ivy hedge, turned right, and WHAM. Some cop fuckin' clotheslined me. I was on the ground, could barely breathe, neck hurting like hell. Next thing I knew, the cop was locking me in the back seat of a car that reeked like some kind of fake-orange cleaner. Sat there two hours, running questions over and over in my head as cops came and went, everything lit up in spinning red and blue.

"Finally, two cops climbed into the front seat and started lying to me. You know how cops do." I paused awkwardly. "Well, maybe you don't. But trust me, they do. Thing was, they were driving down Burnside and I stared out the window as hard as I could, knowing we were about to pass Dexter's, the sandwich place where we were supposed to meet if we got separated. The window was foggy and there was a woman with dark brown hair sitting at the counter. At least I think so. And I think it was my mom. Couldn't tell for sure. After that, everything went to hell." I went quiet, staring at the soggy paper coaster catching condensation under her beer.

She touched my arm again. "That was the last time you saw her?"

"Yeah, and I still don't know if it was her." I could see on her face that Jennifer didn't understand what that meant. That if Mom was there, the job had gone wrong but she'd gone to the rendezvous point as planned. If she wasn't, the job had gone wrong and she'd immediately fed me to the cops to cover her getaway. That distinction was intuitively obvious to me and completely opaque to Jennifer.

"You never told me all that."

"Never told anyone, at least not all the details."

84

"And you definitely didn't mention that your mom killed a guy. I can't believe I didn't, like, Google it."

"I don't know if she killed him."

"But—" she started, then stopped herself. She took a second to compose her thoughts, and I fought down my urge to interrupt and explain my viewpoint. "Okay," she said after a moment, "I get that you didn't see who fired the shot, if it was your mom or the other guy. And you're right, that's cause for doubt. But that detective seemed pretty sure it was her, and it feels like she'd know what she's talking about? Or am I missing something?" She was speaking deliberately, sensitive to the fact that we were talking about my mom.

What she was missing was the baseline assumption that cops lie, but I couldn't think of a nice way to phrase that. "It's a conclusion I'm not willing to jump to," I said carefully.

She nodded slowly. "Fair. Fair. So, okay, you don't know if she killed a guy, and you don't know what happened to her afterward. That's... yeah, that's some serious weight to carry around."

That was the most sympathetic thing anyone had ever said to me about that night. It was a good thing I'd never fallen out of love with her, because that would have made me fall right back in.

"I get that there were reasons you never told me that," she continued, "and I'm glad you could tell me now. But it's kind of a lot for me to take in."

I recognized what she was saying, and rephrased it to let her know I understood. "So, after the big exposition-dump scene, you need a little relaxed time before the next plot point?"

She snickered. "Yeah, that's probably it. Bring in some funny secondary characters or a gratuitous sex scene."

I choked on my response to that, and she, embarrassed, leapt into the awkward conversational pause like she was jumping on a grenade. "Tell you what, can we get coffee later this week?"

"Sure," I said, "But why?"

"I don't know. How you are makes more sense now."

I didn't know how to take it. I flashed on the moment when Caraway had stared at me like an abandoned dog in the shelter.

Jennifer wasn't pitying me—not exactly—but it never feels great to hear someone say, *How you are makes more sense now.* Still, even if it was pity, it sounded like something close to a date.

"I'd like that," I heard myself say.

She finished her beer in two long gulps, promised to text me soon, and leaned in for a hug that lasted a tick longer than I expected. I gripped my beer tightly, watching her disappear into the December darkness, on her way to ten thousand steps.

Chapter Nine

Every evening when I returned from work, I walked by Jamila's apartment. Often I could tell what she was making for dinner. That night, the aroma of cumin and garlic hit me the second I turned the corner to our hallway. Taco night. I only had leftovers in the fridge and my stomach rumbled as I walked by her front door.

Something didn't add up, though. When you live in a cheap apartment building with thin walls and cracks under the doors, you get to know your neighbor's cooking habits, especially if their diet includes heavily spiced foods. Jamila didn't cook Mexican food more than once a week, and taco night had been a couple days ago.

The smell grew stronger the further I got from Jamila's door. Mr. Flores, who lived next to me on the other side, had told me once he didn't eat Mexican food anymore, despite being Mexican, because it reminded him too much of his late wife. I didn't know the people in the apartment next to Mr. Flores, the last on our floor, but I figured it must be them.

At my door, I froze. The smell was coming from *my* apartment. I got to my knees and held my nose near the crack under the door. Cumin, garlic, something acidic like vinegar or tomato.

My first thought was, *I don't have a gun*. In truth, I'd never owned a gun. The last couple days had me thinking in terms of crime again, and when there's an intruder in your home, your first thought is either to call the cops or get your gun. No way I'd call the cops.

I got to my feet and pressed an ear to the door. I heard the sound of my own breathing, then... were those footsteps? A gentle *thwack*, like the refrigerator door closing. A few seconds later, a *ping*. Maybe the sound of a ring nicking a glass, or was it a text message arriving? Either way, there was definitely someone in there.

I quieted my breathing and listened again. Nothing. Maybe the sounds I'd heard had been coming through the walls or something, somehow ricocheting around the...

The door opened and I flinched back. In the doorway stood my mom, right hand on her hip. In her jeans, black top, and green apron, she looked like a typical suburban mom, visiting for the holidays. I wanted to be happy to see her, but there was an invader in my house and my instincts kicked in. I scrambled inside and shut the door, not wanting anyone to see her in my apartment. A brown paper shopping bag lay on its side on the counter, and packages of fresh cilantro and sour cream sat nearby. The oven was on, and a small pot steamed on the stove. It wasn't tacos. I recognized the smell now. That was her famous tomatillo enchilada sauce. She was making the dinner I'd declared "my favorite" when I was seven.

I stood in the center of the kitchen, arms out, palms open. Speechless.

She returned to the stove, stirring the pot as though it was the most natural thing in the world. She spoke without turning to look at me. "The front door of your building screeches. Metal on metal. I heard it open, but didn't hear an interior door open or close. Under normal circumstances, I'd have suspected cops and gone out a window, but the cops don't know I'm here. Figured it was you." She tasted the enchilada sauce, then added a dash of salt. "You paused outside your door, didn't you? You could tell someone was inside. Smart, Brand. Smart."

Thoughts scrambled for priority in my brain. What was she doing here? How did she know where I lived? Why did she break into my apartment? *How* did she break into my apartment?

The last question was easy, so I started there. "You still carry that old twenty-seven-piece pick set?"

She waved toward the counter. "Lost that one a while back. New five-in-one multi-pin. Easier to carry and does most of what the old set did."

I picked up the tool, which lay next to the grocery bag and looked like a stubby screwdriver—a short black handle with a complicated, multi-pronged tip. Connected to the shaft were replaceable pins of different sizes. *Not bad.* Setting it down, I asked, "How'd you get in the front door?" The wooden door to my apartment was secured by a standard five-pin tumbler lock. I knew how to pick one of those by the time I was nine. The front door, however, was glass and steel, with a one-inch, hardened-cylinder deadbolt. The tool on the counter wouldn't open that. Even if she had the equipment in her car, she wouldn't have taken the time to pick a highly visible exterior door as everyone was getting home from work.

She didn't reply. Instead, she opened the oven. Steam filled my tiny kitchen, along with the scent of bubbling golden-brown cheese and tart tomatillo sauce. I damn near lost it as she pulled out the casserole dish. Something in the smell brought a wave of emotion I wasn't ready for.

To steady myself, I followed up on the mechanics of her entry. "Lemme guess, you waited until someone walked in and grabbed the front door as it closed?"

She smiled and set the dish of enchiladas on a torn piece of the shopping bag on the table. "Back door near the dumpsters was propped open."

We sat at the table. "How'd you know where I live?"

She spooned a couple of enchiladas onto a plate and poured extra sauce over them, just like I asked her to when I was a kid. "Soup."

"He doesn't know my address."

She slid the plate across the table. "Said you lived on the East Side."

89

"So do a hundred thousand other people. Don't bullshit me, mom."

My annoyance must have come through because she looked directly at me for the first time. "I've got a DMV friend. Staying with her over near Mount Tabor."

For the first time in two days, I was sure it was the truth. "Thanks for not lying again." Then it struck me: if she could find me in a day using her *DMV friend*, she could have found me just as easily at any time over the last twenty years. She'd shown up now, so why not a letter a year ago, why not a visit five years ago, why not... This was the second time today someone had shown up unannounced. All the questions I'd swallowed at the zoo were back, along with a tide of anger slowly drowning my shock.

I pushed the enchiladas back with all the certainty I could muster. "What the hell are you doing here?"

She dropped her head, as though only now realizing that I had every right to be pissed. "I'm trying to reconnect. I want to find out about your life. Your job. Tell me more about that dancer you dated."

"I'm not going to talk about any of that."

She eased the plate back across the table, looking at me pleadingly. "Have an enchilada and give me a half hour. Please."

The smell of the food flooded me with sense memories, transporting me back to my childhood. I stared down at the plate as a train wreck happened inside my body. Reluctantly, I picked up a fork and began to eat.

"That's good," she said.

I don't know if she meant to sound condescending, but that's how I heard it. I resented it, and I wanted to make her hurt. "The job you're in town for, the microchips, was that a lie?"

She studied my face. "Maybe better if you don't know my plans. You don't want to know."

"Hypothetically, if 'microchips' wasn't a lie, I assume the job is Micro Tech. Only high-end manufacturer in town. Their warehouse is heavily secured, much more than the office space, so my guess is you're looking at the Bancorp Tower." It was a prestigious downtown office building I'd wandered through a few times and, because I couldn't help it, thought about robbing. "I don't know why they wouldn't be storing their good stuff at the warehouse, but maybe you have intel on that." I paused to take another bite. "Bancorp's got four unarmed guards in the lobby during the day, two at night. Perimeter security too, but getting past them is easy enough. The elevator is keycard-activated. I assume you have a guy who makes those. Question is, how do you get the master from the guard in the first place? Already have a partner in town? And speaking of Portland, I assume your fence is out of state?"

My eyes had been on my plate. When I looked up, she was staring at me, a mix of shock and what I thought might be pride on her face. "You're not twelve anymore."

It was good to hear. Without a conscious effort, I'd seen the shape of her job as clearly as if she'd sent me a diagram.

"Soup always told me you'd be good at this. Remember that time we got a season of *Law and Order* from the library and watched it with him in one day?"

I smiled at the memory. "And he went off on how unrealistic it was that rich suspects would ever talk to the cops instead of calling their lawyers."

"You still like that show?"

"Nah, always preferred movies."

She went quiet. Her face became stony.

"What?" I asked.

She looked at the table. "I feel bad I let you watch that when you were—what?—eight? Nine? And how I used to drop you off to see movies on your own. It was cheaper than a babysitter. You *know* what I was doing those nights."

"Cheaper than a babysitter and gave you an alibi. But those are some of my best memories. Movies sometimes are all I have."

"What's your favorite?"

I took a huge bite of enchilada, giving myself time to think. I wasn't ready to tell her the truth. "Changes depending on my mood."

"I remember you saw *The Lion King* like ten times in the theater."

"Half those times I snuck into *Pulp Fiction* after you bought the tickets and took off."

She laughed, a real laugh where she rocked back in her chair and showed her teeth. "You little bastard! You never told me that."

"I was eight and sneaking into R-rated movies. Why would I tell you? And look, if I'm a bastard, that's more your fault than mine."

She laughed again and leveled her gaze on me. "Well, the way you scoped my job, I'd say you must have learned something."

I wasn't sure if it was a change in her or a change in me, but for the first time in two decades, I felt real affection for her. If she'd told me the truth about the microchips, it meant she trusted me at least a little. "So, I was right? Micro Tech? Bancorp Tower?"

She nodded.

"Mostly, I learned by watching you. And Soup, and Ricky. And the others. Watching and listening."

"Well, you seem to have a knack for it." The words could have been a compliment, but her tone made them an accusation. Of me, maybe, but more likely of herself. She moved sauce around her plate with her fork, sketching a weird angular pattern of tomatillo sauce with a single prong.

The affection I'd felt a moment earlier twisted into bitterness. "What?"

"I'm not sure I like that you were listening, watching. I'm sorry I exposed you to all that."

"All that was *you*, Mom. It was just... our life."

She folded her hands in her lap. "Well, sorry."

I took my plate to the sink, refilled my water, and sat again. "Do you know if my dad is still alive?"

She didn't seem surprised by the question. "I honestly don't. I'm sorry."

I don't remember the first time I asked about him, but I remember the last. I was eight years old and we were walking out of the downtown theater after watching *Forrest Gump*. I asked where my dad was and Mom said she didn't know, but that I'd never meet him. The way she said it made me drop the question for good.

"What was his name?"

She winced at this like I'd poked her with something sharp. She carried her plate to the sink and began washing dishes.

I said, "I'll do those later. What was his name?"

"Brian."

"Brian what?"

"Crenshaw."

"Who was he?"

"High-school boyfriend." She sighed and sat back down. "Brand, I'm... Look... I was seventeen, he was seventeen. We were dumb as rocks—about how the world worked, anyway. He wasn't able to be a dad, wasn't—"

"What about your mom and dad? Do they know about me? Are they alive?"

"They kicked me out when I got pregnant. Haven't spoken to them since."

"Have you looked them up?"

She shook her head slowly.

"And my dad, you're telling me you haven't looked him up?"

"Wouldn't know where to begin."

"You're so full of shit."

She stood abruptly and returned to the sink.

"I said I'd wash those later!"

She leaned over the sink and flattened her back, resting her forehead and elbows on the counter like she was doing some kind of yoga pose. She sighed long and low. She wanted out of this conversation.

I dug in. "You're telling me you cut ties with my dad, with my grandparents, and you haven't had any contact with them since?"

She didn't raise her head. "Yes."

"You dropped them. Like you did with me." It came out meaner than I'd intended, but not as mean as I felt. The resentment had been building since our meeting at the zoo, and for twenty years before that. Now it was all here, and it had a target.

She was quiet for a long time and, when she spoke, her voice was softer, sadder. "It wasn't like that. That one was... different."

I stood. "Result was the same. Cut ties, never look back." When she didn't reply, I pressed on. "Different how, *specifically?*" My sarcasm was heavy now.

"The first two times I did it for me. To protect myself. The last one I did for you." She turned toward me, then slid her back down the cupboard under the sink. Sitting cross-legged on the floor, she had tears in her eyes. A piece of my heart broke. The rest of me resented the hell out of it. Twenty years of nothing and now here she was, crying in my kitchen.

"For *me?*" I dropped into my chair. "What the hell does that mean?"

"I cut ties with your dad and my parents for my own good. Your dad couldn't help and my parents didn't want to. I was going to have to do it on my own. I left you for *your* own good. So you wouldn't end up like me. When that security guard died... and with the job going bad... and I'd already been thinking about boarding schools for you and... and what kind of mom uses her son to..."

I could sense her closing up again, but that made me push harder. "What happened that night?"

She looked at me briefly before her eyes dropped. She must have known the question was coming, but still wasn't prepared for it.

"What can I say? Job went bad. Real bad." The pinched look on her face made it clear she didn't want to say much. Some criminals like to brag about their crimes, mostly serial killers. Something in their psychological profile makes them want people to know. I'd never met a thief like that, though. You don't brag about your victories, and you never mention your fuck-ups.

I wasn't going to let it drop. "Walk me through it."

"Went sideways." She shook her head and let out a long, thin sigh. "Everything just went sideways. Lotta things I regret about that night, but..." She looked around my kitchen, then gestured to the wider apartment. "But your life turned out pretty good. Better, even. Right?"

I froze, my brain iced over with a cold, silent fury. Mom's attempt at a polite conversation lay on the table between us, decomposing.

Better. She imagined my life had been *better* without her. Every pain, every humiliation I'd felt in the last twenty years welled up inside me. Every time I'd packed my clothes and mementos into a garbage bag to change foster homes, every time I'd knocked on a new door holding that bag, feeling like I should say, *Hi, your new garbage is here.*

She wanted to believe my life had been better without her, then let her get the answer. You want to open that box, you have to accept what's inside. I locked eyes with her to make sure she'd take in what I was about to say, and yes, there was pleasure when I saw the smile drop off her face. "My life is shit, Mom."

"What do you mean?" She gestured weakly toward my living room, as though the beat-up recliner I got at the Goodwill for ten bucks justified her decision. "You've got stability. A solid job, right? An income?"

Something in the way she'd referred to my job struck me as odd. "You looked me up online, didn't you?"

"Checked in on you over the years a little. You don't leave much of a footprint on the web, or maybe I just don't know where to look. Saw in the paper when you graduated high school. You know, that list of seniors they do every year. Saw you made employee of the month at Morey's a couple times. That's so great. You were better off."

"Better off?" I shouted. "You think I was better—"

"You wouldn't want my life, Brandon!" She stood and glared down at me, full of a fury I'd only seen once or twice as a kid. "On the run all the time. People I know got pinched. Got killed. Always looking over your shoulder. Never knowing... never knowing what..." She dropped into the chair, her rage dissipating as quickly as it had arisen. "You wouldn't want my life, Brandon. Trust me."

She really believed it, had actually convinced herself that leaving me behind had been the right thing to do. She was imagining that breaking into my apartment and cooking enchiladas somehow gave her the moral high ground. I had the same thought I'd had earlier about Carebear: *How fucking dare she?* I used the horrible internal calculus I try to never use, and it told me that the cruelest thing I could say was just the truth. "Let me be clear, Mom: I hate my life.

Every second of it. If you got any other impression it's because you *wanted* to. To justify what you did."

The way her face fell will be with me until the day I die. But in that moment, her pain felt entirely deserved. *Let her hurt. Let her hurt like I did, like I have, like I am.*

"Brand, they were looking at me for murder. And I knew you'd been picked up. For two days I stewed in a little hotel off the freeway. Kept thinking about the guy who'd gotten killed. How he'd be alive if I hadn't tried to rob the game."

I wanted to believe everything she said. But she was a professional crook. Lying was half her job description. I didn't trust her—I *couldn't* —any more than I trusted Detective Caraway. "Or maybe you killed him, and *that's* what you couldn't live with."

"I would never—"

I stood, silencing her as my chair clattered back and struck the wall. "Get out of my apartment."

She didn't move. "If you want in on the... the microchip job, I could—"

"Get. The. Fuck. Out. Seriously." I felt ashamed for half a second, and added, "Thanks for the food, but don't break into my apartment again. It's good to see you. Well, not *good*, but, something. I don't know what it is. This isn't working. I need you to leave. Now."

She walked to the door.

I didn't want her to leave. I wasn't done hurting her. "You know Rabbit was the snitch, right?"

She turned, surprised, then a look of recognition passed over her face. "Rabbit Rafferty?"

"I guess he dropped out of your mind as fast as I did. Can't believe you trusted that rat bastard."

She shrugged as though she didn't remember the guy, even though she'd just said his name.

"He dimed you and Ricky on the poker game."

She shook her head slowly. It felt good to know something she didn't. Lording this piece of knowledge over her made me feel bigger, if only by making her feel smaller. "Didn't you ever wonder why there were so many cop cars within a block of the house? Didn't you ever wonder why they seemed to *know* about the game? I mean, they were there *seconds* after the shots were fired."

"I... how did you find out?"

"Soup."

She shook her head quickly, like she was erasing an Etch-A-Sketch, then stared up at me. "I really figured you were... I thought you'd be happier if I ..."

"Happier? I spent *years* obsessing over that night. How the cops knew, neighbors who might have snitched, the guys who were there—Brian damn White, Michael frigging Carusa. Blackstone, Seykes, Masterson. Those five bastards." I stared at the ground, fists balled up like I was about to punch a wall. "My court-ordered therapists told me you ruined my life by exposing me to crime all through my childhood. If that's true, I'd say you ruined it twice. You trained me to be a criminal, then you took that away." Her shoulders slumped, and I twisted the knife. "Now get out, and don't *ever* come back."

She looked at me long and hard, lips in a line like her mouth was poised to open. But it didn't. After a moment that set like concrete in my memory, she left.

Ever the cautious criminal, she didn't stroll out. She cracked the door a half-inch, listened, and peered out cautiously, left then right. She moved briskly down the hall and left the way she'd come in, through the back door.

The Oregonian, June 3, 1999

Players named in Laurelhurst shooting

Timber heir Seykes and State Rep. Blackstone among players

by Dana Murphy

Nearly six months after the fatal shooting in the upscale Laurelhurst neighborhood, The Oregonian has learned the names of the five men present at the ill-fated poker game. Though police have not released the names officially, a source within the department confirmed the identities of the men. The source described the incident as "an innocent poker game that went wrong," and stressed that none of the men are suspects in the death of the security guard.

The men, who gathered to play beginning at 8 p.m. on Friday night, Dec. 13, were Mark Masterson of Masterson Wealth Management, Brian White of KPKX radio, State Rep. Kellen Blackstone, Michael Carusa of Carusa Chevy, and Martin Seykes, heir to the Seykes timber fortune.

Reached for comment, Rep. Blackstone said, "This was a tragedy and I regret my incidental role in it."

Seykes, known for his philanthropy in support of the Portland arts and music communities, said, "This was a tragedy, and I deeply regret that our innocent poker game among friends could turn into the site of deadly violence. We must commend and support our police in their efforts to bring the killer to justice."

Seykes also told The Oregonian that he is offering a $50,000 reward for information leading to the arrest of Wanda Penny, one of the suspects in the case that hit a dead end in early January.

According to police, Seykes, Blackstone and the other three men were each fined $125, the maximum allowable for an illegal poker game at which the host does not profit.

Chapter Ten

My mom had only been gone a minute when I stepped into the empty hallway. She hadn't left a scent. Like most good thieves, she didn't wear perfume. When you rob a place, the last thing you want is to leave behind an identifiable odor. I can hear the enterprising detective now, *Hmm, no forcible entry, no fingerprints, no trace at all, EXCEPT the unmistakable scent of lilac and vanilla. This could only be the work of...*

The hallway was oddly silent, as though the building itself was offering me a moment to contemplate my situation. That was the last thing I wanted to do. During dinner, vines of anger and sadness had twisted together in my chest, and I was quickly reaching a place uncomfortable enough that I needed a way out.

I stepped into the cold night and wandered toward the liquor store. I'd brushed my mom off when she asked about girlfriends, but as I walked the familiar route, staying in the shadows out of habit, the few I'd had danced through my mind, a series of staccato memories tinged with a little happiness and a lot of failure. Besides a few flirtations and an awkward kiss backstage during a play in middle school, my romantic life started when I became psychic at age fourteen. Put another way, that's when I started convincing people I was psychic by using the same tricks magicians and con men had used for centuries: claim higher authority, speak with absolute confidence, validate the mark's existing biases, and never admit a mistake.

I'd learned the basics from my mom's friend Genevieve, who made good money convincing rich ladies their hot gardener was their destined true love. Of course, the rich ladies had to get rid of some of their cursed money before he'd see it as well. Her techniques came in handy when I tried to impress my friends in the various homes I lived in. I guess it was one way I could use my skills without committing any crimes, and it got the attention of some of the girls.

When a new kid arrived, I'd put on an air of distance and wisdom. I'd wait for someone else to bring up my psychic abilities, then I'd hit the kid with something like, *I sense that your family history contains much conflict and pain.* I'd put a finger to my right temple and close my eyes. *I see a police uniform, you're a child... six, maybe eight... but you're crying.* The trick is, after doing a quick cold read on the mark, you need to be vague enough at the beginning that they start offering up clues about themselves. Then you use those clues to say steadily more concrete things that solidify their view of you as psychic.

I had already conned a few people when a girl named Crystal moved into my second foster home, the one after Cemetery Lane. It was a decent house off Burnside, a good neighborhood then, though not the yuppie food Mecca it is today. Tall and skinny, Crystal had the habit of coiling her dirty-blond hair around her finger, then letting it spring free. I took this as a nervous tic, and tried to impress her with my psychic abilities the first night after dinner. *You've had a difficult few years*, I said when she stopped next to me in the hallway on the way to her new bedroom. *I'm seeing a fight between your parents...* I closed my eyes, moving my head in a tiny, profound circle. I let out a long breath. *There was violence. Maybe physical, maybe emotional. It's... it's still a little foggy.*

It turned out Crystal did that thing with her hair not because she was anxious, but as a way of focusing. She curled her hair around her finger for the same reason my mom's partner Ricky tugged at his ear sometimes—as a gesture of pure, intense concentration. The way

Michael Jordan used to stick his tongue out in mid-air while going for a dunk.

She saw right through me. *Bullshit,* she said. *You're full of bull and shit. But you're cute.* She punched my arm and continued down the hallway, pausing long enough at her bedroom door to give me a look. You know the look—it's the kind that keeps teenage boys up at night.

There were only three of us in that house: me, Crystal, and Shawn. Like Crystal, Shawn was a year older than me. He was a smart-ass homeless kid who'd stolen a car when he was fourteen and been diverted into the system. He wore his hair in cornrows modeled after Allen Iverson, even though he wasn't into basketball. Shawn never told us exactly how he ended up on his own, but he was gay and the way he told me made me think his parents hadn't approved. Like most of us who ended up in foster homes, he didn't like to talk about his parents.

We knew what happened to Crystal's parents, though. She was from outside Portland. I don't know where exactly, but she had a feel to her, like the city was too big, like there was too much going on and she was always on the verge of overwhelm, except when she did that thing with her hair. Her dad had died when she was little. Her mom got locked up for meth, which made Shawn joke that Crystal's mom named her after the only thing she loved in the world.

I never joked about Crystal's name or her parents, though. She'd sworn she'd never mess with drugs like her mom, but that didn't seem to include her drinking problem. Her boozing was what allowed our relationship to flourish. Our custodians at the time were Mike and Sandy, and they weren't the strict disciplinarians of Cemetery Lane. They were more oblivious, probably because they had drinking problems of their own. They kept the liquor cabinet locked. Or I should say """"locked""""" with as many sarcastic quotes around it as possible, because I opened that thing in less than a minute.

I let Crystal pilfer only from the vodka and gin bottles because I could refill those with tap water without changing the color. Mike made tiny pencil marks on the bottles to keep track of the booze, but I made sure that after Crystal refilled her flask, the level came back up to the most recent mark. She got worse as I fed her habit—because of course she did—and pretty soon the gin bottle had to be about eleven proof. I was sure Mike and Sandy would notice that. Thing was, they always started with wine before they moved to the hard stuff, so I just painted the neck of the Beefeater bottle with the mineral oil they kept in the medicine cabinet. Next time they killed a bottle of pinot and went to make some martinis, damn if the gin bottle didn't slip out of Sandy's hands onto that hard tile floor. After that, I stopped helping Crystal steal liquor, but by that time she had crawled all the way into her addiction, and I think she started getting it from someplace else.

I lost my virginity to her on a Sunday afternoon. Sandy was out somewhere or other and Mike, after four beers, had dozed off on the couch watching the Seahawks game. I was watching the game, too, even though I wasn't especially interested. I'd never played football, but I liked the storylines. I tried to turn it into a movie in my head. *Can the undersized QB from a small state college rise to the occasion against his superior opponent?* Not much of a storyline, but it kept me busy when I was out of new movies.

I was listening to Mike snore when Crystal came up behind me and tapped my shoulder. *Come upstairs for a second.*

I figured she wanted me to steal booze for her again. Instead, when we got up to her room, she said, *I'm leaving.*

Like, to go where?

For good. I'm gonna leave tonight.

I wouldn't have admitted it at the time—and I probably didn't even really know it—but I was madly in love with her. Like I said, she was a year older and she laughed at my jokes and seemed genuinely impressed by how much I knew about movies. At that point, we'd made out once. More accurately, she'd made out with me. It happened one night after she'd been drinking. She snuck into my bed, smelling of gin, and we kissed for maybe ten minutes before she left as suddenly as she'd arrived. Neither of us mentioned it afterward. I was interested, but in that awkward, half-paralyzed way teenage boys know they're interested in girls and sex. I could lie and fake my way through most things, but sex wasn't one of them.

What do you mean? I asked.

I'm gonna leave tonight.

After a minute, I got what she meant. *What? Why?*

Look around us. You wanna live here?

No, but... I couldn't think of an objection.

She waved me into her room and we sat on her bedspread, which was a hideous yellow-green color, like old split-pea soup. She put a hand on my leg.

She was running away, and it hit me hard. I wasn't going to admit it, so I asked a series of fact-based questions while trying to think of a way to make her stay. *Where are you gonna go?*

Back toward home. Couple girls I know got a place.

Why tonight?

It's just time. She tossed her hair back in a way that told me she didn't want to say more.

I pressed on. *How will you afford food?*

She shrugged. *I can work. I want to say goodbye to you, though. You were nice to me.*

For half a second I thought about running downstairs, shaking Mike until he woke up, and telling him. Maybe he could somehow force her to stay. Lock her up or something. But that would have been snitching. I didn't get too far into the thought because the next thing she did was take off her shirt. After that, any thoughts I had of doing anything other than exactly what she wanted disappeared.

I never asked, but I think she'd been with at least a couple other guys before me. She seemed to know what she was doing. I didn't. It lasted ten minutes, and I'm probably remembering my performance generously.

Afterward, we lay on the floor, listening to the cars whoosh by outside. She was quiet for a long time, then said, *Can we get married and have like fifteen babies?*

It was the strangest thing she'd ever said to me. I panicked for half a second. Had I just gotten her pregnant? I said, *Wait, did I do something wrong?*

She started laughing. She laughed hard and for a long time and

105

way too loudly. Her laughter was fake as hell. She wanted me to know how much she'd been joking. Wanted me to understand that she hadn't meant it at all, not even the tiniest bit. She was a rock, a beacon of strength and independence who didn't need anyone.

But she *had* meant it. She was even lonelier than I was, and in even more pain. I'd like to say we clung to each other and, for a brief moment, everything was right in the world. But that would be a load of crap. We lay on the floor a little longer, staring at the ceiling, not saying a word. We were two black holes, side by side, incapable of ever really touching.

After a while, she said, *Anyway, I'm leaving tonight.*

I didn't say anything.

A few minutes later she added, *I'm never having kids.*

Me neither, I told her.

It was the last thing I ever said to her. As goodbyes went, it wasn't great, but it was absolutely true. She left that night, and that was that.

After Crystal, there had been a few others, including a yearlong affair with an older woman soon after I dropped out of college. I broke it off when I found out she was married and was as good a liar as I was. After that, there'd been no one serious until Jennifer. I guess I was slowly coming to terms with the fact that some people are too screwed up to function in a relationship. In my teens and early twenties, I blamed the women. When Jennifer left, I turned the blame on myself.

I bought a fifth of cheap whiskey at the liquor store and took the first slug a half block from the corner. I was already feeling loose when I fell into my recliner back in my apartment. Sometimes all my rational thoughts, reasonable plans, and therapeutically-recommended coping mechanisms disappeared all at once. Now they were replaced wholesale by a phrase running through my mind, a phrase that had been a big part of my life when I was fourteen, but had faded into memory. My mom's visit had pulled it back, and now it blared in my mind like a siren. *Who was the chismoso?*

Rabbit Rafferty was the snitch, the guy who'd given the poker-game job to the cops. He was the reason they'd been waiting nearby that night, the reason the red-and-blue lights had been all around as I fled. I'd thrown him at my mom out of spite. In my anger, I'd wanted to make her feel stupid for trusting Rabbit. But that was for show. Truth was, I hadn't even considered the idea that there *was* a snitch until a couple weeks after Crystal disappeared. A dude named Hector had taken her place in the house and a reshuffling of rooms landed us together on a bunk bed. It was Hector who launched my crusade with a simple, off-hand question: *Who was the chismoso?*

Hector was a constant and—more importantly—a *bad* liar. He lied so much he made me look like a beacon of truth. He lied about big things and little things and everything in between, but his lies weren't about deception. Not exactly. They were just... *Hector's bullshit.* Every word out of his mouth was like your drunk uncle telling you about a big fish he once caught—he might be exaggerating or making it up completely, but somehow it didn't matter. If that was all there was to Hector, that would be fine. There's a Hector in every social circle, but there was something else about Hector that demanded my attention. Despite all his bullshit, every now and again, he'd throw in a comment so true it seared me to the core.

One night after lights-out we lay in bed talking quietly, each keeping an eye on the crack under the door, ready to go silent if the hallway light turned on. That night we listened to the wind rustle the tree outside our window and he told me about his parents. He wasn't abandoned, he wanted me to know, and he was only going to be in foster care for a short while. His dad had to leave him to play for the Seahawks "up north in Seattle." I remember the exact phrase because the thought of Seattle being "up north" made me smile. It was an odd way to put it. His mom was a famous actress who worked mostly in Europe, so I wouldn't have heard of her, he assured me.

He was bullshitting, but I enjoyed tugging the thread. *I'm actually really into movies, what's she been in?*

Highbrow stuff, nothing you'd know. She's a real A-lister over there, man.

Try me. Like I said, I'm really into movies.

Nah, man, I'm talkin' subtitles, naked French ladies, stuff you never seen.

What part of Europe?

Eh, somewhere in the middle.

Like I said, a godawful liar.

The conversation turned to how I'd ended up in the foster system, a topic I hadn't talked about beyond my court-ordered therapy sessions. I liked Hector, and his transparently bad lies were so sad, I was embarrassed on his behalf. I wanted him to feel okay telling me the truth, so I told him some of mine. Not everything, but I told him about my mom and what happened the night of the poker game. I figured he'd had a few brushes with the law, and that it might be something we could connect over. When I'd finished telling the story, he was quiet a long time. Then he shifted on the top bunk. It creaked something awful and I peered at the crack under the door, poised to roll over and pull the covers over my head.

Instead, his shadowed face appeared, dangling down over the side. *Who was the chismoso?*

Huh?

You said that when you ran there were two or three cop cars?

I thought back to the night, reliving it in the stark terms I remembered, not the cute version I'd told Hector. *Three or four. Maybe even five.*

And how much time between when the shots were fired and when the cops were there?

Maybe a minute. I saw the security guard fall, saw Ricky and my mom, saw my mom pointing west. It had felt like a long time, but it wasn't. *It happened fast. Really it was less than a minute, I think. It was like they knew we were gonna be there.*

The moonlight cut through the window, flashing on his eyes, which were aggressively open, asking, Don't you SEE?

You saying they knew?

That's what I'm saying, B. Of course they knew. Hector called everyone by the first letter in their first name. I was always just "B." I tried calling him "H" a few times, but it felt forced coming from me, so I went back to "Hector."

When I didn't reply, he drove it home. *That's what I'm asking, man. Who was the chismoso?*

I was defensive at first. There was no way my mom was dumb enough to get dimed out to the cops before a job. After a long silence, I said, *If there was a snitch, why didn't the cops stop the job before they went in?*

Catch you in the act. More jail time. Or they only had part of the job. A neighborhood but not an address. A street but not a house number. That's what happened with my p... with some people I knew.

Hector went quiet. Staring out at the moon through the branches that scraped our window, I considered his theory. If the cops had been waiting for us to rob the game, ready to pounce the moment we walked out with the loot, the question was: Who'd told them about the job? As far as I knew, the only people in on it were Mom, Ricky Gat, and me. I hadn't heard them talk about it in front of anyone else, though my mom often shared stuff with Soup. No way it was Soup. Even back then, I trusted him as much as anyone I'd ever met. There in the moonlight, Hector's head hung down as I thought through all the people my mom had worked with, people who'd come and gone over the years. I had no idea who'd given up the job, but as I lay awake that night, my life took a new direction. Hector only stayed in the group home a few months, but his question stayed with me long after he was gone.

After two years cast adrift, I had a plan, a purpose: I'd find the snitch and kill him.

～

I kicked up the footrest on my recliner and took a long pull of the harsh whiskey.

The smell of enchiladas lingered in my apartment. My fists kept ending up in tight balls no matter how many times I unclenched them, and the argument with my mom hung like a dark cloud. I went to the TV and found my DVD of *Paper Moon*. That movie had broken my heart a hundred times, but it had often given me hope, too.

Hope that a happy reunion was possible. That fantasy was gone now. And along with the sadness over the loss of a happy future with my mom was a fog of shame—shame about my own stupidity, my naiveté for believing it was possible in the first place.

No movie was right for the moment. Watching an old favorite would ruin it, as though my foul mood would forever pollute my experience of the film. I tossed the DVD case across the room and returned to my recliner. Box of memories in my lap, I took another pull from the bottle.

My mom claimed to believe that leaving me behind was the best thing for me. But even if she was telling the truth, it didn't make me feel any better. Because she'd been wrong. Maybe she'd imagined me living a happy life with Mr. and Mrs. John Q. America, going to a fancy private school, getting into a good college, and marrying a pretty young woman and having kids named Pete and Sally Q. America. But that's not what happened. I bounced around, never got fully adopted, and landed in the world still Brandon Penny, son of a career criminal and murder suspect.

I tried to put myself in her shoes, to adopt the mindset of a mother worried her son would be better off without her. It didn't work. Sure, she didn't make a living like most moms, but she was a good, loving mother. No drugs, no violence, always went to my parent-teacher conferences at school. Then—BANG—she was gone, leaving nothing but a dead security guard and a son who never heard from her again.

The more I thought, and the more I drank, the less I believed her story. It was convenient—*too* convenient—that leaving me behind just happened to coincide with her escape. She'd gone on to do crimes all around the country while I'd been left with needlework Bible quotes and worse. By my fourth swig, I was convinced she'd planned to get rid of me all along. Didn't she even mention that she'd been looking at fancy boarding schools *before* the poker game job? Teenage boys were notoriously hard to deal with, right? Who'd blame her for wanting to ship me away? She'd been planning to drop me since I was ten, I concluded. That night in Laurelhurst had given her an easy out.

Detective Caraway was on my mind as well.

Carebear was a liar, sure, but every good liar knows to mix some truth in with the lies. My mom *was* a thief and she *was* in town for a heist. Carebear had been right about that from day one. So how could I be so sure she was wrong about what happened in Laurelhurst? I'd never accepted the version in the papers, but I'd never entirely ruled it out, either.

I took my fifth pull from the bottle. Carebear was right. My mom pulled the trigger. She'd had to disappear to escape the murder charge, and ditching me was a happy bonus.

Caraway could make my life a living hell. Without my mom, without anyone, I'd built a life. Not a good life. Not a happy or interesting life. But it was something, and it was mine. I was in a warm apartment with a bottle of booze and a job waiting for me. I had an ex-girlfriend who didn't hate me and seemed to accept my past, now that I'd come clean about it. That was more than some guys had. More than Mikey Shakes. As bad as things were, they could always get worse. I'd lived through worse and *much* worse. Caraway could take it all away if she wanted.

After another swig, my anger faded. My thinking slowed and became circular. Carebear and my mom. My mom and Carebear. It was as though they were in the room, one on each side of me, pressing in on my temples.

I laughed out loud and rocked in the chair. I was close to hammered. If I kept drinking, I'd soon be out of control. I rarely let myself get there because, as crappy as my life was, waking up with a splitting headache wasn't going to make it any better. So I'd created this stopping point in my brain, a little recurring message that said, *Brandon, you're close to hammered.* At that point I'd stop drinking, chug a few glasses of water, eat a little something, and go to bed.

I told that voice to go to hell.

I turned to the memory box in my lap and thumbed through old newspaper clippings and papers, the memories I had instead of a normal adolescence. Each memento was like a twist in my heart, a thorny reminder of pains I wanted to forget but kept returning to anyway. Sometimes you need to pick the scabs until they bleed. I took another pull from the bottle, longer this time, then lurched over to the TV to put on a movie. I riffled through my sleeves of DVDs, but fell back into the chair without making a decision.

On my phone, I tapped a name into Google: Tyler Twomey. This was something I did every few months, usually after a couple drinks. I hear it's common to have a few people you look up online every so often, just to see what they're up to. Friends from childhood you're curious about but don't actually want to contact. Exes who dumped you who you mostly don't think about. Exes you dumped who you claim to be totally over, but you want to know what they're doing, see if they got married, had kids. See if they ended up with a worse life than you, or a better one. It's not stalking but it's not *not* stalking.

There was nothing new on Twomey—he was still the assistant manager of a failing sporting-goods store in Eastern Washington. He was still divorced, still had no children, still only posted scores from college baseball games and complaints about his crushing student loans. I pulled his large, friendly dad from the door that night for what was supposed to be a couple minutes while Ricky and my mom took down the poker game. A quick in-and-out. Instead, Tyler Twomey, only a few years younger than me, had lost his dad.

I was still shaken by Twomey's sudden, violent death. I hadn't wanted it, hadn't planned it, hadn't expected it. But I *had* caused it. If I hadn't pulled Thomas Twomey off the door that night, his son would have grown up with a father. I did what my mother told me to. Ever since, I'd been unable to escape the consequences. One of those consequences was the awareness that this guy was always one click away on social media, living his life blind to the fact that I was the reason his dad was gone.

I peered into the bottle and swirled the last couple ounces, getting lost in the tiny waves of brown liquor. I opened a Facebook message to Tyler Twomey and began typing. I only got a couple sentences into my confession before deleting it. A drunk person at a keyboard is a dangerous thing, so I decided to close my computer, finish the bottle, and go to sleep.

July 1, 2001

Dude,

I know we said we'd keep in touch but I've been bounced around all over for the last few months. Found your address on a slip of paper in a magazine and thought, what the hell? New "parents" won't let me use the computer but were "nice" enough to offer me a stamp, so here goes...

How you been? You still a movie nut? You ever find the Chismoso?

I'm more into cars than movies these days. Got a poster of the 2000 Mustang on my wall. Saved $2,100 working at Subway and planning to get something used once I move out on my own.

Good memories, sneaking out to watch flicks with you.

I SEE DEAD PEOPLE...

THERE IS NO SPOON...

Ha ha!

Remember that night we stole a pint of vodka and you did the best lines from Pulp Fiction in the voice of the little kid from The Sixth Sense? SAY WHAT AGAIN (whispered mysteriously). I still laugh every time I think of it.

Write me sometime. Let me know where you're living now and maybe we can get together.

Later man,

Hector

Chapter Eleven

I woke to a ringing phone and a splitting headache. I fumbled between the sheets and under the pillows, then checked the crack behind the bed. The ringing stopped and I chugged a large plastic cup of water, which I must have set next to my bed after blacking out.

I rubbed my eyes as blurry memories of the night before drifted through. Whiskey and anger. Had I messaged Twomey? Had I called my mom? Christ, I hoped I hadn't posted anything stupid on my dormant Facebook account. My invisible phone beeped. I looked around again and found it in the pocket of the pants I'd left on the floor. A voicemail.

"Hey, Keyser, it's Eric. Got your J-Pay email and visiting hours today end at 10:45 A.M. Afternoon visiting hours got canceled for a few weeks because of a stabbing. After today, Tuesday is the next option, so come today if you can. Be great to see you. Bye, kid."

Eric, who everyone called "Ricky Gat," had gotten away just like my mom, and I hadn't seen him since. Throughout my teenage years, I'd considered tracking him down more times than I could count. I'd even asked Soup about him once or twice, but his responses had always been vague. Probably didn't want me to connect with a dude like that. Ricky was a professional criminal and, according to Soup,

114

Mom was willing to work with him because he'd done multiple armed robberies and never killed anyone. He took more risks than my mom and, up to a point, that had brought him greater rewards. That point came a few years ago, because he was arrested and sentenced to a dozen years at the Oregon State Penitentiary.

I splashed water on my face, drank a cold cup of coffee still in the pot from the day before, and threw on black work pants, the only pair I owned that weren't jeans. The inmates in Oregon prisons wore jeans, so visitors were warned not to. In case there's a riot, the guards need to know who not to shoot.

I had enough room on my credit card to pay for a Zipcar. And since I only had an hour to make it to visiting hours, I found one a few blocks from my house and hit the road. I cracked the window and flipped on the radio, hoping the fresh air would dry the whiskey-sweat beading on my forehead and the music would distract me from the ice-pick pain stabbing my temples. The radio was set to the news, which only made my head pound harder.

"In Salem yesterday, a town hall meeting with U.S. Representative Kellen Blackstone of Oregon's Fifth Congressional District turned rowdy, when protestors interrupted the event. Over two hundred citizens had gathered in the auditorium at Durban University when the Congressman appeared, dressed in the classic Stockman boots and Wranglers the 'Cowboy Congressman' is known for.

"The dust-up began when a man asked Blackstone a pointed question about so-called 'corporate donors.' Before he could answer, a coordinated team of protesters unfurled a banner on the mezzanine. Blackstone, always quick with a quip, told the audience, 'Probably paid agitators, planted by my opponent.'

"The blue-dog Democrat, who frequently noted his bipartisan accomplishments..."

The combination of a wicked hangover and the report on Kellen Blackstone broke my brain. I turned off the radio and rolled down the window the rest of the way, allowing the wind to batter my face. My reflexes felt slow, like I was driving through a swimming pool, so I needed to take it slow, especially heading out of town on the freeway south. The Terwilliger Curves kill a lot of people every year; no reason I should be another victim. I took it easy as I passed through layers of suburb—Tualatin and Wilsonville—until the freeway believed I was heading south and straightened out. By then, the cold air had cleared some of the cobwebs and I sped up, but only to four miles an hour over the limit. I locked in the cruise control and watched the memories play like a movie in my mind.

~

The last time I went to Oregon State Penitentiary, I was sixteen years old and out for blood.

It had started two years earlier, when I was a freshman in high school. Crystal and Hector had moved on and Mike and Sandy sometimes let me roam free on weekends, so I decided to track down my mom's old friend Soup. Not for sentimental reasons, I told myself, just because I'd heard he was dealing these days.

I found him on a hot Saturday in September. I'd walked two miles in an eighty-degree wet heat, and I still remember the feel of the air conditioner blasting my sweaty skin as I ducked into the pizza shop he used as a home base.

Keyser, good to see you. Soup was at a table in the back, reading the *Willamette Week,* a half-eaten slice of pizza soaking a paper plate with grease.

I slid into the booth across from him. For the first ten minutes, he asked questions about school and where I'd been living. I asked him about people we'd known, people my mom had done jobs with, but I made sure not to mention her directly.

After a few minutes, I got to the point. *Heard you're dealing.*

Where'd you hear that?

Around.

He laughed. *That guy "Around" has a big mouth.*

I didn't laugh. Laughing was for suckers. *Just looking for a dime bag.*

He thought for a long time, finishing his greasy slice and staring at me to the point where I grew uncomfortable. All he said was, *Been thinking.*

I gave him my best *so-the-fuck-what?* look, eyes wide in annoyance. I was hard as nails, like only a fourteen-year-old boy can imagine himself to be.

Wasn't your fault, kid. You probably feel bad you got pinched your first time on a real job. Just wanted to make sure you know, it wasn't your fault.

I didn't know it at the time, but rage and sorrow are two sides of the same coin. Like most blustery teenagers, I had no idea how angry I was inside, or how broken.

What the hell are you talking about? I said it like he was a total idiot, though the truth was I knew exactly what he was talking about. He'd read me like the menu of the pizzeria that hung crooked on the wall behind us. The other half of the reason I'd come to see him was to find out whatever I could about the poker game. I guess learning about that night was my way of learning about my mom without admitting I cared. By the time I found Soup, Hector's question had been burning a hole through my heart for weeks.

Soup ignored my bluster, but he read my heart. *I wasn't going to tell you this unless I needed to. Guess I need to. Remember Rabbit Rafferty?*

I shrugged as though I didn't give a damn who he was. I was hanging on every word.

Rabbit was a part-timer, remember? Part-time bookie, part-time fence, part-time thief, part-time a lotta shit. Anyway, he'd moved some stuff for Ricky Gat and done an okay job, so Ricky and Dolly thought about involving him in the poker game. Figured he was a right guy, y'know? First version of the plan had Rabbit pulling the security guy off the door. But the more they talked to him, the less they trusted him, so after a while, they just cut him right out. Told him they cancelled the job, put you in on pulling the security guard. What they didn't figure on was that Rabbit was also a part-time snitch.

My knuckles hurt. I'd dug my fingernails into my jeans while he was speaking. I slowly moved my hands onto the table, trying to come off as calm, like I was taking this all in stride. I didn't want Soup to know the thoughts going through my head. I said, *You sure? I mean, it makes sense. I wondered why it went wrong, why there were so many cops there. I ditched the first couple cars, but... Are you sure?*

Sure I'm sure. He looked at me hard. *And I'm only telling you so you know it wasn't your fault. Don't want you getting any stupid ideas.*

Where is he now?

Jail. Rabbit finally got got. Year ago.

I nodded as though that was enough, as though that could possibly make it okay. Inside me, the notion was planted. The man who'd taken my mother and my life away had an identity now, had a body someplace. A body that, someday, I could kill. *Well, fuck him. About that dime bag?*

Soup eyed me, and I flushed with teenage shame at being assessed and judged. Finally he said, *No problem. I got some Northern Lights I can let you have at friend prices for old times' sake. Anything else you need?*

I was about to say *Nah* when something happened that didn't happen often, maybe a couple times a year since I was ten. A crime came together in my mind instantly. Opportunity, security, risks, payoff, alibi, everything. I'd always just let those sail past, usually because I wasn't in any position to act on them. This time, though... this time something felt different. *You know where I could get a pick set?*

I died of old age a couple times during the pause before Soup answered. *What the hell, you can have mine. Never use it any more. Forty bucks. And ten for the Lights.* Say what you might about Soup, he was a penny-pinching old bastard.

Two days later, as school was letting out, I buttonholed the girl who'd replaced Hector and told her to let Mike and Sandy know I was going to catch the 6 PM show of *Boiler Room* at the Lloyd Center, so I wouldn't be home until late evening. Then I hung around the halls until the school was quiet and, once I was quite unobserved, stuffed myself into my empty locker.

I had to scrunch down and twist a little bit to get in there, but I made it. Then all I had to do was wait, nearly motionless, for three and a half hours. That was how long it took for footsteps and floor-polishers to stop echoing in the halls, as first teachers, then administrators, then custodians finished their jobs. When the big steel front doors whanged shut for the last time, and nothing else made a sound for ten minutes, I pulled on the jimmy I'd put in the locker latch, clambered out, and stretched.

Being the only person in the high school was an intense rush. Part of me wanted to go nuts, run up and down the halls hooting and hollering. That was the dumb fourteen-year-old piece of me, though. I was listening to the smarter part of me, the part warning that there might still be someone in the building, that I should keep my ears open and my feet quiet.

In that year of someone's Lord 2000, the computer room at my public high school had racks of cheap, low-end PCs with CRT screens. During classes, all those units were monitored and, if necessary, controlled by the teacher's computer, a recent-model Sony laptop with quite a few turn-of-the-century bells and whistles. I figured they'd chosen a laptop so that, between classes, it could be closed and locked in a secure closet.

The foster home had a PC all the kids had to share, loaded with Net Nanny software. It was out in the open in the living room and we got it for a max of half an hour a day. I'd wanted a laptop for a long time, some little piece of my life that I controlled, that wasn't subject to someone else's approval. And now I needed one to find out everything I could about Rabbit Rafferty, and to make my plan to kill him.

The computer room was locked, but I had Soup's pick set in its worn nylon case. Getting in took two minutes. The secure storage closet had a much better lock, and that took closer to fifteen. If you've never picked a lock, it's hard to understand how it feels when it works, when you defeat a system designed to keep you out. The moment when it clicks, when the rake brushes that last pin just right and the wrench suddenly moves after being stuck immobile... it's a release of built-up tension, like a sneeze. Or an orgasm.

I grabbed the laptop, stashed it in my backpack, let myself out of the school, made it home ahead of my alibi, and slept like a log. The next day, at lunch in the cafeteria, I heard that the computer teacher opened up the locked closet, hunted through it in increasing desperation, then sheepishly announced that class was cancelled. And what changed a lot of things was that Richie Cortman happened to be looking at my face when I heard that story. I thought I'd done a good job acting shocked by this unfathomable mystery theft, but he told me later that when I first heard about it, just for a second, I smirked.

After lunch, Richie caught up with me. I was a freshman and he was a junior, but I liked him because once when I was haggling with White Jimmy, the school weed dealer, Richie stepped in and bought me an eighth of kush on his own dime. His family had stupid money and he attended a public high school as some kind of punishment for fucking up at a private middle school.

He said he saw how I reacted to the news about the break-in, I denied it, we went back and forth a little, and then he dropped the question: *Do you think you could break into a safe?*

If I hadn't been smug, if I hadn't been flattered, if I hadn't been fourteen, I would've answered, *I can't break into anything and it's insulting that you'd ask*, or I might've said, *I don't want to get involved in your shit, dude.*

Instead I said, *What kind of safe?*

Turns out Richie's grandpa had left him a 1930s wristwatch in his will, but Richie's dad had intercepted it and locked it in a home security safe, saying that Richie could have it if he got into an Ivy League college. Richie felt the watch was his rightful property, and wanted it now. In response to my questions, he said he'd seen his dad open the safe with a key, it wasn't an especially big key, it wasn't round, he didn't remember how many bumps were on it, there weren't any wires coming out of the safe, and of course his dad didn't have security cameras in his den, why would I even ask?

I said I'd give it a shot.

On the drive to Richie's, a castle of a house in Eastmoreland, I asked the question I should have asked first: *What else is in the safe?*

A few things, he said. *I saw a gun in there, maybe a few thousand bucks, and some legal documents. I know the deed to the house is in there, and dad and mom's Social Security cards. I think maybe some of mom's jewelry. But that doesn't matter, all I want is the watch.*

I had to restrain myself from cursing. *Okay*, I said as kindly as I could, *but I can't just take the watch. Because, no offense, literally one person on earth wants that watch and nothing else in that safe. So if only the watch goes missing, like, the suspect list is pretty short.*

I remember he took his eyes off the road to look at me in surprise and revelation, and we damn near hit a parked car. *Oh shit, you're right. What do we do?*

I just grab the watch and anything else obviously valuable, I explained. *Leave the legal documents, and it looks like a professional burglary.*

Right, yes, that makes perfect sense! He was delighted. *Let me keep my mom's jewelry, and we'll split the cash fifty-fifty.*

I almost asked to be let out of his car. Nobody sensible had the brass balls to demand that kind of split for doing essentially nothing. But Richie didn't understand money the way fish don't understand water. Fifty percent would still be more than I'd ever had in my pocket in my life, and it wasn't worth arguing over. Mostly I wanted to get a look at this safe.

Before we entered his house, I pulled on a thin pair of latex gloves. Richie looked awed at my professionalism, and yeah, that felt kinda good. I knew the gloves would make the pick more difficult, but I didn't feel like getting arrested.

The safe was in Richie's dad's home office, which had a wood-paneled, deep-carpeted aesthetic I would come to recognize as Suburban Macho. A large wooden desk faced a pair of French doors that offered a nice view of the backyard garden. The safe itself was a steel door the size of a toaster oven, set into the rear wall about chest height. Sure enough, it had a regular keyhole, and I pulled out my pick set and got to work.

The lock was high-quality, very little give in the cylinder, and the pins just did *not* want to set. The gloves weren't helping, but I was making slow progress when a loud, shattering CRASH came from behind me. I jumped half a foot and nearly snapped the pick I was using. I turned around, and there was Richie, standing outside the shattered French door with a hammer and a pleased expression.

I figured I'd help, he had the balls to say. *If the door's broken from the outside, it looks more like a burglar did it.*

I kept my voice level, but only with great effort. *A burglar who can pick the lock on this safe, but not on a French door? THAT burglar?*

Oh. He looked so crestfallen that, for a second, I could almost feel bad for him.

Never mind, just let me finish this. I decided to try a different pick for these shy pins, and started over. It was taking forever, and it didn't help to have Richie standing awkwardly in the room, shifting from foot to foot and looking jumpy every time a car drove by.

Suddenly there was that soft, beautiful little *click*, and the lock popped. I opened the door of the safe, and the rush was incredible. I'd done this, me, fourteen years old and opening a safe full of cash and gemstones like a pirate treasure cave. It felt good, felt *right* in a way nothing had for two years.

I reached in, pulled out an absolutely gorgeous Rolex Oyster, and handed it to Richie without a word. Likewise I handed him a nicely minimalist ruby pendant and an over-designed sapphire-and-diamond necklace. There were two stacks of twenty-dollar bills, each in a violet bank wrapper, meaning $2,000. I handed Richie one and stuffed the other in the pocket of my jeans. There were the legal papers he'd mentioned too, but I ignored those. There was a market for Social Security cards, but that was a can of worms I didn't want to open just yet. Instead I picked up the nickel-plated .357 revolver and felt its weight in my hand. I imagined a life where I held one regularly, and it was easy to picture. I imagined pointing it at Rabbit Rafferty's face.

I put it back. That was another can of worms I didn't want to open. Just yet.

According to Richie, who was now as much my buddy as a junior could be to a freshman, neither his father nor the police ever mentioned the incongruous detail of a smashed window and care-fully-picked lock. Hell, the cops probably figured it was better than fifty-fifty that this was a rich idiot going for an insurance payout and being sloppy about it.

A couple months later, a friend of Richie's from a different school got in touch with me on a Friday night. He'd ordered some stuff online, but accidentally used his dad's business address for the delivery, and he needed someone to get into that address and make one particular package disappear before Monday morning. So I did.

That job led to another, and another, and another. For two years of my high school education, while I absorbed basic algebra and the *we-left-some-shit-out* version of American history, while I was bounced into a group home and then back into a foster situation and then back into another group home, I occasionally got calls from other teenagers.

I didn't excel academically. I was never on any sports team. I wasn't in the nerdy clubs or the student government. High school is, to some extent, about finding what you're good at, about building your identity. The identity I built was strictly off the record. Most of the kids I worked with never heard my real name. I never became part of a crew, never worked with a partner more than twice, never left a fingerprint or did a job I wasn't invited on.

And for all that, between my freshman and junior years, I stole nearly everything that wasn't bolted down, and a couple things that were. I made money, and that was nice, people thought I was cool, and that was nice, but mainly it just felt *so damn good* to do something I was so damn good at. I stole like a greyhound runs, like a bloodhound hunts. I was doing what I was *made* to do.

After a while, I started asking for only a fraction of the take I was rightly due. The truth was, I would have worked for free, but the kids who hired me wouldn't understand that. They'd never trust a thief who didn't want a cut. And I didn't want to explain the other reason I didn't need the money, which was that I didn't have a future.

My future ended with the death of Rabbit Rafferty. I would walk up to the prison, ask to see Rabbit as a visitor, and once we were in the same room, I'd stab him until they pulled me off his corpse. I even spent some of my ill-gotten gains on a ceramic knife. I just needed something that would get through a metal detector, but I splurged for an exquisitely pointed chef's knife, pried off the handle, and went through a lot of friction tape carefully wrapping and rewrapping the tang. If I was going to kill a guy with a prison shiv, let it be the Excalibur of prison shivs.

I never imagined a scenario where I walked away from Rabbit's death. This was a suicide mission, plain and simple. Even if I didn't get killed by Rabbit or shot by the guards, they weren't gonna say, "We just watched you stab a dude, but he was a snitch so I guess you're free to go." Might as well just say, "Put me away for murder, boys, I know for a fact a cell just opened up." I didn't like the idea of life in prison, but it was less appalling than the alternative, which was knowing that Rabbit stole my life and doing nothing about it. Most teenagers are nuts in one way or another: you can have adolescent hormones or rational thinking, but you can't have both. For me, all that teenage testosterone didn't manifest in sports or mosh pits, it coalesced into a single-minded hatred of Rabbit Rafferty.

It came to a head when I was sixteen and, for the first time, one of my idiot clients got seriously busted. A few of them had gotten in trouble with their folks, but whatever, anyone can lie to their parents. Teenagers can't lie to cops very well, though, so when word got around school that Gemma Green had been seriously-no-shit-arrested in connection with a car theft she'd paid me to commit, I took for granted that she'd give me up. Serious crooks often break down when the cops start in on them, and Gemma wasn't a serious anything, just a teenage girl with a vindictive streak and dubious money management skills.

So when I got home from school and the cops weren't there yet, I prepared to go out for the last time. I put on a hoodie with a front pocket big enough to hold my knife, wiped the search history and several file directories from my laptop, stuffed my cash into my pants pocket, and bade a mental farewell to the Bridwells and their house.

At the downtown bus station, there was an old Black guy with a trumpet sitting on a stool, a trumpet case open at his feet with coins and a few bills in it. He wore an immaculate white tuxedo and, for some reason, Mickey Mouse ears. I'd seen him around for years; nobody knew where he lived, but if you passed through downtown Portland, sooner or later you heard him play.

As I waited for the bus down to Eugene and the prison, he was playing "When The Saints Go Marching In," up-tempo and cheery. It didn't suit my mood at all. I wanted something ominous and minor-key, and I most certainly did not want to be in that number when the saints went marching in. I'd already chosen my side, and it was not that of the saints.

Despite buying a new laptop, some really good sneakers, new clothes, and an iPod, as well as a couple quiet but lavish gifts for other kids in the foster home, I still had nearly $8,000 in cash. The rich kids always paid me in twenties because that's what ATMs dispense, but I'd converted most of it into fifties and hundreds for ease of storage. When the bus pulled up, I tapped the trumpeter on the shoulder.

Hey man, I said quietly, *good music.*

He grinned. *Thanks! I gotta stay working, right?*

During the second that his attention was on my face, I slipped the entire wad of bills into the breast pocket of his tuxedo. I wasn't about to drop that in his trumpet case where just anyone could see it. I hoped he'd check the pockets before he sent it out for cleaning. I got on the bus with nothing left behind me or ahead of me.

When I got to the entry gate of the sprawling complex of the Oregon State Penitentiary, I learned that sixteen-year-olds are great at fantasizing about revenge, but not at planning it. They wouldn't let me in. I wasn't on the list of approved visitors for Jerome "Rabbit" Rafferty. I was standing there with my expensive knife in my pocket, all ready to cruise through the metal detector like a super-spy, because I'd executed the cool part of the plan, the awesome undetectable weapon, but not the boring part, where I was an unaccompanied minor, without parental permission, asking for access to a prisoner I had no relationship to. I will wince with embarrassment at that moment until the day I die.

Look, okay, sorry, I finally said to the guard, *but can you at least ask? Like, I'll wait here, can you call someone to ask Ra—, um, Jerome if he'll add me to his approved list? Even if I have to come back another day? C'mon, I took a bus all the way down here, don't send me away with nothing. Please?*

I must have looked pretty pathetic, standing there in my baggy hoodie, because the guard told me he'd make a call.

When he came back a minute later, he wore an odd frown. *I'm sorry, kid, Jerome Rafferty is no longer an inmate here.*

What the hell? Where is he? I'd find him at whatever prison they'd transferred him to. I was sixteen years old and full of testosterone and action movies. I'd hunt him across the earth if necessary, like Clint Eastwood in *Hang 'Em High,* or—

He's dead. Somebody shivved him last week. The guard could have been telling me the bus was on time, for all the emotion his voice carried. He closed the window of his little booth and returned to the paperback he'd been reading when I walked up.

I stumbled from the gate and sat on the edge of the highway. I rested my head on my knees as the sun beat down on my neck. The thing I'd built my life and my identity around for two years didn't exist. I had no other plan. All that lay ahead of me now was the long ride back to Portland, and the cops coming for me when Gemma dropped her inevitable dime.

The bus ride was numb, the stumbling back into my bedroom at the Bridwells' was numb, everything was numb. What could there possibly be left to feel? I should have been afraid of my imminent arrest for car theft, but that emotion seemed like too much work, so I just waited.

And waited.

By the third day, I realized I'd given Gemma too little credit. She hadn't said a word about me. The cops weren't coming. So I kept waiting, but now I didn't even know what I was waiting for. I'd leapt from a cliff to kill my enemy, not expecting to survive the fall. Instead, I'd landed safely with no plan for survival. All I got was the fall.

I looked back at the person I'd been over the last two years, the tight bundle of rage and intention who'd transcended his boring, everyday life of foster parents and school and girls who wouldn't give me the time of day. That version of me had felt things intensely and lived with a clear purpose, but he'd gone on a suicide mission and now he was dead.

I never chose to stop being a thief. It wasn't a clear decision and I wasn't "scared straight." I just went a week without stealing anything, then two weeks, then three. About a month later, I got a call from Richie, saying a friend of his needed a favor. He'd "found" a safe and needed help opening it, and did I want the job?

I still remember how easy it was to say, *Nah, man, I don't do that anymore.*

Richie was graceful about it, but it took me a couple days to understand what had happened. I'd had a drive inside me, an engine that kept me going. With that switched off, all I had to replace it was the ersatz conscience that had been beaten into me by every authority I'd known since December 1998. The *follow-the-rules-because-other-wise-we'll-hurt-you* model of life. It was a piss-poor replacement for the engine of my mind, but it was the only other thing I had. So theft became something for other people to do. I still read about crime and thought about crime, but that was as far as it went.

About a year after Rabbit died, I mustered the energy to get myself out of foster care for good. I found just enough of the focus and intention I'd had when I set out to kill the snitch who'd ruined my life. Then I was living on my own for the first time, and that was enough to keep me straight a while longer. I had to hold down a regular job or the judge would have thrown me back in foster care. By the time I graduated high school I resided in a world of stifled impulses, of mediocrity, of banality. A world where everything had been reduced to a dull grind. It was a world where making things right wasn't possible, so why bother trying?

And that was the world I knew until Detective Joanne Caraway picked me up for a friendly chat.

Associated Press, October 6, 2002

Skinhead Leader Suspected In Brutal Prison Stabbing

by Mariah James-Clarker

The body of Jerome Rafferty was discovered in the Oregon State Penitentiary late on the night of October 4, stabbed repeatedly in the chest with an unknown weapon. Rafferty, 33, had served almost three years of a six-year sentence for possession of stolen goods.

A source inside the prison said that "most of the guards and all the inmates" believe the killing was either performed or ordered by Michael "Mickey" Crispin, who is serving a life sentence for murder. Crispin's arrest two years ago drew courthouse protests and death threats from fellow members of the White Aryan Resistance and affiliated neo-Nazi groups.

The source went on to say, "There's no question in my mind that Mickey's capable of it, but of course nobody saw a thing."

This is the seventh murder in an Oregon prison this year.

Chapter Twelve

I sat at the visiting booth, which was separated from the others by makeshift dividers big enough to block your face without offering real privacy. My headache had transformed from a series of staccato pain pulses to a deep, thunderous throb, the kind of all-consuming ache that makes you swear you'll never drink again. I rested my hands on the counter and peered through the glass divider, where another guard stood next to the door leading into the bowels of the prison. His stare made me nervous, like he wanted me to know he was watching, maybe even listening.

On the way in, they'd searched me, making me stand for two minutes with my arms in the air while going through all my pockets. Not as bad as the strip searches required for full contact visits on the weekends, but still. Every minute or so, a short, stocky guard shouted out the remaining time to one of the booths. Given that there were twenty booths, it made for a lot of shouting. And given my state, each shout hit me like a brass-knuckled punch to the ear. Soup told me once that their aim is to make visitations as unpleasant as possible to discourage visitors from coming back. If my experience was any indicator, he had it right.

Ricky Gat had been one of those larger-than-life figures when I was a kid. Good-looking, charismatic, and he also had guns, which made him cool in a dangerous way. The simple fact that his name was Eric but everyone called him Ricky Gat was badass for an impressionable kid. He'd traveled, too. He talked of New York City and Mexico and even Mauritius, a little island in the Indian Ocean where he planned to retire someday. I'd never left Oregon. Around Ricky, my world got bigger. He exuded a confidence that made me feel like my options were unlimited. A few days before the job, when my mom wasn't listening, I asked him how he became a thief. Turned out, Ricky had followed a pretty common career arc.

Started with retail theft, he told me. *Easy targets. But the key when you're starting out is to put your own unique spin on it. For me, it was tee-veeeees!* He'd said it in an ironic-salesman voice, but the man did love TVs. He'd given us our first flatscreen in 1997, well before anyone I knew had one. It brought my movie-watching game to a new level and was one of the things I missed most after my mom disappeared.

The story Ricky laid out stuck with me as a potential career path, and I thought about it as I waited. *Started when I was driving behind one of those big-box electronics stores. Saw a truck, y'know, unloading big-screen TVs through the back door. Saw their system. One dude would get the TV from the truck to the sidewalk, other dude would cart it in on this four-wheel dolly thing. The kind hotel valets have for luggage. Watched them for a couple days, cool-like. The guy on the truck always stayed with the TVs, that was the key. Except one day he didn't. That one day the dude hopped down from the truck and followed the other guy inside. Maybe to use the bathroom. Hell, don't know, don't care. I stopped my Jeep right next to that truck and slid a sixty-incher into the back. From there, I developed a whole system around TVs, usually using inside guys to make it easier. After that, I got a few reliable fences, all in the electronics world. And here's the thing, kid: Once you have three or four reliable fences, you get exposed to the whole underside, the hidden stuff. You start hearing about bigger fish. You see, the fences are your customers, and the customer is always right, right? They start telling you about cars, houses, even drugs, though there was no way I was getting into stealing drugs from dealers. Do a good job with your fences for a year or two and people start looking at you for the big stuff. Art, vaults, corporate assets.*

Even at twelve, my mind went immediately to what those bigger jobs might look like. I asked, *You never did any of that, did you?*

He waved a hand dismissively. *Nah, I broke off on my own. I think of it like running a little corner store, y'know? The money ain't huge, but I'm getting by, and I'm my own boss.*

I probably should have guessed that he never made it to the big time not because he wanted to run a mom-and-pop criminal enterprise, but because he screwed up a job. I also should have known that he left out the last phase in the career arc of most thieves: Getting caught.

The aroma of the visiting room filled my lungs and turned by stomach—stale air and body odor, mingled with an odd perfume that reeked like artificial bubblegum. It smelled like institutional repression and human desperation. I watched the door for a minute, then two, then five. I was beginning to think Ricky wasn't going to see me. After all, prisoners aren't required to accept visitors, though most are eager to see anyone who shows up. By design, prison life is a slow death by monotony. Any break in the routine is usually welcome. After I'd lost track of how long I'd been watching the door, the guard stepped aside and opened it. Another led in a prisoner, but it wasn't Ricky Gat.

As the man sat, the guard barked that I had an hour maximum, the prison's limit. I doubted I'd need that long. The prisoner had ashy skin, deeply lined with age. A jagged scar ran down his left cheek and veered toward his jaw making a backwards L. He tugged his ear, studying me. A look of surprise spread across his face as I recognized his light green eyes. Oh God, this was Ricky.

"Keyser." He damn near whispered into the phone, one of those old corded things only prisons still use.

"Ricky?"

"It's me, kid."

I didn't know what to say. This was Ricky Gat, but a broken

version of the man I'd looked up to. He was the "After" photo in every before-and-after picture they showed you in school to make you Say No To Drugs. In addition to the scar on his face, his nose was crooked, bent to the right like it had been broken at least once.

Physically wrecked though he was, his mind was still sharp and he read my reaction. Pointing to his nose, he said, "Gets a little rough in here sometimes." He grunted. "Funny thing is, outside I wasn't a violent person."

I smiled. That's how I remembered him. He had a dark sense of humor, but he never got rough with anyone, not counting when we'd act out fight scenes from movies for fun.

I tapped on the counter in front of me, thinking of where to start. "How long you been in?"

"Three years."

"What for?"

"Armed burglary."

Same kind of job he'd run with my mom. "How much longer?"

"Three more—two if I get parole. If there's any way you could write a letter for me"—he sighed like the request was physically painful—"I'd appreciate it. Public defender says the more letters of support I get from non-criminals, the better."

"Um... Yeah, I'll do it." I didn't know if I would. "You know why I'm here, right?"

"How's Soup? Still a cheap old bastard? What's he up to?"

"He's... *retired*. Bought that pawnshop west of Eighty-Second. Ace's Quick Cash."

"Retired? That's not retired. Pawnshop? If it ain't in the game, it's game-adjacent."

I laughed, and there was a little twinkle in Ricky's eye. He'd always gotten a charge from making people laugh.

He kept going. "Soup was so cheap, one night after a good day at work, me and him and your mom went downtown, to one of those nice business hotels. Steakhouse. He drove and we decided to use the valet parking because we felt pretty flush right at that moment. So Soup asks me if I'd tip the valet. He *didn't have any cash*." Ricky used air quotes to communicate that Soup had, in fact, had plenty of cash. "When we got out of the car, dude gathered all the change from the cupholders in his busted-ass '91 Civic. Probably had three bucks in quarters and he was worried the valet would steal it." He looked down, smiling. "Cheapest bastard I ever knew. Dude will never retire. Only way you get Soup out of the game is to pry him out with a crowbar made of money."

I laughed and Ricky slapped his knee, delighted. We smiled at each other and, for a second, I forgot about my queasy stomach and throbbing head. Then the guard shouted at us, "Booth ten, you have fifty minutes!" and, just like that, I felt worse than ever.

I leveled my gaze at Ricky, trying to focus. "Like I was saying, you know why I'm here right? I—"

"Your mom, how's she? *Hellooooooo*, Dolly. People still call her that? I haven't seen her in... well, a long time. Figured that's why you were coming when I saw your name on my list. Brandon Penny." He shook his head. "Little Keyser Soze." His eyes were pleading, *Don't just get your answers and leave, man.* He was lonely. Far as I knew, Ricky didn't have any family. I was probably one of the only visitors he'd had since he got locked up. He wanted to make it last.

I didn't. Sure, I felt for the guy, but all I wanted was to get answers to my questions and get out of there as fast as possible. The thought of going to jail had never scared me before. What it had done to Ricky Gat, though? That scared the living shit out of me.

A light flickered and we both looked up. "They do that a lot," Ricky said. "Still makes me nervous every time. Don't know why."

I met his eyes, hoping to communicate a question with the lie I was about to tell. "You asked about my mom. Haven't seen her in twenty years. *Exactly* the same as you."

He shook his head and let the phone fall away from his ear, wrapping the cord around a finger, then unwrapping it. When he brought it back to his mouth, all he said was, "Damn."

He'd put the chronology together in his mind. I'd always assumed that when the job went bad, he and my mom had gone their separate ways and never had contact again. He hadn't imagined she and I had done the same.

"Yeah. *Damn.* And that's why I'm here. I need to know what happened. That night."

He waved a hand dismissively, brushing the bulletproof glass between us, which got the attention of a guard, who barked, "No touching the glass!"

He set his hands on the table, scrunching the phone up against his ear with one shoulder. "They half-broke me, but I'm not stupid enough to... I have no memory of anything you're talking about." He smiled, shifting gears. "What I will tell you is your mom was—you're old enough to hear this now, right?—hot! Not gonna lie, I used to be pretty damn good to look at, too." He brushed a hand through what was left of his hair. "Never had a shortage of lady friends. And your mom, whoo boy! But there was just no way in with her. She'd be perfectly nice up to a point and not an inch past."

I knew where he was headed. "Did you and my mom ever..."

"Nah, that's what I'm saying. Your mom was all business. I tried and she was always like, 'Nah, I don't shit where I eat,' or she'd just put me down, 'You're not half as good-looking as you think you are, Ricky.' Truth be told, I thought she was kind of a bitch. Rejecting *me?* C'mon. Sittin' in here gives you time to think, though. She had it hard. Harder than me, harder than Soup. Didn't have anyone, and she had you to think of."

"That's all, I mean, thanks for sharing all that. But is there some way you could... I..." I didn't know how to formulate the question. Like my visit when I was sixteen, I hadn't thought this through. Just because he was in prison didn't mean he'd happily discuss the details of previous jobs, or attempted jobs. After all, anyone around us could overhear, and I wasn't sure the line was clean. It was illegal to record visitor sessions in prisons in Oregon, but illegal didn't mean much. In this context, "illegal" just meant "inadmissible in court." Cops do all sorts of things they know full well won't hold up in court, but that doesn't mean they can't use them to screw you over.

"You still into movies, Keyser?"

"Yeah, got my own DVD player." It was a ridiculous thing to say, since most of the world had moved to streaming. But sitting with Ricky had pulled me back to 1998, when getting my own DVD player felt like an impossible dream.

"Hell," Ricky said, "we have one of those in here."

"What's the best movie you've seen since you've been inside?"

He tugged his left ear, concentrating. "I know." He whacked his knee with an open palm. "*Shawshank Redemption.*"

I was stunned they'd let a bunch of felons watch a movie about escaping from prison. "They let you watch that in here?"

The guard yelled at Booth #1, damn near rattling the floor. The shout jolted me upright, but Ricky ignored it. I guess he was used to shouting.

"Sure. And the next day I locked the warden in his office and played Mozart over the loudspeaker." He stared at me, stone-faced, then broke out laughing. "Why wouldn't they let us watch it? You think it's gonna make us angry about life inside prison? We're the only ones who actually *know*! And it ain't like it's an instructional video on escape." He pointed to the wall, thick blocks painted white with a sad coat of primer. "You think I'm tunneling out of here with a rock hammer?"

"Still, I thought they might... I don't know what I thought."

We were quiet for a minute, but it wasn't a silence. A loud woman to my right told a story of her recent trip to the grocery store. To my left, a man spoke more quietly but occasionally raised his high voice, which came through the divider like the squeak of a mouse.

And the guard kept shouting. "Booths four and nine, you each have ten minutes left. Ten minutes only!"

"So," Ricky said.

I drummed the counter in a little patter with my fingers. "Yeah."

The stools were bolted to the floor, but Ricky leaned back a little and put his free hand behind his head, like he'd do in a comfy recliner in his own living room. Something in him had shifted. "You're trying to get me to talk about a crime I was never charged with. I'd be pretty dumb to do that."

I nodded. "True, that would be pretty stupid. The thing is, I've been wondering about that night for a long time. From your reaction before, you didn't know that my mom and I split up after that. Or, well, she split up from me. They got me, put me in... *homes*. Ain't seen her since."

He looked at the floor with something that bore a strong resemblance to shame. "I'm sorry about that. I didn't know."

"Are you sorry enough to get over yourself and tell me what happened?"

"Like I said, don't know anything about any night where anything happened."

I put a hand on the window. A guard shouted, "No touching the glass!" and I pulled it back.

It was enough to get Ricky's attention, though. He looked at me and I pleaded, "C'mon, a guy got killed." I felt terrible about doing it— begging is embarrassing and asking a con to confess to another crime is immoral—but I didn't have time for anything slow-played or subtle.

He must've taken pity on me, or maybe he figured out a way to answer my question that felt safe. "When I got picked up for the robbery I'm in for now—which I didn't do, by the way—I had to make a statement before the court." He looked from side to side, then leaned in, his head an inch from the glass, the antique phone pressed up against his skull. I saw into the lines on his face, saw his pores and the pink scars on his skin. "Now, I don't know what night you're talking about, but I've done some things wrong in my life. Never killed anyone and I never would. Don't know what you're even talking about with 'a guy got killed.' But I'm no saint. I've owned up to that and I'm paying for it big-time. Anyway, when I made my statement before sentencing... well, I'll tell you what I told the judge." He closed his eyes, thinking, then opened them and lowered his voice. "Kid, I *never once* took a *loaded* gun on a job." He paused, as though imploring me to listen. "And neither did *anybody* I worked with."

When you lie as much as I do, when you've been lied to as much as I have, it's easy to assume everyone around you is lying at all times. Distrust starts in the head, an automatic picking-apart of motive and tone that sometimes lands on a definitive answer—true or false—but more often leads to a general sense that nothing is real. That nothing and no one can be trusted. From there, distrust works its way down to the heart, where it sticks, coiling and twisting and tightening, until it's difficult for truth to land at all.

The thing was, Ricky was telling the truth. I was sure of it. In the week leading up to the job, he'd warned me, *Brand, treat every gun like it's loaded*. I'd taken that to heart, and it was good advice. But I'd assumed it meant they actually *were*.

His eyes were still on mine. "You feel me? Brand, you feel me, right?"

I nodded slowly.

"Booth number eighteen, you have twenty minutes remaining! Booth number ten, you have forty minutes remaining!"

The callous shout of the guard smacked me back into myself. I opened my mouth to ask the obvious follow-up—*If you're saying the guns weren't loaded, then you didn't shoot the guard and my mom didn't shoot the guard, so who did?*—but something in his eyes stopped me. He'd gone out on a limb saying as much as he had.

Instead, I planted what he'd told me in the back of my mind and shifted the conversation to more trivial matters. "You still follow hoops?"

He perked up at this. "Blazers heading for the playoffs again."

"How much do they let you watch?"

"Maybe a game a week."

"Well, don't worry about it, they'll choke in the playoffs. It's tradition."

"Dame Lillard don't play like he believes in that tradition."

"Ah, so you're saying Tom Johnson's ghost will break his knees."

That last was an old inside joke of ours. The piece of property where the Blazers played had once belonged to Tom Johnson, a mobster who ran Black crime in Portland back in segregation days. Ricky's theory was that Johnson's ghost felt he was owed a cut of that Blazers money, and every year he didn't get it, he'd pull a typical gangster move and bust someone's knee. If you looked at the history of knee injuries on the team, it explained a lot.

We talked basketball and bullshit for the next half hour. As much as I wanted to get out of there, my hangover had reached a stage where I felt like I'd puke if I moved. Besides that, every minute I kept talking was another minute I could put off thinking about what he'd said. I told him about the new concession stands at the Moda Center —he'd been a bit of a foodie and was happy to hear that hot dogs and hamburgers weren't the only options at a Blazers game. Distracting myself only half worked, though. The whole time, as my mouth moved with descriptions of the sauce at the Tennessee BBQ place, or the fact that there was a s'mores stand, the memories played over and over in my mind, no matter how hard I tried to hit pause.

A few months earlier I'd watched a documentary about World War Two in which all the old black-and-white footage had been colorized. I'd been skeptical at first, being a film traditionalist, but it had changed the meaning of the war for me, changed the meaning of the past. It made the war feel closer to the present day, made the people more real, the scale of the horror more tragic. It had changed everything. What Ricky had said was like that. All my memories were updating in real time, tinged with new meaning.

After we exhausted the food talk, we hit a lull in the conversation, one of those half-awkward pauses when you've covered every shared interest and you both realize there isn't more to say.

Breaking the silence, Ricky gave me an odd look, like he was puzzling something out in his head. "You got a job?"

The triviality of the question didn't match the complexity of his look, but I decided to answer straight. "Pharmacy job. Cashier."

"How long you been there?"

"Few years. Before that, I worked at a Plaid Pantry for a while."

"They still got that slushie machine where you can mix different flavors?"

I nodded.

"Booth number ten! You have ten minutes!" The guard's shouting didn't make me jump this time. Apparently I could get used to prison life pretty fast. "And Soup? Well, you said you didn't see him much. What about Mikey Smooth?"

"Gave him forty bucks a couple days back. He's homeless now."

He crinkled his already wrinkly forehead. "And... damn... what was his name? Dude with the bird tattoo on his neck. Jamaican dude?"

"Raoul?"

"Yeah, you see him much?"

He was a guy my mom had worked with from time to time. When I was eight, I thought of him as the guy with the cool accent who always smelled like spices. Later I figured out he was the guy my mom passed jobs to after scoping out houses. "Haven't seen him in, I don't know. Years."

He nodded, smiling a little. "So, you're just kinda chillin', sounds like." He'd taken the long route to figuring out whether I was a crook. He seemed happy I wasn't.

"Yup," I said. "Just living a normal life. Straight and narrow."

"Your mom would be happy to hear that. She never wanted you to... well, you know."

I knew.

She'd never wanted me to become a thief. And I hadn't. Problem was, by the time the guard called out the end of my time, the main reason I had for *not* becoming a thief had dissolved into thin air.

Therapeutic Evaluation, 4/3/03

Requested by: Judge Marsha Bowman

Purpose: Emancipation Hearing Consultation

Evaluator: B. Parscales

Subject name: Brandon Penny

DOB: 4/1/86

Sex: M

Years in foster care: 5

Hours of evaluation: 3

As requested by the court, I conducted three hours of evaluation with Brandon over three days. His cooperativeness with therapy is good, up to a specific point, past which it drops to zero. Though he seems eager to learn about himself, this investigative process stops when it touches on a certain area.

Subjects Brandon avoids talking about include: the night he was arrested, his mother's internal motivations (he will discuss his mother and his memories of her, but shuts down entirely when asked to speculate about what made her do the things she did), his experiences with the police, any illegal actions by himself or any other children in foster care, and any participation he may or may not have had in his mother's crimes.

At the risk of making an educated guess, my professional opinion is that Brandon will not talk about these things because he absorbed a "code of silence" ethos as a young child. He is therefore unwilling to discuss anything that could possibly incriminate someone else. He denies this, but if this hypothesis is correct, of course he would.

Brandon has clearly sustained substantial trauma from his experiences in the foster-care system, and has been taught to accept that trauma as normal. It is no wonder that he now seeks emancipation from the state care system. How much pain he bears from his experiences before being taken into foster care is difficult to determine, for the above-described reasons. He appears well-adjusted on a superficial level, and is capable of normal social interaction without apparent difficulty. It must be considered, though, that a child of such intelligence could be demonstrating adjustment on a visible level without experiencing such an adjustment on a primal level. That is, he could be harboring deep traumas, as yet unseen. It cannot be precisely determined whether this is the case in this specific instance.

All that said, Brandon is highly intelligent and capable of interacting with people and society in a healthy and responsible fashion. It remains possible that this presentation is a facade, but that opens epistemological questions that are ultimately irrelevant. I recommend granting his emancipation request and mandating ongoing therapeutic treatment, though the specifics of any such treatment plan are outside the scope of this evaluation.

Chapter Thirteen

I drove home slowly, keeping to the speed limit and staying in the right lane. My stomach felt better because I'd thrown up in the parking lot on my way out of OSP, but my thoughts were swampy as I considered my chat with Ricky.

As far as I knew, my mom had never taken a gun to work before the poker game. I didn't know the details of every job she'd done, but I knew the types of jobs, and none required guns. They were short cons or well-planned thefts, jobs that required skill instead of force. Until that night. What made that job so special that it warranted risking violence for the first time in her career? Nothing, because the gun wasn't loaded.

Ricky's admonition to *treat every gun like it's loaded* had started playing in the back of my head in the prison, and it hadn't let up. Dull silver on red is where the memory started. We were in a hotel somewhere on the East Side. The gun was on the bed. Silver, not especially shiny, sitting on a red bedspread.

My mom was in the bathroom getting ready. I was all set in my costume—fake freckles, puffy jacket, hair a little mussed because nine-year-olds don't care as much about their hair as twelve-year-olds. My pawnshop bike was already in the car. I'd practiced riding it in the hotel's parking lot before dinner because when you're going to take a flop off a bike that's too small for you, you want to make sure you do it on your own terms.

A horn blared as a line of cars passed me on the left. I checked my speed. I was driving fifty in a sixty zone, so I sped up and locked in the cruise control. Last thing I wanted was to get pulled over for going too slow.

I stood over the gun and looked up at Ricky, asking with my eyes, *Can I touch it?*

Ricky glanced at the bathroom door and I knew he was thinking exactly what I was thinking. *Your mom wouldn't approve.* But she was locked in the bathroom.

I cocked my head to the side, trying to look mature, studious. I gave him a look that tried to convey *I got this*, but probably communicated more childish pleading.

Ricky nodded cautiously. *Carefully, kid. And just for a sec.*

It was heavier than I expected.

I felt Eric's hand on my shoulder. *Treat every gun like it's loaded.*

I held it up with both hands, aiming at the spot on the wall. You ever shot someone?

Won't come to that. Never has, never will.

My mom emerged from the bathroom then, heavy jacket on, scarf and hat in hand. It was the last time I saw her face clearly.

When she saw me holding the gun, she frowned. *Brand, don't touch that. It's dangerous.*

I quickly set it on the bed. *I wasn't doing anything. I was just...*

I know, but still.

Ricky patted me on the back. *Listen to your mom, kid.*

Minutes later, we left for the poker game.

I flicked on the radio and half-listened to a song or two, five minutes of local news, and a few commercials. It was enough to move me away from the memory of that night, but not enough to grab more than a fragment of my attention. My mind had moved on to something else.

The guns weren't loaded, which meant one of the men at the

poker game killed the security guard. There were five players, and each had been part of the background noise of my life for the last twenty years.

Brian White was a political shock jock on KPKX radio. Ads plastered with his severely punchable face graced half the buses in Portland right now. Mark Masterson was a financial manager, the owner of Masterson Wealth Management Services. His job was to help millionaires and billionaires avoid paying taxes and carry out other shady financial deals. Congressman Kellen Blackstone represented Oregon's Fifth Congressional District. He was a former prosecutor whose every word sounded like a lie, even more so than your average politician. On the night of the poker game, he'd been a state representative, but had risen steadily in power and prestige. I'd read he was considering a run for Senate. On the night of the poker game, Michael Carusa owned a single car dealership. Now he owned a handful throughout Oregon and Eastern Washington. *C-A-R-U-S-A, Drive-The-Car-You-Deserve-Today!*

The wealthiest of the five was Martin Seykes, heir to the Seykes timber fortune. Maybe he had a complex internal life full of meaning and nuance, but his public persona was every bit the cliché of the privileged rich boy who only avoided burning through the pile of money he inherited because the pile was so damned big to begin with. He'd collected multiple DUIs, all followed by large charitable donations to clean them up, and two messy divorces in which he'd settled for millions. He also fronted a vanity jazz band in which he played mediocre guitar at "gigs" he personally bankrolled.

Over the last twenty years, as my life spiraled downward, then meandered sideways, these five respected members of society flourished. One of them shot Thomas Twomey, and they *all* let the cops try to pin it on my mom.

I crested a hill and the highway opened before me, entering a wide valley with a lake on my left. The day was gray, but a sharp sliver of light had cut through the clouds, hitting the lake like a sword of fire. Another thought hit me like a slap to the face. I'd been on the verge of believing Caraway over my mom. For twenty years I'd lived with the uncertainty—the nagging little hint that *maybe my mom had fired the shot*. Carebear had arrived to fill in a few blank spaces, but Carebear was a liar—I'd pegged her for a liar the first time I saw her—so she'd filled in those spaces with lies. I had nearly believed a cop over my mother.

A hundred little memories hit me all at once. All the crimes I'd stopped myself from doing since the day I went to kill Rabbit Rafferty. In one, I was seventeen, standing in the aisle of a convenience store with Becca, a girl I was trying to impress. Two security cameras, one in each corner. I knew the models, knew the angle of the lenses, knew where the camera's blind spots would be, if they were recording at all. I told Becca to buy a pack of gum and I'd steal us some food, then I walked into the blind spot, planning to steal whatever was in that aisle, just because I could. Standing there, hand on a bag of beef jerky, I froze. I didn't do it.

When I was twenty, I took a few classes at PSU and one day a girl left her laptop on the seat after class. I was alone in the room, just me and the two-thousand-dollar MacBook. All I needed to do was walk out with it and I could replace the one I'd bought four years earlier at the end of my reverse-Veronica-Mars phase. I sat there like a fool for five minutes, a war raging in my mind, before finally bringing it to the professor's office so she could return it to the girl.

The next semester, I met a dude using a keycard replicator to add money to his student ID card. Guy was a techie who just wanted to have enough imaginary digital cash to dine out of the vending machines whenever he was hungry. Within a couple days I'd involuntarily sketched out a campus-wide program for selling credits to students for thirty cents on the dollar. We could have made thousands and been campus legends. I stayed quiet. Never mentioned it to him. The idea faded into the back of my mind and disappeared entirely when I quit school over the summer.

Then there was Jennifer's ATM card, and don't even get me started on the pharmacy. Drug dealing is one of America's oldest businesses, and just because that dealing takes place under fluorescent lights doesn't make it somehow less lucrative. The opportunities for quick and easy profit were endless.

It wasn't only the fear of getting caught that turned me straight after my high-minded fantasy of killing Rabbit had crashed back to earth. There was something else that had held me back, an invisible rope that had bound me one loop at a time. Cops and judges and therapists and foster parents had tightened it over and over with a thousand suggestions and warnings.

You don't want to end up in jail or on the run like your mom.

There's still time to get your life on track.

Don't take the easy way out.

Laws are what hold society together, Brandon.

Your desire to steal is a manifestation of your defiant personality disorder, Mr. Penny. When you want to commit a crime, it's simply because you're rebelling against a perceived external authority.

The last one was partly true, but it wasn't the whole story. Truth was, I was born to be a thief. My mom's buddies knew it when I was a kid. I'd known it my whole life—*feared* it my whole life. I'd fought my criminal instincts every day since I was sixteen. Fear and inertia had always tipped the scales toward inaction, toward the straight life, toward boredom and mundanity.

It was time to tip them the other way.

My phone buzzed. It was Caraway, and I swiped to reject the call. A minute later, it buzzed again with a voicemail. The voice-to-text preview read, *Brandon, I need some more info on...* so I swiped to delete it.

My mind was clearer than it had been all day. I felt new. Each intricate detail of the world had come alive with significance, like the walk home after a date where you fall in love for the first time. The fake-leather grain of the steering wheel, the weight of my body on the seat, the smell of the pine air freshener that dangled from the rearview mirror, the way a sliver of light cut through the stand of conifers on the hill—all the insignificant things had become big, colorful, *real* things. The world was alive because, for the first time in years, *I* was alive.

The five men at the poker game forced their way into the clean, empty space of my mind. One of those guys was a killer, the other four accessories. For the last twenty years, each had grown richer and more respected. My mom abandoned me and spent her life on the run for a murder one of those five men committed.

Following the rules had done nothing to address that. It was time to try something else.

My phone buzzed again. My first reaction when I saw Jennifer's name on the caller-ID was excitement. We'd always been a text-first couple, and I couldn't remember the last time she'd called me. But as I reached for the phone, a familiar knot re-tied itself in my stomach. The Brandon I'd become in the last hour didn't fit with the Brandon I'd shown Jennifer for the last three years. As far as I could tell, it never would. I answered, but couldn't find any words.

"Hey," she said.

I decided to let her take the lead. "Hey."

"So, I've got the evening off with nothing to do. Just hanging at my place. I was thinking about everything you told me the other night. Maybe we could talk more. If you want, I mean. Feel like stopping by after six?"

I thought about saying no, but I needed to break it off with her for good, and in person. I owed her that. "I'll be there. Few things to take care of first, but I'll see you tonight."

Emancipation Hearing Transcript, June 18, 2003

Petitioner: Brandon Penny

Age: 17

Judge: Marcia Bowman

Current Guardian: State of Oregon

State-Appointed Counsel: Sergio Flores

Judge: And the mother is not here to protest the emancipation petition?

Counsel: No, Your Honor.

Judge: And the father?

Counsel: Whereabouts unknown. As we outlined in the petition, he's had no relationship with my client.

Judge: All right, then, let's get started. Mr. Penny, the court has reviewed your petition, and I'm going to ask you a few questions. Okay?

Mr. Penny: Yes, ma'am.

Judge: I've reviewed the financial documents, apartment lease note, job records, and psychological evaluations. You and your counsel did a thorough job. And I see you've received good grades in school.

Mr. Penny: Yes, ma'am.

Judge: Can you confirm that you understand all the records you submitted to the court?

Mr. Penny: Yes, ma'am.

Judge: And they are all truthful to the best of your knowledge?

Mr. Penny: Yes, ma'am.

Judge: Good. In an emancipation hearing like this, the application is generally the main thing we need, but your situation is a little different given that you're currently under the protection of the state of Oregon and given, well, who your mother is.

Counsel: Your Honor, we addressed that in the application. Mr. Penny can't possibly be held accountable for the actions of his mother, and given that she was removed from legal guardianship over five years ago, I can't see how she is relevant to—

Judge: Sit down, Mr. Flores. No one is holding your client responsible for anything. But it's this court's job to determine Mr. Penny's financial and emotional maturity in order to release him from state guardianship. Having a mother who's a known criminal is certainly relevant.

Counsel: Agreed, Your Honor. I only ask that you keep in mind that my client has not seen, spoken to, or heard a single word from his mother in over five years. He has no knowledge of any alleged crimes. He is ready to stand fully on his own two feet.

Judge: The court will determine that, Mr. Flores, but first I need to ask my questions. Please sit down. Now, Mr. Penny, I'm going to ask you a few questions about your mother. Typically, the court would give her three months to object to your petition, but since you've been under the custody of the state for, what was it again?

Counsel: Five years, Your Honor. A little over five years.

Judge: Yes, so we can waive the waiting period. Normally, emancipation requests separate a child from his or her parents legally. In your case, Mr. Penny, you're requesting separation from the state, which has acted as your legal guardian for the last five years. Is this correct?

Mr. Penny: Yes.

Judge: And you understand that if I grant this request, you will no longer have state support to fall back on?

Mr. Penny: Yes.

Judge: You will be responsible for your own financial contracts, phone bills, taxes, and so on. You understand that?

Mr. Penny: Yes. I took a financial literacy elective, so I understand about all that.

Judge: And you understand that most laws applying to minors still apply? You must still complete high school. Child labor laws and statutory rape laws still apply. Voting and alcohol laws do not change. You are not an adult even in the event that this court grants your petition and emancipates you from state guardianship. Understood?

Counsel: I've counseled him, Your Honor. And if I may say so, Mr. Penny is one of the brightest seventeen-year-old boys I've ever—

Judge: Please don't interrupt, Sergio. Brandon, do you understand?

Mr. Penny: Yes.

Judge: Just a few more questions. Why do you want to be emancipated, Mr. Penny?

Mr. Penny: Well, I've been in group homes and foster homes for five years now. Some bad things happened in some of them. Where I am now is okay, but I'm able to make three hundred dollars a week while going to school full-time. I've had no issues with the law since, well... you have the files. I found an apartment I can afford if I'm allowed to move, and I feel it's time to be on my own.

Judge: Good, good. I'd like to ask you a few questions about the incident that separated you from your mother.

Mr. Penny: I, um...

Judge: It's my job to make sure emancipation is in your best interest and that your sources of income are legal.

Counsel: Your Honor, we've provided pay stubs and—

Judge: I understand that, but Mr. Penny's mother is wanted for crimes in at least three states, including this one. I do not wish to litigate the past, but to grant this request I need to ask some questions about her. It would be irresponsible of me to release Mr. Penny from state guardianship if I thought there was the slightest chance he'd resort to crime to get by. Understood?

Counsel: Yes, Your Honor.

Judge: Mr. Penny, understood?

Mr. Penny: Yes.

Judge: Were you ever involved in criminal activities with your mother before the night of December 13, 1998?

Mr. Penny: No, Your Honor.

Judge: Never?

Mr. Penny: I...

Judge: Keep in mind, you are in no legal trouble here, but it's important you answer honestly.

Mr. Penny: When I was a kid I knew she stole things sometimes, but that's all.

Judge: Good, thank you. But you have not committed, been arrested for, or accused of any crimes since the incident back in 1998?

Mr. Penny: No, ma'am.

Counsel: With all due respect, Your Honor, this is all in the report.

Judge: As are Mr. Penny's grades and test scores, the former of which are above-average, the latter exceptional. Have you applied to college?

Mr. Penny: No, ma'am.

Judge: Do you plan to? I'm sure you'd get a scholarship.

Mr. Penny: Um, not sure. I might try a few classes at PSU.

Judge: I've also reviewed the reports from one of your social workers. She says you are of above-average intelligence and—

Mr. Penny: Thank you.

Judge: I wasn't finished. She says Brandon Penny, and I'm quoting here, "possesses an agile mind, intelligence well above average with flashes of brilliance, and a deep understanding of human nature for his age, but he sometimes exhibits oppositional thinking," end quote. She says you talk about an ordinary life like it's a prison sentence you're stuck with.

Counsel: Your Honor, "oppositional thinking" could be a description of any teenager on earth.

Judge: "Any teenager" doesn't have a mom wanted for murder. Back to before the night of December 13, 1998. Mr. Penny, you said you were sometimes aware of her thefts as a child.

Mr. Penny: I really didn't understand as a kid, judge. I figured out that not all the money she made was honest, that sometimes she was stealing things. It was wrong, and I didn't know it at the time or even understand it.

Judge: And Mr. Penny, what were some of the things she stole?

Mr. Penny: I...

Judge: Mr. Penny, did you hear the question?

Mr. Penny: Sorry, judge, I...

Counsel: Your Honor, might we have a brief recess?

Judge: For the Good Lord's sake, Sergio, this is a quick hearing and I've got a full docket. Mr. Penny, I'm just trying to get a sense of your past. Now tell me, what were some of the things she stole?

Mr. Penny: I...

Counsel: A brief recess, please.

Mr. Penny: I, I...

Chapter Fourteen

I ditched my Zipcar near Duniway Park and powered down my
phone.

The gadget the cops use to track them is called a Stingray. Cell
phones constantly search for the strongest available signal, and, on
any given day, they connect with dozens of different cell towers as you
move around. The Stingray is designed to emit a stronger signal than
any cellphone tower, forcing every phone within range to connect to
it, thereby giving up your location to the Stingray operator. Just like a
cell tower can ping your phone even when you're not making a call or
downloading data, so can a Stingray. In the wider world, state and
local police departments were battling with the ACLU and the Electronic Frontier Foundation to determine whether the use of a Stingray
without a warrant should be legal. On the ground, I had to assume
they were using one, especially now that I was going to find my mom.

I hooked down an alley and walked to a plaza three blocks east.
Then I took four right turns, changing pace on each block and pausing
at random times, eventually landing back where I'd started.

From there, I ducked past a DO NOT ENTER sign into a basement parking garage, rode the elevator to the third floor, then took the
stairs down on the other end, a block away. I checked the skies. If

Carebear had guys tracking me on foot, I could likely ditch them. If she had aerial surveillance, that would be tougher. No helicopters in the air, though, just a couple crows flying by. Didn't think they'd rat me out, but you can never be certain with crows.

I was almost sure I was in the clear, but I did another lap around the block for good measure, stopping into a coffee shop along the way. After the fourth right turn I noticed something. A woman in a red jacket had been in the coffee shop, in line behind me. Now she was half a block ahead. I stopped, staring right at her. I figured she was fronting me, which meant she was even better than the Eisenhower jacket guy had been. She walked a few paces, then stopped at the corner.

After a long pause, she turned right and disappeared. Not a tail.

My brain buzzed. I'd never done Ecstasy, but from what I'd read the experience sounded like how I felt ditching cops. Every little detail mattered. And not only did every detail matter, every detail brought pleasure. The mundanity of life faded away, imbuing all the little moments and images with beautiful meaning. The movement of my eyes as I scanned for tails, the feel of my feet on the sidewalk as I changed direction, the synapses firing as I compared this situation to every other one I'd been in or seen or read about.

I walked to a bus stop and hopped on the 8, which would take me into downtown. I doubted they were tracking my bus pass, but I paid cash just in case. I leaned on the headrest and stared out the window, allowing my mind to go blank except for the job. I needed to figure out where my mom would be, what she'd be doing, how she'd be dressed, everything. All I knew about Micro Tech was that they had offices in Portland's most famous office building, and that's where I'd start.

Approaching from the south, the Bancorp Tower came into view as a slim, pinkish-gold contradiction in the sky. Viewed in isolation, it was beautiful. Spanish pink granite, sleek and slender, with windows that absorbed or reflected the light depending on its strength and direction—sometimes it was liquid gold, sometimes pink, sometimes a soft gray. Big Pink, as everyone in Portland called it, was built on an irregular lot, a parallelogram with no right angles. When you approached from the southwest, the building's massive face blocked the view of the river. Taken in the context of the downtown, it didn't fit. And since it was built on the site of the former Salvation Army building, Mikey Shakes referred to it as the city's middle finger to Old Town and the homeless.

I hopped off the bus, circled the block twice, and cut through an underground parking garage, coming out on the southwest of the building. Next I bought a Portland Timbers baseball cap and wore it low on my forehead to shield my face as much as possible without looking like I was shielding my face.

I did a few laps around the tower, stopping occasionally to pretend to look at my phone, which was still powered down. Hyperaware of my surroundings, attuned to every sound and detail, I memorized the security guards on my first lap. On the second lap I let them fade into the background, allowing me to focus on the others. Most of the people on the street were coming to and from work. They walked with purpose, talking on cell phones or looking worried about some unseen responsibility. There's a big difference between people who look busy and distracted, like the ants marching in and out of Big Pink, and people pretending to look busy and distracted, like the Eisenhower jacket guy. By my third lap I was satisfied there were no cops around.

With the confidence of a salesman who'd just made his monthly quota, I strolled into Bancorp Tower. A huge, three-story area that had been recently renovated, the lobby was all marble, with minimalist staircases that gave the space an open, airy look. The banks of elevators were off to the right, and to the left sat a security desk, which I scanned quickly, not letting my eyes settle on any one spot for too long. Past the security desk, a wide hallway led to a row of retail stores, which took up the rest of the ground floor. I checked them one by one—a coffee shop, a mini-spa, a fancy handbag store, and a "gourmet" deli selling mediocre, overpriced sandwiches designed to rip off busy office workers who didn't have the time to find a decent lunch. It made me miss Dexter's. I strolled into the deli and grabbed a soda from the cold case, trying to look impatient but reveling in the opportunity it gave me. I studied the men at the security desk and tracked the mall-cop-level oversight provided by a solitary dude in a gray polyester uniform who wandered the hallways.

There was no video surveillance in the common areas of the building, and a careful glance around revealed no camera blisters in the lobby or adjoining hallways. Made sense: the building had gone up before the age of ubiquitous surveillance, and the companies that had owned it since weren't the types to spend money installing new infrastructure. This way, each individual company in the building could pay for monitoring its own offices.

I paid cash for the soda and headed for the elevators as though that had been my plan all along. The only floor that allowed access without a key card was the thirtieth, home of City Grill. As I rode the elevator, I watched a few people get off before me, waving their key cards past a magnetic sensor before punching in the number of their desired floor. I got out on the thirtieth floor, used the bathroom, then asked a few pointless questions of the hostess: *How late are you open? What's the signature dish? Would this be a good place to bring a group of old friends from out of town? What about a first date? What would you order?* Satisfied that I'd lingered long enough, I took the elevator back to the ground floor.

To the right of the elevator was a large placard listing all the building's tenants, each name printed on a clear plastic strip. Micro Tech was located in Suite 1809, which meant that my mom must have already obtained keycard access to the 18th floor, or was confident she could. But how? I scanned the other businesses listed on the eighteenth floor, looking for ways in. Without keycard access, the easiest way up was to find the most publicly facing business, one that had lower security than Micro Tech, one that would be easier to fool into letting you up. The only other business listed on the eighteenth floor was another tech firm, Bio Chip, Inc.

The stairs were also an option. The problem was, the stairwells *also* utilized keycard access points. The doors in the lobby had scanners just like the elevators, and so did the emergency doors by the restrooms at the City Grill. Maybe some of the other floors had less security? It was worth a shot. The keycard issue made me wonder how up-to-date Mom's tech knowledge was. It was one of way too many things I didn't know about her and it made me think of a time when I'd come close to being the brains of one of her jobs.

I'd been eavesdropping on her and Soup talking about a shipping warehouse. Soup had a duplicate set of keys and a big van, Mom had the security patrol schedule, but what they didn't have was the inventory. Without that, it was tough to know what night the job would be profitable enough to be worth doing. I'd been spending a lot of time in the computer room at school, any period I could get an excuse to be in there. I'd taken to hanging around the corners of Usenet where hackers gathered, and while I quickly learned that the more involved code was beyond me, there were an awful lot of tricks that qualified as stupidly easy. I had to poke around a bit to find the warehouse company's system, but AltaVista was surprisingly helpful, and a few minutes later, I was logged in as "admin" with the password "password." I came home from school that day with a printout of the warehouse's scheduled inventory for the next two weeks. I didn't produce it until Soup came over after dinner, and he whooped and guffawed most satisfyingly, but Mom asked me in a serious voice if I'd printed it out on a school computer. I admitted I had, and she thanked me for being a big help and said never to do that again. Even so, my info meant they could target a shipment of the new Nintendo 64s, and guess who got one for free?

Looking around Big Pink, I didn't think it'd be as easy as "password: password" this time, and I had doubts about my mom's knowledge of the tech necessary to crack the key card system.

I headed for the door, planning to make another lap around the outside. Still alert for tails and undercover cops, my gaze stopped on the coffee shop where a woman sat at a metal table. Her blonde hair was cut into a nice bob and she wore pink sunglasses and a neck scarf that made her look like a 1950s movie star. I'd seen her at least twice in the last hour. Once by the elevators and once near the security desk. Her shoes and handbag implied wealth, and her demeanor did the rest. When she picked up her coffee cup, she moved her pinky beneath it for balance, then splayed it out like a fancy British lady drinking tea. Then her pinky curled back under, then back out. It was a strange tic, almost like she was doing reps with her pinky finger. She'd done it when I was a kid, too. It was inadvert. Unconscious. That was my mom. The hair was wrong, the build was wrong, but it was her, and she was casing the target.

I entered the coffee shop, making sure she noticed me on my way in. I doubted I'd surprised her. Once she had her game face on, she wouldn't break it for anything.

With my back to her, I examined a Portland-branded coffee mug. "Unless you've got a reliable partner, you're going to have trouble getting the key card. I've got a fix for that." I spoke softly, watching her face in the reflection of a silver pitcher, the kind used to foam milk on an espresso machine. As expected, she showed no surprise. Just stared at her phone like she was scrolling Instagram or checking her bank account.

The last thing I'd said to her in my apartment was *Get out and don't ever come back.* Now, here I was, interrupting her job and offering to help. I set down the coffee mug and ordered an espresso to go. On my way out, I knelt a yard away to tie my shoe. "Meet me at Giordano's," I whispered, "two blocks west."

I didn't wait for her reaction. Son or not, when someone makes you as you're scoping out a job, it grabs your attention. I knew she'd follow.

The Oregonian, November 7, 2002

Blackstone mistress scandal not enough to derail reelection

Jackie Morningstar

Congressman Kellen Blackstone of Oregon's Fifth Congressional District won reelection easily yesterday, despite being dogged by constant rumors of a secret mistress in Bolivia for the last two years.

The second-term congressman beat Republican challenger Mark Stedford by twenty points, the widest margin ever for the Portland native and the highest margin of victory in the Oregon Fifth since the midterm elections of 1978.

Stedford's campaign made hay over Blackstone's alleged affair with Maria Taylor, a model whom Blackstone admitted to meeting in the Bolivian capital of Sucre as part of a Congressional trip for the Foreign Affairs Committee in 2001. Though he denied the affair, the married father of four was photographed with Ms. Taylor in 2001 and early 2002, both times in a variety of Bolivian bars and nightclubs.

Reached for comment, Blackstone called his campaign's victory a vindication. "No matter how many vicious lies were spread about me, the good people of Oregon are sending me back to Washington, because they know that what truly matters is that I fight for them."

The Congressman raised unprecedented sums of money in this election, including record donations from the media, timber, and financial sectors.

Chapter Fifteen

I arrived at Giordano's first. A windowless, second-floor pizza joint, it had a wood-fired brick oven that required a vent fan powerful—and loud—enough to carry the smoke and heat into the alley. It was a holdover from an earlier Portland and would probably be remodeled as a vegan ramen house any day now. When I was too broke to afford three squares a day, sometimes I'd walk through the alley to get a whiff of the charred crust and caramelized cheese wafting from the vent fan. I grabbed a booth in the back so I could see the entrance, and ordered a pie for the table, plus two waters and two sodas.

In my early twenties, I worked security on the graveyard shift in a downtown office building for six months. I must have been going through an identity crisis—*me, working security?*—but it was an easy gig for which I got paid ten bucks an hour and didn't have to carry a gun. I was terrible at the job. I got fired for not chasing enough homeless people away from the warm grates around the base of the building, which is what I was supposed to be doing between ten at night and six in the morning. I didn't mind getting fired. I'd made a deal with myself early on that I'd do the job well if it ever came to real criminals. If someone busted into the building—someone like me or my mom, for example—I'd have done my duty and called the police. I don't think I'd have felt any animus toward them, but, hey, it was my job, and I was trying like hell to be a decent citizen. But being a decent citizen meant I wasn't gonna make an old lady move off the only source of warmth she had available to her on a cold winter night.

One of the things I learned at that job was that companies will spend millions of dollars on server security, encrypted Wi-fi, anti-virus software, firewalls, and email protections, but often forget about the first line of defense in any office: the front door. This is because companies are responsible for their own cyber-security, but usually rely on the building's security guards for the physical safety of their offices. Keycard vulnerabilities are often missed because the people working in the building become comfortable with their surroundings. After all, there are uniformed guards in the lobby. Seems safe enough, right? Most companies with offices in buildings like Big Pink assume the building itself is secure, so they focus on cyber.

Even when office buildings *do* get hit—which happens more than you think—companies rarely make the crimes public. It's bad PR. A building like Big Pink has over a hundred tenants and a high turnover rate. The last thing management wants is to become known as the building that got robbed. So when heists *do* happen, the owners use their connections to keep them out of the news.

There's another reason office tenants don't focus on physical security, and it's the same reason office-building heists aren't as common as they used to be: offices rarely have anything of value inside. Not cash, not jewelry, not much of anything that can easily be fenced. Computers, sure. But who's going to break into a skyscraper for ten or twenty grand worth of laptops? You're better off robbing a nice old Victorian in Laurelhurst.

Most of the property in this type of office building is *intellectual* property, which is another reason companies focus their security dollars on their email systems and networks. My mom had found an outlier with the microchips—physical goods that were compact and valuable. My scan of Big Pink told me that Carebear and company weren't watching the building, but my hunch was that my mom's job was flawed for other reasons. That's where I came in.

165

My mom arrived after fifteen minutes, just as the waiter set down the pizza. The cheese was still bubbling, the steam wilting the fresh basil they'd sprinkled on top. An intoxicating perfume filled the air.

"Smells amazing," Mom said as she sat.

"What took you so long?"

"Doubled back a few times." She said it dismissively, picking up a slice and quickly dropping it onto the plate in front of her. Giordano's pizza came out hot every time.

I felt there was more to it than that. "Mom, for once, be completely honest."

"I did double back, but not to lose a tail. I was having second thoughts. You showed up out of nowhere."

"And?"

"I don't know. I want to think it's because you want to... I don't know... reconcile?"

I absorbed what she said before I responded. "You *want* to think. But you're scared that—"

"Brand, I didn't say—"

"What you're *scared* of is that I might be working for the cops." I said it with all the injured pride I could muster, so she'd feel guilty for even thinking it.

It worked. She looked down a moment before she met my eyes again. When she did, she was angry. "You said you're living square and you didn't want to see me again. And then you show up out of nowhere—at *my* job—and say you want a secret meeting in a location you know well, but I don't. You're goddamn lucky I gave birth to you, because that's the only reason I'm here."

"I'm not working for the cops."

"So why *did* you show up?"

I didn't want to tell her about my visit with Ricky. "I want in on this job. I doubt you've got the right tech."

She eyed me over her slice. "Oh? How so?"

"I'll get to that. First, I need some answers."

"I don't want to talk about that night."

"Fine. Fine. Remember the Lying Game?"

She smiled. "Sure."

We'd played it with Soup when I was a kid. One person asks three questions, the other person answers all three, but has to lie on one of the answers. The player who spots the lie gets a dollar from the liar. Most folks use Two Truths And A Lie as a friendly icebreaker at corporate events or college orientations. We played for money.

"If I don't ask about that night, will you play?"

She offered a sideways nod, a reluctant acquiescence.

"One: which state did you live in the most over the last twenty years? Two: what's the biggest job you've done, in terms of dollar value? Three: What's the *coolest* job you've done?"

She closed her eyes and smiled, trying to figure out the lie. "One: Wisconsin. Two: nine hundred grand. Stole a painting for a guy in New York City. Three: On a cruise ship from Texas, I nabbed a dude's sixty-thousand-dollar cell from his penthouse stateroom, then tossed it into the Gulf of Mexico."

"Last one's gotta be the lie. No way you'd toss a phone like that."

"No dollar. The first one was the lie."

"Wait, so then why'd you toss the phone?"

"Guy was rude to me at the bar. His phone was one of those gem-encrusted ones they make for people with way too much money. Did it just out of spite."

"So you didn't live in Wisconsin?"

"I did, but Texas is where I lived longest. Actually, Mexico, but you asked which state?"

"Why'd you live in Mexico?"

"Shouldn't we talk about the job?"

"C'mon, Mom?"

"Went down there for gallbladder surgery. After, I stayed. Had a little issue with the pain pills they gave me and, well, I don't have that issue anymore."

I nodded. Medical tourism and pain pills. I understood a little better why she'd said I wouldn't want her life. "Sorry about your gall-bladder, I guess. Are there any, uh..." I couldn't think of the word.

She smiled. "Complications? Other than having to get off vikes and percs, no. I'm fine."

"Can we play again?"

She nodded.

"One: Do you have any other kids? Two: Would you have found me this week if I hadn't had Soup find you? Three: On a scale of one to ten, how strongly did you consider coming to get me at some point, busting me out of foster care?"

"No, no, and ten. And before you guess, all three of those are true." She reached across the table and took my hands. "I was shitty in a hundred ways, but in that first year, once I knew you were in the foster home, I came back to Portland. Sat outside that big house you lived in—Cemetery Lane, right?—and waited, and watched. They had security cameras but... I mean, you know those weren't gonna stop me."

"What did?"

"I honestly thought you'd have been worse off with me." This time I could hear the self-loathing in her voice when she said it.

That was still something I couldn't absorb, but I no longer wanted to hurt her like I had in my apartment, so I changed the subject to safe territory: the heist. "I think I saw a flaw in your job, and I couldn't let it slide."

"Like what?"

"Building security. But first"—I drank half my soda in one long chug—"Micro Tech?"

"Encryption tech company, but you already knew that. Barely even know what that means, but I have it on good authority the chips are worth half a mil at least."

"They are." I frowned. "But you have to get in first. Got a clean phone?"

She slid her bulky black phone across the table. I'd envied the thing since I saw it at the zoo. To a regular person, it would look like an out-of-date hunk of junk, the kind your grandpa shouts into before accidentally dropping it in the toilet. It was the single best phone for her line of work. It didn't have any bells or whistles, didn't integrate with any social-media accounts or sell data to advertisers. It did block most attempts to intercept calls, it encrypted every message, and alerted you if a call or text had been intercepted. I bit my upper lip. "You don't have another one of these, do you?"

"No, but..." She lifted her water glass and took a sip, turning casually and locking in on each person in the room one by one. The move sparked a flood of memories. She always liked to do something else, something normal like drinking a glass of water, when she checked a room.

Setting down the glass, she pulled another phone from her purse. "Standard trash phone." On her own device, she tapped out a text and sent it. "When you power it on you'll have a text from me. Use mine for now."

The screen was small and the browser slow, but it worked. First thing I wanted to do was check out the other tech firm that shared the eighteenth floor with Micro Tech. A quick Google search informed me that Bio Chip was a health-tech company developing implantable chips to carry a person's medical records with them everywhere they went. They were primarily a research company, and I figured they'd have tight security, though not as tight as Micro Tech because their individual chips were valued only in hundreds of dollars, not tens of thousands. I didn't need to know how she knew Micro Tech would be stocked with high-end chips. I trusted her on that. Getting onto the high floor was the issue, and that brought me back to my read on Big Pink's keycard security. "How were you planning on getting in?"

"Keycard clone."

"Show me."

Again she scanned the room, this time while tentatively biting into her slice. She froze and looked at the pizza as if seeing it for the first time. "Whoa, this is delicious."

I chuckled. "Right?"

She pulled the device from her purse and slid it across the table. It was a handheld RFID writer that looked like a miniature version of the speed guns state patrol officers use on the highway. A few inches tall, it worked by holding it up to a key card, scanning the data, then transferring the credentials to a blank key card. There'd been one like it in the office when I worked security. Back then we used it to test our keycard access codes. Thieves used the same device to swipe those codes. Since leaving that job, I'd learned more about them. Some folks read about celebrity gossip, some folks read about historical murders, others read recipes for lemon cakes or beef Wellingtons they'll never make in real life. My leisure time involved a lot of security and infosec blogs. That's how I knew that this device wouldn't work at Big Pink.

I slid it back to her. "You're gettin' old, Mom."

"What do you mean?"

"Well, are you planning to break into a college dorm room?"

She held her slice halfway between her plate and her mouth. "What?"

"This is for 125-kilohertz systems."

"I have it on good authority this will work."

"Whose authority? And in which decade?"

She looked offended. "You're saying my information is outdated?"

She'd never been a tech person, and the fact that she didn't have a regular crew only compounded this. Every thief needed to know some tech because, chances were, if there was something worth stealing on the other side of a door, it was controlled by some sort of computer chip. That made breaking in harder in some respects, but much easier if you understood how they worked. "A keycard is just a device that stores a password. When you wave it at the reader in the elevators, and at the individual suite doors, the password and its access credentials are transmitted to the reader. The door unlocks if the access credential number is correct. It's that easy."

"And that hard. So what did you mean about 125 hertz?"

"Most low-security buildings run on 125 kilohertz systems. Lower cost, easier to clone." I nodded down at her RFID writer. "That thing would be perfect if you wanted to steal a couple laptops and a bong from a dorm room at Lewis and Clark."

She looked hurt. "You don't have to rub it in."

I was beginning to feel disappointed in my mom and pissed at whoever had scoped out the tech for her. I'd unlocked the mysteries of the system with a ten-minute Google dive. "Big Pink works on a 13.56 megahertz system, which makes it harder to swipe the data. The basic technology is the same, but the amount of data that needs to be transferred is much higher, which means it takes longer. And the scan distance is shorter, so it's harder to do without drawing notice."

"When you found me in the café, I was about to try the scan on the guard doing laps in the building."

"Yeah, that wouldn't have worked."

Mom scowled and looked sideways at someone who wasn't there. "Damn it, Valerie. That's the lady who... never mind. What can we do about it?"

I've always loved crime movies. I was a teenager when YouTube appeared and still remember the day someone uploaded *The Great Train Robbery* in its entirety. I've watched *The Sting* and the *Ocean's* movies more times than I can count. But there's a big difference between heist movies and actual heists, and it's not only that I'm no Redford or Clooney. As I ran scenarios through my mind, I landed on all sorts of clichés and tired tropes I'd seen hammered home in movie after movie. The blonde bombshell pulls the goofy security guard away from the door, for example, or the sneaky duo steals outfits from a city maintenance crew to gain easy access to the building. My mom was still a bombshell of sorts, and sure, we could steal some outfits if we had to, but neither of those would solve our problem, nor would they get us the keycard access we needed. Real heists often hinge on mundane technical details like the frequency of your RFID scanner. The issue was tech, and tech rarely makes for good cinema because it's hard to explain to an audience and not even the best cinematographer can make the inside of a computer look cool.

I said, "Transferring the passwords and access credentials means more time standing next to the security guard. With the older system, I could have strolled by the security desk while you chatted up the guard, and in half a second, I'd have scanned his card from two feet away, and that would be that."

"And now?"

"We need two or three minutes, and close proximity. Hold on."

I couldn't find complete architectural schematics online, but they'd published a PDF detailing Big Pink's 2011 renovation, which included a redesign of the three-story atrium, modernized bathrooms, and new elevators.

Elevators.

At forty-two stories, the ride from the ground floor would take roughly a minute, two round trip. That might do it. All I needed was to get the security guard in the elevator with my mom and me. I needed to think, so I threw out some small talk. "Did you know Big Pink is actually forty-one stories, but the top floor is listed as the forty-second story because they don't have a thirteenth?"

Mom shrugged.

"Partially because the builders worried some of their renters might be superstitious, but also to make it seem taller than it is."

I finished my slice, then my soda. Mom watched me as a waiter refilled the drinks. She was deferring to me, waiting to see what I'd come up with. It made me feel good, but also nervous.

When the waiter left, I said, "I've got an idea."

She leaned in. "What?"

"Do you have anything different to wear?"

We built our new plan over the next fifteen minutes, talking in low voices and pausing every time the front door clanged. By the time we'd finished the pizza, there was little left to say. The business was out of the way, which left us with only our past. We'd gone quiet. We each knew what needed to be said, but neither wanted to bring it up. We were like a divorced couple, meeting after a long break. We'd filled in some blank spots about the intervening years, but we were more comfortable talking about our child because we couldn't bear discussing all the ways we'd ruined one another. Crime was our child.

I started to sweat, gripping my soda harder. I didn't look at her when I broke the silence. "No bullshit. What happened that night?"

"You don't want to hear about that." She turned away, like that would end it.

"That's *all* I want to hear about. Don't you get it? You leaving that night broke me. Everything after that went bad..."

"I'm sorry." She wouldn't look at me.

"Tell me what the hell happened inside that room."

She was quiet for a long time and, in the silence, I realized something. She wasn't trying to hide something from me or shield me from some unpleasant truth. She was hiding it from herself. She didn't want to face it. She'd been running from that night just as relentlessly as I had.

She looked at her watch.

"You got somewhere to be?" My voice was pointed, accusatory. "Let's play the Lying Game one more time."

She turned to me slowly, her face pinched like she'd just smelled something unpleasant. "I won't make you play it. I'll tell you. You have to understand, I'd been looking into boarding schools for you. Nothing too far away, but there was one over in... Damn, I don't remember. But I'd found one that looked good and I thought it would be better for you. You were always too smart for regular school and I knew it wasn't gonna be best for you to stay with me. How are you supposed to do homework at night when we're out doing what we did, right?"

If she wanted me to consider her side, she was going about it all wrong. I'd never been a fan of school. I'd gotten in trouble a few times, most notably the time I launched a homework-for-hire scheme. It started off with me paying a girl named Sarah ten bucks to do my math homework for a month. My friend Seth asked why I was suddenly doing so well in math and, when I came clean, he asked me to arrange for Sarah to do his work as well. Seth paid his ten bucks a month, Sarah accepted seven bucks to do his work since it was mostly the same as mine. I took the remaining three bucks as a transaction fee. Long story short, the damn thing snowballed into a school-wide scandal. By the time it came crashing down, I was making fifty bucks a month, getting all my work done for free, and corrupting half the fifth-graders at East Side Elementary. I served a two-week suspension.

Mom's mention of boarding school wasn't the way to bring me over. I almost launched into a forceful rebuttal, but the pained look on her face kept me quiet. I had to hear her out.

"If we had more money," she continued, "I could afford the school. I think it was nineteen grand a year or something." She looked up. "And it wasn't one of those ones for troubled kids or anything. A *real* boarding school for fancy kids. They had a *lacrosse* team, for Chrissakes." She sighed, wringing her hands tensely. "I remember thinking that was something. Never met a poor person who plays lacrosse, y'know? Anyway, that's why I took the job with Ricky. I'd never worked a job with a gun before."

"Ricky told me the guns weren't loaded. I went to see him."

Her eyes went wide and her mouth fell open. She looked like she'd just had the wind knocked out of her. "You didn't *know* that?"

"I—"

"You honest-to-God didn't know that? Did you believe all that crap in the papers that I might be..." She choked up, swallowing a couple times like she was fighting tears.

"I never really *believed* it, but how was I supposed to know? You disappeared. I was twelve."

Her face went through a series of contortions. I understood. It's a hell of a thing to absorb the fact that the stories we base our lives on aren't true. I was still working on it myself, and it wasn't doing me any favors. "I can't believe you even thought I *might*..." Her face softened. "That why you joined me? Why you came to find me today?"

"Partly.... But why even have the guns? A threat?"

"We'd heard there'd be over a hundred grand in cash at the poker game. Maybe more. That was gonna be the job that took us out of the daily grind, got us some working capital. Got you into boarding school." She snapped her fingers. "I remember now! It was in Cedar Hills. Twenty minutes from our old apartment."

"You know I wouldn't have wanted to go, right?"

She considered this, but didn't respond. "We took the guns to make the whole thing go faster. We had it that the security guard was for show, that he wasn't armed. And he wasn't. *He* wasn't the problem."

"So what happened?"

"When you got the guard off the door, we busted in as planned."

She paused before continuing, and for a second she almost smiled. "By the way, I never got a chance to tell you, you did a great job on that. Played it just right."

I smiled. The part of me that had wanted so badly to do my part well still craved her approval. Then it seemed ridiculous, given everything that had come since.

"So we busted in. They were playing in the living room, not more than fifteen feet from the front door. Right away, Ricky pulled the gun and demanded money. Everything on the table was chips, but when he said that, all five of 'em looked straight at this cash box sitting on a bookshelf behind the table. Ricky looked at me, then held a gun on them while I crossed that big front window and went for the box." She closed her eyes and spoke slowly. "From there, I don't remember exactly how it went down. My attention was on the box, so the whole thing is kind of choppy. One guy leaned to his side, like maybe he was reaching for the floor. I only saw the gun for a second. His arm was bent at the elbow and the first shot went into the wall between me and Ricky. Everyone started scrambling. I was on the other side of the table from Ricky. He was closer to the door and the guy was shooting at him, not me. Ricky ran to the door, which he never should have closed in the first place. We had to get the hell out of there, but the door kinda snapped toward us and hit Ricky when he tried to open it. He stumbled back into the room. Dude with the gun tried to shoot Ricky in the back. Shithead missed and hit the guard in the chest just as he came through the door. Everyone stopped for half a second. The guard staggered out to the porch, same way he'd come in. Ricky bolted past him and I followed." Her voice was slow and monotonous, like she was telling me the plot of a boring movie. My guess was it was the only way she could get through it. "That's what I remember."

"Which guy fired the shot?"

"Five white guys, all in their thirties and forties. I was wearing a mask."

"You don't know which one?"

"He had brown hair."

That ruled out Martin Seykes. "But you don't know more than that?"

"Why does it matter? It wasn't me and it wasn't Ricky."

I didn't hide my incredulity well. "It matters."

She didn't say anything, so after that, I went quiet, turning my mind back to the job, back to Big Pink. After a while, I gave her a look that said, *It's time.*

Mom got up, but stopped halfway across the restaurant and came back. She leaned on the table. "You're really good at this, Brandon."

I couldn't tell if it was a compliment. It sounded more like a statement of fact, but I heard sadness in her voice.

I told her "Thanks" and watched her go, waited a minute, then paid, circled the block, and found the back entrance of the building we were going to rob.

The Oregonian, July 5, 2006

Timber heir Seykes donates to victims fund

Samuel Drebben

Portland timber heir Martin Seykes donated $75,000 on Tuesday to the Oregon DUI Victims Association (DUIVA), a non-profit that supports the families of those killed by drunk drivers in the state.

Seykes, who last month was cited for driving under the influence, received a suspended sentence and apologized publicly after the incident.

According to DUIVA, each year over 10,000 Americans die in drunk driving accidents, and more than twenty percent of the victims are not the impaired drivers.

Reached for comment by The Oregonian, Seykes said, "Everyone makes mistakes. I made one, and I've acknowledged it. This donation is the least I can do."

Chapter Sixteen

B
ig Pink had an open first floor spanning a whole city block. Because of the odd-shaped lot on which it was built, the base had no right angles, which was disorienting.

I did a couple laps through the lobby, pretending to look for something, before grabbing a cup of coffee in the café. I sat at a small table that gave me a good angle on the security desk, the foyer, and the hallways. I'd told my mom to head through a parking garage or two, just to be sure she wasn't being followed, and to give me a few minutes to prep. I scrolled on the trash phone, one eye on the screen, one on the action. There were four security guards on duty. Two at the main desk—one of them a walrus-sized white dude, the other an older Asian woman. Another guard patrolled the perimeter of the building, passing by a glass door every few minutes. The last guard was wandering the building, mostly giving out directions to hurried visitors. Usually, he'd send them to the security desk, where the walrus-sized dude would call up to an office to get them access.

While I waited, I readied the app that would make or break our plan. The phone Mom had given me was older, but the app was small and simple, and I'd downloaded it at Giordano's. Its sole purpose was to lift the passwords from keycards, and that's all I needed it to do.

My mom appeared after about five minutes. She looked five years younger. As promised, she'd created a different look, doing her hair up in a ponytail, which stuck out the back of the Timbers cap I'd been wearing earlier. Her shirt was tucked into her jeans, which she'd pulled up, giving them that mom-jeans look. She'd also removed her makeup and put on an air of being—how to describe it?—flustered. Every bit of her energy gave off a vibe: *I'm in a hurry and I can't find my keys.* No longer an elegant, wealthy woman, she looked every bit the aging, minivan-driving soccer mom just trying to get through the day.

I tossed my coffee cup in the trash and ambled toward the desk, where she was already speaking with the massive security guard. His oversized front teeth had a gap between them like Michael Strahan's, and, honestly, he looked dumb as a rock. That would help us, but it wasn't why she'd approached him instead of the woman sitting next to him. Like Thomas Twomey, he had that gentle-giant look. The kind of guy who might take pity on her.

"Well, usually, ma'am," he was saying when I approached, "if you're meeting someone, we ask that they come down and meet you in the lobby."

"Yes, of course. You seem nice." My mom flashed an understanding smile. "I don't want to get you in trouble with your boss or whatever. Or are you the boss? I don't really know how it works. I'm sorry. I've got three teenagers in the car..." She waved in the general direction of the street. "...and, damn, I don't have the number and..." She waved her phone in the air as though proving the number wasn't in there.

"You can use our phone to call up and..."

"I know, and thank you, but I don't remember the name, either. I know it was the twenty-sixth floor and I remember how to get to the door coming from the elevator, just not the suite number. Any way you could take me up?"

"Um, uh, sure, I'm allowed to do that, I think." The guard seemed to be convincing himself, which was exactly how we'd planned it. Whenever possible, you want the mark to think it was their idea to give you what you want. He glanced at the woman, who looked up from her monitor and nodded. She was in charge.

He smiled, relieved. "I can take you up, ma'am."

"If you're sure it'd be okay... thank you. It's very nice of you." As they headed for the elevator, mom kept going. "You're sooooo nice! Most people these days don't want to help anyone, y'know? Only looking out for themselves. Bunch of thieves and crooks out there."

I followed, far enough behind to not be suspicious, but close enough that I'd be sure to make it to the elevator before the door closed.

When I was a kid, I was often the distraction while my mom did the crime.

Brand, pretend to be sick.

Brand, start crying loudly over there. I'll be standing next to that table of fancy watches.

Brand, fall off your bike and wait for the big security guard to come running for you.

Now, our roles were reversed.

As we waited for the elevator, I scanned a little placard displaying the names of all the businesses with offices on the floors above. My eyes stopped on one of the four companies occupying office space on the twenty-eighth floor: *Masterson Wealth Management Services.* Interesting. Mark Masterson—money launderer to the stars and possible shooter at the poker game—also worked out of Big Pink. I didn't let it percolate long, but I filed the information for later use.

"Oh, again, thank you so much," my mom said as I slipped the phone out of my pocket. "If I take too long my kids will be doing doughnuts in my minivan on Burnside." The big guard chuckled dutifully.

My mom led the way into the elevator, standing such that the guard had to take the spot by the buttons. I leaned past him and pressed 30 with one hand, holding the phone by my side and pressing "Scan" with the other to start the app's sixty-second cycle of looking for a password it could clone.

"Either of you had the burger at the restaurant?" I asked. "I'm famished."

"It's good," said the guard with a professional, friendly grin. "Get the one with gorgonzola. It's weird at first, but it grows on you."

"Thanks." I was standing a little closer to him than would be normal with only three people in the elevator. I felt him inching away but we boxed him in as much as we could without being obvious about it. I extended my arm slightly, worried my phone wasn't close enough to the pocket where he'd stashed his keycard.

"What about salads and stuff?" I shrugged. "I'm meeting a date."

"Took my girlfriend there last month," he said. "She got a pasta dish. Said it was pretty good. Mushroom something?"

At the fifth floor, a couple joined us. Like a pro, my mom skootched toward us, giving me the excuse I needed to crowd the guard even more. I frowned at him as if to say *Sorry*, but it was close enough now to get the scan. Three, maybe four inches, that's the pickup range on the 13.56 MhZ chips. While the elevator slid slowly upward, the app went to work, copying the guard's master keycard. Once it had that data, the same app would let it broadcast an identical signature, allowing us the same access as the building's own guards.

At the twenty-sixth floor, Mom followed the guard out of the elevator, stopped short, and pulled out her phone. She gaped at the screen in disbelief. "Damn kids."

I held the door open as she jogged back to the elevator. The guard followed her. When I got off on the thirtieth floor, she was halfway through a story about how one kid had just punched another and she'd have to reschedule.

The screen on my phone flashed with a message: SUCCESS! CARD SAVED AS 001. As planned, my mom and I would exit separately and have no more contact until the next day.

Walking to Jennifer's, the world looked different. Each alley was a potential getaway route, every underpass a possible switch car location. Instead of businesses and homes, I saw attention points, strong points, and weak spots. I was fully awake on levels I hadn't been in a long time. I'd done and felt and lived more in one afternoon of real work with my mom than I had in the previous sixteen years of empty drudgery. I could do anything. As I approached Movie Madness, I saw how easy it would be to blind their cameras, bust in through the side door, and steal their entire memorabilia collection, which was displayed proudly in glass cases secured by weak-ass diecast locks. I'd never do that, but I could if I wanted to, and that feeling was intoxicating.

I stared up at Jennifer's second-floor window, recalling a hundred times I'd looked down from it while she studied or took a shower. I used to play a little game where I tried to catch a glimpse of the movies in people's hands as they came and went, as though a quick cold read, plus a second-long glimpse of a DVD case was enough to tell me what they'd rented. *Thirty-something hipster carrying a case in seventies yellow and brown? Must be The Criterion Collection edition of Harold and Maude.* I never knew if I got it right, but that wasn't the point.

Walking around the side of the building and up the stairs, I felt strangely grown up, like in a movie when a character returns to the house he grew up in and says, *I remember it seeming bigger.* As Jennifer opened the door, though, her place didn't seem smaller, it seemed *drabber*, and that was because I felt so alive. I had to remind myself that I was here to break things off between us for good. I'd chosen the path of crime, and it was not a path she could walk with me.

As much as the place looked drab, Jennifer did not. She was in jeans and a big sweatshirt—her usual chill-at-home attire—and her hair was wet. The living room smelled faintly of mint and jasmine, the scent of her regular shampoo carried by the steam from one of the long, hot showers she took every day.

She led me to the couch, an old leather sectional she'd gotten from her parents, which clashed with the newer bookshelves. Her apartment was nicer than mine, neater than mine, the walls lined with Ikea bookshelves stacked with DVD cases and books on film history. And still it looked banal. Distressingly normal. I tried to imagine what my own place would look like with this new clarity of vision, and found the prospect too depressing to think about.

Jennifer stared up at me from a fancy beanbag facing the couch, saying nothing. As I settled into the comfortable, overstuffed cushions, it was as though I heard a whisper of another Brandon, the one who'd watched a lot of movies on this couch, had a lot of sex on it. The one who'd tried to eke out a little happiness in his stifled, miserable life. That Brandon wanted simple comforts and ease. There were two Brandons now, and I didn't have the power to make either one of them leave.

"You were wrong about my mom," I began.

"What?"

"It's not your fault. Most people would have thought... Hell, I almost... never mind that now. The point is, my mom's not a murderer." A quiet part of my brain whispered, *She wasn't a murderer in 1998, but you don't know what she's done since.* I ignored it. I was here to break things off with Jennifer for her own good, and this was no time for quibbles.

"Um, okay?" She stood and moved to the other end of the couch, stretching her legs out between us. "Not sure what you want me to do with that."

"I found out today her gun was never loaded." I was hoping for a look of revelation on Jennifer's face, but it didn't happen, so I added, "Which means the entire case against her is not only false, it's *deliberately* false. They know who did it, and they've covered it up for twenty years. Now that she's in town, they're trying to find her so they can pin it on her."

Jennifer took a good long moment to blink. "All right, but who's 'they' in that sentence?"

"The police. Or... maybe not all of the police, but at the very least...." I didn't want to say Caraway's name. "Anyway, that's not the point. The point is, I'm about to leave Portland for good, and I don't want to do that without saying goodbye."

Jennifer jerked back. "Whoa whoa whoa, what? Sorry, you're clearly seeing a connection between 'My mom didn't shoot that guy' and 'I'm gonna leave town forever' that makes sense to you, but I don't see it. Help me out?"

Help me out? was one of the catchphrases in our relationship. Every time she couldn't understand the way I saw the world, or every time I didn't get something in her weird normie point of view, we'd say *help me out?* A kind, no-pressure way of asking for a bridge between our worlds. It mostly came up in relation to movies, when I'd call an ending too pat, or she'd call a plot twist too farfetched when it seemed obvious to me. I hated and loved that she still trusted me enough to ask that.

I took a breath and carefully edited the information I was willing to share. "My mom is doing a job a couple nights from now. Never mind where. But—"

She interrupted me. "Sorry, but by 'job' you mean a *crime*, right?"

I sighed. "A major one. So starting a few nights from now, I'll need to be somewhere else, I'll be... well..." I didn't want to come right out and say I'd be part of the heist, but I needed her to know.

Jennifer stood slowly and did a couple laps around the couch. I saw her putting pieces together in her mind, saw the question forming. She leaned on the window, watching a crow that was perched on the windowsill. "What haven't you told me?"

I sighed. "A lot. I never lied to you about anything big. But I left stuff out and hid a lot more. I told you about the night my mom and I got separated. After that, I did all sorts of little thefts while in high school." I stopped, pondering whether to walk her through the Rabbit Rafferty saga. I decided against it. "Not gonna lie, I was pretty fucked up for a few years. When I was sixteen, I stopped. And I've been straight ever since."

"I was getting worried you'd been... that all along you were..."

"No, nothing like that. I really did stop when I was sixteen. But here's the thing. All along I *wanted* to be, *needed* to be. I'm so damn good at it that—"

"Wait, good at what?"

The crow flew away and she began pacing again.

I noticed her bare wrist. "Your steps thing. Did you forget to put it on after your shower?" She looked down, and I smiled. "You're not gonna get credit for all the pacing you're doing."

She chuckled. "Nice topic change. Good at what, Brandon?"

I sighed. "There's a lot that... I can... Don't really know how to explain it. Remember that time you locked your keys in here and called me from school, asking me to meet the locksmith at your door and pay him?"

"Yeah."

"I called the company, canceled the job. Picked the lock myself."

"You can pick locks?"

"Locks, safes, pockets, purses, cars, combinations, cons..." I forced myself to stop listing things. "That's the least of it, and that's what I'm saying. I've hidden a lot of things from you. Stifled a lot of impulses."

She looked at me sideways, trying to figure out what I meant.

I moved to the edge of the couch and leaned toward her. She was halfway across the room, but it felt much further. "I'm better at this than I am at anything else. I'm better at this than most people will *ever* be at anything. My whole adult life, I've pretended that isn't true."

Jennifer crossed the room, and I thought she was going to sit next to me, but she stopped short. She crouched, her eyes meeting mine. "Don't you see? That's a *good* thing, Brandon. Of course you'd want to do the stuff you were raised around. That's normal. Part of growing up is breaking free of the shit our parents did to us. Kids who were abused are more likely to abuse their kids, and they need to do the hard work of breaking that cycle. Same with kids of alcoholics." She must've seen the skeptical look on my face because she tried another approach. Standing to pace again, she said, "Most people think about cheating on their partners every now and then, right? Nothing exactly wrong with that." She chuckled. "Hell, when we were together, I thought about it every time we saw a Chris Evans flick. We don't have to *act on it*, though. Stifling our impulses to do something wrong makes us good people."

She flopped down on the beanbag chair, as though making her

case had exhausted her. She was trying to convince me, but she was also trying to convince herself that I was a person she could be with.

I wanted badly to agree with her, but I couldn't. I'd tried for sixteen years to live in that world, and it had slowly sucked the life out of me. I wanted her to know that she'd been the only good thing in that stifling, exhausted life. I wanted her to know that I *wanted* that to be enough, but it wasn't. All I said was, "It's hard to explain. I'm sorry."

"So if your mom was a serial killer and..." I tried to interrupt but she raised her voice... "and you'd grown up learning all the little tricks to hunt down and murder your victims and get away scot-free, then what? You'd have to embrace that as your destiny or whatever?"

Her sarcasm hurt me. I knew she was right, but also that it didn't matter. "I never hurt anyone."

She smirked. My response had sidestepped her question, and we both knew it. "So, what, now you want to join your mom on her job?"

I didn't look at her. "That's right."

"And then leave town?"

"Right."

Jennifer considered her words carefully before she responded. "What if you *didn't*, though?"

"What if I didn't what?"

"Didn't do whatever you're talking about doing. What if you were just the smart, sexy boyfriend of a college professor?"

I stared at her.

"I don't even know if I'll get the job yet, but just try it on." She sat next to me, her thigh against mine. She continued, a little awkwardly, "You're all lit up right now. I don't know if you see it, but I do." She put a hand on my knee. "I've never seen this kind of energy in you. I believe that it's the real you, and it's *very* hot, but I don't see why you need to use it to be an actual thief."

The way she said "hot" gave me a flashback to our first date. She'd been working the counter at Movie Madness, and we'd chatted a few times when she invited me to continue the conversation over a meal. At dinner, I'd asked why she'd asked me out, and she'd shrugged. "You can talk movies intelligently and I think you're sexy, so why not?" She didn't understand, then or now, how that sentence had ripped me open in the best way. I'd always been passive when it came to women. Even as far back as Crystal, I was the type who needed the woman to make the first move, and usually the second one as well. I'd never in my life been called sexy, and the casual ease when she'd said it felt like a miracle.

In other words, Jennifer picked a hell of a time to remind me why I fell in love with her in the first place.

"I'm just saying," she continued, "maybe there's an alternative storyline where you can still be engaged with the world, which I'd love to see, but where you don't toss out your whole life and disappear?" Her dark eyes were warm and inviting and when she reached out for my hand, I let her take it.

"It's not like I've never thought of that, it's..." My brain went fuzzy, shortcircuiting as it tried to reconcile Jennifer's vision of Brandon with the one I was barreling toward at a hundred miles per hour.

"Can you take some time to think about it, or do you need to go steal something right this minute?"

"I can take some time," I heard myself say.

And then she leaned in fast and kissed me, just once, then a slight pullback, a tilt of her head, and another, longer kiss. My free hand went to her shoulder, hers to my side. My mind had gone blank, which was a wonderful place to be. All I was aware of was the scent of her hair and her slightly cracked lips and the softness of her shoulder.

She pulled away reluctantly and leaned back, pressing her thigh into mine. "Yesterday there was this couple browsing the romance section and doing cheesy lines from movies they'd watched together. You would have loved it. They were super cute, and I knew like half the lines they were doing. The guy did one in a cheesy-ass British accent: 'Neither of us has to be perfect, Annie. All we can do is help each other become the best version of ourselves.' No idea what movie that's from, but it got me thinking. I'm heading in that direction, and you helped me get here. I think you have more options than you think."

I was barely taking in her words, but I noticed myself smiling, leaning in. She swung her legs up over my lap and scootched forward. "Maybe we can catch a movie later, for old times' sake. And, y'know, kill some time before the movie. For old times' sake."

I knew exactly what she meant when she said, *Kill some time before the movie.*

"Okay," I said.

"You see what's playing." She leapt up and headed to the bedroom. "Just give me a minute," she called, "and make sure the movie is at least a couple hours from now."

I missed whatever she said after that because I was turning on my phone, then absent-mindedly scanning the email notification that popped up. The subject line was *Re: my mom,* and it was from Caraway. My sense of hearing, my sense of time, my sense of the world in general, all fuzzed out as I flicked my thumb to open the email.

Brandon,

Thanks, I knew I could count on you to do the right thing.

-Detective Caraway

What?

I read it twice, then scrolled down. Her email was a reply to something I'd written. My stomach twisted. Something I'd written last night. My jaw tightened. Something I'd written last night while blackout drunk.

Subject: my mom

Carebear, if that's even your real name

It pisses me offf that you came into my work today. I said I'd help you and now you're messing with my job, which is aLL I HAVE AS SAD AS THATIS

So here's the hjelp. I haven't been able to find my mom, and I'm done looking. I asked around all her old freinds accomplices People I know and used to know. Kept hearing microchips and Friday night. I think you can figure out the only place in town that sells the good stuff.

She was probably lying about it she's a big liar. I swear that's all I have now please leave me alone.

I won't be looking for her or talking to her ever again. You were right about one thing that day we first talked she abandoned me and I've always wanted to forgive her. Now I know I can't

Brand.

Even blackout drunk and unable to write without typos, my instinct to lie had been working. Half the email was BS aimed at getting Carebear off my back, but I'd let a small piece of truth slip in. The microchips, and Friday night. The resentment I'd felt toward my mom over the last few days—freshly exhumed after twenty years—had gotten the better of me. In the world I grew up in, there was one unbreakable rule, one unforgivable sin. No matter what, no matter how bad a grudge you hold, no matter what they offer you, no matter how scared or angry or desperate you are, *you never snitch*. A snitch is the lowest thing there is. It had never crossed my mind that Rabbit Rafferty's fate was anything less than he deserved. And now I'd crossed that line.

I don't remember leaving Jennifer's, but presumably I did, because I was jogging home when I remembered to turn off my cell phone.

Chapter Seventeen

I paced my apartment like a methed-out madman, half-broken by emotional whiplash. I'd been yanked from the incredible high of working with my mom to the consuming guilt at betraying her, via my crippling confusion around Jennifer. Somewhere in there, I'd lost the ability to maintain my cool.

I was tempted to contact my mom, tell her the job was shot, but I couldn't. She'd know it was my fault, that her only son had grown up into a goddamned snitch. I'd never see her again. Would that be so bad, though? What if Jennifer's pleasant fantasy was right? What if I could just be a regular person?

I put on a movie and flopped onto my recliner. Tonight it was *Thief*, an early-eighties heist flick starring James Caan. I had no intention of watching it, but having something familiar on in the background often settled my nerves.

Judging by her message, Carebear believed I was helping her, likely assuming that her friendly visit to Morey's pharmacy had swayed me. Though my scans of the Bancorp Tower hadn't revealed any increased security, I had to assume she'd figured out our target. Carebear's primary motivation would be grabbing my mom for the Twomey murder, so she probably wouldn't bother tipping off Micro

Tech. My guess was that on Friday afternoon she and a half-dozen undercover cops would begin lurking around Big Pink with a simple plan: arrest Wanda Penny on sight. But that didn't mean my mom had to skip town with whatever she had in her pockets. I'd screwed up her job, and I owed her a new one.

I could put together a new heist. I didn't know what or how just yet, but I knew I was capable of it, and I knew where I'd start my research.

I turned my phone back on since I needed another screen to supplement my laptop and I didn't mind if the cops traced me to the apartment. There were three more missed calls from Caraway, but I wasn't interested in her right now. More importantly, there was a stack of missed texts from Jennifer.

You okay?

What the hell, Brandon?

Seriously, are you ok?

I stared at the messages, guilty and ashamed, knowing I needed to explain myself but unwilling to tell the truth. *So sorry*, I replied. *Some stuff came up out of nowhere. I feel really bad about running out on you.*

Both intentionally and unintentionally, I'd kept tabs on the five men from the poker game. Living in Portland, it was hard to avoid seeing them everywhere as they rose to prominence. Martin Seykes was a more-money-than-sense wastrel right out of a P.G. Wodehouse novel. Between alimony to several ex-wives, a few crashed sports cars, and charitable donations to cover his various screw-ups, it was amazing he hadn't managed to spend the entire Seykes timber fortune. Kellen Blackstone was smarter, but no better. He always led the state party in fundraising, and a little digging revealed that an awful lot of those funds came from his one-time poker buddies. And he gave his pals a lot of value for their donations. Michael Carusa had gotten some favorable land rezoning when Blackstone was in state government. Mark Masterson lobbied Blackstone every time there was a proposed law limiting shady financial dealings, and Blackstone always voted Masterson's way. They functioned as a mini-fraternity, a bunch of rich guys making sure society continued to run for their benefit, and theirs alone.

Just as that structure was clicking into place for me, my phone pinged with a new message from Jennifer. *What happened?*

I took a second to go over what she knew and what she didn't know before I tapped out my lie. That extra second is what keeps you out of trouble, in my experience. *The guy I met at the prison this morning had a heart attack. I got a text saying he wanted to talk to me before he died, but he was dead before I got to my rental car.*

I paused because the next bit of research I needed to do would take some time and attention, and it would help if I front-loaded an excuse for that time and attention to Jennifer. *Gotta drive out to the prison, identify the body because he has no family. So, y'know, it's gonna be a shitty night. I'm really sorry I didn't say something, or text you. I was in a panic.*

My half-assed excuse would collapse if Jennifer contacted the prison system, but I knew she'd never do that. I deliberately made my alibi too emotionally fraught for her to check on, and at the same time I observed that it was a terrible thing to do. But I did it anyway, running entirely on instinct. Knowing the truth about what I was and what I was doing would not make Jennifer's world any better. In the moment, it honestly felt like I was being kind.

I sent the text and turned back to my laptop. Brian White was the kind of shameless radio host who could be loud-wrong on issue after issue, then move on like he'd never held the position in the first place. It had taken me a few years to realize that his audience didn't care. For his listeners, the show was an emotional exercise, a discharge of energy, like yelling at a sporting event. Brian White wasn't a newscaster; he was an artist of performative outrage, aimed at whatever target fit the fears of his audience that week. His most recent viral clips were about his crusade against Portland's homeless population. He'd even coined a catchphrase around it: *Get 'em off the street and KEEP PORTLAND NEAT!* It was a not-so-subtle jab at the most popular bumper sticker around the city: *Keep Portland Weird.*

Jennifer texted again. *I'm sorry that happened, I really am. And I get that you're going through a lot now. But maybe it's time to leave that life behind for good?*

Maybe it is, I replied.

Her next text arrived only a few seconds later. *So, I've got my fingers crossed for this job in Seattle. Do you think I'd like it there? Do you think you'd like it?*

Not really sure, I replied. *Never been.*

I wonder whether a new city might be the thing you need to get past all the stuff we've been talking about. I've been looking at rents and they're higher than here, but I'll be making more money, assuming the job comes through, and they do have a pretty good movie place.

Jennifer was the type of person who liked to try on different lives. She was picturing us in Seattle right now, probably had photos of a little apartment pulled up in one browser window, mapping walking distance to the university in another, distance to the video store in a third. On my laptop, I had half a dozen windows open, trying to get to the bottom of a deadly shooting while my criminal mind worked overtime to find a new heist. But despite myself, I was in Jenifer's fantasy, too. There weren't only two Brandons at work, though. There was a new Brandon, one who was trying desperately to figure out how to make the other two come together.

Not gonna lie, I wrote, *it sounds kinda nice.*

I've never seen you like you were today. Could you ever see yourself using what you know, what you are, in the regular world?

I pictured myself packing up a lunch box, grabbing an umbrella, and trekking across Seattle to a locksmithing job. Breaking into homes and cars for $60 an hour. I hated the thought, but at least I'd be able to meet Jennifer for a movie after work. After a year or two, we'd have scratched together enough money for me to start a security company. *For $10,000, Brandon Penny and his team will identify any and all holes in your company's security system—both physical and digital—and create a comprehensive report. Call BP Security today!*

I wanted to want that life. I really did, but as much as I wanted to shut my laptop and go back and forth with Jennifer, I couldn't. *I gotta crash, but I really hope you get the job.*

193

I searched for Brian White in combination with Martin Seykes and Michael Carusa. Nothing came up, but when I searched White's name alongside Mark Masterson, some YouTube clips appeared, including a five-minute segment about how to shelter your income from taxes using various shady but legal financial tools, such as overseas corporations and second homes. Next, I found a link to a podcast episode, a longer interview between White and Masterson. I paused the film and played the podcast on the trash phone, pacing my apartment as I listened. Most rich folks believe they're smart, that they got rich through superior skills, intelligence, and hard work. Sometimes it's even true, but usually it's a combination of birth, nepotism, and luck. Many rich assholes also think they're invincible. It makes them overconfident, and that's what makes them easy to rob. It's what makes them say things they shouldn't in podcast interviews. White and Masterson were exactly that breed of rich asshole.

They spent the first five minutes talking about the Blazers, which pissed me off because I resented the thought of sharing a fandom with those two guys. They were the dudes who swooped in and bought courtside seats for two grand a pop when the Lakers came to town, then stared at their phones for half the game while I craned my neck from the nosebleed seats.

Next they talked about local politics. Though White was known for taking aggressive political positions to stir controversy, Masterson was more reluctant to get into political issues, choosing instead to walk the middle. It made sense. All sorts of people have money they want to hide. Why alienate potential customers over politics?

Brian White: *Now Mark, where are you on so-called 'gun control' issues?*

Mark Masterson: *It's a tough one, Brian. Look, I understand that public safety is important. I'm a big supporter of the police unions and the Fallen Badge Foundation. And I think cops get a bad rap in the news, if we're being honest. Anyway, I know Americans want to feel safe, and for some that means getting all the guns off the street. But for others, and I count myself in this group, responsible gun ownership is what brings that sense of safety. Personal protection, am I right? It's* *just as important. As you know, Brian, I've been forced to use a firearm for personal protection in the past, I've had to defend myself and my property against criminals, and I'm glad I was able to do so. I strongly believe in safety training and keeping guns out of the hands of domestic abusers and the insane, but for law-abiding citizens like you and me, self-defense should be paramount.*

I stopped in the middle of my living room and sat cross-legged on the floor. I tapped the screen to rewind thirty seconds. *As you know, I've had to use a firearm for personal protection.* I lay flat on my back, spreading my arms wide like somehow that would help me take in what I was hearing. *I've had to use a firearm for personal protection.*

Mark Masterson and Brian White were speaking about the poker game. Granted, it was in a way no one would understand. No one but me. Their willingness to discuss that night made me wonder: If Caraway was lead detective on Twomey's murder, she had to know as much about that night as anyone other than the people in the room. That meant she knew my mom hadn't fired the shots. What I didn't know is whether she knew who had, or whether she even cared. I ran a series of searches trying to link Masterson to Joanne Caraway, but found nothing other than a couple police banquets where they both appeared on the guest list. That didn't mean much, though. They were both smart enough to keep any connection off the internet.

What I did find were hundreds of links to mentions of Mark Masterson. I read interviews on obscure financial blogs. I scrutinized photos of the financial advisor on Google Images. His hair was mostly gray rather than brown these days, and he had a weirdly rectangular face, usually framed above a silk tie and tailored suit. His Instagram account was private, but I found his Twitter handle, which he used to promote Masterson Wealth Management Services. I read a few press releases about MWMS and found photos of him looking serious, staring out at Portland from his office at Big Pink. I scanned transcripts of more podcasts. It was clear Masterson wasn't a major-league player in the financial industry. He wasn't having lunch with executives at Goldman Sachs. He was a self-promoter who managed a solid boutique firm catering to clients who wanted to shield their money from taxes in ways that were *legal, but aggressive.* He used that phrase over and over in interviews.

I perked up when I landed on something that got the criminal side of my mind churning. It was an interview he'd done after the Mossack Fonseca papers—also known as the Panama Papers—had broken worldwide. If you haven't heard of them, the Panama Papers were a stash of over ten million documents, stolen and leaked, chronicling both the legal financial transactions and the crimes of hundreds of people over a forty-year period. The documents named a dozen current or former world leaders, over a hundred other public officials and politicians, and hundreds of celebrities, businessmen, and other wealthy individuals from two hundred countries. In addition to using offshore shell companies for all sorts of technically legal but ethically questionable tactics, they illustrated hundreds of cases of fraud, tax evasion, and evasion of international sanctions.

In the interview, Masterson condemned the leak and defended the financial institutions being raked over the coals. "Bearer shares are a secure and valuable instrument," he argued, "and this trumped-up so-called scandal just shows that they need to be handled with care and discretion. Of course, care and discretion are our watchwords at Masterson Wealth Management. Working with bearer shares allows individuals to avoid the overreach of government and taxation by keeping ownership anonymous and transactions off the books. They do bring slightly more risk than other financial instruments we can employ, but sometimes you have to take a little risk if you want your finances to really rock and roll."

I'd never heard of bearer shares, but he seemed keen on them, so I read a handful of articles to get the basics, then a few more to confirm they were *actually* legal, because I honestly couldn't believe they were.

Bearer shares appeared to be Masterson's specialty. He'd even testified before the Oregon State Legislature when they tried to pass a law to regulate them more forcefully. Kellen Blackstone had lobbied against the bill and, predictably, it didn't pass.

Normally, if you own shares of a company, those shares are held in your 401k, or your eTrade account, or at a brokerage. Each purchase and sale is recorded, and you pay taxes on profits. Bearer shares work differently. Whoever holds the actual stock certificate—the physical piece of paper—also owns the corresponding shares of the company. Shares are anonymously owned, unregistered, and untraceable. The only way to tell who owns them is to find out who is literally holding them. When the owner of the piece of paper changes, so does the owner of that portion of the company. Most importantly, if that company is a shell, incorporated in a small country whose entire legislative agenda is purchased by billionaires, its entire ownership may be held in bearer shares. That lets rich bastards move money between one another without involving any names, and without paying taxes to any legitimate government.

I've got above-average search skills, but I'm no hacker. Luckily, you can dig up a ton on just about anyone from a series of well-conceived online searches. Social media is a good place to start because most people leave clues they're not aware of. Location tags, license plate numbers or addresses in the backgrounds of images, those sorts of things. And you can get a good sense of someone's routines by studying the times at which they post. If you're willing to sit in front of a laptop all night and dig deep, interesting things appear. The key is knowing where and how to look. Masterson's public posts led me to links he'd posted to less-public places. Some of those links were clearly written by the same man, tagged with a different user name. Turned out that Mark Masterson also posted anonymously as Masterclass69, and that term helped narrow my search. I found comments on old financial forums, even an archived MySpace page. I created a fake account on a blog called Wealth Management Elites, where Masterson was a frequent commenter as MrMasterclass.

The more I looked, the more I learned how specialized his services were. He wasn't the type of guy who moved your money from stocks to bonds, who built a diversified portfolio aiming for a steady rate of return. He was no Bernie Madoff either. This wasn't some big Ponzi scheme designed to rip off his investors. From what I could tell, he was good at his job, even if that job was making shady moves for select clients in special situations:

Getting ready to divorce your wife and need to hide ten million in assets before the judge rules on the case? Call MWMS. We'll convert equity in a business into untraceable bearer shares and hold them for you until the divorce is finalized.

Got inside information on a stock you want to capitalize on, but don't want to trigger an SEC investigation? Call MWMS and let us set up a series of shell corporations. We'll buy the stock on your behalf and split the profits.

Company had a banner year and you don't feel like paying taxes on that income? Let MWMS re-route the money to Ireland via Denmark, using the tax treaty network. After all, if Apple can stash its profits overseas, why can't you?

Want to slide your tax bracket from 37 to 32 percent? No problem! We'll maximize your IRA and 401k contributions to lower your take-home pay. That not enough? We'll buy a second home through a shell company and front-load mortgage payments to bring your income below the magic number.

Need to "clean" a million in illicit cash? Call MWMS and we'll use a shell corporation to buy a nice waterfront lot that just happens to be in a development zone overseen by our pal, Kellen Blackstone.

And this was just what I could figure out from six hours of reading.

I scoured every mention of Masterson in the press and read every interview I found. Officially, MWMS held over eighty million dollars in assets. That meant the *real* number was at least twice that. Standard investment brokers made one or two percent of the total value of the money they managed. Masterson's specialized services would get him more, making him a millionaire many times over.

I looked for other businesses registered in Masterson's name, or in the name of his firm. Turned out that MWMS was Masterson's only asset, but the company itself owned six smaller companies, each of which owned several holding companies, each designed to hide money in various ways. The bottom line was that lots of millionaires trusted this guy with their money. Not only that, they trusted him to execute their shadiest manipulations of the tax code, their most aggressive sheltering of their wealth.

My eyes were drooping by the time I found a quote that popped them wide open in an online forum called Wealth Managers United. The free account I set up allowed me to read old threads, but not make comments of my own. Searching a variation of Masterson's favored username, I found dozens of posts, mostly repetitive advice or views I already knew. But in one thread about security and safe deposit boxes, I found something different.

He'd been arguing with an investor who liked to hold capital in gold and gems, as well as bearer shares and bearer bonds, stashing them in multiple safe deposit boxes all over the city. The other guy called it "diversifying your locations." After arguing back and forth for a while, Masterson summed up his feelings with a short, pithy comment: "Bank vaults aren't actually safer than protecting your own shit." There he was, admitting in a forum he believed to be anonymous, that he protected his own assets. Assets that were untraceable, and worth millions.

I read those smug, clever-stupid words, and I was fourteen again. I could almost smell the pizza in the little place Soup used to deal from. For the first time since that day, a job coalesced in my mind in a single instant, fully-formed from setup to getaway. The rush of insight was dizzyingly intense, and the pleasure of it settled into me like the full feeling after a good meal. Why in hell had I ever turned away from this?

At some point I dozed off. I was used to my dreams being murky or upsetting—odd jumbles of people and events I couldn't understand, or didn't want to. That night was different. The dream felt more real than reality, even after I woke.

It started with me as a teenager, but instead of living a sad life on Cemetery Lane, instead of busing out to the prison to find Rabbit

Rafferty and ending up crying on the side of the road, I was an international criminal. It was as though all the scenes I'd missed, all the crimes I hadn't committed, were occurring in real time.

And in the dream I grew. From a teenager to an adult, and all the way to the present day. The dream didn't show the payoffs of my crimes. I didn't get rich and sit on a pile of money on a private island. There were no harems of women, no mounds of cocaine, no flashy houses or cars. In the dream, I'd simply figure out crimes and execute them. I found holes in security systems, opened locks, conned marks with easy charm, and put together small crews. The pieces of the caper always fell together perfectly. I was a conductor, and the music I made was beautiful.

When I woke, the sky was dark purple, a color that belonged to five in the morning, a couple hours before dawn. In my mind there was a split between the two Brandon Pennys. It felt physical, like the front half of my brain was careening forward, researching, making connections, scoping out the shape and the pace of the crime, the escape, the fence. In the back of my mind, a finger wagged. A hesitance lived there, a voice that said, *This is not what is done, Brandon.* It wasn't Jennifer's voice, but I felt her nearby.

I cracked the window to let in a breeze. Birds chirped and an occasional car splashed through a puddle. The cold air felt good on my face.

The split in my mind carried on a conversation, and I watched it in slow motion, as though viewing an odd, Technicolor dream of my life. The front half of my mind was composing a note to my mom, using our secure app, of course. The back half told me to get in bed and go to sleep. A gust of cold air hit my face, jolting me into action.

I watched myself walk back to the chair and pick up the phone mom had given me. I tapped out a message. *The microchips aren't the job. I've got a better target. The job is on a different floor, and it's a day earlier.*

The Daily Barometer, June 2, 2007

Twomey Belts Beavers to Semi-Finals

By Darren Bakkar

Tyler Twomey, OSU's star first baseman, batted in all five runs against Washington State yesterday, leading the Beavers to a 5-2 win and bringing the team one game away from its first PAC-12 title in six years. Twomey batted 4-for-5 with three doubles, adding a diving catch in the sixth inning with runners on second and third that saved at least two runs.

After the game, Twomey credited the pitching performance of junior Michael Voltario for the win. "We played well," he said, "but he [Voltario] was pitching with a lot of confidence out there, and that gives us a lot of confidence at the plate. When you only need a few runs to get the win, you can swing freely."

The Beavers are now 31-19 on the season, their best record in six years.

Chapter Eighteen

They say the truth will set you free. I felt freer than I had in twenty years.

I stepped into the cold dawn, high on the intoxicating feeling of seeing through something that had been opaque. Mark Masterson was a money launderer and tax evader, as well as a killer. And I was fairly sure that Caraway's special interest in my mom went beyond a misguided attempt to solve an old murder.

Payday had hit that morning and I had a fresh $850 in my account, most of which was spoken for, but I was going to treat myself. I hadn't eaten since Giordano's, so I aimed toward the corner store for a six-pack and a chicken pot pie. The new heist had formed in my mind faster than I could control. As I walked, every star twinkled just for me, a secret message that I could break into the Bancorp Tower. Every gust of wind blew only to let me know that I was destined by God to rob Mark Masterson.

I noticed the blue-and-white following me before rounding the first corner. It was half a block behind, cruising slowly in my direction. It wasn't a tail, I knew that right away. If the driver had been trying to disguise the fact that he was following me, the car would have crept forward, lights off, until I turned the corner. Instead, it pulled up right alongside me, headlights on.

I glanced at the cop behind the wheel, whose face was shadowed so I couldn't get a clear view. Judging by the shape of the head, it was a large man, not Carebear or the dude in the Eisenhower jacket. The man kept turning his wide face to look at me, then back to the road, then back to me.

There was no need to try to ditch them. After all, I was just out for a six-pack and a pot pie. I didn't run or even change my pace as he rolled down the window.

"Where ya headed?" he asked amiably. With the window down I got a better look at him. He was in his mid-twenties, clean-shaven, and had the look of a guy you'd get to play a generic meathead in an Eighties movie. His forehead was broad and his hair was one of those square buzzcuts you don't see much anymore.

My brain naturally reached for appropriate lies, but I was hungry as hell and saw no reason not to tell the truth. "Corner store. Dinner time."

Another cop leaned forward in the passenger seat and rested his elbow on the dashboard. "At five in the morning? Pretty late for that, no?" His face was sharp, marked by irregular angles, as though his cheekbones, jaw, and nose had been broken and healed crooked. Light from a nearby streetlamp reflected off his bald head, making it shine like a cue ball before the break.

I shrugged.

He shook his head slowly, like a disapproving parent. "Really no reason to be out so late."

Officer Meathead had slowed the car to keep pace with me as I walked, and the store was only half a block away. A car alarm wailed nearby. The street was dark and deserted, which worried me when combined with the officers' casual but snarky tones.

Officer Cueball said, "Sure you're not out to *steal* something?"

My face tightened and I slowed my walk involuntarily. Up to that moment I'd hoped they might be harassing me on general principle, figuring I was a dealer or something. But the way he said the word "steal" told me that Carebear had sent them. I've met some friendly, hardworking cops who aren't on the take and are just trying to do a day's work for a day's pay, which I can respect, even if I wouldn't trust them to change a dime for two nickels. These dudes were different. Everything about them exuded corruption. Caraway wasn't trying to frame my mom as her personal pet project, now she was using other officers in the department to do her dirty work.

"Just out for a six-pack and a pot pie." I said it with as much bravado as I could muster, but I was nervous.

Officer Meathead put his hand out the window and struck the door of his car with a kind of *yee-haw* flourish. "Sounds delicious."

The car rolled alongside me as I entered the store's parking lot. Meathead and Cueball watched me walk into the store. I browsed the beers, studying their reflections in the fridge as Cueball spoke into his radio.

I pretended not to care, but I was roiling inside. Something had changed. They weren't here to arrest me. If they were going to do that, they would have done it. And they weren't trailing me to try to find my mom or catch me in a crime. This was intimidation, plain and simple. I wondered if Carebear knew about my line of research. My laptop had full VPN protection, better than anything the PPB was going to break. My apartment could be bugged, but not this quickly. Anyway, I'd listened to the podcasts on my earbuds, so a bug would have just heard me typing and occasionally muttering the phrase "That bastard!"

Assuming they didn't have anything solid on me, it was possible they'd already arrested my mom. Hell, by now Caraway might even have pinned the Twomey murder on *me*. I was being ridiculous, but it's surprising what goes through your mind when two cops are watching you through a convenience store window.

I walked out with my food and beer in a brown paper bag, eyes straight ahead but fully aware of the location of the cops. The long, dark block stretched before me like an ominous shadow. They followed in their blue-and-white, staying a few yards behind me. Each of my steps was heavy, each breath echoed. Time slowed, like when you pass a speed trap on the highway and watch until you're sure no flashing lights are going to appear in your rearview mirror.

Turning the corner onto my street, I felt relief. I was half a block from the safety of home.

The engine revved and the car sped up, suddenly pulling twenty feet ahead of me. For a glorious instant I thought they'd received an urgent call and were leaving so they could race toward the scene of the crime. Then the car stopped, right in the center of the road. The lights flashed and, before I could make a move, Officer Cueball was walking toward me with long, determined strides. "On the ground," he barked.

Startled, I dropped my bag. A beer bottle shattered.

I considered running, but Cueball was fast; he moved like an athlete. I didn't think I could outrun him, and even if I could...

I didn't have time to finish the thought. He was in front of me. He knocked my legs out from under me with a swift kick and I fell back, barely protecting my head as my side hit the remaining bottles of beer and I tumbled into the street. I rolled up against the curb, then onto my back, smelling gutter filth and the hoppy, floral notes of my broken IPAs.

Cueball stared down at me.

A car door slammed. Meathead appeared, standing next to Cueball. He was a lot taller than his partner, but much less threatening. Even lying on my back in the street, my shoe wet with beer, I read the guy as soft.

Cueball, on the other hand, looked vicious. His cheek was scarred where before I'd noticed irregular bone angles. And his scowl showed real contempt. "He tried to run." His voice was sharp and certain.

Meathead looked side to side as though making sure no one was watching. "Resisting arrest, Brandon?"

Gathering myself, I asked, "Am I under arrest?"

Cueball kicked me in the ribs, so swiftly that it took my breath before I felt the screaming pain. "Not yet."

Everything in me burned to grab his leg and pull him down. But I'm not much of a fighter. I got in a few scuffles in the foster homes, but I always preferred to talk my way out of trouble. Sometimes, I ran and lived to fight another day. But the thing with cops, especially ones who are trying to intimidate you, is that if you run, you give them a reason to arrest you. If you fight back—no matter what they're doing to you—you give them an excuse to kill you. And the more I looked at Cueball's scowl, the more I thought he was a fighter. He had the cauliflower ears that wrestlers and MMA fighters develop through years of having their faces pressed into mats. If I was right, he could break any number of my bones, and he was clearly anxious to do so.

I put on my most polite tone. "Then am I free to return to my apartment?"

"Not yet." Meathead raised his voice to compete with Cueball's. "We want to talk to you, Brandon."

"Can I stand up?"

Cueball crouched next to me. "No, you can't." His breath smelled like pepperoni. "You're not going to move, hear me?"

I felt a trickle on the side of my face and a sharp pain above it. I'd cut myself on a bit of broken bottle. I reached up to touch it and he grabbed my wrist, twisting it back and to the side.

"Okay okay okay," I cried out, trying to turn with the bend of my wrist.

"Were you reaching for a weapon, Brandon?" He pinned my arm to the ground with a bony knee and twisted my wrist harder. Pain shot down my forearm and into my shoulder. He smiled, then looked up at Meathead. "I think he was reaching for a weapon."

"Should we take him in?" Meathead asked. "Reaching for a weapon in the presence of an officer is attempted murder."

"I'm not armed," I offered weakly. "I've never owned a weapon."

Cueball twisted harder. "Did I tell you to speak, boy?"

I closed my eyes, let my body go limp. I hated him, hated *them*. Fantasies of bloody murder moved through my mind, maybe just to distract from the pain. After what felt like forever, he let go.

Cueball's voice was cold and calm, letting me know he was in control of the situation, not me. "Don't say another word until I tell you." It was the voice of a man doing a normal job on a normal day.

I said nothing.

He leaned in close, lowering his voice to a hard whisper. "There's a very nice person who is trying to help you, but you're being incredibly disrespectful to her. Ungrateful. She's trying and trying to help you, and you can't even give her a phone call. I can't *believe* the rudeness of people like you. When someone is trying to help you, you're supposed to accept that help and show *gratitude*. But a piece of shit like you can't even do that. You can't understand kindness even when it's being shown to you, so I'm telling you in terms you *can* understand. Call her back. Do what she tells you to do. Got it?"

"Yes."

Cueball waited until I met his eyes. "You *really* don't want to see us again, do you?"

"No, sir."

"Why not?" Meathead asked. "Don't you like us?"

"Yes, sir."

Meathead let out a heavy, wet laugh that reminded me of Jabba the Hutt. "Yes you *do* like us? Or yes you *don't* like us?"

I said nothing. Cueball twisted my wrist harder. I tried to turn with the twist, but he ground my arm into the pavement with his knee. He was vicious and well-trained, and I was glad I hadn't run. He would have beaten the living hell out of me, if he hadn't shot me in the back.

Something in my mind snapped and I opened my eyes, somehow removing myself from the pain. "How far are you going to take this?"

Cueball sneered down at me, a look of hatred and condescension. I was the lowest scum on earth. "Answer my friend's question."

"What question?"

"Do you like us or not?"

"I do not."

Putting all his weight into his knee, he raised up on my arm, digging the bone into my bicep. I squirmed in agony, but kept looking at him as tears filled my eyes.

Meathead cleared his throat and Cueball looked up. I couldn't see what he saw but the way he eased off made me think someone was coming. As much as he was enjoying this, he was smart enough to know that a concerned citizen with a cellphone camera and a Twitter account could ruin his week.

He let go of my wrist and knelt beside me.

Not wanting to make a sudden movement, I slowly moved my wrist in small circles. He leaned in and whispered in my ear. "Our friend says you need to deliver your mom's location in the next twenty-four hours. Don't fuck with her, Brandon. Truly."

He leapt up like a fighter springing off the mat. I rolled onto my side and watched from the street as they hopped into the car and pulled away. They drove the half block back to my apartment building and parked exactly where they'd been before.

An old guy shuffled down the block. He looked at me in the street and smiled as he leaned over my broken six-pack. Finding the two unbroken bottles, he asked, "May I?"

I nodded and he pulled me out of the gutter, then continued down the street, stuffing one beer in each pocket of his baggy jeans.

I tucked the soggy pot pie box under my arm and trudged back to my apartment.

Chapter Nineteen

M om was running late. I'd arrived at McMenamins Chapel
    Pub in North Portland right when they opened for lunch,
and had already been waiting ten minutes. I chose McMenamins
because it's a Portland institution and I wouldn't be living in Portland
much longer. The joint had a long history. The brick building in
which it was housed had once been the Little Chapel of the Chimes.
The place was cavernous, with an old tugboat-shaped mahogany bar,
tin ceilings, and a second-floor wraparound balcony with a gorgeous
ironwork railing. Even the chandeliers were the originals from 1932, a
frosted-glass art-deco style that looked like large Christmas ornaments. I had a sentimental fondness for the bar because it's the first
spot I used my fake ID when I was eighteen. It had over fifty craft
beers on tap and I'd ordered two pints of what I'd ordered then,
because only McMenimans had it: Ruby Ale on draft.

I tried to pick up my beer and my wrist barked in pain, sparking a
flash of memory and anger. When I'd messaged my mom before my
ill-fated trip to the corner store, I didn't say much about the new job.
Maybe I was being cautious, or maybe I hadn't been sure I was willing
to go through with it. Crooks don't just wander around all day stealing
stuff at random. Most thieves have an on-off switch that has to do with

lines he will and will not cross. For some it's connected to a moral code: *I'll steal, but I'll never use violence*, or *I'll rob, but only those who are rich*. For others, it's a simple calculation of what he can get away with: *I can rob two houses in this neighborhood in a month, but three or more would bring too much heat*, or, *If I can pay off both security guards to stand down, I'll roll that jewelry store. If not, I walk away*.

Most people who think of themselves as non-criminals have the same switch. *I can jaywalk and get away with it, but not right in front of a cop. Weed should be legal anyway, so I'll smoke this joint. Sure, downloading this movie violates copyright laws, but those companies have tons of money. I can claim a few grand in fake expenses for my small business. After all, the big companies do it, but if I get TOO crazy, the IRS will catch me.*

These are the little calculations we make every day to break the rules we don't agree with or think we can get away with breaking. Professional thieves make the same judgments, but with higher stakes and harsher penalties. When Ricky and my mom decided to use unloaded guns the night of the poker game, they made the following calculation: *We are willing to use guns, opening us to armed-robbery charges, while at the same time making our theft more likely to succeed. But we're not willing to load them, so we won't end up with a murder or attempted-murder rap.* Of course, the second part didn't really work out.

For sixteen years I'd fallen on the conservative side of these calculations. My crime switch was firmly in the "Off" position. Ricky Gat's revelation had put a finger on that switch. Getting roughed up by Meathead and Cueball had flipped it for good. One way or another, I was leaving Portland—either on a plane with a fake ID and a bag full of money, or in the back of a cop car to join Ricky in prison. Unless... I thought of Jennifer. I was still trying to merge my two lives into one. But our messages from last night felt like they'd been sent in another time, by different people.

I finished my pint and started on my mom's, wondering whether she'd show up. The beer was helping, but my sliver of doubt widened with every tick of the clock. *What if she'd been picked up by Caraway?* I doubted it. If Carebear had nabbed my mom, she wouldn't have sent those two guys to intimidate me. *What if she'd gotten to know me enough over the last two days to realize she wanted nothing to do with me?* That thought was harder to sit with. As much as my rational brain told me it was ridiculous, the twelve-year-old in me expected her to disappear again. By the time she arrived a full half hour late, I'd finished her pint and ordered another round. I decided this would be my last beer. Three pints was enough to numb the pain, but at four I'd start making bad decisions.

I narrowed my eyes as she sat. "Why are you late?"

She gripped the beer, then ran her hand through her hair without taking a sip.

I studied the prints her warm fingers had left on the frosted pint glass. "Where were you?"

"Physically, I was walking the riverfront. Mentally, I was..." She trailed off, taking a long, slow sip of beer.

"You were thinking about ditching me."

She nodded. "When I got your message, I thought, we can't go down this road again. You're gonna end up in jail or—"

"*You* never did."

"I'm good at this, and I've been lucky. It takes both."

"You said yourself I'm good at this, too."

"But you may not be as lucky."

I couldn't argue with that. No matter how good a thief you are, no plan is perfect. In the movies, criminals are often up against a dogged detective who's just as smart, or smarter, and their battle often comes down to a dramatic confrontation of wits and physical prowess. In real life, whether you get caught more often depends on whether someone snitches, or whether you get unlucky. Soup had a saying about being a criminal. *It's fifty percent what you know and fifty percent who you know. The other fifty percent is dumb luck.*

"I don't have a choice any more, Mom. What I didn't tell you yet is that I was in touch with a detective. She was on the job that night. Pulled me in for questioning. Been riding me for information. Still wants to pin the murder on you and—" She raised her hand to object, like she still needed to convince me that she and Ricky hadn't killed the security guard. "No, lemme finish. She came to my work a few days ago. A threat. Last night, two cops were outside my apartment." I pointed to the scabs on my cheek where my face had ground into the pavement. "They roughed me up."

She stood, fists clenched. Her eyes darted wildly around the pub, like she was ready for a fight. I thought she was mad at me, then realized she was mad at the cops. She loomed over the table, a mama bear protecting her cub from danger.

"It's okay," I said. "Sit."

When she finally sat, her eyes surveyed the place suspiciously. I'd only seen her like this once before, when I got in a fight in school in fourth grade and we had to attend a meeting with the other boy and his parents. He'd blackened my eye and while she said all the right things, she had the same suspicious, protective crazy eyes she was displaying right now. "Really, I'm fine. But it's nice to see you care." I didn't mean it sarcastically, but I could tell I'd wounded her.

Her eyes stopped dancing, dropped to the table. "I always cared. Lemme tell you something, Brand. You asked whether I looked you up, whether I thought about coming to find you. And I know you may not believe me, but I really did think it was the best thing for you. But there were the nights." She cleared her throat. "You see, by daylight I was always able to convince myself I'd done the right thing. When I tried to fall asleep, I lost the ability to believe that. I'd lie awake for hours, thinking I'd done something unforgivable. And I *had* done something unforgivable. Either way was unforgivable."

"So in your mind, there were two options: be a crook while dragging me along, or be a crook while leaving me behind?"

"That's right."

I waited for her to catch my look, but her eyes dropped away and she took a sip of beer. She seemed somehow embarrassed.

"And?" I asked. "The third option?"

"Just being a normal person was never really an option for me. I'm starting to think it was never an option for you either."

"I tried," I said. "I really did."

"We're natural-born thieves."

We sipped our beers, both allowing the truth of what she'd said to land.

Finally she said, "Tell me about the detective."

"Joanne Caraway. Dirty as hell, and she wants you."

She stared into her pint glass. "I don't understand. Anything on you and that night is ancient history. Until yesterday you hadn't done anything, and even the keycard thing isn't much."

"You're talking like things are fair or rational. Why would you think that?"

"I—"

"Here's what I think: when she first brought me in, Caraway had a convincing story that you shot that security guard."

"I never even—"

"Mom, I believe you, but here's the thing. If Caraway was involved in the investigation of the poker game, she *knows* you didn't do it."

My mom was right there with me. "And if she knows I didn't do it and was trying to pin it on me, she did it either because she wants the collar, or because she knows who *did* do it."

I rapped the base of my pint glass gently on the table, a quiet tap of affirmation. "Exactly." I didn't want to tell her that I knew who did. We'd softened on each other, but that didn't mean I had to tell her everything.

"What else do you know about the detective?"

"Not a lot, but I've got a few ideas for how to find out. Point is, we're doing this job tomorrow night. You want to hear about it or not?"

She nodded, which gave me permission to dive into the research. I told her about bearer shares and MWMS, including everything I knew about their office at Big Pink. I explained how I planned to move the stolen items, assuming the job was successful. Finally, I connected MWMS to Mark Masterson.

She'd been with me up to that moment. She said, "Wait, Brandon, Mark Masterson from the poker game?"

When I was a kid, she rarely said my entire first name, preferring "Brand," or "Keyser," or another one of the half-dozen nicknames her friends and associates tried out on me. "Brandon" was reserved for when I was in trouble.

Did you eat all the chocolate-chip cookies when I specifically said you could only have one, Brandon?

Brandon, did you really start a homework-for-hire scheme and get suspended from fifth grade?

I was in trouble now because you do not—you *do not*—do crimes for personal reasons. That's how idiots get busted for torching their ex's truck. It's how dumbasses get arrested for stealing from someone against whom they have an ugly public grudge. Doing crimes for personal reasons is just handing the cops a signed envelope labeled *Motive.*

When I didn't answer immediately, she continued. "Tell me you switched up the job because it's a better heist with lower risk and a higher payout, and not because you want to get back at Masterson. Tell me that, Brandon."

"He was the shooter."

I hadn't planned to tell her that and, to my amazement, she didn't even flinch. She'd always known one of those five men was the shooter. To her, the specifics didn't matter.

"Even if you're right, we can't... we don't do crimes for revenge."

"Mom, this is a better job, easier, and for more money. Probably *way* more money." I didn't tell her I'd burned her microchip job with my email to Caraway. And I wasn't going to admit to wanting revenge. "This. Is. A. Better. Job."

She stared at me long and hard, and I wondered whether she suspected I was holding something back. All of a sudden, her shoulders shot back and her demeanor changed. She was in work mode. "Escape plan? I had one, but it's different with you involved."

"I'll need a passport. I have an idea of where we can go, and how. It'll allow us to get out of the country and move the bearer shares." I wrote the location and the name of the only airline that flew there on a scrap of paper and slid it across the table. "Can you get tickets, paying cash?"

"Sure. I've got a passport. You?"

I was way ahead of her. "I can get one. Might have to wait out of state somewhere for a few days, depending. That a problem?"

"Not if nothing else screws up, no."

"Car?"

"Already have one parked a half mile from the job. Across the river at Southeast Third and Market."

"Good."

"What name do you want on the ticket?"

I thought awhile, jotted the name on another scrap of paper, handed it to her, and walked out.

I paused on the curb, squinting into the winter sun and thinking about Jennifer. In my mind I composed a series of texts. In one I told her I'd left town for an emergency pharmacy conference, which made me chuckle bitterly because there was no such thing. In another I asked to get together next week, as though I'd still be around next week. In the third version I told her the whole truth about me, my mom, and what we were about to do.

I didn't send her a text. I had to find a way to break it off completely, but couldn't bring myself to do it. I hopped a bus and headed for Ace's Quick Cash.

December 9, 2017

Dear Brandon,

When we met, my first impression was that I'd finally met my soulmate when it came to movies. I've had a great time this last year, and I hoped our relationship would open up into something else, something more. But after talking last night, it's obvious that our futures don't align.

I believe in a future where the past is fixable, or at least can be overcome. I don't think you believe this, but the truth is I don't know what you believe because you're so closed down about everything. I don't want to be with a man who can't open up, who can't face his past honestly, a man who can't see a brighter future on the horizon.

There was a time when I thought it was enough for a partner to be faithful and decent to me, but I know now that I want more. You're a special person. Smart and kind and fundamentally good. I thought that, in time, you'd be able to trust me, to trust yourself, to trust our relationship. It's best we part now and learn to live without each other instead of going on together knowing it will end. I hate that it has to be this way. Even though it hurts right now, this is what's best for both of us.

I'll always care for you,
   Jennifer

Chapter Twenty

I hated involving Soup any more than necessary, but he was my best shot at getting a passport on short notice. That is, if I could ever get him alone. When I walked into Ace's, he was in a spirited debate with an old lady about the value of a particular six-string guitar. She was trying everything she could to get the price down: *There's a crack in the fingerboard. My grandson is turning nine. I only have eighty dollars.* By the time they settled on a hundred bucks, there were two people in line behind me. I stepped to the side, allowing them to go ahead. And I waited.

Getting roughed up by the cops made me think about Oregon's distinguished criminal history, some of which is quirky and weird, like the story of the murdered lions or that time the Rajneesh cult poisoned a salad bar in The Dalles. There's a bleaker side, too.

In the pioneer days, most of the crimes in and around Portland involved either timber, gold, or racism. Often, it was more than one at the same time. In May 1887, thirty-four Chinese gold miners were murdered by a gang of white horsemen in what became known as the Hell's Canyon Massacre. That's appalling, but it wasn't even atypical. Even as Oregon banned slavery in 1844, the government passed a law requiring that African-Americans leave the territory. Any Black person who remained could be flogged publicly every six months until he left. When Oregon adopted its state constitution in 1857, it officially banned Black people from coming to the state, residing in the state, or holding property in the state. Like I said, the biggest crimes are always legal. Finally, after a stylish young guy in front of me paid for an old vintage coat and left, Soup said, "Thought you'd be back. How's your mom?"

From the way he asked, I thought it unlikely that he'd been in touch with her since he arranged our meeting at the zoo. I walked a little square around the store, trying to decide how much to tell him. "She's... it's complicated. We reconnected. I need an ID."

Soup grabbed a roll of paper towels and a spray bottle of cleaner from behind the counter. He crouched, still limber despite his age, and began wiping down the glass. "I hate when people lean on my display cases. You see that? Windex ain't free."

There were a few smudges and fingerprints, but nothing I'd have noticed if he hadn't mentioned it. I watched him clean, growing more and more worried that he hadn't responded to my mention of the ID.

Finally, he said, "So you're back in it?"

"Yeah."

"With Dolly?"

"With my mom, yeah. We're—"

"Don't want to hear it."

I walked another square, guilt building inside me. I could find someone else to get me a fake ID, but I couldn't find anyone I could trust the way I trusted this creaky old crook. "So, can you help?"

Soup stood and set the cleaning supplies on the display case. "How does she look these days? Still a beauty?"

"Can we not talk about how my mom looks?"

"Sure, but she's doing well and everything?"

"Yeah, she's good."

"She need anything?"

It took me a moment to understand that he was asking if she needed an ID as well. "Nah, she's good."

"When do you need it?"

"That's the thing. As soon as possible. I need a passport, not just a DL."

Soup walked around the counter and plopped on his stool. "I got you."

"You do?"

"Yeah, don't worry. Come by around dinner time."

"Cool, I can... Wait, dinner time *today*?"

He shrugged. "What I said."

Dots connected themselves fast in my head—how Soup kept hanging on with a pawnshop that few people patronized, the way he changed the subject when I talked about certain things, why giving up dealing had been so easy for him.

For years, I'd believed Soup had gone straight, just like me. The truth was, he'd never joined me in the club of *People Who Used To Do Crime But Stopped*. I'd only added myself to the list of *Chumps Who Believed Soup Stopped Doing Crime*. The first club was small enough, but I may have been the *only* member of the second one. He *had* stopped dealing weed; he'd just moved to dealing high-end fake IDs instead.

Knowing he'd lied to me had the bizarre effect of making me trust him more. When he thought he was talking to a kid who'd had "law-abiding citizen" beaten into him by the system, he'd fed that kid what he wanted to hear, needed to hear. Now that he was dealing with a fellow criminal, he had no need to be dishonest.

I slid an envelope across the counter. Inside was a slip of paper with my new name on it, plus a passport-sized photo I'd gotten in the vintage photo booth at the retro arcade on my way over. That photo booth wouldn't remember me the way a drugstore clerk or big-box store photo-department worker would.

Soup opened the envelope and thumbed through its contents. "Nice name. But there's no money in here. I want a piece."

"Of what?"

"Of whatever you and Dolly are up to, which I don't want to know anything about."

"Sure," I said. "If it works, you'll get a nice piece, but I want something else."

"I could tell, y'know. There's two kinds of energy in you. Theft energy and revenge energy. You got the second popping out of your eyes."

"Wait, what do you mean?"

He shoved his plastic toothpick in his mouth and stared at me. Soup had watched me closely when my mom was around, but probably even more closely since. He'd kept an eye on me back when he was selling me weed. He'd known me when I was angry, known when I wanted to track down Rabbit Rafferty. And he'd known I went straight, maybe even hoped it would stick. He knew me better than I knew myself. And he knew all along that, if I ever learned what happened that night, I'd want revenge.

I dove into the topic I'd only dipped my toe in for two decades. "I've never actually asked this, but what do you know about what went down that night?"

"Been waiting for that question for twenty years." He smiled. "Not gonna say I know everything about it, but I know a little."

"And that little is?"

He set the envelope on the counter and shoved his hands in his pockets. "So there was the snitch, right? Rabbit. And that's why you got pinched, but there are a couple things about it. First, police were stupid as all hell, letting the robbery go down and gettin' that dude shot just to try to sting your mom and Ricky. But that's a separate issue. I read all the papers after and I like to think I'm pretty good at reading between the lines. There was never any solid evidence leaked to the press that your mom or Ricky shot the guy."

"Because they didn't."

"I *know* that, but that's not my point. My point is"—he narrowed his eyes— "the cops would have leaked it if there *was* anything solid. Trust me, every cop who worked that case knew who fired that shot, and they covered it up all along."

"Mark Masterson was the shooter."

Soup shrugged. He didn't care who fired the shot any more than my mom did. There were crimes that could be connected to him and crimes that couldn't, and he had a professional aversion to knowing anything about the latter, including the murder of Thomas Twomey.

"You know anything about a detective named Joanne Caraway? She was—"

Soup held up a hand, cutting me off. He paced for a full minute, then dug his cellphone from under an old magazine and passed it from one hand to the other. "You want to go there? I mean, there's doing a job with your mom and then there's... digging into a crooked detective is a whole other..." He leveled his gaze on me. "You sure you want to go there?"

I looked down. "Want's got nothing to do with it. I *have* to go there. What do you know?"

Soup nodded soberly. "I know a guy who... well, he was there that night. And I can get him to talk to you." He flipped open his phone. "You familiar with the Shanghai Tunnels?"

"Does this guy know more about Caraway?"

He nodded again, and for an instant it looked like he was suppressing a smile. "Oh yeah. But you didn't answer my question. Do you know the Tunnels?"

Chapter Twenty-One

Beneath Portland's original downtown ran a series of passages and secret rooms known in local lore as the Shanghai Tunnels. Begun in the 1840s, they were used to hide and move booze during Oregon's first failed experiment with Prohibition. Expanded continuously after that, they were, at the very least, used by bars and restaurants to keep goods out of the rain, and just as likely out of the way of health and tax inspectors. But more nefarious purposes were rumored as well. The maze of interconnected basements and tunnels stretched from downtown all the way to the waterfront in what is now Chinatown. They were used by organized criminals through the late 1880s all the way into the 1950s to smuggle goods on and off ships. Other stories said the tunnels were used to ferry people in and out of opium dens and brothels. The most popular stories are of "Shanghaiing"— the practice of drugging and kidnapping men, forcing them through the tunnels and onto a ship. They'd wake up ten miles out to sea, bound for China, enslaved to the ship's captain. Or so legend had it.

Most of the tunnels had been collapsed with dynamite or boarded up, but a couple of local companies ran tours of what was left of them, using basement entrances in restaurants as launching points for the tours. There were a couple of other ways in, though. I'd learned about one from Mikey Shakes back when he was still Mikey Smooth. I'd learned about another from Soup an hour ago when he told me to meet his cop buddy there.

The meeting point was a compact "room," if you could call it that, in the western section of the Tunnels. To get there I had to pass through an entrance that reminded me of a medieval dungeon from the movies—a slatted metal gate with a busted lock, half-hidden in a stone wall under an overpass in a downtown park. I'd been waiting ten minutes, shifting my weight from one foot to the other, trying to find a way to stand that didn't exacerbate the soreness from the beating I'd taken.

The cop I was supposed to meet was named Jackson Forge. Soup said he could be trusted, and Soup telling me I could trust a cop was so impossibly strange I had no choice but to believe him. It violated everything about his three rules. It violated, well... everything. And it made me conclude that Forge was on the take, that he looked the other way when it came to whatever Soup was running in addition to his pawnshop. I didn't know for sure, but I didn't need to. If Soup said he could be trusted, I'd trust him.

Footsteps crunched on the gravel walkway, then the gate screeched open. Officer Forge walked in and closed the gate behind him. I stepped back and stood in the corner of the room, which wasn't exactly a room, more of a hollowed-out space in the dirt and rock. Everything around us was dark but for a soft gray light cutting through the spaces between the metal slats.

Forge pointed over my shoulder. I turned, but saw nothing. I flicked on my phone's flashlight. The dark tunnel seemed to go on forever.

"Let's walk," he said, his voice low.

I moved down the tunnel carefully, Forge trailing me. Shards of broken glass crunched beneath my feet, breaking the thick, underground silence. The glass was of all different colors, and the larger bits suggested beer bottles from many eras.

The stone and dirt tunnel widened and lightened. It was starting to resemble a normal hallway. I passed under a seam indicating the beginning of a new section, where the ceiling was high enough for me to stand up straight. A murky gray window at the top of the wall let in a trivial amount of light. From where, I didn't know.

Forge leaned on the wall opposite me. "Soup said you want to talk." He didn't look like the macho cop ideal, and that made me give him the benefit of the doubt.

A middle-aged Black guy, he stood a good bit shorter than me, and while he clearly still had some power in his frame, his muscles had been slowly turning to fat for years. He wore a regular patrolman's uniform, and a firm-looking but substantial gut pushed his gunbelt down to an angle. Mostly, it struck me, I'd known him less than a minute and he'd spoken eight words, but he already seemed tired of me. Everything about him screamed *I'm not here for your bullshit*. He wasn't aggressive or combative, but he gave off an aura that he'd heard it all, seen it all, and you better get to the damn point. That's probably why he got along with Soup, and why he let my old friend operate. Soup's business wasn't doing any real harm, and Forge couldn't possibly be bothered to do the paperwork required if he busted him.

He eyed me, waiting for me to get the ball rolling.

"He told me you might know something about me, about the night I got arrested."

"I do."

I kicked a small rock and watched it bounce down the dusty tunnel. "First I gotta ask: Why talk to me? What's in it for you?"

"Smart. You don't trust cops. Just like I don't trust crooks. Except for Soup." He laughed loud—too loud—and the echo filled the cavern. I imagined the sound moving down the hallway and into the park, but I had no idea how the acoustics actually worked in a space like this. "Me and Soup owe each other half a hundred favors. He called one in." He held up both hands, warning me off. "But you should know, I ain't gonna say much."

"That's fine. I'm not out to get you in any trouble. There are just some things I need to know."

"Let's walk."

"How deep does this go?"

225

"Not far." He took the lead this time, producing a flashlight that illuminated a crumbling stone walkway. I let him go ahead a few steps. His flashlight was the kind that works pretty well as a club, and I didn't intend to step in range of it. The walls transitioned from stone to brick, then back to stone as we reached an arched portion where the hallway widened, like we were passing beneath a bridge. We stopped at what looked like a prison cell, maybe six feet by six feet, like half a cage built into a crumbling brick wall.

I tapped on the bars, which let out a dull, echoless ring. "What was that used for?"

"They say that's where they held prisoners before Shanghaiing them."

"You think that was real?"

He shrugged. It was one of the most hotly contested bits of local criminal history. Forge couldn't care less. He truly didn't have time for this shit.

I walked on, gesturing for him to follow. I wanted him to think it was to move to an even more private spot. I had a half dozen questions burning to be answered, but the truth was, I was buying time.

About a year into my relationship with Jennifer, a friend told me he'd seen her out with another guy. The news triggered a kind of paranoia I'd never felt before. I ruminated all day at work. When I got home, I fidgeted on my couch, waiting for her to get back from class so I could confront her. I was angry. I was hurt. Mostly I didn't know what I was feeling. When she opened the door that night, I panicked. I didn't *want* to know the truth. *What if she's in love with him and leaves me? So what if she was out with someone else? She's here now. Why am I so insecure and petty?* As bad as it was not knowing what happened, knowing might be worse. That's how it was in the cavern with Forge. I stood on the edge of something new, trusting a cop to tell me something that could change my life.

The hallway terminated at a room that was likely the former basement of a bar or restaurant. A steep wooden staircase led to nowhere, stopping abruptly where it ran into a boarded-up ceiling. Along the wall, a wooden shelf sat empty but for a thick layer of dust. The place felt lifeless. There weren't even any spiderwebs.

Forge seemed annoyed. "Ask what you wanna ask."

"What did Soup tell you?"

"He said you're the kid."

"What kid?"

"The kid I arrested that night. The night of the Laurelhurst shooting back in ninety-eight."

"You were the..." I dropped heavily on the second step, remembering the muscular cop who'd clotheslined me as I sprinted from the house. "You put me in the car. You drove me into the station that night."

Forge rested his flashlight on a shelf at neck level so it illuminated his torso but left his face shadowed. "No hard feelings, right?" He laughed suddenly, out of nowhere. "You were fast as hell, I remember. Good thing I got the jump on you or you would have been in the wind. Not sure whether that would have been better or worse for you." His chest moved in a way that made me think he was shaking his head. His chin dipped into the light, then disappeared again.

So many questions ran through my mind at once, it nearly short-circuited.

Forge moved dirt around with his toe. "Ten minutes, kid. Told Soup I'd give you ten minutes. Go."

I took a deep breath to calm myself. The smell in the tiny room was dank and musty, an earthy, ancient smell that's not possible above ground. "How'd you guys know we were gonna rob the poker game?"

"Snitch. Bunny something."

"Rabbit Rafferty?"

He snapped his fingers. "That was it. He wasn't my snitch, but that was him. Jo-Jo called him Double-R. She got him on something or other—drugs probably—and he fed her half a dozen tips. Made her career. One great snitch sometimes makes the difference in a career."

"Jo-Jo?"

"Jo Caraway. She snooped out the poker-game. Was my partner for a few years after that, early 2000s."

I swallowed hard. "She was there, in Laurelhurst?"

"There? It was *her* bust."

Sometimes knowledge doesn't land in your mind. Sometimes it appears in your body so suddenly it feels as though it's been there the whole time. Everything Caraway had done over the last few days made sense. I understood it in my bones. She wasn't only the lead detective on the case *now*, it had been hers for days before I'd hopped on that bike in Laurelhurst.

I didn't want him to know how important the revelation was, so I turned away and said, as casually as possible, "Anything else you can tell me?"

"I *could* tell you a few things, what I *will* tell you is this: Rabbit gave her the tip, but she set it all up. I was backup, along with a half-dozen others. Pissed her off to hell when it went bad and we only snagged you and not the other two."

He fidgeted with the flashlight, easing it back and forth on the shelf. I couldn't see his face, so I didn't get a great read on him, and I assumed he wanted it that way. I was pretty sure something was bothering him.

"What else can you tell me about her?" I worried that a more specific question would make him clam up.

"Her specifically? You didn't hear a word from me. But let me talk about cops in general. You like movies?"

I nodded, no idea where he was going with this.

"In movies and TV back when I was a kid, the heroes were usually private eyes, but the cops weren't necessarily bad guys. Nowadays the cops are the heroes on all the shows my dad watches, and it's hard for me to tell him that isn't how it works. When I took all the tests and everything to become a cop, I thought it was like on TV. The good guys versus the bad guys. And maybe some of the cops were bad guys, but that was okay because the good guys would win in the end. You following me?"

I weighed my answer. "No, sorry. I get that's probably been rough or whatever, but I don't see what that has to do with Jo Caraway."

He sighed. "The nasty truth is, the line isn't between good guys and bad guys. It's between cops and *everyone else*. If you're a cop and you commit a crime, no other badge will testify against you. If you're a civilian and someone with a badge accuses you of a crime, every other cop will back up their story, whether it makes sense or not." He waved a hand dismissively, as though waving away a hundred people he was pissed at. "Even if there's pushback on this or that, it's all kept in-house. That's how it's supposed to be. That's how it is."

"Well, that sounds like a real proud way to make a living."

He shot me a harsh look. "Oh, you can talk, *thief*. You take money from people who worked for it, and you cover up for everyone like you, exact same as we do. Bet you learned how to say 'snitches get stitches' before you could walk. And you're gonna criticize *me*?"

"I'm not here to criticize you," I shot back, "and all I want to know is what's going on with Caraway."

He looked down and sighed. "Fair enough." He took a moment to gather his thoughts before he spoke again. "Look, the boring-ass truth is, cops are people like everyone else. Most of us are normal folks trying to do our job—we make mistakes, sure, and occasionally one of us does something heroic. Mostly, we grind away at life, at paperwork, and try to stay alive. Just like every other asshole out there." He picked up his flashlight, and for a moment it hit the side of his face, which I noticed for the first time had a few deep, angular scars, like he'd been slashed with a knife long ago. "But there are some people I've met, just a few, who are rotten to the core. In my business, lots of us make compromises with the law, or with the truth. We take shortcuts, just like your plumber or Uber driver, like every kid who buys Cliffs Notes instead of reading the book. But some are the *bad* kind of dirty. Corrupt. Truly wicked." His dark eyes were locked on mine, open wide in the dim light, communicating more than his words. He was talking about Caraway.

"I think I know who fired the shot that night."

He held up a hand. "Don't tell me."

I stared at him hard.

"Figured it wasn't one of the perps, but I honestly don't know who it was, and I don't want to."

"You knew it was one of the players all along?"

"Suspected as much. If the perps were going to kill the security guard, why not take him out from the jump? Why pull him off the door?" He shook his head. "Plus, two shots fired, both *toward* the front door? The way it went down never added up."

I nodded vigorously.

He continued, "So I figured it had to be one of the players. Self-defense. Don't know which. I might *guess*, but I don't *know*. Like I said, I was backup. There to grab anyone who ran, which, you know, turned out to be you."

"Why didn't you ever look into it?" It came out more accusatory than I'd intended.

He kicked the dirt. "Wasn't my case, and one thing you learn quick is that you don't last long when you start messing with other people's cases."

"You said you 'might guess' who the shooter was."

He shrugged. "Might, but I don't really care. Two perps busted in, a player fired in self-defense and hit the wrong guy. Involuntary manslaughter. Not like I was turning my back on a serial killer or something. Fucking tragedy, but wasn't gonna keep me up nights."

"Would Mark Masterson be your guess?"

His lips made a tight line. He was being careful, closing down.

"Would he?" I demanded.

"Might be."

"Why? I mean, why would he be your guess?"

He crossed his arms, refusing to answer.

I sighed. "If Masterson actually did shoot the security guard, and it was Caraway's case from the beginning..."

He shrugged.

"She was covering for Masterson for twenty years. When my mom came back to town, Caraway got spooked, right? Figured the coverup of that night might come back to bite her. She wanted to put the case to rest by busting my mom for the murder. Protect her client once and for all."

He shrugged again, looking more disengaged than ever. "I'm not saying anything about any of that. Don't know specifics of what she's up to now. But remember what I said. Most cops are decent folks. But just like in the general population, occasionally you get one who's only in it for the money. You want to know the real reason I'm helping you?"

"Sure."

"Soup said you're a good person. That you didn't deserve all the shit that happened to you. I knew there was something wrong with how things went down that night. You're one of a hundred things that never felt right in my career. Small things, but they add up, you know? Used to be I thought I could fix them all, somehow make things right, make things feel whole." He snorted. "But that never happens. Those things just sit inside you, festering, until you retire or die. So if I can spend ten minutes to give you closure... good." He toed the dirt into a small pile.

I wanted him to say it. "Caraway's bent? She's one of the scary ones?"

He shrugged again: *You said it, I didn't.*

"So how are you okay with that? Wouldn't you like to help take her down?"

He shook his head as though ashamed of me. "When I told you five minutes ago that a cop never turns in another cop, were you not listening? Did you take a piss break when I wasn't looking?"

"Okay, yeah. But you know she's bad news."

Forge pursed his lips, like he was searching for the right words, then met my eyes and lowered his voice, communicating more about Caraway with his look than saying her name ever could. "Some people are capable of any wicked thing."

"And you'll say that to a crook in a tunnel, but not ever to someone on the record."

"It's a tough world out there, no doubt about it. A man can't be proud of everything he does." He turned away and walked back in the direction from which we'd come. He'd been sick of me since before the conversation started, and he wasn't going to say anything more.

I followed, walking slowly to allow Forge to exit the tunnels well before me. I felt stupid, just as I had when I'd been jealous over Jennifer. When I finally got around to telling her that my friend had seen her out with another man, she laughed. She kissed me. She'd been doing an assignment with a guy from her postmodern film class. She wasn't cheating on me, and we spent the night talking about Christopher Nolan and Wong Kar-wai. I learned that not everything was about me, that the lives other people live are not the ones we imagine. The way Forge talked about Caraway told me this was about much more than me. I was an ant, probably one of a hundred, playing in the dirt on Caraway's lawn.

And without saying it, Forge had confirmed my hunch that Caraway and Masterson had been allies for two decades. By the time I stepped into the cooling night air, one thing he'd said about Caraway was playing on repeat in my mind: *Occasionally you get one who's only in it for the money.*

When I got home, I collapsed into my chair and reached for my laptop. It was near midnight and I had under twenty-four hours until the job at Big Pink. Minutes after I got picked up in 1998, Caraway started working the coverup for Masterson. But she'd heard about the job from Rabbit, which made me want to look at possibilities.

Had she told Masterson in advance that she was gonna use his game to bust Ricky and my mom? Was that why he'd had his gun ready? Or maybe she'd only met Masterson that night, and had taken the opportunity to "partner" with him. The first to the scene, she would have had a damn good sense of what went down within minutes. Maybe he'd pulled Caraway aside—or had she pulled him aside?—and struck a deal on the spot. *Oh, Mr. Masterson, I know it wasn't your fault. You're a good, honest person and it would be terribly unjust if people called you a murderer. Let's say one of the robbers did it. Cool? Oh yeah, sure I'll offer you a lifetime of police protection. What's in it for me?*

Then she threw in a few leaks to the press to move the story toward my mom. Nothing definitive, no manufactured evidence that my mom fired the shot. Just suggestions, rumors. That my mom actually *had* tried to rob the poker game made it a lot easier. Not much of a leap to believe that, when things went wrong, she killed a guy. In the end, it didn't matter how Caraway and Masterson had become teammates in the coverup. What mattered was how much he was paying her, and whether I could prove it.

I opened my browser and stared at the blank search box. A good team of investigative journalists could probably dig up a hundred crimes she'd committed, but I wasn't a good team of investigative journalists. I doubted she'd left an easy trail. And what would I do if I found any evidence?

It was pretty damn simple, actually. Caraway was, as Soup used to say, crooked as a pig's dick. But what was I gonna do, turn her in to... the cops? Seek justice via the court system? I stifled a laugh. Even if that could have worked, it wasn't what I was good at.

My eyes were closing involuntarily when my laptop dinged with a message from Jennifer. *Got the job in Seattle. They want me to start winter quarter, a month from now. I'm going to take it, and I want you to come. I've got enough saved for the move. You could take a little time before finding a job or starting something new. I know you think your life has to go the other way, but it doesn't.*

Her text hit me like a message from a different world. I shut my laptop and stared into space. As much as I wanted him to, the Brandon she was inviting to Seattle didn't exist. Or did he? I was too tired to think, too tired to feel. Before I knew what I was doing, I kicked back the legs of the recliner, just to shut my eyes for a moment and consider my options.

I was asleep within seconds.

Chapter Twenty-Two

NFL players say Tuesdays are the worst. When you play a game that requires a three-hour beating every Sunday, you're gonna be in pain afterward. By Monday morning, you're sore and bruised. But by Tuesday morning, getting out of bed is damn near impossible. Turns out the same holds true when you take a beating from cops. It had been almost forty hours since my dance with Meathead and Cueball, and the pain woke me up, an ache so deep it was cellular. When I tried to move, the all-body throbbing morphed into flashes of pain that shot up my legs and down my arms and shoulders into my back.

Even worse than the pain was the fear, a mental paralysis that had taken up residence in my brain as I slept. The job at Big Pink was in twelve hours, and I had details to finalize. Game-day jitters are common among thieves, and the successful ones learn to work through them. But this was something more. All day yesterday I'd been operating on anger. Now I couldn't stop replaying the scene with Meathead and Cueball. More importantly, I couldn't stop imagining something worse happening when I stepped back into Big Pink.

I staggered stiffly to the kitchen and put on a pot of coffee, my mind darting away from the fear and landing on Jennifer. Standing as still as possible, one hand on the counter for balance, I listened to the steam rise in the coffee maker, then gurgle as it forced the water through the grounds. Listening to those familiar sounds—waiting for the coffee to brew as I had a thousand times before—I felt as though all the excitement and passion of the last few days had been an illusion. The mundanity was back. My crime switch—fully activated yesterday—had flipped off overnight.

Then Jennifer's offer flashed in my mind like a bolt of lightning in a heavy fog. Maybe Seattle *could* work. Like my mom had said, lifting the keycard had barely been a crime. I could come clean about busting my mom's Micro Tech job, call off the MWMS heist. She could still disappear from Portland, never to return. And I could leave for Seattle tonight, get a headstart on Jennifer and scope out the best movie theaters in our new city. Caraway might control portions of the PPB, but she couldn't follow me two hundred miles north.

I reached for the coffee as it sputtered its last breath of steam. I could still back out of the heist and start over with Jennifer. I could still—

Tap tap tap.

I received few visitors, and most of the time it was a neighbor. I could usually tell which neighbor because I'd hear their door open, then track the number of footsteps down the hallway toward my apartment. When Jamila invited me for dinner, the scent of whatever she was cooking would already be wafting into my apartment. I'd hear her door open but not close, then hear eighteen light footsteps. I'd be at my door before she knocked, and I never made her ask twice. I rubbed my eyes, headed for the door, and cracked it an inch.

The door flew open violently, knocking me back into the apartment. All the pain in my body sang out in chorus as I crashed on my side. I rolled onto my back, sliding up on my elbows as the door slammed.

Joanne Caraway stood over me.

"Brandon Penny, you're under arrest!" She said it louder than necessary, like it was part of a performance. She wanted the neighbors to hear. But she kicked the door closed behind her, which meant she didn't want them to see. "I just came here to talk, I can't believe this."

In half a second, she was at my side. She dropped, pressing a knee into my thigh and twisting my right arm. She moved efficiently and, before I could respond, my wrists were zip-tied behind me.

She hooked a hand under my armpit and yanked upward as she barked, "Stand up!"

I did. My shoulders were pulled back uncomfortably by the tie, intensifying the pain already coursing through my arms and neck.

From her pocket she pulled out white latex gloves and put them on. Next she took out a small baggie full of a pink crystalline powder and stepped behind me, pressing the baggie between my thumb and index fingers. She placed the bag on my laptop, which sat on the table next to my chair. She repeated this, moving swiftly, like it was a perfectly normal set of actions she'd performed often. Each baggie contained at least a few grams of what I assumed was crystal meth.

She said, still loudly, "This looks like intent to distribute, not just private use. That's serious. We've been looking for the dealers of this pink crystal for months."

"Intent to distribute" eliminated any possibility of a drug-treatment diversion program. It meant years in prison, maybe a decade. As she leaned in to attach my prints to a third baggie, she whispered, "Brandon, I do not like being fucked with. Have I not made that clear?" She smiled her sweetest smile yet as she pulled away and set the baggie next to the other two on my laptop.

Had she found out about my meeting with Jackson Forge? I doubted Forge had run his mouth, but someone else could have. Maybe a tail followed me despite my best efforts, or maybe Carebear had a tail on Forge. More likely, she was pissed I hadn't come crawling after she sent Cueball and Meathead to knock me around. The whole point was to intimidate me, and it hadn't worked.

Loudly again, she began the Miranda spiel. "You have the right to remain silent and refuse to answer questions. Anything you say may be used against you in a court of law."

My mind raced. She moved her hands from one pocket to another, looking for something. She found her phone in the back pocket of her slacks. Positioning herself so the ceiling light hit the bags of meth just right, Caraway continued. "You have the right to consult an attorney before speaking to the police and to have an attorney present during questioning now or in the future."

Stepping to the side, she snapped photos of the meth and inspected them, probably wondering how they'd play when printed on poster boards at my trial. I could see her now. *Yes, Your Honor, I came to speak with Mr. Penny and saw the baggies. Probable cause. He must have been high himself to be so careless as to leave them out in plain view when answering the door. Most dealers are users as well, sadly. And, given his troubled past, it's really no surprise where he ended up...*

Caraway knelt before the door, arranging the last bag of meth artistically on the floor, judging the angle carefully so she could claim it had been in plain view from the hallway.

Tap tap tap. Caraway's head shot up to the door, then to me, eyes wide, asking whether I was expecting someone.

My first thought was that my mom had come to talk about the job, or maybe to call it off. I almost shouted for her to run, almost dashed wildly to the door. Carebear had been hunting Wanda Penny for twenty years, and I had no doubt she'd shoot her on sight if she couldn't arrest her cleanly. Hell, she might shoot her even if she *could* arrest her cleanly.

Caraway stood, but didn't open the door. "Who is it?"

"Um, it's uhh... Is that, um, Mrs. Penny? Is Brandon home?" Oh God. It wasn't my mom's voice. It was Jennifer's.

Caraway's eyes on me again, demanding an ID.

I whispered, "It's an old friend, just tell her to go away. She's got nothing to do with anything."

I wriggled my bound wrists behind my back. Quietly, I felt around on the bookshelf behind me, groping blindly. A couple of quarters, no, a DVD case, no... there. The cheap ballpoint pen with *Morey's Pharmacy* printed on the side. Silently, carefully, I picked it up.

Caraway seemed to make an internal calculation and opened the door. Jennifer's eyes landed on me immediately, then scanned to the baggies of meth on my laptop.

Caraway said, "Mr. Penny is under arrest. Methamphetamine."

Jennifer took a step back. "He... I... There must be some mistake."

Gripping the pen tight, I got my thumbnail, then my thumb, under the metal clip. I couldn't flex my hands much, but I pried the metal clip away from the body of the pen. It snapped off with a gentle *click*. Caraway's head moved like she'd heard something, but she didn't turn around. She was busy setting up Jennifer to be a witness at my trial.

"No mistake, ma'am. What's your name?" Caraway shoved her phone in her back pocket and pulled out a notebook.

Jennifer's eyes searched my face, then my apartment. She'd been taught by a thousand movies to believe every word out of a cop's mouth, but in that moment she wanted to give me the benefit of the doubt.

"Jennifer, my name is Jennifer." She took another step back, almost imperceptibly.

Shimmying my shoulders hurt like hell, but it let me work the clasp of the zip tie around to where my fingers could reach it. A zip tie isn't as secure as a pair of handcuffs. All that holds it closed is a tiny plastic tongue. That little bit of plastic can withstand a couple hundred pounds of pulling or torque, or it can bend out of the way with a couple ounces of pressure in just the right place. The harsh plastic bit into my skin as it rubbed back and forth, but then I felt the angular knot of the clasp. Gently, working blindly, I needled the clip of the pen into one side of the clasp and squeezed my fingers, providing gentle pressure. With a whispery hiss, the tie loosened. I had to clutch it with my fingers to keep it from dropping to the floor.

"Weren't you at Brandon's job the other day?" Caraway asked, her tone almost friendly.

"I... what's he being arrested for?"

"Last name?" Caraway demanded. She didn't like being questioned.

I used to bug Ricky to teach me to fight, but he was always reluctant, probably because mom made her feelings about violence clear. He'd given me one good piece of advice, though. *When it comes down to it, everything is a weapon.* Jennifer's eyes landed on me. I kept mine blank, but offered a tiny get-out-of-here nod to the right. I didn't want her to see what was about to happen. Jennifer didn't move.

"Last name?" Caraway demanded.

I leaped toward my chair. Caraway swiveled, her notebook falling from her left hand as I grabbed my computer and lunged forward. Her right hand was almost on her gun as I swung my laptop at the side of her head. *CRACK.* The hard plastic case busted across her temple. Caraway fell to the floor face down, her limbs splayed out like an unconscious drunk.

Jennifer ducked through the door into my apartment. "Oh my God, Brandon."

I knelt over Caraway. There was no blood, but she was out cold, her shallow breaths barely audible.

"Brandon, what..." Jennifer's voice was more panicked than I'd ever heard.

"Just wait."

I cast a look—a *last* look—around my apartment. I grabbed the phone my mom had given me, as well as my own. I grabbed the DVD of *Paper Moon*. I considered bringing my box of memories, but there was no way I was gonna carry it across Portland. I'd hauled it around my whole adult life, too long already. I threw on a pair of shoes and cracked the door. My fear was that Caraway's noisy entrance had gotten someone's attention and that a crowd might have gathered outside. Luckily, the hallway was empty.

I grabbed Jennifer's hand, shut the door behind us, and pulled her into the alley behind my apartment.

Chapter Twenty-Three

W e stood silently in the alley for a long, frozen moment.
Her eyes searched my face. She had more questions than we had time. I said, "All the stuff I tried to hide from you, it was this."

"So you *are* a meth dealer?"

I took her hand. "No, she was framing me because of my mom. I..." My ears caught the sound of sirens in the distance and the math changed again. No chance Caraway had woken up yet, so she must have called for backup before arriving at my apartment. "We don't have time for me to explain."

"I believe you," Jennifer said, "but you just flattened a detective."

"A *crooked* detective."

She shoved her hands in the pockets of her jeans and paced in silence. "That means we could still, I don't know, go to the cops. If she's crooked, we could—"

"Jennifer, she *is* the cops."

"Or get a lawyer, I don't know. Something."

I touched her forearm so she'd stop pacing. "You hear those sirens? Within two minutes, Carebear and a dozen others will be looking everywhere for the meth dealer who assaulted a detective. If caught, that meth dealer won't see life outside a prison for a long, long

240

time. You say you want me in your life. This is my life. After tonight I'll either be in prison or I'll be going far away for a long time. If you want to be part of my life, *this life*, show up at Southeast Third and Market Street tonight at 11 PM."

"Third and... Why?"

"If I'm not there, it means I've been arrested. If I am, it means I'm leaving Portland for good with a shit-ton of money."

The sirens grew louder.

Jennifer seemed not to notice them. "But we could... Seattle. There must still be a way to—"

"No." I put my hands on her shoulders and met her eyes. "Jennifer. I have to go. Now. And so do you. Go back to your apartment and don't talk to anyone. I doubt they'll come looking for you. If they do, say nothing and get a lawyer. I'm sorry."

"But—"

I gave her a little push down the alley. "Go."

She turned. "Third and Market? 11 PM?"

I nodded. "Will you be there?"

Jennifer stared at me, assessed me. I searched her face as I had a hundred times before, expecting to read an answer in her dark brown eyes, her flushed-red cheeks. But she'd activated her superpower, that hard-faced neutrality that told me nothing at all. The sirens were right on top of us now and their wailing cut through me, but not half as bad as Jennifer's look. Tires screeched on the other side of the building. I turned instinctively as the sirens stopped suddenly. When I looked back, Jennifer was walking away.

I watched her for a second, then ran down the alley in the opposite direction, slowing as I hit the corner. Two blue-and-whites had parked in front of my building, lights flashing. I waited for the officers to disappear through the front door before hopping a fence into another apartment complex.

Four blocks east, I hit the ATM at the 7-Eleven, withdrawing everything I could. It was only eighty bucks because that's how they

241

do you at the 7-Eleven ATM. I didn't have time to hit my bank. Ace's was a mile away, so I took off jogging. In a situation like this, speed is more important than anonymity, so I was willing to be more noticeable to get there sooner. Jogging hurt like a bastard, but since everything hurt like a bastard anyway, I endured it.

As I ran, my thoughts turned first to the job, then to my mom. There was no way to be sure, but I had to assume wherever she was staying was busted. Caraway had come for me and failed. I had no doubt she was still coming for my mom as well, if she hadn't already reached her. Problem was, I didn't know where my mom was staying. All she'd said was that it was "near the mountain." She meant Mount Tabor, a small volcanic cone surrounded by a park in southeast Portland. I'd scanned my brain when she'd said it, trying to remember friends or associates she'd had in the neighborhood, but hadn't hit on anything. I'd need more to go on if I wanted to find her.

I was sweating hard when I reached Ace's. The run had hurt, but had actually loosened up my stiff muscles. I yanked the door. Locked. I peered through the large window. Empty. It was nearly ten in the morning. I ran around the block to the back entrance and banged on the metal door.

As the clanging echo faded, I considered what I was doing. The smart option was to boost a car or hop on a bus, to get the hell out of town. If Caraway had been willing to frame me, she'd be willing to do anything else she needed to do. *Yup. Leave now and never come back.* There'd even be some poetic symmetry to it, ditching my mom like she'd ditched me. That wouldn't bring me any satisfaction, though. Hurting Mom further was pointless, and the real problem was Caraway. If I left town, she'd shake down Soup or anyone else she could tie me to, as much for retribution as to find me. Plus, there was a chance—however slim—that Jennifer would show up at the stash car tonight.

The door opened. "I was on the can," Soup said. "Why are you breathing so hard?"

Without a word, I slid through the back door and bolted it behind me. "Can you stay closed a few minutes longer?" I checked to make sure no one was watching us through the front window, then rummaged through jackets on a rack at one end of the shop.

"What the hell are you doing?"

"Did the ID come in?"

"It did, but—"

I pulled a leather jacket off the rack. It was clearly a relic of the '70s, with reddish-brown leather, oversized buttons, and ostentatious white stitching. It was the kind of thing you'd usually see on a young Portland hipster or a dude in his sixties.

Turning to Soup, I said, "Listen. I'm not gonna tell you why because you'd be more of an accomplice than you already are." He put up both hands as if to say, *Accomplice? Say no more, Keyser.* I kept going. "I need a disguise, I need that ID, and I need to know where my mom is staying. I can offer you eighty bucks, and, if I'm not in jail by the end of the day, that piece of the score we talked about."

His eyes shifted to the front door and I turned, half panicked. It was only a jogger, pausing to check her watch. Looking back to Soup, I asked, "Will you help?"

He tossed me a passport, which he'd pulled from under the cash register. At first glance, it looked as real as any fake I'd seen.

Soup said, "Document of that quality would normally be two grand, and that's the friends-and-family price."

There are two ways to fake a passport. The first is impersonation: you steal a real passport and you're either lucky enough to look like the dude in the picture, or you swap it out. But most countries don't use actual photos any more. Instead, they print the photo digitally, then laminate over it, so you can't just duck into the Rite-Aid photo booth and tape it over the existing photo. You've got to replace the whole page, which brings us to the second way to fake a passport: counterfeiting. That's the method Soup had used. Passports are hard to counterfeit because of the special paper the government uses, but it's a more reliable method if you have the right equipment. Down to the hologram and the data bar they'd added in 2007, this thing was spot-on.

Impressed as I was by the quality, something else struck me. Soup was deeper in the game than I thought. "I'll owe you."

"Damn right you will."

I fumbled through a barrel of miscellany, pushing aside a set of golf clubs and a beach umbrella before finding what I was looking for. A crutch.

Soup tossed me a pair of wide sunglasses with ridiculous, round lenses and bright red frames. I put them on, then threw the jacket on over my t-shirt and buttoned it. Next I found a wool newsboy-style cap to complete the outfit. It was lightly worn but didn't stink and it was big enough to cover most of my hair.

I'd done everything I could to not match the description of me that Caraway had almost certainly circulated through the Portland Police Bureau network. I looked up at Soup. "How do I look?"

"Like you're on your way to a bangin' new kale restaurant, or the Reed theater department. Or one of those weed shops that drove me out of business."

I laughed. "I wish." Behind him on a shelf, I spotted a pick set. "Toss me that."

He did. "Add forty bucks to your bill."

My eyes landed on the gun case. *What if I...* I shook off the thought before it formed. Loaded or unloaded, no way I'd use a gun to get myself out of this.

I met his eyes. "Where's my mom staying? Please tell me you know something."

"I—"

"She said something about Mount Tabor, if that helps."

I shot a look out the front window. Across the street, a couple dudes walked by. Their dark suits made me think they were detectives; you didn't see a lot of men in suits in this neighborhood. But they didn't glance in, stop, or even slow down. A moment later they disappeared from view.

I looked back to Soup, sitting on his usual stool. He crinkled his forehead into a half-dozen little folds of skin, the way he always did when thinking hard. "I really don't know. Don't think she had any associates in that area, but she might have. She could be renting, or Airbnb with a fake ID. Could be a lot of things."

"Soup, think. Did she ever mention someone in that neighborhood? I'd bet it's someone she used to know, someone in the game. She said something about a DMV person."

He closed his eyes. "There was one woman."

"A woman?"

He stared at me. Our eyes met and a memory triggered in my brain. "Some woman with a red house. But she wasn't a crook."

He stood and paced back and forth behind the counter, holding up a finger like a name was on the tip of his tongue.

It was on the tip of mine as well. "She used to babysit me when I was super little. Veronica? Monique?"

"Holy hell, *Monica. That* was it."

The memories were cloudy, but I think she was a housekeeper like my mom and, as far as I knew, she'd never been involved in the jobs my mom pulled.

Soup said, "I don't think the house was red, though. Maybe dark orange, or, wait, no..." He squinted, and the skin crevices on his forehead deepened further. "Purple?"

"Do you remember anything else about it?"

"Was only there once. Don't know, exactly, but it's near the tennis courts off 60th."

That rang a bell. "I owe you forever, Soup. Sorry in advance for anything that comes to bite you in the ass in the next few days. You'll hear from me." I gave Soup one last look and hobbled out the front door, relying on the crutch for balance.

I scanned while moving my head in the opposite direction of my eyes behind the sunglasses. There was a single blue-and-white across the street. I didn't know whether it had been there ten minutes ago. I limped away, waiting to hear sirens or see flashing lights, to hear the screech of tires beside me. They never came.

I turned a corner, then another, then another. A few minutes later, I was on a bus, heading across Portland to Mount Tabor.

~

"We gotta go. Now!" Finding my mom had been easier than I expected, but getting her out of the house was proving difficult. The bus had dropped me off facing the mountain, the same direction we used to come from when we'd walk here from our old apartment. The view had triggered a memory. I remembered watching tennis from Monica's front porch and, when I asked if we could play, her telling me it was a game for rich people.

Walking as fast as I could while keeping up my appearance of a dude with a bum leg, I'd headed up SE 60th to Salmon Street and recognized the house immediately. It was no longer red, but the porch had a low railing covered with overgrown vines, just as it had twenty-five years ago. Monica had a two-bedroom apartment in the front half of the house, which was split into two separate living spaces.

My mom stood in the doorway. "How'd you find me?"

"Is Monica here?"

"She's at work."

"Good." I forced my way past her into the house.

"What's happening?"

"Detective tried to frame me, I knocked her out. I don't think I was followed but—"

"Why the hell do you have that crutch?"

"Mom, listen. I am *burned*." I leaned the crutch against the sink and paced the kitchen. "Grab what you absolutely need and let's leave out the back door."

"Where are we gonna go?"

I hadn't thought that through. "I'll think, you pack. Only what you need for the job and your flight."

She hurried to the bedroom. I walked to the window that over-looked the porch. In the distance, the tennis courts off Salmon Street were empty, as was the street. So far, so good. I relaxed for half a second, just long enough to realize how much pain I was in. Turns out walking unnaturally on a crutch you don't need makes your back sore as hell, especially if a cop worked you over pretty hard the night before last. I snuck into the bathroom and swallowed five aspirin, washing them down with sink water.

Mom returned a minute later with a small leather duffel full of clothes and equipment.

"You got my outfit in there?" I was still in the vintage jacket from Ace's, and it wasn't ideal for the acting we had to do later.

"Used clothing shop down the block."

"Good."

The bag had a nice leather strap and, thrown over her shoulder, it could pass for a large purse. She'd thrown on shoes and sunglasses and wore a long, dark coat. "That movie theater still nearby?"

"What?"

"We could hide out there. The one that used to serve food."

She was talking about the Academy Theater, one of my old favorites. It was a three-screen independent joint that showed a great mix of classics and new releases. The perfect spot to lay low. "Let's go."

We bought tickets for the 11:30, the 2:30, the 4:40, and 6:35 showings and took seats in the back of the theater, near the emergency exit. We hadn't been tailed and we'd paid for the tickets in cash, so we were reasonably confident we were safe, but you always plan your escape.

Assuming Caraway had woken up, my apartment was now a crime scene. Every officer in the PPD would have heard about the white, brown-haired, thirty-something meth dealer of average height and weight who'd assaulted a detective and fled his apartment in Felony Flats. He was likely armed and dangerous and could be working with known thief Wanda Penny. Caraway herself would be incensed in her cloying, chilling way. I imagined her tight smile, concealing an icy rage as she went about the business of trying to ruin us. Even if she didn't know I'd partnered with my mom, Carebear probably thought I'd warned her off the Micro Tech job. Still, I had to assume Carebear had her eyes on Big Pink. And everywhere else in the city.

Mom tapped my forearm. "Brand, your head is cocked to the side, the way I do when I'm thinking about a job." I winced. Count on your mother to point out the embarrassing tell you didn't know you had. She glanced around the empty theater. "Let's bag it," she said definitively. "The job, I mean." There was pain in her eyes. A big part of her was hooked into this score, and it wouldn't be easy to let it go.

"No."

"Don't tell me you haven't considered it. I have four grand in cash on me. That's enough. We can split up or go together. But the job is too risky."

"No." Almost to my surprise, I said it with a certainty that reflected exactly how I felt. "I had the chance to back out last night. I almost took it." I'd been furious when Mom told me she'd thought I'd be happier living a normal life. And just that morning I'd been ready to try the same thing, to bail on everything and head to Seattle. But that version of me seemed impossible now. It was a fantasy when she wanted it for me, and a fantasy when I wanted it for myself. A fantasy that never had a chance of becoming real, no matter how hard I tried.

She squeezed my hand. "You sure?"

"If it wasn't Caraway, it would have been something else." It was depressing to say. It was a relief to admit. It was both. I'd shut the brilliant, devious kid they called Keyser inside a locked closet in the basement of my mind for sixteen years, until Carebear Caraway had blustered in and demanded to speak with him. But if she never had, someone would have. Something would have pushed me too far, someone would have said the wrong thing sooner or later. I spent sixteen years telling myself I'd locked up the criminal inside me, but deep down I always knew the little bastard could pick locks. And I realized now that my mom had seen that long before I ever did. She'd gamed out this scenario and hoped it wouldn't shake out this way, and she'd been wrong.

She smiled sadly, as a young and amorous couple entered, holding hands and whispering. We couldn't say any more after that. We each shifted uncomfortably in our seats, eyes flicking up every time someone else came in. It was never a cop—there was no reason to think it would be—but we had to look anyway. Family tradition demanded one of us get popcorn and drinks five minutes before the official showtime. Via nonverbal gestures and eyerolls, I conveyed to Mom it should be her.

The movie was one of the second-runs the Academy specialized in, a sweet animated feature about the importance of family. Had I not been keyed up and in physical pain, I probably would have enjoyed it. As it was, I stiffly endured it, all the while keeping one eye on the doors.

After the credits, I hauled my aching body into the lobby to make sure there were no badges hanging around. There weren't, so I gave Mom the signal to join me. We had fifteen minutes until the next show, so we got a couple of hot dogs and salads from the surprisingly well-supplied concession stand. It was the most well-balanced lunch I'd had all week.

In between bites, I said, "Someone may join us at the stash car." I'd considered not telling her about Jennifer to save myself two kinds of embarrassment. First, inviting a civilian to join us on the back end of a job was not okay. And second, there was a pretty good chance Jennifer was smart enough not to show up.

Mom eyed me over her soda cup. "Huh?"

"Don't worry, she doesn't know anything about the job. I didn't—"

"She the one who almost made you back out?"

I nodded.

"Is it Dani? The dancer you mentioned?"

"Her name's Jennifer. She's gonna be a teacher. Film studies. There was never a Dani." I chewed slowly and watched her face. If I'd been anyone else, she would have walked out of the theater and never spoken to me again.

Instead, she let out a long breath and gave me a reluctant nod, the type of look a parent gives a kid when the kid has screwed up in an unfixable way, but the parent has no choice but to love the kid anyway. "She must be special."

The second show was a big-budget superhero blockbuster, and even six months after release, it drew a large crowd of teenagers, superhero fans, kids, and comic book aficionados. Mom and I stayed packed into the corner near the emergency exit, but this time it would have been tough to find two seats together otherwise. No longer even able to whisper without being overheard, we had no choice but to watch the film.

The energy of a crowd in a theater is its own thing. Shocks are shared, laughs become infectious, and you become part of something bigger than any of you individually. I've heard church is like that sometimes, but I don't have a church. I have movies instead.

Most superhero flicks don't ask the audience to feel anything new or unfamiliar. They draw on effective story beats, centuries old, that endure because they work reliably. In that room filled with geeks and children, it was easy to forget cynicism and metatext. When the villain made a solemn pronouncement and the hero turned it back on him with a cutting remark, the whole room laughed. Despite myself, I laughed along with them. When it looked like the hero was doomed, but rose up at the last moment to give the villain hell, a hundred fans hooted and hollered unironically. Mom and I were right there with them. We let ourselves fall under the spell of the movie, and for ninety minutes we enjoyed a world where good and evil were clear and uncomplicated, and evil got the living shit beaten out of it.

The next show was an old classic: *The Addams Family*. Out of pure nostalgia, I got a large popcorn and Red Vines. The only other people in the audience were a couple in the front row and their three squirmy children, so Mom and I could talk in low voices without being overheard.

I offered her a Red Vine. "This is what you got the first time we saw this movie together."

"Wait, really? I don't even remember that."

"I was six. It was the first day we did the *put-that-necklace-back* con."

Mom made a delighted shriek that she was able to turn into a natural-sounding laugh at what Raul Julia and Anjelica Huston were doing on screen. Grabbing control of her voice back, she whispered, "Oh my *God*, you're right. This is the movie we saw that night!"

"And you got a large popcorn and Red Vines. First time we ever got them at a movie, first time I ever helped you with a crime, first time I saw Christina Ricci. Guess I got addicted to all three."

She looked down. I couldn't make out her expression in the darkness. "I feel bad about that. I should never have gotten you involved."

I grabbed another Red Vine from the box. "Mom, seriously. Red licorice is delicious, and my best childhood memories are helping you with crimes. You want to apologize for something that night, apologize for the Christina Ricci thing. Smart crazy girls who are clearly trouble have cost me a lot more than licorice."

Good thing Raul Julia was at it again, because Mom's laugh that time couldn't be disguised.

After the Addamses finished their antics, we had half an hour before our next ticket. It was early evening by then, and the lobby was full of people coming and going and standing in line for snacks. Mom and I sat at a table in the lobby sipping sodas, the duffel bag on the floor between our feet.

Somehow we landed on the subject of all the lousy food I'd had. "Seriously, that bland-ass tuna casserole haunts my dreams, but I have to admit, I don't think I could make a better one."

She shook her head sympathetically. "I should've taught you to cook when you were small. Don't know why I didn't."

I shrugged. "I get by. Sometimes this lady named Jamila invites me over for food. She lives across the hall. Mainly I eat cheap. Make a big pot of soup and live off it for a week, that kind of thing. Except once in a while I'll see something on TV that looks delicious, and I'll get this temporary delusion where I think, *Yes! I can cook that!* So I buy more ingredients than I can afford, make something totally underwhelming, and then it's ramen and lentil soup for two weeks because I blew the grocery budget on hubris."

Mom snickered. "That won't be a problem after tonight."

"True. No matter what happens, buying groceries won't be a worry for at least the next ten to fifteen years."

. . .

I could feel the countdown going on inside me, and I knew Mom could, too. *In 182 minutes, we'll be walking into Big Pink to commit the biggest theft of our lives. In 178 minutes we'll be slipping the five-pin on Mark Masterson's office door. In 170 minutes, we'll be on the lam for life under phony names, or we'll be under arrest.* We couldn't talk about it directly, and I didn't want to. The tension of the approaching job and the weight of the duffel bag's contents were there, but more importantly, Mom was there. Soon we'd be thieves, but that was still 182 minutes away and I was sitting with my mother, talking about movies and food and old jokes. Life made sense in a way it hadn't for twenty years.

Our last ticket was for the same animated flick we'd seen at the matinee. You buy four tickets at a three-screen theater, that's what happens. This time around, I let myself laugh at the cheap jokes, and when the big tearjerker scene came, I let myself cry. I glanced over, and Mom was crying too. As the credits rolled and the theater cleared out, a lump formed in my throat. There was something I wanted to say—needed to say—but I wasn't about to say it aloud. Taking out the trash phone, I found my mom's number and composed a text.

The reason I came back and found you at Big Pink... I snitched. Kinda by accident but also maybe kinda not. I was drunk. Wrote to a detective. Mentioned a microchip job and she put two and two together. That's why I found the other job.

She read it slowly, twice maybe, then looked up. "It's okay."

I nodded down at her phone, and read the credits as she typed. A minute later, my phone vibrated.

You made a bad decision and you feel terrible about the hurt you caused. You want to make it right. I know that feeling well.

The credits ended, and the movie theater lights came up. The cleaning crew arrived.

Mom and I wandered through the lobby, pulling up our collars at the same time as we walked out into the chilly Portland night.

Chapter Twenty-Four

W e heard the crows before we saw them. Greeting us as we approached from the northeast, the cawing sounded like a hundred yattering gossips at a cocktail party. We saw no blue-and-whites, but the crows had Big Pink surrounded. Between the caws were hoarse and grating coos, rattles, and clicks. Every branch of every tree bowed beneath their weight. Every telephone wire was thick with them. The night was cold for a Portland winter, low thirties or so, and I wondered if the crows were complaining about the weather. The paranoid part of my brain figured they'd seen us scoping the place out and were warning the security guards.

My breathing quickened and I slowed my walk. "Hold on." I had to get right before going in.

My mom touched my forearm.

I took two deep breaths. Soup had told me once that being a great thief is like being an elite athlete. You make a game plan and you stick to it. You have to know in advance that fear is going to arise. It exists to keep us in line, to keep us from doing dangerous things. That's its evolutionary purpose. Theft is inherently dangerous, so you need to expect fear. Being great requires the ability to set that fear aside, but not in a tough-guy, *I-fear-nothing* way. You simply need to accept that the fear exists, separate it from the part of your brain that trusts the plan, then execute the plan. That's what great basketball players do in the fourth quarter of a close game. Afraid of missing the big shot? That's natural. Set it aside and take the shot anyway. That's what I had to do.

I closed my eyes, looking at the fear in my mind as a separate person. I said hello to it, then set it aside.

We passed beneath an especially thick band of crows crowding a telephone wire that ran into the tower. All of a sudden, their cawing stopped. The night fell silent save for a car alarm in the distance and the low conversation of a couple who'd spilled out of the building and turned away from us, arm in arm.

I looked up. Ten thousand gleaming black eyes looked down silently. I didn't know why they'd stopped talking any more than I knew why they'd been talking in the first place, but I wasn't afraid they were ratting on us any more. It felt like the crows were on our side.

At the door, Mom asked. "You ready?"

"Ready."

Her demeanor changed suddenly and she led us in, waving merrily at the two guys behind the security desk as we strode toward the elevators. As we'd expected, they were different from the two who'd been there when we swiped the keycard data. No chance they'd recognize us. Any smart security team mixes up their shifts to be less predictable to criminals, but this place didn't have a smart security team.

One of the guards looked up briefly and smiled. The other kept his eyes on his computer screen. Our job required some basic technical skills, but it also required acting. We were both dressed well— me in black slacks and a dark blue dress shirt, Mom in a black dress with a white shawl. We looked like a mother and son out for a pre-Christmas dinner, or maybe a cougar and her boytoy out on a date. Either way, apart from the small duffel bag that passed as a large purse, we looked like a dozen other pairs who'd headed to the thirtieth floor that night, seeking beautiful views of Portland accompanied by New American cuisine and inventive cocktails.

What you have to understand about security guards is that, for the most part, they don't care about what they're protecting. In movies, you always see them in action. The bad guys break in and the security guards try to stop them. They call the police, they run down halls, they fumble for their weapons as the smarter criminals get the drop on them. You're conditioned to think of them as fundamentally interested in preventing crime, like it's their calling or something. It's not. What little they do, they do to protect their jobs. They don't want to get fired so they have to pretend to care, especially if they're being recorded. In a building like Big Pink, security staff are making fourteen to fifteen bucks an hour. They're not cops, they're certainly not detectives, and they rarely see action. Most are barely making ends meet. The last thing they want is to put their asses on the line to protect the office of some guy who makes half a million a year. For the two schlubs at the desk, a bad night might mean dealing with a belligerent tech-bro who drank too much at the restaurant and puked in the lobby. They're simply not prepared to handle professional thieves. Even if they wanted to stop us, which they didn't, they wouldn't know where to start.

At the elevator, Mom punched in the thirtieth floor, home of the City Grill restaurant and the only floor in the building that didn't require a keycard. Of course, we could have used the keycard data on my phone to access any floor we wanted, but it was ten at night and the elevators at Big Pink displayed the floor numbers on the ground level. We didn't want the guards glancing up and wondering why we were headed to a floor of offices. One of them might be bored enough to be curious.

The elevator opened into a hallway lined with black-and-white photos of old Portland. Around the corner to the left was the hostess stand and the restaurant's main entrance. To the right was the stairwell door, and farther down the hall, the bathrooms. We paused in front of a large, ornate mirror. Mom adjusted her shawl and took her sweet time doing it.

I placed all my attention on the hostess stand and the patterns of noise coming from the restaurant. Next I listened for bathroom noise —a toilet flushing or a door creaking.

I was about to give the signal to proceed when I heard it. "Just down the hall." Faint, a woman's voice from the restaurant. The hostess. "Past the elevators where you came in."

I cleared my throat. Mom took an earring off, frowning into the mirror and fussing with it as though she just couldn't get the damn thing back in.

An older gentleman shuffled behind us. She put the earring on as he disappeared into the men's room.

Hand on my phone in the pocket of my slacks, I scanned for sounds. Everything was clear. I tapped my foot twice and swiveled toward the door between the elevator and the bathrooms. Mom was right behind me. I whipped out my phone and held it up to the keycard scanner. The light blinked green and beeped. Half a second later we were through the door. Mom pulled it gently closed behind her.

We were in. From there, things moved quickly. The stairwell was echoey bare concrete, unheated, and shockingly cold after the warmth of the restaurant lobby. There were no security cameras, which made our job easier. Hurrying down two flights, we arrived at the landing of the twenty-eighth floor. The two-way keycard system required another scan to enter the hallway from the stairwell, then two right turns took us to a blue door marked with a placard: *Masterson Wealth Management Services.*

Mom pulled out her picking tool and crouched. She lifted the tool to the lock, and froze. "Brandon." She tilted her head and I looked down, my eyes falling to the lock when I saw the concerned look on her face.

Most insurance companies require a minimum of a five-pin lock on exterior doors. Same way your car insurance company might give you a discount if you have a fancy alarm. But pin locks today use the same technology they used when they were invented during the Civil War. Mostly they provide the *illusion* of security and add a couple minutes to the time it takes a professional to break into your home or office. They're a slight deterrent, maybe, but not real security. Anyone who's serious about getting in is getting in.

Photos of Masterson's office that I'd found on Twitter showed that this door had been "secured" by a five-pin lock. But something had changed.

"Not the same lock." Mom's tone was brisk, her voice full of tension.

I dropped to one knee. "Six-pin." Even though the difference between a five-pin and a six-pin lock was substantial—each pin raising the difficulty exponentially, not linearly—the extra pin wouldn't have presented her much of a challenge. Her newfangled tool probably could have busted it in under a minute.

Still, it worried her for the same reasons it worried me. A hundred permutations ran through my mind. *When had Masterson changed the lock? Was it specifically to protect the items we were here to steal, or had it been a general security upgrade?* Most importantly, *If he'd made this upgrade, had he made others? What the hell were we walking into? Security cameras? Tougher locks? Armed guards?*

The questions passed through my mind in seconds that felt like hours. I locked them away in the room with my fear. "Stick to the plan," I said, for me as much as for her.

I tapped her knee and she slid out of the way as I whipped the pick set from my back pocket, reminding myself I owed Soup forty bucks, plus a whole lot more. I could have used her pick, but I wasn't familiar with it. This set was old-school, like the ones I'd learned on. Tension wrench in my left hand, rake in my right, I went to work, just like I did on that school computer lockup, just as I had on Richie's dad's safe. In twenty seconds, the wrench gave, turning to the right and clicking like a key. The door opened and Mom led us in without a word.

Masterson Wealth Management Services lived in a four-office suite with southwest views. The reception area was nice, designed to impress clients with a glass-fronted fridge filled with Voss, cold brew, and Diet Coke, and it had a wide reception desk framed by potted plants. We found Masterson's corner office quickly. It had the five-pin lock we expected. Mom popped it in ten seconds, and we were in.

Through the gaps in the blinds, the moon was bright enough to cast slivers of light onto the wide oak desk and the three filing cabinets, which were the reason we were there.

The first two cabinets were standard beige three-doors protected by simple key-lock systems. The third...

"Oh no," I said.

The third was a five-drawer made of heavy-duty black metal. Not easy to carry out, but we'd expected that. The worrisome part was the electronic fingerprint security system. In my research, I'd seen images of Masterson's filing cabinets, but there had always been someone standing in front of the locks. The first two were easily pickable, but the stuff we were after was likely in the third. There were ways to defeat a fingerprint lock, but I hadn't prepared for it.

"It's fine." Mom reached into her bra and pulled something out. I couldn't see it in the darkness. She held it next to the fingerprint reader, and the lock clicked open instantly.

"You always keep a rare-earth magnet in your bra?" I asked.

"Yes."

In the movies, we would have had to kill Masterson, cut his finger off, and use his unique print to open the lock. But movies lie. They go for what's dramatic and visual, rather than what works. Thieves go for what works.

No matter how fancy they look, security systems are put together by people. Regular people with all their laziness, shortcuts, budgetary limitations, and stupidity. You're supposed to look at a fingerprint lock and think *Opening this lock requires a fingerprint.* That's a lie. Opening that lock, as with almost any lock, requires a latch to move out of the way. Suckers are impressed by how secure the fingerprint sensor *appears.* What they don't know is that the manufacturer cut costs on the nickel-plated solenoid that holds that latch in place, the valve my mom had sprung in half a second with a ten-dollar magnet. Masterson had probably shown off this filing cabinet to clients a hundred times, cold-brew coffee in hand. *Go ahead, try it with your finger. See? I'm literally the only person in the world who can open this filing cabinet, because I take security seriously.* In practice, the 150-year-old technology in the pin locks had taken us longer to open.

Starting at the bottom of the cabinet, mom leafed through files. Starting at the top, I did the same. We were looking for three kinds: files to go on the floor, files to go in the trash can, and files to go in the bag. The first kind we threw in random directions around the office, making the sort of mess a three-year-old might. Mom even stepped out into the hall to toss a few up and down the hallway.

I riffled through folders as fast as I could, looking for the handful we planned to steal. Finally, from below, my mom gently whacked my hip. "These?"

I grabbed the folders and turned toward the window as I opened the one on top, letting the moonlight shine against the embossed seal "MWMS" on the certificate inside. The five folders she'd handed me were full of certificates stamped with the same seal, and that was plenty.

I shoved the folders into the back of my waistband, then a few more unimportant files into the bag. Mom closed the drawer and headed for the door.

I wasn't done. Thumbing through the top drawer of the cabinet, I stopped on a fat folder vaguely labeled, "Legal." Looking through it, I found a set of thin, unmarked folders of different colors. I checked the green one, then the red one, then the yellow one.

"Brandon, what are you doing?" Her voice was an urgent whisper.

"Just a sec."

As a general rule, thieves have to be honest with one another, and that goes double when you're in on the same job. Everyone needs to understand the plan. For a job to succeed, everyone needs to stick to it. I hadn't shared this part of the plan with my mom. I'd assured her this job wasn't personal, but I'm an excellent liar.

I found the folder I was looking for, shoved it in my waistband with the others, and closed the drawer. Wordlessly, we removed our wigs. Mom pulled off her shirt and jacket and tucked one inside the other. I took off my glasses, then turned my reversible jacket inside-out. Instead of a black leather jacket, I now wore a blue liner-style field jacket.

Heading out through the unlocked doors of Masterson Wealth Management Services, we strolled to the elevators, and I pulled out my phone to activate our ride down to the ground floor.

I'd been holding it next to the sensor for a few seconds before we realized it wasn't working.

Chapter Twenty-Five

W e stared at my phone—first in confusion, then in a steadily building horror—as it refused to unlock the damned elevator. I made sure the RFID app was open and active, but it wasn't doing anything. I mashed the touchscreen with my thumbs in an attempt to get the app to admit it had the master keycard code for this building, but it denied knowledge of any such code. It was possible Mom's rare-earth magnet had gotten too close to it. Those things will fry a cell phone just as fast as they'll fry a lock. For half a second I wondered whether Carebear had convinced security to disable the whole system to trap us, but that made no sense. The depressing fact was that the app simply choked on its own code at the worst time. For whatever stupid, glitchy, meaningless electronic reason, our exit plan was broken.

Luck. Like Soup said, half of being a successful thief was sheer, dumb luck. Sometimes tech fails. On occasion, apps crash. And once in a while, your bad luck leaves you stranded on the twenty-eighth floor of a high-rise with no way out.

Mom said, "We can still take the stairs, except—"

"Yeah. The stairs are behind emergency-only doors, which are alarmed."

"So if we open one of those, security immediately knows which door it was, and where to meet us."

"Right." I struggled to move past the fact that an idiotic software hiccup had turned a beautiful plan to garbage.

"Unless..." From the tone of her voice, I knew what she was thinking.

I responded before my brain fully caught up. "Unless it's not the *door* that triggers the alarm."

"They don't monitor doors if it's a real fire alarm."

"There are metal trash cans in Masterson's office."

"I saw a shredder, too."

We walked back into the office and sent most of the documents in the bag through Masterson's top-grade shredder, turning them into expensive confetti. It might have been possible to reconstruct them if he was willing to take the time and trouble, but we were about to eliminate that option. We dumped the confetti into the metal trash can next to Masterson's desk, then placed a stack of other documents from the bag on top, ones I hoped would burn just enough to be partially identifiable. On the very top layer, we placed the wigs and clothes we were leaving behind. Shreds, paper, clothing. Tinder, kindling, logs. That's how you build a fire.

Glancing at the ceiling, I estimated the angle of the sprinkler system. I dropped to my knees and shoved the can further under the desk.

Without looking, I reached back to my mom like a runner grasping for a baton in a relay race. She pressed a tiny book of matches into my hand.

The pieces of paper we were about to torch represented the entire legal existence of dozens of shell companies, and we were about to erase them from the world. The plan had always been to burn a portion of the bearer shares and the files that went with them. We'd thought to do it outside, where the fragments of paper would be identified later, maybe by city authorities. Instead, fate had forced us to do it here, in Masterson's own office, just to get a clean exit.

I played our escape in my head one more time, like watching a movie of our next ten minutes on fast-forward. Once I was sure we'd done everything right, once I'd seen it happen the way it was supposed to, I said, "Ready?"

"Ready."

I lit a match and let it slide down the side of the trashcan to the hungry confetti at the bottom. The tiny yellow glow grew, and grew, and deepened into orange. Black smoke rose from the can, gathering under the desk and spreading into the room.

We hustled into the hallway, not bothering to close the doors behind us. We stopped at the door marked:

EMERGENCY EXIT ONLY

ALARM WILL SOUND

My mom touched my arm. "Brand?"

"Should be any second. A minute, tops."

"No, there's something else."

I was alarmed by the look in her eyes. "Are you okay, Mom?"

"I'm..." she paused, making her voice come out casual. "I'm thinking of all the idiots I've worked with, and that if I'd been working with you instead, we'd both be retired by now, lying on a beach fanning ourselves with wads of cash."

My face flushed hot. I didn't need to listen closely for the alarm. We wouldn't be able to miss it when it came. "Mom, just because you feel bad about running out on me—"

"I do feel bad about that, but right now, I feel sorry. If I hadn't let them take you, if I hadn't let them teach you their sick rules..."

"C'mon, Mom, let's stay focused on—"

"No, you listen to me, I'm your mother. I'm wanted for a dozen felonies in a dozen states. I've worked with every kind of hustler and grifter and gangster that exists. And you're better at this than all of them."

I heard myself asking the question I'd been sitting on for three days and twenty years. "That night, did you go to Dexter's?"

She stared at me, blank-faced. "Of course I did. How could—" She stopped mid-sentence and reached into her bra again, pulling out a small piece of what looked like laminated paper.

Suddenly, the fire alarm exploded around us—a harsh, high-pitched blatting designed to make people get out of a building fast. Before I could get a good look at the paper, she shoved it into the back pocket of my jeans and smashed through the emergency-exit door.

I darted past her, taking two steps at a time. Mom took one at a time, our alternating pitter-patter of rapid steps filling the space between the shrieks of the alarm. Now all we had to do was descend twenty-eight flights of stairs and creep through the exit before the fire department arrived.

One floor, then two, then three. Everything was playing out exactly as planned, at least exactly as I'd planned since the keycard app gave up the ghost. Five floors, then six, then seven...

I smelled something sweet and musty and damp. Weed. Someone was vaping weed in the stairwell. I slowed, then stopped, holding out my arm so my mom, who was tight on my heels, wouldn't pass me. Craning my neck to peer around a corner, I saw nothing. The scent grew stronger.

I glanced up the stairs in the direction we'd come from.

"What?" my mom whispered.

"Someone's there. I—"

"Hey." A flight below, a security guard emerged from around the corner. His left hand held a vape pen, his right was on the radio on his belt. He looked up and my eyes met his. He stuffed the device in his pocket. "I... What—?" He said something else, but it was almost impossible to make out over the alarm.

I'd prepared various lies for different situations that might arise. But I was still surprised. This dude was even more of a slacker than the two guys at the front desk. Fire alarm went off, and firefighters had already been called. He wasn't paid minimum wage to be a hero. Why not chill in an unmonitored stairwell ten stories below and get lit during what was almost certainly a routine false alarm? I understood. I used to have his job.

The shrieking blat of the alarm continued to pound our ears, and realization dawned in the guard's eyes. Anyone legitimately evacuating from the restaurant—the only business still open in the building

—would be in a big group, in a different stairwell. We were in a place we had no excuse to be. If we could have talked, we might have been able to bullshit him, but the alarm noise made that impossible.

I leapt forward, shoving the guy back. He swiped at me half-heartedly, but I jumped down half a flight of stairs and he didn't try to stop my mom as she pushed past him. He only cared enough to call someone above his pay grade, shouting into his radio as we disappeared a floor below him. "Two people, southeast stairwell, twenty-first floor. White male, age thirty or so. White female, fifty or so."

If every cop in downtown Portland wasn't already headed to Big Pink, they would be now.

We hurried down three more flights in silence. I heard something below. A door closing? I stopped and went flat against the wall, listening in the tiny spaces between the alarm's shrieks. My breaths were heavy. No other sounds came. Not from below and not from above.

"What did you hear?" Mom asked.

"Thought it was a door, but..." I shook my head, walking slowly down the next flight, then picking up speed for the next ten. At the fifth floor, my mind clicked on the office listings I'd read online. I crashed through the emergency door and emerged on the unoccupied fifth floor, which was in the middle of a renovation. Mom followed without a question. Clearly, she trusted me to get us out of here. My bet was that security would concentrate their response at the base of the stairwell we'd been in when we ran into the security guard, *not* the stairwell at the opposite corner of the building.

It was a vast, unfinished space of about ten thousand square feet. Automatic lights flashed on as we sprinted through, swerving around boxes of tools, pallets of sheetrock, and five-gallon jugs of paint. We busted through the door and into the northwest stairwell, which appeared empty. From there, it was thirty seconds of adrenaline, straight to the ground floor. We were both panting by the time we reached it. I leaned on the wall.

Mom bent over, taking a series of deep breaths. After our breaths had slowed, I reached for the doorknob. "Wait," she said. "Maybe we should split up."

"Not a chance."

She touched my hand. "Think about it. There's—"

"No," I said. "Other side of the door is the back lobby. No security there at night. Elevators to the right, glass doors to the left that exit onto Burnside."

"Got it."

"Once outside, we follow the plan."

She looked skeptical, but nodded.

The plan was simple. The getaway car was on the other side of the Willamette River, half a mile away. There we'd change clothes and cross into Washington state. Then I'd drive us ninety minutes to the Sea-Tac airport. If she showed up, Jennifer would ride shotgun.

As I cracked the door, my stomach twisted. Along the street were flashing lights, at least two fire trucks and three blue-and-whites. It was more of a response than I'd expected. More than was reasonable, and it had arrived faster than I'd thought possible. This time there was no *chismoso*, just Joanne "Carebear" Caraway, who'd likely had a half-dozen patrolmen on standby just in case.

I closed the door. "Should we try the other side of the building?"

She met my eyes. "Probably *more* of them on the other side. You were right to lead us across. Just... we have no choice."

She stepped in front of me and opened the door.

Chapter Twenty-Six

W e burst into the night, greeted by an assault of sirens. The building was surrounded, but no one was within fifty feet of the door. To the south, two cop cars were parked sideways, blocking the street. To the north, a fire truck screamed to a stop and three men jumped out, heading into Big Pink. Above us, crows took to the sky. Dozens of them at first, then hundreds. It was as though all the crows in Portland had gathered at Big Pink and picked that moment to flee. Their flight temporarily blocked the glare of the streetlights, blocked the stars. The sky was black with feathers.

Everything slowed. I had seconds to make a decision, and I was fully aware that this moment would define my next days, months, and probably years. My senses went electric.

Just across the street was a small plaza. Half of it was a parking area, the rest a wide brick walkway lined by a handful of tents. A homeless man had just emerged from his tent to see what the commotion was. On the side of the plaza nearest us stood a thirty-foot modernist statue. Made of chunks of square and rectangular iron, it looked like an abstract Lego man—angular, blocky, and vaguely person-shaped.

Kitty-corner to Big Pink sat a three-story parking garage that had once been a factory. In the renovation, the window panes had been taken out, leaving the black iron frames empty and making it look like a burned-out building. From my research, I knew you could park there for thirty bucks a day. Not a bad place to hide, especially when compared to the wide streets around us.

I turned to my mom, whose eyes danced up and down the street. She was scanning for a moment, a break in the circling of cars, a waning of the sirens. I pointed at the parking garage.

"There are more coming," she said. "There's not a way."

Just then, a shout came from the north, barely audible over the wailing sirens. "There!"

We turned at the same time. Three officers and a security guard had emerged from a side door to our left. One pointed our way. I looked to the right, where another cop car had parked at the end of the street, blocking both lanes.

"Brand." My mom put her hand on my arm gently.

I turned. We shared a look, the kind where, in theory, two people have the same thought at the same moment. Truth is, I don't know what she was thinking. I don't know how much of what I saw in her eyes was pain, how much was regret, how much was atonement, and how much was cold-blooded calculation. It was only a second, and things were happening fast. They say there's no greater pain than that of a mother whose child dies before her. I imagine that not far behind is the pain of a mother who knows her decisions ruined her child's life. I think her look had something to do with that.

She shoved the duffel bag into my arms and pointed toward the parking garage. "Run."

I heard it as *We should run.* Or maybe that's just how I wanted to hear it, how I wish she'd said it.

But she meant something else.

She took off toward the group of cops, walking at first, then breaking into a full sprint. I didn't have time to object. She was gone.

I saw her run toward them, saw them run toward her. But only for a second. I darted across the street to the plaza, ducked behind the iron statue, and paused.

"I am the notorious Wanda *damn* Penny," I heard her yell. "Come and get me, coppers!"

I stared into the sky, where the last of the crows had disappeared, leaving only a dull blackness dotted with a few washed-out stars.

She didn't go quietly. Like me, she wasn't much for violence, but she wanted to take more of their attention, so she put up a fight. I didn't see it, but she let out a barbaric grunt as she struck the first cop she could hit. More shouts followed, but I couldn't make out any words. She didn't stand a chance, but she was trying to buy me time. She knew that, when faced with an assault, cops converge quickly to protect their own. And that's what they did.

When I peeked out from behind the statue, four or five officers stood in a circle, one bent over her flailing body, another kicking wildly.

I bolted across the street into the ground level of the parking garage, which ran parallel to Big Pink, taking up a full city block. By entering it I was getting closer to the building, closer to the cops. I was betting that after they subdued my mom, they'd focus on the direction from which she'd come, then assume I'd escaped down that road, away from Big Pink. Hugging the concrete barrier that separated the different areas of the garage, I stayed low, creeping in the shadows. Shouts and hurried orders drifted in from all directions. I listened for Caraway's voice, and for my mom's, but heard neither.

I reached the end of the parking lot, just across the street from the north end of the building, where two fire trucks had parked. Red and blue lights flared off cars all around me, but I was crouched behind the low concrete barrier, not visible from the tower.

I peeked over the top of the wall. Someone burst through a side door of Big Pink and moved in my direction. The glare from the lights of the firetrucks damn near blinded me as I tried to get a clear look at the figure. Judging by the size and stride, it was a man of average height, square-shouldered and walking briskly in a dark suit. Probably a detective, and he was coming right for me. There was no way he could have seen me, unless he happened to be looking out a window when I made my dash from behind the statue to the garage. The way he walked in my direction made me realize that's exactly what had happened.

I heard him call something to the cops, who must've been cuffing my mom right about then. I spied a staircase in the far corner of the garage and, abandoning any hope of secrecy, sprinted for it. I busted through the door into the stairwell, ascending the two flights three stairs at a time.

On the roof of the garage, I headed for the opposite corner, where there was another staircase. Looking back as I ran, I heard a door screech open, but saw nothing. If the guy was behind me, it was far enough that I could lose him.

I had twenty yards on him at least. He was huffing it in his off-the-rack suit and leather Oxfords, but tonight I was lightning and Silly Putty again. And this time there was no Jackson Forge to clothesline me. He might shoot me in the back, but there was no way in hell he'd catch me.

I leapt down the three flights of stairs, two jumps per flight, and spilled out into the opposite end of the parking garage, back near the statue I'd been hiding behind five minutes earlier. I didn't take the time to look back. Streets were blocked all around me. Like a running back picking a hole in the defense, all I could do was find the weakest spot and run as fast as I could. I looked for darkness. There were lights in all directions. All but one.

The patch of darkness was behind the group of homeless people now gathered outside their tents. I ran toward them, ducked between two tents, and jumped the low iron fence into another parking lot. From there, it was a straight shot east toward the river. I slowed after a block. I heard no footfalls behind me, and inconspicuousness was now more important than speed. All I heard was a cacophony of voices, gradually fading with distance. It was probably my imagination that insisted I could make out Caraway's voice in that chorus, sounding furious and cheated. It probably wasn't her, but just to be on the safe side, I raised one hand and flipped the bird in what I hoped was her general direction.

Halfway across the Hawthorne Bridge, I checked the time.

Despite the complications, it was only ten minutes after eleven, and my mind shifted to Jennifer.

I jogged across the rest of the bridge, cut back toward the industrial neighborhood and slowed as I reached a bar with people smoking out front. The car was in front of a gourmet cheese shop a block away. It was a newish Ford sedan. Reliable but not fancy, my mom had probably rented it sometime in the last few days with a fake-ID and matching credit card. Easier and safer than boosting one.

The car was exactly where it was supposed to be. Jennifer wasn't. She often ran ten to twenty minutes late, but almost never more than that. Scanning the deserted block, ears searching for sirens, I decided to give her ten minutes.

I leaned on the car, pulling out the small paper Mom had stuffed in my pocket. It was a receipt, preserved with what looked like carefully-applied packing tape, the poor man's lamination. Leaning in, I squinted to make out the faded dot-matrix printing in the orange-yellow glow of an old streetlamp.

Dexter's Sandwich Shop
  12/13/1998 10:18
  Ticket #637-0
  1 Pastrami
  Rye
  Coleslaw
  Hot Mustard
  1 Corned Beef
  Sourdough
  Sauerkraut

1 Medium Diet Coke
  1 Medium Root Beer
  Total: $15.75
  Paid: $20.00

Change: $4.25

She'd pointed west that night to send us in opposite directions for our escape, planning all along to meet me at Dexter's to mourn a job gone bad and celebrate our escape from the cops. She even got my favorite sandwich so it would be waiting for me when I ran in. I stared at the receipt for a long time, listening for sirens and, strangely, listening for my mom. I knew by now she'd be cuffed in the back of a police car, but some piece of my mind still expected her to walk up behind me and say, "Let's go."

After five minutes, I found the magnetic hide-a-key near the rear bumper, right where Mom had said it would be. I got in and adjusted the seat and mirrors, leaving the door ajar to listen for Jennifer's hurried footsteps. Every few seconds I'd check all three mirrors. The piece of me that had been formed by a thousand movies wanted her to run up at the last second, hastily-packed bag slung over her shoulder, hair disheveled. But all I saw was an old homeless woman smoking a cigarette and a thirty-something guy in reflective running gear, going for a late-night jog with his dog.

It was twenty minutes past eleven, and Jennifer wasn't running late. I could wait all night, but she wasn't coming. I thought about driving to her apartment, making my case one more time, but that could put us both at risk. I considered sending a text only she could understand, offering to send for her when things cooled down. But she'd made her decision, and I had to respect that. In the end, it was pretty simple: Mom showed up at the rendezvous point and Jennifer didn't. So I started the engine and eased down the block, keeping to five over the speed limit the whole way out of town.

The Oregonian, December 21, 2018

Fire at 'Big Pink' ruled arson

Sonia White

A small fire reported early Tuesday morning at Portland's famous US Bancorp Tower—affectionately known to locals as "Big Pink"—has been ruled arson.

Firefighters responded to the call around 10:45 Tuesday night, and the two-day investigation has determined that the fire was deliberately set in a twenty-eighth-floor office.

The tower, near Southwest 5th and West Burnside, is Portland's second-tallest building and home to over fifty businesses.

Downtown Security, Inc., the firm that manages security in the building, released a statement claiming the fire might have been set by a deranged homeless man.

Fire Department sources disagreed. According to three members of the department, access was deep enough into the building to suggest that a robbery may have occurred, in addition to the arson. Downtown Security, Inc., disputes this. "There was no robbery," their statement read.

Sources within Portland Fire and Rescue tell us it was a small fire in a garbage can, and that nothing of value was damaged. Investigators say they could tell the fire was intentionally set.

The investigation is ongoing.

The Oregonian, December 22, 2018

On the run for twenty years, murder suspect arrested in Portland

Wanted for 1998 Laurelhurst murder

Connected to "Big Pink" burglary and fire, investigators now say

Sonia White

Late Friday night, a man and a woman broke into an office in the US Bancorp Tower and set a fire to cover their escape. One of the suspected burglars, Wanda Penny, has been wanted for twenty years in the unsolved murder of Thomas Twomey, a security guard who was shot to death outside a home in Laurelhurst in 1998. Ms. Penny was apprehended by police while attempting to flee the scene, and is currently in custody.

According to police records, Ms. Penny is being held for assaulting officers, breaking and entering, arson, and first-degree burglary. Though police would not confirm what was stolen, the fire started in a twenty-eighth-floor office leased by Masterson Wealth Management Services, so the crime is thought to be connected to financial instruments.

Reached for comment by The Oregonian, *Masterson downplayed the burglary, calling it a "minor break-in." He went on to say, "My offices are secure, always have been. And I trust law enforcement to get to the bottom of this."*

In what may be a coincidence, Mark Masterson was present at the poker game at which Mr. Twomey was killed in 1998, but declined to comment on the shooting.

Police say the fire did minimal damage and was set to trigger alarms to cover Ms. Penny's getaway. Building security officials had previously denied that the fire at Big Pink was related to a burglary.

According to police, Ms. Penny's suspected accomplice is her son, Brandon Penny, an employee of Morey's Pharmacy and lifelong Portland resident. Reached for comment, his supervisor Kevin Peterson said, "Brandon has always been a conscientious employee. Even won employee of the month a few times. Can't see him getting caught up in anything illegal."

Police tell a different story. Mr. Penny is wanted for questioning in connection to both the burglary and the assault of a detective that, sources say, occurred the day of the break-in at Big Pink.

Ms. Penny is scheduled to be arraigned Monday morning.

Chapter Twenty-Seven

A few days later, a man named Michael Keyser stepped out of a taxi in front of Nevis International Bank and Trust in Pinney's Beach, a small town just south of Charlestown in the West Indies. He was my height and my weight. He walked like me and talked like me. But Michael Keyser had light blond hair and deeply-tanned skin that made him look like a longtime resident of a sun-drenched state. More importantly, he didn't have my past.

When people think of a bank, they usually picture a generic square building with an ATM out front and a few bored tellers inside. A nice little Wells Fargo branch, or a credit union you stop by after work to deposit a paycheck, take out some cash, or apply for a mortgage. It's probably located downtown, or maybe at the corner of a suburban shopping plaza. That's not the kind of place where the super-wealthy bank.

Nevis International looked like a decadent clubhouse on the eighteenth green of a fancy golf course. Surrounded by rolling lawns that led to the ocean, the grounds were dotted with palm trees. It was a sprawling white building in the island Victorian style, designed to remind rich visitors of colonial days. It was the kind of place where you could clean your cash while enjoying a Nevis Delight, the island's famous cocktail made of rum, honey, passionfruit, and club soda, garnished with tangy starfruit segments. I'd had two a day since my arrival on the island, and I wasn't sick of them yet.

The bank was founded by the Brits over a hundred years ago, specifically for the purposes of laundering money. Run by ruthless British bankers, but "licensed" and "regulated" in the federations of St. Kitts and Nevis, it was the perfect spot to park money you wanted to keep away from the British government. In the fifties, it opened its doors to the rest of the world and became a well-respected, mid-tier offshore bank. It was the kind of place Mark Masterson would have loved if he wasn't back in Portland, scrambling to figure out what happened to his life and, more specifically, his bearer shares. Bearer shares I now held securely in a handsome brown-leather attaché, all but the ones we reduced to ashes on the twenty-eighth floor of Big Pink.

Masterson Wealth Management Services had a complicated structure, built around a single guy shuffling large amounts of other people's money from shell company to shell company, money that couldn't be accounted for in any legal way. That was the whole point: take millions of dollars and shield it from governments, ex-wives, and former business partners. You remove a single company from a structure like that and Masterson can shift the money from that company to any of a dozen others. But if you take a *lot* of that structure, and if he doesn't know what you've taken, and you destroy a bunch more of it, and he doesn't know what you've destroyed, he's paralyzed. Half the imaginary companies he owns are financed with debt held by the other companies he owns. Some of them are subsidiaries of others, entwined in weblike structures that mean no one's legally responsible for any of them, because that's the point.

Most importantly, if the bearer shares for a company are *stolen*, someone still owns the company: whoever's holding the shares. That's a tough situation, but maybe one he could cope with. If the bearer shares are *destroyed*, though, nobody owns the company. It doesn't exist any more. Masterson would probably suspect we'd stolen some of the shares, but he'd know for a fact that we'd destroyed others. All those companies ceased to exist, and he couldn't even know which ones. How many share certificates were burned? Which companies were now vulnerable, and which were nonexistent? How many millions of dollars burned up in that trash can? All he had were unanswerable questions and a bucket of ash. While he was scrambling to figure it out, I was on a plane to the Bahamas. Sure, he could reassemble some of his house of cards from whatever documentation he still had. Over time, he might be able to lawyer up hard enough to extract money from some of the accounts owned by companies I'd torched. But all the while he'd be trying to fend off enraged clients even richer than him, and who had even less respect for the law. His professional reputation, and his career, had literally gone up in smoke. It was like the old con of burning down a warehouse for the insurance money, but getting the best goodies out first. The guys sifting through the ashes had no way of knowing which stuff burned, and which stuff rolled away in the back of a van. It was a hell of a situation to be in, and I didn't envy him.

Dressed in a red silk shirt and black slacks—professional but still island-friendly—I strolled into the lobby and up to the first person I saw, a man with long dreadlocks and a magnificent blue suit. He greeted me in a friendly British accent. "Hello, how can I help you, sir?"

I held up the attaché. "I have a few companies with holdings at your bank that I'll be transferring to my personal account." These financial instruments were designed to let people like Masterson move money around with no friction or oversight. I was going to use them exactly as designed.

"Do you have an account with us, sir?"

"I do."

"Name please."

"Michael Keyser."

He looked back and forth from his keyboard to the computer screen, presumably pulling up the checking and brokerage account under my new alias. "I see you applied online two days ago. And will you be using the transfers for your initial deposit?" He didn't blink an eye.

"Yes."

"Very well, sir. I'm Rivera Blakely, private banking consultant. Please follow me."

If I'd walked into a Citibank in Portland under the same scenario, I would have been hauled away in handcuffs, assuming the teller making forty grand a year even understood what I was talking about. Out here, it was par for the course. I smiled as I followed Blakely to a large private office with a view of the water. "Heard there was no bank on the island more professional than Nevis International."

"We like to think so."

I sat across from him and readied my documents as he pulled up my accounts. "I see you filed all the documents electronically. I'll just need your passport to verify."

I handed him the passport Soup had created. It had taken me a day to forge the rest of the documents I'd needed to set up the bank account under my new name. I'd needed a second form of ID in addition to the passport, so I created an Arizona driver's license, as well as reference forms from my lawyer and my local banker back in Arizona, both with numbers that forwarded to my new cell phone. I'd also created a lease agreement that proved Scottsdale was my permanent address.

He handed back the passport. "Very good, Mr. Keyser. And the shares?"

I slid a small stack of stock certificates across the table. "Hammerstone Holdings, Lightspear Holdings, Greenbriar Holdings, December Holdings, and Masterclass Holdings. Just go ahead and transfer it all to my brokerage account for now."

He checked them over, crinkling his nose as he inspected them, his lips curling.

Bearer shares have been used for decades for all sorts of nefarious business, ranging from tax evasion to funding terrorists. In fact, it was 9/11 that finally convinced the U.S. government to really go after them. Since the Patriot Act passed, they've become harder to deal with, but each state and each country has their own laws regulating them.

As though reading my mind, Blakely lowered his glasses and stared at me. "You know it was 9/11 that finally caused the U.S. to start restricting this kind of instrument."

"That's what I hear."

"And you want to transfer everything held by these companies to your own account?"

"Yes, sir." I held up a hand preemptively. "I know, *I know*—I'll get slaughtered on taxes, but with everyone cracking down on bearer shares these days, it's just not worth the headache."

"If it's your tax situation you're concerned about, you might want to establish legal residency here on the island. Quite a few gentlemen of means find that advantageous. They enjoy our climate, and also our *financial* climate, if you see what I mean."

"I'll give that serious consideration. I appreciate how you don't crawl down a guy's throat with rules and regulations." I was in character as the kind of guy who'd do business with Masterson, but my God, I wanted to punch myself in the face.

While Blakely typed, I watched the sun cut through a mountainous bank of white clouds, turning the ocean into blue fire, and I thought about Jennifer. I saw her presenting her thesis, arguing about the value of obscure nineties movies before a panel of stodgy old professors, and teaching classes in Seattle. She'd write interesting books and spread her fast-talking enthusiasm to a new generation of movie buffs. Thinking about her future left me strangely satisfied. As much as I wished she was sitting beside me, I knew she'd made the right decision.

My hunch was that Caraway would spend a few days making Jennifer's life difficult. She might even haul her into that dusty interrogation room with grooves worn in the wall. Unfortunately for Caraway, she didn't have any leverage. Even the true version of my past I'd shared with Jennifer had been devoid of names, dates, and places. In the end, Caraway couldn't do much to Jennifer.

"All right, Mr. Keyser, I think I've got this set up. Before I commit, is this right?" Blakely turned his computer screen around so I could see the structure of the transfer. The accounts of those five holding companies would be closed, and their balances sent to my new account with this bank. The bottom line on the screen showed what my account would be worth.

It was an eight-digit number.

"Y'know—*hem*." My mouth was suddenly dry. I swallowed and tried again. "Y'know what, go ahead and put two million into checking. Walking-around money."

"Of course, sir." Blakely clicked a few more times, then put the transaction through. And like that, I was filthy stinking rich.

It didn't feel much different. It didn't take away any of my memories. Didn't fix any of the things I'd done wrong. I'd have to do that myself.

Blakely clicked his mouse a few more times, then stood. "Anything else I can do for you today, Mr. Keyser?"

I shook his extended hand. "Thank you, Mr. Blakely. There is one more thing." I pulled a large yellow envelope out of my attaché. "Can you add this to your outgoing mail?"

"Will it need postage?" He took the envelope. "Ahh, I see, prepaid. Happy to do so, Mr. Keyser." He read the address. "The *Oregonian*? What's that, one of your businesses or—"

"No, no, nothing like that. It's a newspaper. Just a little scoop I want to share with the press back home."

I walked out into the warm tropical sun and thought about Mom. She was in a Portland jail, awaiting charges. That was all I knew for sure. I'd do everything I could to remedy that, but I had to believe that me being here would make her happy, that she wouldn't regret the tradeoff. I knew she wouldn't give me up to the cops, but Caraway would do everything she could to make her life a living hell. For as long as she was able to, anyway.

Carebear was about to have much bigger problems.

The Oregonian, January 7, 2019

Detective under investigation

Corruption, money laundering suspected

By Susi Vega

Detective Joanne Caraway, a long-tenured detective in the Portland Police Bureau, is implicated in a litany of violations, including corruption and money laundering, according to three sources close to the internal investigation.

Caraway, the youngest woman to be promoted to detective in the Bureau's history, has been placed on paid administrative leave, pending the investigation.

Although the department confirmed the action, no official statements were made about the reason for the investigation.

Caraway declined to comment.

Financial Transfer Receipt, January 8, 2019

Bank/Wire Transfer Payment Details

Order reference number:

7199011

Sender:

Michael Keyser
P.O. Box 8181
Pinney's Beach, Charlestown,
Nevis West Indies, Caribbean

Recipient:

Rose City Commercial Lenders
11677 SW 5th Ave
Portland, Oregon, 97204

Bank:

Nevis International Bank and Trust

Routing Number:

323181993

Account #:

38900112

Amount:

$245,166.17

Memo:

Please apply this payment to mortgage #3478122, under the

name Franklin Kitchens. It is for the building located on NE Humboldt Street and NE 82nd, Ace's Quick Cash, and the apartment above. This should bring the mortgage balance to zero.

Financial Transfer Receipt, January 8, 2019

Bank/Wire Transfer Payment Details

Order reference number:
4899923

Sender:
Michael Keyser
P.O. Box 8181
Pinney's Beach, Charlestown,
Nevis West Indies, Caribbean

Recipient:
Tyler Twomey
26778 Park View Lane
Eugene, Oregon, 97401

Bank:
Nevis International Bank and Trust

Routing Number:
323181993

Account #:
38900112

Amount:
$1,000,000

Payable To:
Tyler Twomey

Memo:

Pay off your student loans and build yourself a life.

The Oregonian, January 30, 2019

Detective Caraway fired, arrested

Local financial advisor Mark Masterson also arrested

By Susi Vega

In a shocking conclusion to the month-long investigation into PPB detective Joanne Caraway, the long-tenured detective was fired and immediately arrested yesterday.

Caraway turned herself in at the downtown police station at noon, was booked and released on bail just after 4 p.m. Reached for comment, Caraway told The Oregonian, "This is all a misunderstanding. Bureau politics gone bad. Having served the city of Portland with dignity for nearly thirty years, I expect to be fully vindicated."

An official statement from the PPB, however, said she was charged with "Corruption and money laundering." The release went on, "For a hundred years the PPB has aimed to serve the citizens of Portland, so when one of our own commits a crime, we must investigate and prosecute as we would any other."

PPB spokesman Mark Jarreti declined to say what evidence the arrest was based on, but said, "Prosecutors would not have brought charges if they didn't have the evidence to convict."

Sources within the department say the arrest of local financial advisor Mark Masterson is related, though they would not confirm how.

Masterson, the owner of Masterson Wealth Management Services, was arrested Friday on federal charges of bribery and money laundering.

According to documents obtained from an anonymous source and confirmed by the Oregonian, Detective Caraway had over three million dollars under management with Masterson Wealth Management Services. Masterson's attorney, Ronin Kraft III, vowed to defend his client vigorously: "Mark Masterson is a valued member of the Portland community and has committed no crimes. He will be fully vindicated."

But one veteran officer, who wished not to be named, said, "She [Caraway] has been crooked from the jump. On Masterson's payroll, that I've known for years. Framed at least three people I know of. Some people are capable of any wicked thing."

February 1, 2019

To:

Wanda Penny, SWIS ID 768439
C/O: Multnomah County Sheriff's Office
11540 NE Inverness Dr.
Portland OR 97220

From:

David Graziano, Senior Partner
Graziano and Pike Law Group, LLC
177 Southwest Morrison, Suite #200
Portland, OR 97204

Dear Ms. Penny,

We received your signed copy of the contract for our firm to represent you in any and all matters related to the alleged recent events at the US Bancorp Tower, as well as any other charges that may arise. Thank you for being so prompt with the paperwork, as we understand that the corrections system tends to make things difficult. Graziano and Pike, as you may know, has a well-earned reputation as the best criminal defense firm in Portland. Your case will be handled by Susan Blankenship, one of our most experienced defense attorneys. Please make sure her name is added to your list of permitted visitors. Her first visit is scheduled for this coming Monday, the 4th.

As per your request, the person paying our fees has authorized a deposit of $5,000 into your inmate account via the TouchPay system, to use on snacks or personal items. The prison is legally required to give you access to these funds. Please write to our firm at the address above if you need more money for any reason. As you know, all letters in and out will be read by prison staff.

Your anonymous benefactor has asked us to pass along this brief personal message:

Dear Wanda,

When you asked what my favorite movie was, I lied. I said I didn't know. Actually it's a 1970s flick called *Paper Moon*. It's about a little girl and her dad grifting their way through Dust Bowl Kansas during the Great Depression. They pull some short cons, swindle a bootlegger, get chased by crooks and cops. All the good stuff. In the final shot of the film, they're driving down a long, winding road into the future —maybe to live a nice straight life, maybe to continue the grift.

We should watch it together sometime soon.

—The End—

A Note From the Author

Thanks for reading *The Things She Stole*. I traveled to Portland dozens of time to research this book and, like Brandon Penny, I fell in love with the city. In fact, here's a photograph I captured on a recent visit. You may recognize Steel Bridge from chapter 6 and "Big Pink" from the second half of the book.

"Big Pink" and Steel Bridge, Portland, Oregon.

If you enjoyed *The Things She Stole,* I encourage you to check out the sequel, *The Lies We Live* (releasing summer, 2023).

You might also enjoy my mysteries, the Thomas Austin Crime Thrillers. Each book can be read as a standalone, although relationships and situations develop from book to book, so they will be more enjoyable if read in order.

In the digital world, authors rely more than ever on mysterious algorithms to spread the word about our books. One thing I know for sure is that ratings and reviews help. So, if you'd take the time to offer a quick rating of this book, I'd be very grateful.

If you enjoy pictures of corgis, the beautiful Pacific Northwest beaches, and other landmarks of the Pacific Northwest, consider joining my VIP Readers Club. When you join, you'll receive no spam and you'll be the first to hear about free and discounted eBooks, author events, and new releases.

Thanks for reading!

D.D. Black

Also by D.D. Black

The Brandon Penny Heists

Book 1: The Things She Stole

Book 2: The Lies We Live (Coming Summer, 2023)

The Thomas Austin Crime Thrillers

Book 1: The Bones at Point No Point

Book 2: The Shadows of Pike Place

Book 3: The Fallen of Foulweather Bluff

About D.D. Black

D.D. Black is the author of the Thomas Austin Crime Thrillers, the Brandon Penny Heists, and other Pacific Northwest crime novels that are on their way. When he's not writing, he can be found strolling the beaches of the Pacific Northwest, cooking dinner for his wife and son, or throwing a ball for his corgi over and over and over. Find out more art ddblackauthor.com, or on the sites below.

f facebook.com/ddblackauthor

instagram.com/ddblackauthor

tiktok.com/@d.d.black

BB bookbub.com/profile/d-d-black